MYSTIC SOULS

PARANORMAL WORLD BOOK FOUR

C. C. SOLOMON

CatDog Publications

Mystic Souls is a work of fiction. Names, characters, places and incidents are either the product of the author's imagination or are used fictitiously, and any resemblance to actual persons, living or dead, business establishments, events or locales is entirely coincidental.

ISBN: 978-1-7336259-9-9

ACKNOWLEDGMENTS

Thank you to all my friends and family who supported my dreams. Thank you to line editor, Judi Soderberg, who has helped me since book one. Thank you to my beta readers, Charlie and Alesha. Thank you to my editors at Real Indie Author, you push me to be a better writer. Thank you to my proofreader Madeleine at Mad Skillz for your great eye and my formatters at Yours Truly Book Services for your awesome services at every level. Your quick work and professionalism have consistently come through. And thanks to my readers for keeping me going. Your enthusiasm and feedback has made a huge difference.

FOREWORD

To keep updated on C.C.'s prior and future books and her travel and lifestyle website, go to: www.ccsolomon.com

CHAPTER 1

"Ok. The fact that I even have to have this conversation with you at all is insane, but this needs to be resolved once and for all," I announced, pacing in front of the women sitting in the werepack conference room. It was actually a party room in my apartment building, but it served its purpose.

I wanted to make this a woman to woman chat, so I didn't invite any of the male pack leaders. Seven women, who were foolishly throwing in their hats to be Erik's concubines, sat about the room on couches and chairs, curious faces aimed at me. Raya Ortiz, third in command of the pack, stood to my left and I asked Faith Thomas to attend as my support. Like me, she wasn't a were. Still, she was one of my besties, so I bent the rules for her.

Why I needed to be at this stupid meeting was, as I just shouted out loud, truly crazy and unnecessary in light of the many other things I had going on. However, Raya had stopped by my place the night before and told me, in her usual less than friendly way, to "boss up." She also mentioned that I might have to 'choke a bitch'. That was her lane more than mine. However, if push came to shove...

Ever since my boyfriend—man, mate, partner? Did calling one your boyfriend really work when you were a full-grown adult living in a magical post apocalypse? Eh, it was going to have to do. So, ever since my boyfriend, Erik Bennett, had justifiably killed the prior leader of the pack about a month before, he'd become the new leader.

They wanted one thing: to be the wives to the new pack leader, Erik. With me as head wife, of course.

Hell to the no.

Ok, Amina, time to put on your big girl panties and act like all 5'3 of your non-were self is something scary, I told myself.

I let out a nervous breath and stuck out my chin like I dared someone to come at me. Fake it till you make it. "This is the last time that I will say this, so please listen closely. Erik and I are a monogamous couple. Despite the ridiculous rumors, we don't have an open relationship. We aren't polyamorous. It's just the two of us. And, despite the gossip, I also know Erik hasn't been with anyone else." I was confident of that. Erik was loyal to a fault. I had been banished for three months, with no hint of my return and even with the many plays for him, he'd remained faithful.

Raya was one of those women who had been after him, and she confirmed that he'd been faithful to the point that he almost died due to our separation. Since we were in the early stage of being mates, we needed to be together, so my banishment caused him great harm. I only went unharmed because I have a soul mate, though not of my choosing. A fact that really wasn't helping my cause right now.

"I am not interested in the future possibility of sister wives should we get married. Got it?" I looked around the room at the women whose frowning faces seemed like they were not registering what I was saying. In particular, the former wives of Seth.

Seth, during his reign of terror, had taken not one, not two, but five wives. At the time of his drugged-out phase, he'd killed two of them, leaving us with three women who'd served no other purpose in the community other than catering to Seth's needs. Now that the barbaric ass was gone, they had no idea what to do with themselves.

A Seth widow, a petite woman with black hair gave me a snotty smile. "I heard you're also seeing Phillip. If you can have an extra man, why can't he have an extra woman?"

I threw all my power into my stare, hands on my hips, and she just blinked her eyes slowly and crossed her arms. So much for intimidation. "Regardless of what you may have heard, I am not with Phillip. We are just friends." Barely friends but it was growing. What it wasn't and what it wouldn't ever be, was a romantic relationship.

That was met with some cackles and whispers. Not surprised. Few people in town believed we had a platonic relationship, and I was sure Phillip didn't help squash the rumors either.

I raised a hand to silence the group. "Look, it doesn't matter what any of you believe. Erik has also told you no."

I thought the women would respect our mate bond and just eventually go away on their own, since Erik was doing a nice job of turning down his growing fan club. However, Raya let me know that behind my back the women were sauntering in the police station where Erik worked as the chief of police to drop off tons of food while dressed in scantily clad outfits.

Another Seth widow, a woman with honey-blond hair, stood up giving her best innocent face as if she wasn't about to stab me with a word knife. "He could change his mind. The world is different now. Why not just accept an open arrangement? We know you're busy with that big battle we heard about. We could cook for you, do laundry, watch Brandon."

Yeah, and have sex with Erik. They were really pissing me

off now. How had this become my life? I felt like the wife of a NBA player fighting off groupies.

A short red head, raised her hand, not standing up. "Erik can change his mind. He could get bored with just you. And to be honest, we don't really have to listen to what you say. You're not one of us." She gave me a tight smile that I wanted to slap off.

Choruses of agreement spread throughout the room.

Faith let out a loud cough with wide eyes, clearly in as much annoyance as me.

Raya turned slightly to me. Her face held amused chocolate eyes, and her lips were set in a smirk. She tucked a lock of her bob length, wavy brown hair behind her ear as she leaned towards me. "You're losing the room. Might be time to do the choking of the bitches," she murmured through clenched teeth.

Apparently, Erik turning down their proposals and food wasn't enough. Raya informed me that as "queen" of the pack, I needed to put my foot down since they were clearly disrespecting me. What putting my foot down meant was probably something violent. It was becoming clear to me because I wasn't a were they weren't going to respect the rules. I didn't know their struggle and I wasn't going to get automatic buy-in just because I was mated to a were. I'd have to prove I was dedicated to the pack…by fighting. This was more than a guy issue. They were testing me as one of their leaders.

I scratched my head and frowned in mock confusion at the group, ignoring Raya's advice. I had enough fighting to do that was serious. This still seemed silly to me. "I'm sorry. I'm Erik's mate. I'm a part of the leadership."

"So," said a tall brunette. "We didn't have to listen to any of Seth's wives. Just because you're Erik's mate doesn't mean you run the place."

"It does make her part of leadership," Raya cut in.

"Thank you," I replied with a curt nod. I could see my game at playing polite was failing miserably. I was starting to think it was time to do the ugly work I wanted to avoid.

"But they aren't exactly obligated to listen to you."

I cut my eyes at Raya. Just the other day she was calling me the night boss, and now I was a nobody?

"You aren't even a were," said a pink-haired woman. "You aren't strong enough to lead on Erik's behalf or even beside him. It's an insult for you to think you can boss us around."

A chorus of agreements came around the room.

Yup, nice guy role play was a wrap for the day.

"Are you fucking kidding me?" I shouted, throwing my hands to the side. "I'm fighting every other damn day, and you all are saying I'm not strong enough?"

Their faces seemed dead and unimpressed. They had no idea of what I'd been doing.

I wanted to drop kick and throat chop just about every one of them. I'd fought a man who came back from hell, dark fairies, a jinn, elves, giant beasts, and man-eating plant-life. I was not a weak bitch. I was a tired bitch. I was an over-thinking bitch. I was definitely a stressed-out bitch. But I was not a weak bitch.

"It's not that, Amina," said another red0head with long hair, Brittney. She gave me sympathetic eyes and her fingers knotted together in front of her. She was another of Seth's widows who I happened to like before today. "We know your powers are nothing to mess with. Only with us weres, physical strength is what matters."

"Yeah," said the tall brunette. "You can wave a hand and make things happen, but can you throw a punch to knock a person on their ass?"

I put up a finger. "Excuse me, it's not like you all aren't strong because of your were magic."

Silence. Clearly, they didn't care about my very valid point.

I shrugged and shook my head, at my wits end. "What do you want me to do? Fight you all?"

Murmurs filled the room.

"Might be a good idea," Raya said to me, crossing her arms. "Show them who's boss like Erik and I had to do for our positions. We weres work differently. They need to respect you, and that's shown through kicking someone's ass."

Raya and Erik were built like athletes. Raya could have been a professional volleyball player in the time before magic. I still got winded from jogging one mile.

Faith leaned into me. "Just turn these bitches into frogs and let's go. Tell them to respect *that* shit." She shook her head and squinted her violet eyes at the group, crossing her arms, her tattoos peeking out of the edge of her sleeves and the neckline of her shirt. She could have been a model in another time, tall with a toned physique and a short, dirty blond haircut that complemented her features. In this world, no one took her good looks for weakness.

I wished others would stop taking my girl next door looks as a joke. Several women called out the word 'challenge' over and over again until it became a chant from the whole room. I looked out at the group. "You want me to engage in a fistfight. Over a man? Ladies, has it really come to this?"

"Yes," they cried.

I rubbed the bridge of my nose. The last time I got in a fight over a guy I was a sophomore in high school and this mean girl, Janice Mills, shoved me in the back in the cafeteria because she'd heard I was flirting with her boyfriend, whose name I could not recall. I was not, in fact, flirting with the guy. I hit her back. She wound up with a black eye, and I wound up getting a reputation as a kick-ass fighter. Neither Janice nor any of her friends ever bothered me again.

Turns out you're never too old to fight after school over a boy.

"How about this." Raya turned to me and bowed her head, her eyebrows raised. "You fight one of these women. Whoever submits first wins. If you win, they all lay off Erik and respect you for good. If the other woman wins, then it's business as usual, which means they don't have to listen to you about Erik."

I rolled my eyes at her.

She gave me a quick shrug, unperturbed.

Of course, she'd be enjoying the hell out of this. We used to hate each other, what with her disrespecting my relationship with Erik. Now we'd come to a sort of unspoken truce, and I didn't hate her as much. Maybe even kind of liked her. Until right now.

I shook my head. "So, who wants to fight?"

The tall brunette stood up. No one else moved. She was built like a basketball player. All legs and definition. She had to be at least six feet tall. My heart sank.

"Fine." I was going to die. Everyone would be mad because this was not what I was all powered up to do. Fight for a man. My mom would be so disappointed.

"Good," Raya replied with a head nod. "You can't use your magic."

I pointed at her. "That's a lie." If I was going to die, it was going to be a fair fight on my way out. I darn sure *was* going to use my powers. "You weres are naturally powered up. A normal human without assistance could never win against you. Now, I won't use a spell or a weapon, but I'm powering myself up to at least be able to take a hit and hit back."

Raya looked like she was pondering that for a moment and then she gave a curt nod. "Fair enough."

The other women got up and moved the couches and chairs back to clear a space to fight. Panic gripped my heart. I hope I didn't die like this.

The brunette gave me a cocky smile. "This will be fun," she replied, cracking her knuckles.

"Don't get ahead of yourself, Melissa," Raya interjected. "I've seen Amina fight, and she's no weakling." Raya nodded and patted my shoulder. "Don't die because of this. It'd be embarrassing. For you."

I swore and closed my eyes. She really wasn't good at giving pep talks. I summoned my magic from my core and felt its heat spread through me. Technically, I was what you called a life or earth mage. This meant I could control every form of life and everything made of the earth. I could make an earthquake or a man walk. I could give strength or take it away. Now I was using my magic to control my own body and enhance it.

I closed my eyes and closed my fist as I forced my magic through me, whispering a spell to boost my strength. It was similar to the spell I'd put on Erik when he was fighting for his pack position. Feeling the burning spread through me, I was beginning to doubt that he really didn't know what I was doing.

"Melissa," I said, opening my eyes. I felt strong and light on my feet. I wasn't sure I could do a backflip, although I did feel like it was possible. "What type of were are you?"

She smiled, exposing sharp teeth and her gray eyes bled a full deep brown with no whites to her eyes present. "A werebear."

Son-of-a-bitch. That's fine. I was strong. I'd faced a man that had returned from the dead, an evil fae queen, an alpha weretiger and an elven king. I could take on a random werebear.

And with that, she body-slammed me into the ground. My back hit the hard tile floor, and I swore my soul jumped out of my body for just a moment. Before I could get my bearings, no pun intended, Melissa picked me up and raised me over her head like I weighed nothing before tossing me into the nearest wall.

Pain in my back reverberated through my body, and I fought the urge to play dead to stop the bear from coming at me. Luckily, my body was harder now, and nothing was broken. I got to my feet and jumped out of the way, just as Melissa charged towards me. She clumsily slammed against the wall, and I punched her hard in the middle of the back. She arched forward then swung around, lashing her arm out. Unexpected claws sliced across my stomach, just as I jumped back.

I shouted from the pain and heard Faith scream my name. I ignored her, pushing through the pain as I ducked another swipe of Melissa's claw. The werebear kicked her foot up, and it connected with my shoulder, dislocating it. I bit my lip hard, feeling warm blood trickle down as I took the pain.

If I was going to win this, I'd have to throw in a little offense. I would have to use my lack of heights to my advantage by staying low. I rammed into Melissa and knocked her over a side table. She grabbed me by the waist and ripped me away from her, elbowing me in the nose. I felt a crunch and knew it was broken. Pain was becoming my constant companion. I felt like I was going to die. If I dropped out now, I'd never be rid of this problem. Through blurry vision, I saw Faith take a step towards me, so I put my hand out to stop her.

What is going on? Phillip's voice boomed in my head.

I'm fine. Go away. I shouted back through my mind.

As my fated soulmate, Phillip Leal was attuned to me, and an internal alarm would go off when either of us was in danger. Was I losing this fight? No, I just had a few minor setbacks, I could still win.

Doesn't seem like you're fine.

I'm fighting for respect in the pack. I can't have you help me. Ok, gotta go.

What? Amina–

I shut his voice out of my head having grown in the ability to block him out.

I wiped the blood from my face, or rather smeared it around my face. Alright. Time to try this again.

Melissa charged at me with a smug grin. I waited until she got just close enough, then spun out of her way, zooming behind her. Crouching low, I sliced across her tendons on her left and right ankles with sharpened nails that were tough as claws.

Melissa screamed and dropped to her knees. I couldn't let her heal. It was act now or she'd gain the upper hand again. Standing straight, I kicked her in the shoulder. She fell to her side and then onto her back. I stood over her as she reached up, swiping wildly. She slashed across my arm, but I ignored the pain and aimed for both of her wrists, slicing deeply. Blood sprayed across my face, which I ignored. I balled my fists and began to punch the werebear in the face, again and again. She tried to block me and strike back, but I'd cut deeply enough to weaken her arms. She leaned forward and bit my fist. With my free hand I punched her in the side of the face repeatedly until she let go, spitting out blood and teeth.

I continued to hit her. Again and again. I had to win. I had to beat her. She had to stay down. "Stay down. Stay down. Stay down," I yelled with each contact of her face with my hands. I would win. I was strong. I was the boss. I would rule.

Far off voices circled around me, only I couldn't make out their words. I could only focus on hitting. At keeping her down.

A hand grasped my shoulder, but I shook it off. Another hand on my arm prevented me from hitting. What was with this resistance? I looked to Melissa, except she lay immobile, both her hands to her side, eyes swollen. Who was stopping me?

I dropped my hands and looked up to see both Raya and Faith standing over me, both holding my arms back. I frowned and looked back down to Melissa. Suddenly the horror of what I'd done to her hit me, and I felt sick.

"Oh my God!" I cried. "Did I–"

"No, but you were about to," Raya said in a worried tone.

"Let go of me. I have to heal her," I said.

They didn't move. I looked up at them again. "Please! I can heal her faster than she can heal herself."

Raya and Faith exchanged worried glances before slowly releasing me.

I quickly hovered my hands over Melissa's body and poured my healing magic over her, feeling the warmth move through me and into her. Moments later, her wounds began to heal, the swelling in her eyes reduced. She looked up at me with terrified eyes and slid away from me.

"I said that I yielded!" she cried. "Didn't you hear me?"

I shook my head quickly, pushing the pounding out from my ears. "I'm sorry."

"Don't apologize," Raya stated, lifting me up by the arm. I allowed her to pull me up and stood beside her. "You kicked her ass properly. You just have to know when to stop."

I felt sick. How had I not heard her tell me she yielded? Where had my mind gone? I didn't recall anything after my first punch when we were on the ground. Just darkness and one focus. Winning. I could think of nothing else.

I covered my mouth, my stomach queasy.

Faith put her arm around my shoulder. "You ok, hon?"

I nodded, not speaking.

"Spread the word, ladies!" Raya shouted, looking around the group. "Amina is not to be messed with. You will respect her and her orders from now on. That means no flirting with her man. For any of us."

The women nodded and murmured, fearful expressions on their faces.

"We're sorry we doubted you," Brittney stated, solemnly.

Melissa, looking no worse for the wear, nodded her head. "You're a good match for Erik. We'll let the others know."

I lowered my hand, my frozen mind coming to life again. Melissa seemed ok and not at all as horrified as I was. Maybe as a were she was use to the violence. I wasn't sure I would be. Wait. "There are others? There are a lot of eligible bachelors in this town, what is the deal?"

Raya shrugged. "What can we say? Power is attractive. And Erik is pretty hot."

"Maybe I'll take another look at Phillip since you say he's available," Melissa said with a smirk.

I shook my head, then immediately regretted it. My adrenaline had subsided, and the pain from my cut up stomach and hands, my bruised back and broken nose, all of it flared front and center. I slowly walked to a nearby seat that was tossed to the side, lifted it upright, and sat down.

"What's going on here?" came a familiar male voice with a delightful deep New Zealand accent.

I looked up and smiled at my mate.

Erik's hazel eyes grew as round as saucers, and he raced over to me, kneeling his tall, broad frame down in front of me. "What happened? Who did this to you?"

I didn't look to Melissa, not wanting to get her in trouble. "We were just playing a game," I replied with a toothy smile trying to downplay the very serious situation.

He cocked a dark brow. "Did this game involve trying to kill each other?"

"A little bit. You should have seen the other guy." I scrunched my eyes in pain, tightening my lips. I wasn't sure my acting was coming through right now.

"You got a bad bitch, Erik" Raya commented, patting Erik on the shoulder.

"I know," he replied, still looking me over. "I'm going to

pick you up in my arms and take you to the infirmary. Do not argue with me."

I sighed. I just fought to get respect, and he was going to ruin that by taking me out of here like some sappy heroine in a romance novel. To let him pick me up now would undo everything I'd done, even though I felt like death was leaning on my back.

"Don't pick me up. You're gonna ruin my street cred."

He titled his head, giving me a confused look. "What?"

"Just let me walk out of here with some pride." I struggled to my feet, swatting away his help, while internally screaming in pain.

The honey-blond haired former wife of Seth stepped forward. "We're sorry about disrespecting you. You too, Erik. We respect your relationship and won't bother you again. We're getting jobs, so you don't need to support us anymore. It'll be good for us to start again, find our own way," she said, hands clasped in front of her.

The other women murmured in agreement behind her.

Erik gave the women a nod and then lowered his voice when we left the room. "What did you do to them?"

"Just gave them a good talking to."

CHAPTER 2

Instead of going to the infirmary, Faith offered to heal me and instead we went back to my apartment.

Once healed, and after Faith left, I sat up on my bed and looked at Erik as he strolled back in my room with a cup of tea. I didn't blame the other women. He was gorgeous. Look up the description for 'rugged good looks', and you'd find a picture of him. He just had on jeans and a simple black shirt that fitted well to his defined chest and arms. It was like he was made of smooth marble with just enough softness to not hurt me. His straight black hair was buzzed on the side and back and longer on the top, and he had a trimmed, short beard which gave him a slightly bad boy appearance that I found very attractive. Well, the hair and his tattoos.

He placed the tea on the bedside table. "It's still hot," he said before sitting down on the edge of the bed. "Now tell me why you thought you needed to fight for respect?"

"Who told?"

He gave a lazy smile and a wink. "Your BFF, Phillip."

"That snitch."

Erik snorted and shook his head. "You didn't need to fight. I was handling it."

I clapped my hands together. "Yeah, I shouldn't have had to fight like some crazy woman on *Jerry Springer*, except Raya was telling me that women were coming to the station in scantily clad outfits trying to feed you."

He put his head in his hands. "I can't believe she said anything."

"I can't believe you didn't. So yeah, I had to go all WWF and fight a bitch and get my respect!"

Erik chuckled. "Street cred, snitch, fighting for respect. What are you a drug lord now?"

I shrugged. "You had to fight for your position; I had to do the same."

"I had to fight under Seth. I was voted in after he died."

I rolled my eyes. "Let's be honest. You killed the alpha, rightfully so, so the vote for you was pretty easy. Those women never saw me in hand to hand combat. I got my nose broken, not for you but for me. This is a different world. Eloquent words at a podium don't work anymore."

He took my right hand and lifted it to his lips. "I'm sorry I put you in that situation."

I shrugged. "Eh, it had to be done. We're asking people to fight alongside us and possibly die. They don't know anything about these first soulmates and their following. I have to gain their trust and respect if they are going to put their lives in my hands."

Erik tilted his head and grinned at me.

"What?" I asked with a frown.

"You're changing."

I rested my head against the headboard, exhausted. "I can't fight like that again," I whispered. "I lost control."

"I'm sure it wasn't that bad." He gave my hand a slight squeeze.

"I healed her. You didn't see her before. Raya and Faith

had to pull me off of her. I could have killed her. Something's wrong with me."

Erik pulled me to him and wrapped his arms around me. "Nothing's wrong with you. It's just this new world. It's making us harder."

He rested his chin on top of my head. "Who'd you fight?"

"Melissa."

He let out a low whistle. "She's a beast. Used to be a firefighter, I think."

Glad I didn't know that before or else I'd have run out of their screaming with my hands in the air. "Well, that werebear kicked my ass sufficiently."

"How'd you even fight her without using your magic?"

"I did. I gave myself a physical boost."

"You have been training, haven't you?"

Between meeting with my mentors in Hagerstown and Galway, I was getting a tremendous amount of training, thankfully. "It's all I do. Help run the town, get allies, train, take care of Brandon. Rinse and repeat. I just hope I'm done with the in-fighting. I don't want to have to do any more unnecessary fighting. I don't want to lose control like that again."

Erik kissed the top of my head. "You won't have to. They'll all spread the word after today. You aren't just someone who sits on a throne and points their finger to make things happen. That they will respect."

"We now have over two thousand people living here. I need everyone to get on board with protecting our town. They don't have to like me, but they've got to at least respect what we're trying to accomplish."

"That's going to be harder than we thought."

I pulled away from him and looked up at his eyes, suddenly clouded with concern. I was guessing he was busier than I thought. "Still dealing with Seth loyalists?"

He nodded slightly. "Some I'm dealing with, some are just

leaving town. It's where they're going that's concerning. If they're going to anyone that might be following the original soulmates, that's going to be a problem."

"We'll figure it out. Raya and Carter have been continuing damage control. People seem to like the counsel set up instead of just having one person run the place. We're also growing our own ally numbers from all over the world. We're in a better position than before." I scooted closer to him. "I wish that–"

"I could stay," he cut in, finishing my sentence.

I raised an eyebrow. There was no privacy anywhere, including my head. "Reading my mind?" As part of the Six, a group magically brought together and linked for a higher purpose, we had a talent for being able to speak telepathically. It hasn't yet translated to mind-reading, but I wouldn't be surprised if it did.

He shook his head. "Your eyes." He moved in and kissed me, and for one small moment, the world melted away.

I felt nothing else but his soft lips on mine and the touch of his strong hands on my arms. I inhaled the spicy scent of him. It was the best smell. I lightly nipped at his upper lip, sending him into his familiar growl, before lowering my hand to his thigh and moving slowly upward.

"Woman, what are you trying to do to me?" he groaned into my mouth.

I kept moving my hand up, inch by inch. "Nothing."

He moved from my lips and rested his forehead on mine. "It's getting late, Mina. I don't think we have time."

I sighed. Although it wasn't even dinner time, I knew what he meant. Dusk was quickly being replaced by nightfall, and that meant he had to go. If I didn't have Brandon, I would go to his place. Ever since Erik had gotten the virus, which only happened to paranormals, he'd kept his distance from our ward, Brandon, and unfortunately from me.

The worst of the symptoms, primitive behavior and

mindless violence, came out in the evening and night, so Erik decided to live outside the protective steel walls of the town to keep others safe. Brandon, having run in fear when Erik went loupe under the virus, was still a little apprehensive around Erik, and that mainly kept him away. Even though Phillip and I were able to pause the regressive virus from moving forward in Erik and a few others, the virus remained, and there was no cure, only a test.

When we came up with a test to discover who was infected, we were able to determine that a new black market drug had the unhappy side effect of causing the regressive virus. A person with the regressive sickness could then infect another without them ever having taken the drugs.

Erik stood up suddenly, and moments later, I heard the front door open and Brandon stomping into the apartment.

"Shit," he muttered.

"Take your shoes off first, son," came the voice of an older man. Mr. Johnson, the only other werehyena in our town, had taken to training Brandon some afternoons. It was, in part, so he could learn the hyena way, and also to ready him for battle. Brandon was only seven, and I had no intention of having him anywhere near the fighting. However, we didn't want him defenseless either. Erik and I basically adopted Brandon when I saved him from going loupe during his first shift into a werehyena. Both his parents were deceased, and the boy needed some stability and peace.

"Hey, Mr. Johnson I'm getting up," I called from the bedroom.

"Oh, don't worry about that, Rocky. Rest up!" he shouted back with a laugh.

I laughed as I heard him shut the front door. Looks like word of the fight got around quickly.

Erik looked to the window. "Maybe I should leave through the window before he sees me."

I laughed again. "You're going to jump out of a window to avoid seeing a kid? Do you know how high up we are?"

"I don't want to scare him."

I heard Brandon walk down the hall.

"Then don't jump out of a window and plummet to your death."

Brandon jumped into my doorway frame with a growl, hands out as if he had imaginary claws.

I jumped, pretending to be scared, and threw my hands up. "Oh no!" I cried.

Brandon paused in the doorway, lowering his hands as he stared up at Erik, his light brown eyes large and frightened.

"It's ok, Brandon, Erik was just taking care of me. I got sick at work. He helped me get better."

The curly-haired boy looked up to Erik, who stood absolutely still in front of the window. When had he moved over there? Erik held his hands out at his sides. He gave Brandon a slight smile before saying hello.

Brandon didn't respond at first. He looked over to me as if seeking permission.

I didn't blame him for his caution. He'd been through so much in his short time in this world. His father had been killed in a fight for a high-ranking spot in Seth's pack, then Seth, while under the influence of the new drug, had killed his mother, and he'd seen his idol, for lack of a better word, go loupe and try to kill him. My main desire when it came to that boy was to protect him.

I gave Brandon a slow nod, and the little boy looked back to Erik with wide, unsure eyes. "Hi," he said in a tiny voice. "Are you back now?"

"No, just visiting," Erik replied, still frozen.

The little boy seemed to ponder that over in his mind, his eyes moving to the left, lips twisting. "You going to eat with us?"

Erik scratched his head and gave a sheepish smile. "I can't. I have to…do some work."

Brandon nodded before shrugging. "Next time, ok?" he said before moonwalking away.

I let out a relieved breath. Kids just bounce back better.

"That's not what I expected," Erik said in a careful voice.

"He's a kid. They're resilient, and time heals. We hope, right? He needs you."

"He has you and Mr. Johnson."

I sucked my teeth. "That's not enough. It was your idea to bring him in. Now we're a packaged deal. Come have lunch with us this weekend. He needs to spend time with you again. I need to spend time with you."

Erik looked away, a frown on his face. "It's getting darker out. I need to go."

I reached my hand out, calling out his name. However, Erik was already a blur of supernatural speed, leaving my bedroom. Soon after, I heard the front door close.

I let out a jagged sigh, loneliness creeping throughout my insides and settling like a boulder in my heart.

CHAPTER 3

Later that night I was doing a little meditative magic I'd learned from one of my mentors, Liz. Meditation had become a helpful crutch to quiet my mind of self-doubt and to deal with my growing anxiety issues. It also helped me concentrate on and strengthen my gifts. When I wasn't helping to run the town, spending time with Brandon, drumming up allies to help me fight the first soulmates, I was training. Mind, body and soul.

I went to bed, ready to sleep with a little of this anxiety abated. I'd just gotten comfortable when someone knocked on my door. I threw off the comfort of my covers and quickly walked down the hallway to the foyer. Looking through the peephole, I was ready to drop kick whoever it was at this hour.

Charles.

I swung open the door and frowned. My brother stood leaning a hand on the door frame, the other hand on his hip. His brown eyes were bloodshot. His honey complexion was ashen, and his face was covered in a beard which he'd grown out the last month, and I still wasn't sure that I liked it. His curly dark brown hair was longer and it was twisted in braids, with the top reaching almost to his eyebrows and the sides and back shaven. We could have been twins except my curls were shoulder-length, and he was tall and lanky where I was short and curvy.

"What's going on?" I asked, opening the door wider.

Charles walked through. "Came here for dinner. You invited me."

"Dinner was at seven. It's almost eleven!" I exclaimed.

He walked into the kitchen. "So, I don't get to eat?" He opened the refrigerator.

I scratched my head, perplexed at his sudden brotherly visit. "Uh, no. I invited you over just to spend time. There's a jug of blood in the back though."

Charles was a vampire and a technology mage. He'd started off as just the latter but then had come back from death as a vampire still maintaining his earlier powers. Most people who changed into vampires with magic had many humanistic qualities. They had an easier time going out in the sun, could procreate, and eat food. People made into vampires by drinking vampire blood, and then dying were more limited. No procreation, the sun could kill them or give them a bad sunburn at the very least, and they did not eat.

Charles had gone into a dark place since coming back from the dead, and an even darker place after killing a close friend of ours who had been possessed by the soul of one of the original soulmates. He'd saved my life, but that didn't mean he felt good about it. I was pretty sure he was going through some form of depression or PTSD, but he refused to talk about it, and he would not allow me to use my magic to heal him emotionally. It was as if he wanted to feel the pain.

I watched him open a container, take out a piece of chicken, and bite into a drum leg.

I poked out my lower lip and squinted my eyes, confused. "What are you doing? You can't eat."

"I took something that allows me to eat one meal each

time I take it," he said with a mouthful of chicken. He rolled his eyes and let out a sigh. "I forgot how well you make chicken. The seasoning is just everything."

"What kind of 'something' did you take?" I asked, taking the container from him and closing the lid over the chicken.

He reached up to the nearby cabinet above the counter and took down a plate, holding the chicken between his teeth. He put the chicken on the plate and opened the other two containers filled with the collard greens and cornbread. "Just a pill I got from this girl who works at the apothecary," he replied, piling his plate and then putting it in the microwave.

That sounded shady as hell. "So, it's just a pill that gives vampires the ability to eat?"

"Yeah, and ghouls, too."

"That's all it does?

Charles tilted his head, narrowing his eyes. "Why does it feel like you're grilling me? Someone's trying to do something nice for the good people of this town, and you want to make it an issue."

Apparently, he thought I was stupid. "If this is so nice, why are your eyes bloodshot?"

He shrugged. "Side effect."

"You're so full of shit, Charles." There was a new magical drug that was slowly growing in popularity throughout the world, but I hadn't seen him regress like Seth. At least not yet. That didn't mean that he wasn't taking another type of magic drug or magically enhanced weed. He hadn't been himself. At times he had all the tell-tale signs of someone strung out. His eyes seemed dead, with lids that barely stayed open, and his energy was low. He rarely seemed alert anytime I was around him. It frightened me.

The microwave beeped signaling the food was heated, but before Charles could open the door, I went up to him and wrapped my arms around my brother. "I need you to be good, Charles. We got a war to fight. I need you to be good. I need you to be," I whispered, my voice breaking along with my heart.

I felt Charles' arms surround me. "Sis, I'm good. I just wanted to eat food again." He moved me to arms-length and looked in my eyes. "I got your back, sis. Don't worry about me. I won't let you down. I'm going to kick these original soulmates' asses, and I'm going to get my girl back from that pointy-eared dick."

But I did worry. I couldn't help it. He was my little brother, and I wanted to do everything I could to make things right for him. I just didn't know how. I gave him a small smile, moving away as he went to get his food from the microwave. "If Lisa wants to come back, she can," I replied, changing the subject. We weren't going to solve this problem tonight, but I wasn't giving up, either.

"You don't believe that. That elf, Jujube–"

"Joo-won."

"Whatever, that elf king fucker is holding her captive." Charles picked up a piece of cornbread and bit into it.

"She ran off with him to prevent him from killing Erik and me. She's staying because she thinks she can convince him to be an ally with us against the first soulmates since he's so into her."

Charles grumbled something unintelligible and took his plate to the dining room.

"You can't be mad, Charles. You did hook up with Blake."

Charles shoved a forkful of greens into his mouth before speaking. "I know, we aren't even seeing each other anymore."

I frowned as I watched the contents of his food swirl around in his mouth as he talked. Had he forgotten proper table manners in the few months he'd stopped eating? "Did you really like Blake?"

He shrugged. "Not like I did Lisa. We were each other's

escape. I was infatuated with her, and she liked the attention from someone new. I was a plaything to her. Lisa hates me now." He took another bite of chicken, and I wasn't sure he'd even chewed, just swallowed it like some cartoon character.

"Did you forget table etiquette when you became a vampire?" I asked, sitting down.

He looked at me with blatant annoyance. "Yes," he replied before opening his mouth wide.

I was just about to reach over and pluck him on the forehead when I heard the loud scream of a child.

Brandon.

We both jumped from the table, Charles zooming past me in a blur of vampiric speed.

By the time I got to his room, Charles was already sitting on the bed with his arms around a crying Brandon. I turned on the light at the bedside table and sat on Brandon's other side, rubbing his back. "What's wrong, honey? Bad dream?"

Brandon sniffled and wiped at his face. "He tried to get me."

"It was just a nightmare, little man," Charles assured him, ruffling the boy's hair.

Brandon shook his head swiftly. "No, the man tried to pull me away. He wanted me to do bad things. He tried to make me change." He looked behind him.

I looked over him and saw that his sheets were sliced up. A cold fear washed over me. "Did you do that?"

Brandon nodded. "I'm sorry. He made me do it."

"It's ok, honey." It was not okay, but he didn't need to know that.

Charles looked over to me with questioning eyes.

"Who made you do it, Brandon?" I asked, but I already had an idea. At this stage, anybody messing with us came from only one source.

"He said his name was Gedeyon."

Gedeyon. Just as I suspected. One of the original soulmates.

"Can he do that?" Charles asked with wide eyes.

I had no clue. The ability to control someone via a dream was horrific, but they were shockingly strong, so I didn't doubt it. "How'd you fight him off?"

Brandon didn't respond, his eyes still watery. That monster must have really terrified him.

"I warded him," I replied softly. I'd tried warding a person, which worked as an invisible shield, when we fought Seth and Joo-won. It'd helped Erik when he'd needed time to heal before getting back in the fight.

When I found out that Gedeyon was an ancient werehyena, I had immediately put a ward over Brandon so that he wouldn't be controlled by the more powerful Gedeyon when he finally appeared. I had no clue it would work as protection even in a dream state. That was good to know. It might be a good idea to ward the others in our circle as well.

When we finally got Brandon back to sleep with a promise for me to sleep next to him when Charles left, we headed back to the dining area.

Charles looked down at his food but didn't touch it. "I don't get it, sis. If this Gedeyon dude has the power to control people in their dreams, why would he come for the weakest of the bunch?"

I rubbed my eyes with the heel of my hands, weariness burning them. "When he entered my dreams, he didn't harm me. I got the sense he wasn't strong enough to. Instead, he tried to persuade me to join him, so he could use me to grow his power. He threatened me, and I ignored him. He's starting with Brandon as a teaser."

Charles sucked in his breath and put his hands on his waist. "When he gets strong enough, he could control the whole pack, without even moving from wherever the hell he is. Or maybe every werehyena in the world."

"He's powerful, but we won't let him get any stronger." I should be scared, but I was too pissed. That ancient asshole had come after a small child. I was responsible for Brandon, and I wasn't going to let him get hurt. Gedeyon could have a problem with me, but he would not harm an innocent child. He'd just made a huge tactical error. I'd been scared before, but now I was mad.

CHAPTER 4

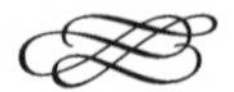

A couple days later, I received another knock on my door. I opened the door to Phillip Leal. He walked right in without an invite. This was becoming an unfortunate habit among my friends. He turned and gave me a self-satisfied smirk. I would have asked him why he was so cocky that day, but it wasn't any different than any other day.

"Don't smile at me like that. I've been trying to reach you to practice our bond magic and beat these original assholes," I huffed, crossing my arms. "They came for Brandon, or don't you care?"

Phillip rolled his light brown eyes that were usually deceivingly innocent. Almost puppy-dog-like. They'd certainly fooled me in the beginning, along with the fact that no one could deny that he was cute. He was slightly taller than average, toned, clean-shaven bronzed skin with short wavy black hair cropped close to his head. He was a beautiful asshole, and I was stuck with him.

It wasn't totally his fault he'd been an ass up until recently. When I first met him, he had been the tyrannical ruler of Silver Spring, torturing and maiming any who defied him or were a possible threat to him. Then Lisa had banished us to Ireland, and I had found out that he was under a dark curse or spell of some sort, which the first soulmates were behind. I had been able to lessen the effects of the curse, which made him pretty likable. However, he wasn't totally in the clear. We had learned he was very susceptible to the female half of the soulmate pairing, Rima.

This didn't put us at a total disadvantage. Since she could body hop, if she was nearby, Phillip would know because he'd go all googly-eyed for whatever body she was in. We worked on keeping our bond as powerful as possible so that we could hopefully dull down Rima's control over him.

"I was trying to gain us followers. I wasn't ditching you. I told you I'd be back Sunday. I wouldn't leave you hanging. Not anymore." He gave me dramatic innocent eyes.

I twisted my lips in annoyance. I knew he had a job to do. We needed support, but we also needed to hone our power. "Whatever."

Phillip nodded, still smiling. "You know, while I was out there rallying the troops, it wasn't an easy task. I had a target on my back. I was often attacked. But I survived because I had my power source with me."

I cocked a brow having no idea what he was talking about. "What was that?"

"Gary. We really haven't been using our familiars enough. Granted taking a griffin everywhere you go isn't the easiest thing to do but I can mentally call him. You can probably do the same with Poppy."

Well, that made sense. "So, I could just teleport my kitten when I need her?"

Phillip nodded, looking way too proud of himself. "Yup, like your own personal battery. When we fight, we need to always have them in the vicinity. I don't know if the original soulmates have familiars, but if they don't, that's a one up. And you should also think about upgrading your cat."

I rolled my eyes. "I'm not getting rid of her."

"No, I'm not saying that. Your cat is a reanimated familiar of a soulmate. She needs to be in training too. You never know what a magical kitten can do."

That was a fair point and one I hadn't considered. Guess it was time to wake the kitty.

"By the way, you didn't ask why I came back a day early."

I turned and walked further in my apartment, Phillip following. "Why are you back early?"

"Have you seen your friends this morning?"

"It's Saturday. I didn't have any plans with anyone." I didn't mention that I was still holding out hope that Erik would show for lunch. I hadn't heard from him in the last two days since my fight. His keeping his distance really made this whole relationship thing challenging. "Why are you asking?"

He shrugged. "If my friends were all meeting without me, I'd be pretty pissed."

I gave him a slow blink. What in tarnation was he talking about? "Is this your indirect way of saying the others are doing something without me?"

"A little birdie told me that she saw the four of them, sans Lisa, of course, outside of town headed towards Mae's place."

That was odd. "By little birdie, do you mean Blake?"

Phillip threw his hands out to the side.

Ok, maybe he was instigating things. It was probably a misunderstanding. How could they meet without me? "We don't know they went to Mae's."

"We don't know they didn't."

I narrowed my eyes. "Why would Mae call a meeting and leave me out? What did I do to her? She didn't call you to meet either. She's your godmother!"

Phillip raised his eyebrows. "I know. I think we both know this was not a coincidence. I love Mae, but she can be sneaky."

"You don't have to tell me that. Having us drink vampire

blood unknowingly, knowing you and I were soulmates, working to keep us banished..."

Phillip nodded. "Yep. Gotta love her. But I'm not mad at her. She has her reasons, I'm sure. What would bother *me,* though, is why they all were ok with meeting without *you.* Even your loving brother and your furry mate."

I tightened my lips together again. I was bothered. I'm sure he could read it on my face. I never could play poker. Maybe I had a fear of missing out.

Phillip leaned towards me. "Want to hear what's going on?"

~

I hadn't gone invisible in a very long time. The last time was when I had escaped from a prison for the paranormal. It just seemed sneaky to use it any other time than when absolutely necessary. And I suppose teleporting into someone's home while invisible was the very definition of sneaky.

Also, because Erik had a were's nose, we also concealed our smell. We were basically flies on the wall.

"I've never seen her like that before," Faith stated seated on the couch of Mae's living room. She ran a hand through her short hair, her face scrunched together in apparent worry. "She scared me."

"She scared herself," Erik said, leaning on the wall next to a bookshelf. His eyes were dark and face set in a scowl. "Why are we here without her?"

Good question.

Mae walked from the kitchen of the small home with a plate of what looked like snickerdoodles in her hand. She was older, perhaps in her 60s, with short coily, black hair and wise, deep brown eyes. She wore jeans and a long bright red cardigan over a black blouse with a chunky colorful necklace adorning her neck. "Because there are things you should know. Things that are meant just for you."

What the hell? What did they need to know that I didn't?

The town head medical mage, Bill Locklear, followed behind Mae with a big pot of coffee in one hand and some cups in another. He was tall, with short gray hair and a solemn face. That day, he wore slacks with a gray sweater that said, Don't Worry, Be Happy. He wore this signature necklace with a turquoise pendant around his neck.

Felix Gonzalez took some of the cups from Bill and put them on the coffee table. He was our local gentle giant at 6'7 with the frame of a wrestler. He was the heart and soul of our group, and now that we knew he was half-angel, his kind heart made sense.

Felix was also half-demon. We'd only found out his identity recently when his guardian angel, Azrael, showed up out of nowhere and returned Felix's lost memories. Apparently, Felix used to be a hitman for a demon, and the angels put a stop to that by wiping his mind, knowing his greater purpose was to become part of The Six.

Mae sat down in a gray loveseat near the couch. "I'm not surprised she went berserk. Soulmates are very powerful. They can be of the greatest good, but also of the greatest evil."

Charles pffted. "What are you getting at? My sister's not evil. Now that other guy..."

"That much power, uncontrolled, can lead one astray. It's the reason I called you all here. And why I could not invite Phillip or Amina."

"Why can't they hear this?" Erik asked. He looked like he was biting back a snarl, and it was more than clear that he was upset at being there without me. This is why I loved him.

Mae placed her hands on her lap and looked down as if contemplating her words before she spoke. "Because there are things that you might be called to do that they cannot stop. Do you think that soulmates being so powerful is not a risk to humanity?"

"No, we don't," Charles said, laying on the carpet, sunglasses over his eyes. This would be his bedtime so I was sure he wasn't in a great mood to be up. "We know the story of the first soulmates. They started out like saviors, went crazy with power and tormented the world."

I always knew I could count on my brother to defend me.

"Right," Mae stated, nodding. "And it can happen to any soulmate pairing. If the other pairings lived long enough, it could have happened to them. The soulmates before Amina and Phillip were only alive long enough to do good. They were killed by Gedeyon and Rima before they became something else."

That was disturbing, but it didn't mean it was our future. Things would be different for us. They had to be.

Erik growled, pushing himself from the wall. "What are you trying to get at, Mae?" His voice rumbled through the room. For a moment, I felt a bit of calm at his anger. He seemed just as upset as me, and it was comforting.

Mae looked to Erik with saddened eyes. "If Phillip and Amina beat the original soulmates, they could live long lives and continue to do amazing things."

"That's what we want, right?" Felix asked, pouring himself some coffee before sitting on the couch next to Faith. He looked so confident that what Mae was alluding to was not going to happen that it made me smile, in spite of myself.

"Yes," Mae began looking around the room. I could have sworn her eyes lingered on Phillip and me, but she didn't seem to be affected. Instead, she looked past us to the others. "It's possible. It's also possible they could go evil even sooner, especially with Phillip tainted. This situation they are in is very stressful, and they are very new to magic. Amina's fight greatly concerns me. I've had disturbing visions."

My heart caught in my throat. Mae and her visions. That did not bode well for us.

"Why are you just telling us and not them?" Erik asked, his eyes clouded over in darkness.

I knew before Mae even answered, and my heart sank.

"The Six were brought together to stop evil in the world. Soulmates can be that evil. There might come a time when you have to stop them from doing wrong. I didn't invite them because this message isn't for them. It's for you. Lisa already knows. The Fairy Queen Arwa told her this. Now you must know."

Felix put his coffee down and suddenly his happy-go-lucky disposition dissipated. "What do you mean by 'stop' them?"

"If you can't subdue them you might have to..." Bill grasped his pendant and rubbed it before saying the next words. "...kill them."

I wanted out. I wanted away. How had I become the enemy? This wasn't the way it was supposed to be.

Charles jumped up. "If you think I'm fucking killing my sister you're out of your goddamn mind. Fuck this Six."

"Young man!" Mae shouted, standing up as well. The room shook slightly, reminding me that Mae wasn't just all talk. As we had learned when she first showed signs of the supernatural illness, she could manifest a psychic earthquake and possibly other telepathic movements. "I have told you before to watch your mouth. Now, I understand you are upset. I am not chomping at the bit for anyone to kill Amina or my god-son. What we are talking about is a worst-case scenario. What we haven't had a chance to say is that since Amina is part of the Six she might have better control over herself and Phillip, or you all may have an easier time subduing her if she were to go mad with power like the originals."

Bill rubbed Mae's back in support. "We are simply saying

to prepare for the possibility so that you know what to do if the worst were to happen. This is the best-case scenario for them. They have the Six, mates in Blake and Erik, and Amina has Charles. Just look out for them. Protect them both, not just from the original soulmates, but from themselves."

His ominous words hung in the air, and the nervous looks between them made me queasy. They were worried. About me. Maybe even scared. They weren't the only ones.

CHAPTER 5

After teleporting out of Mae's house, Phillip and I sat at the bar of the local pub and restaurant, drinking whiskey silently beside each other. In the supernatural apocalypse, alcohol was more limited, but almost ten years in, companies were starting to resurrect and create their products again. Alcohol was one of them. These companies were mainly controlled by the growing government. This gave the government bargaining power to have us non-government communities fall in line if we wanted any comforts of the past. Many non-government towns ended up making their own liquors as a result. Our town made a craft beer and cider that we sold to other towns for various foods, drinks and items, like the whiskey we were now drinking.

We were on our second glass. It was barely after 12 p.m. It didn't matter.

"We're the bad guys," Phillip said before taking another swig of his drink.

"You're the bad guy. I'm just guilty by association." I looked around the almost empty pub. It was just the two of us, one bartender and a couple in a booth across the room. I didn't need anyone hearing us self-doubt. If we couldn't trust ourselves, why would they?

Phillip leaned into me. "You think your friends are going to tell you what they learned?"

I leaned back and glared at him. "Oh, they're my friends now?"

"I didn't see Blake in that room."

"Touché." I stared down at my drink. I had no idea if they would confess. I'd teleported right after Bill had finished speaking and for the almost hour we'd been at the bar, no one had tried to reach me. Brandon was at a friend's house, and Erik had never responded to my lunch invite, so that was canceled.

I shrugged my shoulders back and sat upright. I needed to get myself together. This was a distraction from the bigger issue. "We shouldn't be at this bar full of self-pity. We need to keep preparing. We just have to make sure that whatever we do is for the greater good."

Phillip turned to me and bit his lower lip in thought. "If I go bad, feel free to put me to sleep. Not like you would a dog, I mean more like a male sleeping beauty."

I chuckled slightly feeling mildly relieved that I could even laugh at all. "I wasn't confused about that."

He gave me two thumbs up. "And you can have Gary."

I turned my upper lip up. "I don't want your bird lion thing. I don't even know where you house it."

"He sleeps in the farm area in a barn with horses."

I did not care. I didn't want to talk about what we should do if we went bad. I didn't plan for that to happen. "That does not sound safe for the horses."

"Anyway, I just want to make sure that you know I'm fine with being put to sleep, the snoring kind, if I show signs. You should be free to live your life and have fur babies with Erik if he doesn't go loupe from the illness."

It seemed so odd to see Phillip give up hope like this. He

was supposed to be the overly cocky one. Now he was preparing for his demise. "Thanks."

"And if you go bad..." He stopped and looked at me, expectedly.

I ignored him and took a sip of my drink. He could keep his negative thinking to himself. I was not coming out of this the villain. We were heroes, damn it.

He cleared his throat, persistent.

I rolled my eyes. I just wanted this conversation to be over so I would appease him for now. "Ok, put me to sleep, too. The snoring kind, not the six feet under kind. But you can't have Poppy. She's going to Charles."

Phillip gave a shake of his fist like some old man. "Oh damn, that's too bad. I was really–" he paused and looked to the door.

I followed his gaze to find Grace Sarin at the entrance. She spotted us and waved before walking over.

Grace had been one of the first to greet the Six in town. I internally called her a Disney princess because she was always so darn cheerful and beautiful. She was average height, curvy, with long wavy dark brown hair, amazingly arched eyebrows and smooth skin the color of burnt sienna. She was constantly smiling, and when she sang, I felt like birds chirped along with her. She was actually a siren with the ability to control and kill anyone she chose just by singing. To see her sing was both fascinating and horrifying. Though she did have an amazing voice.

She usually wore a dress in some flowery print to top off her princess style. Since we were in the midst of our six-month winter period, another by-product of the new super-natural world, she was more covered in a long beige peacoat, but I could see the material of a long black dress with flower prints peeking from the hem of her coat.

I hadn't seen much of Grace since she and Faith had unceremoniously parted ways. Well, according to Faith, they never broke up because they were never together. Grace was more of a one-person gal, and Faith was more of a free spirit, in part due to her struggle with containing her love as a succubus. Lately, Faith had been cozying up to the angel, Azrael.

Grace plopped down on a barstool beside me. "What are we drinking?" she asked, looking behind the bar at the very limited variety of libations.

"Whiskey," I replied, staring back down at my drink. "What brings you here?"

"I had a craving for their fish and chips," she replied in her bubbly tone. She leaned past me and waved at Phillip. "Hi, Phil."

When he didn't speak, I turned to him and saw him wave at her with wide eyes like he was in awe.

I leaned towards him. "What's wrong with you?"

"Has she always looked this good?" he whispered.

I chuckled. "Like a Miss Universe contestant? Yes."

"You said she's not with Faith anymore, right?"

I looked back to Grace, who was busy giving her order to the bartender. "Well, technically they weren't an official couple according to Faith. So yeah, she's free. What's the deal? It's not like she's new to town. Have you never noticed her before?"

"I guess not because I'm looking at her in a new light." He began to grin, his eyes still glued to her. "Switch seats with me." He elbowed me lightly.

"What? Why?" What the hell was going on here? Was he actually interested in Grace? How could he even focus on such things now?

He tore his eyes from her to glare at me. "You are the worst wingman."

"That's because I wasn't trying to be. Why are you being weird?" I lowered my voice and gritted my teeth. "She doesn't even like guys."

"She might be more fluid like Faith." He tapped my shoulder. "Come on."

I glared at him, as I got up and moved. This was odd even for him. Was he lonely? I supposed it was possible. He still had his BFF, Blake, but then again Blake was her own free spirit, and she'd dated my brother, so perhaps that was too close for comfort for him.

Phillip was acting different. He was being all into a woman he could have flirted with many times before and had expressed no interest in him ever. The last woman who he'd fallen for was an odd choice then too, my friend Chelsea who had hated him. Of course, then he had been under Rima's influence when she possessed Chelsea's body. Not to say that his interest in any woman had to be because Rima had hopped into the woman's body, but we had come too far to ignore signs when we saw them.

I stopped in front of Phillip, my heart froze.

Phillip stood up, his brows raised, and I was sure he was thinking the same thing as me. We both looked over to Grace, who looked back at us with a pleasant smile.

"Something wrong?" she asked, before taking a sip of her drink.

Phillip walked around me and sat down carefully on the stool next to her.

I remained standing, my heart taking off in my chest.

What could I do? I couldn't kill her. She was possessing Grace, and I wouldn't see another friend harmed because of that bitch. I could put her to sleep, but then I'd have no way of confirming that she was really Rima.

"Rima," Phillip said, leaning towards her with a slight grin. Clearly, he was not afraid.

Meanwhile, I was still holding my breath thinking of next steps. I had to be absolutely sure before I made a move, and even then I wanted to be certain I could win.

Grace raised her eyebrows with a look of confusion, and

for a moment I thought we were wrong. Then she lowered her well-arched brows and a soft smile covered her lips. "Interesting," she said in a low voice. She put her drink down on the bar and turned to face us equally. "How did you guess?"

My heart thumped in my ears. It was her! Why had Phillip given away our hand so easily? I wanted to strangle him.

Phillip crossed his arms, a look of confidence spread across his face. "Your little spell you had put on me to make me fall in love with Chelsea slash you, also works as a sort of 'you' detector. I know when you are in the body of someone nearby because I start thinking with the wrong head."

What is wrong with you? Why are you telling her our secret? Now she'll know she can't hide from us! I cried telepathically.

Shit, Amina I don't know! I can't lie to her. She's compelling me. Knock me in the head, so I'll shut up!

I walked towards him to do just that, and Grace turned her attention to me. "Don't be mad at our little Philly. He can't help himself. He has to do what I say." She threw out her hands to the side. "Well, I suppose the jig is up, as they say. Are you going to try to kill me now?" She batted her eyelashes, not looking the least bit scared.

Of course, I wouldn't. She was possessing the body of a friend, but I was going to do something. "Sleep!" I shouted, pouring magic into my words.

She gave a fake yawn, covering her mouth. "You can't possibly think that such a power word would work on me. It's going to take stronger magic than that, honey. But I suppose I should do you the favor, before you bow down to me or die, whatever you decide, of knowing that Grace is not real."

"What are you saying?" I frowned, taking a hesitant step back.

"There is no Grace. Never has been. I'm the real Rima."

She laughed, and I looked to Phillip, whose face was a mask of confusion. "Yes, you silly things. I've been mobile for a couple of years now. My poor Gedeyon was not. *Was* being the operative word now." She picked up her drink and took a sip before speaking again. "I mean, what do you expect? We are ancient, after all. The most powerful soulmates ever to exist. When magic returned, we slowly awoke in different lands. Gedeyon back in Ethiopia and me back in India."

I grew queasy as Rima spoke. She had been under our noses this whole time. Faith had been alone with her. I'd been alone with her. She could have killed us. My mind blared a loud alarm in my head, willing me to act but with Phillip so close and in possible harm, I was admittedly fearful. I hated him sometimes but he was my soulmate. Him dead would do us no good.

"You found us even before we knew of each other. How'd you do that?" Phillip asked, his eyes were slightly glazed over as he spoke, and although his brain seemed to still function, I could see that he was still under Rima's thrall. I'd have to get him out of here if I was going to fight her without him jumping in the way.

She smiled. "When you started dreaming of each other, you put out a beacon. Not a strong one, but it was enough to pique our interest. So, when I was able to move, I came here. To you."

I needed to stall her, to work out a way to kill her before she made another move. "So, you're a siren and Gedeyon is a werehyena and you have soulmate magic."

Hey, guys, so the female soulmate is here at McGaffigans Tavern. She actually is Grace, blah, blah, blah. Help! I cried out to the Six. If I was going to fight Rima, I needed a power boost, and the Six could help.

Grace/Rima tilted her head from side to side, looking up at the ceiling. "Actually, you have our soulmate magic. And we need to get that back from you. Gedeyon would prefer you just work for us and we can siphon your power as we go. He has such a good heart. I say, kill you now. Yes, it might mean less power that we'll receive, but I think it's less cumbersome than dealing with your continued presence."

What? Erik shouted in my mind. *On our way.*

I heard confirmations from the others, except Lisa. Not good.

I balled my hands into fists, forcing my nerves away. "So, then, you aren't that powerful yet."

Rima tsk-tsked me with a wag of her finger. "It would be silly to think that, darling. Our powers are beyond your abilities. You are both babies, still learning. And we still have some of our soulmate gifts. Your strength would be just a boost to aid us in ruling this world as we once did."

Rima tilted her head and narrowed her eyes at me. Shit, did she know I was calling for help? "Phillip, bring Brandon here."

I reached for Phillip, who stepped back, giving me a pained look as he disappeared.

Panic ripped through me. "You bitch! Leave him alone!" I moved towards her.

She held up her hands. "I need to have some insurance. Don't think I don't know you were psychically reaching out to your friends. Tell them to stay back, and your little friend won't get hurt."

Shit, well that answered my question. However, I was not going to stand here like a victim. Maybe my friends couldn't come but my battery could. I shut my eyes and conjured my kitten to me except I placed her behind the bar and out of sight.

I heard the small sound of her purr behind me, and it slightly relaxed me. Sure, I was still on my own, but that little bit of help did something for my confidence.

Phillip reappeared with Brandon, who held his hand, his little face wide-eyed and confused. And my panic rose again.

"What are you going to do?" I asked, staring at Brandon.

"I can sing him a little song," Rima replied, putting her drink back down. "Brandon, what's your favorite song?"

This bitch. "Don't answer her."

Brandon began to look rightfully scared as he looked at the three of us with nervous eyes.

I had to get the others to stand down. If they showed up, Brandon could die. I needed to take care of Rima on my own.

Everyone, fall back. Don't come. She brought Brandon here, and she is going to kill him. She can do it with just a note.

Shit. I heard Charles curse in my mind.

"They won't come. So, you can let Brandon go back home."

Rima tapped her chin, as if in thought. "Or I could keep him here and have him watch you submit to me or die."

"Amina?" Brandon called in a shaky voice. "What's going on?" He struggled out of Phillip's grasp.

"Hold him!" Rima barked.

Phillip, his face now dazed, almost dead, grabbed the boy back by the arm and yanked him back. Rima's hold was too powerful over him. I wouldn't be getting his help today.

"You stay with Mr. Phillip, ok?" I replied with a tight smile.

Brandon nodded slowly, tears filling his eyes. He might only be seven, but he was no fool.

I looked away, unable to bear seeing him so scared.

We have to do something, Amina. Phillip's voice rang in my head. *I'm not going to submit if I can help it. There's two of us and only one of her. If we bow down to her, she will still kill him. She wouldn't want any loose ends. That's how they rule.*

He was right. We'd learned enough about the first soulmates to know that they took no prisoners. We had to attack and make it count. My only hope was that the ward I had surrounding Brandon was strong enough to withstand her power.

Rima folded her arms and gave a pretend pout. "Are you done discussing what to do?" she asked, unfazed by our telepathic communication.

Rima was strong, but she wasn't a life mage. Perhaps a few magic informed words wouldn't work on her, but our mage abilities might. Except I needed my magic to hit hard. I'd only get one shot.

As if sensing my need, Poppy jumped on the counter and butted her head into my shoulder. I grabbed her quickly to my chest and a burst of hot energy coursed through my body. My fingers tingled with an almost electric current that I had no time to wonder about. I quickly focused on the base of Rima's neck and pushed my magic through my body towards her.

Rima's eyes widened, and she let out a blood-curdling scream. The sickening crack of bone filled the quiet restaurant, and the siren dropped to her knees, her neck hanging at an unnatural angle onto her chest, bone protruding through the skin.

I heard the few other people in the pub scream, and the bartender dropped the plate of fish and chips he was carrying. I hoped we weren't scarring people for life here, but this was the new world, I was sure they'd seen worse.

Phillip let go of Brandon who raced towards me. I shoved him behind me, and he clutched my shirt.

However, Rima wasn't dead. She grabbed her head and moved it upright on her shoulders. How was she not dead? Even as a soulmate, we were still susceptible to death if the heart was damaged, airway obstructed or brain stem snapped. Was it because she was a siren? They weren't exactly human. Vampires, ghouls, weres, and some others could live from a neck break if not fully decapitated; maybe she could too.

"What the hell?" Phillip shouted. He pushed his magic towards Rima, and she flew back into the farthest wall, cracking the plaster. He held her body against the wall with his magic, and I was happy for once that something was slowing this siren down.

Poppy hissed in my arms, and I held her tighter to me. However, she was stronger than usual, and she wiggled out and jumped to the floor. If she tried to attack Rima, she would die. She was just a kitten, magical or not.

The cat continued to hiss in Rima's direction and arched her back. I heard bone snap and her body stretched, fur growing longer and expanding before a burst of blinding light hit the room, causing us all to turn away.

What the hell was happening to my cat? Had Rima done something to her, knowing she was my familiar? I looked to Rima, who was also squinting her eyes and looking away. She didn't seem in control right now.

When the light disappeared, we were all staring at a panther sized gray cat with bright yellow eyes that shown like headlights.

"Poppy?" I said in a questioning whisper. The cat was definitely otherworldly. How had I not known?

My cat ignored my voice and sped towards Rima before taking off into a leap and landing on her, pulling her down to the ground.

I watched in open mouth shock as Poppy began to tear and claw at the siren with her monstrous teeth and claws. Splatters of Rima's blood painted the floor as Poppy continued to maul her.

Rima stopped screaming and pushed at Poppy's chest before she opened her mouth again…and sang. Her voice was crystal clear and powerful. Her range was unlike anything I'd ever heard, going from high to low effortlessly. I didn't know the song she sang. It was in another language. However, the melody was entrancing. Before I knew it, I began to sway to her sound.

Amina, take Brandon and get the fuck out of there. Now! Erik's voice boomed in my head.

I'd heard his voice, his words, but, it sounded so distant that nothing connected.

I went rigid and felt a wetness on my cheeks. I touched it and looked down at my finger. Blood. I quickly looked to Brandon and Phillip, who were swaying to her sound as well, inching closer to her, along with the other patrons and bartender.

Panic took hold, and my vision went blurry as blood continued to pour from my eyes, nose and ears, as it did the others. I moved towards Phillip – Brandon still clinging to me – but stumbled as throbbing pain stabbed at the back of my head. I felt sick to my stomach but kept stumbling forward. The pain was blinding. I felt like my head would explode.

Rima was killing us with her voice. It was horrific, and I had no idea how long we had until we'd pop like balloons.

"Poppy, come!" I screamed, feeling the sudden urgency.

Poppy, ever the obedient cat even when in her magic form, jumped off Rima and raced towards me.

The voice of the others rang in my head, pushing me to move faster and get out. Finally, I grabbed Phillip by the arm and touched Poppy with my other hand. I stuttered through the recitation of the teleportation spell and got us out of there, hearing the scream of a patron just as his head exploded.

When we emerged outside of town, I fell, meeting darkness before I hit the ground.

CHAPTER 6

"There's nothing there. No bodies and not a trace of blood," Erik announced hanging up his house phone sitting on the side table. The whole group was gathered at Erik's three-bedroom house beyond the protective steel walls of the town.

I leaned forward on the couch, still feeling woozy. "What are you saying? Brandon, Phillip and I escape with seconds to spare."

"Maybe she stopped singing when you teleported away," Erik reasoned, sitting down beside me.

I shook my head vigorously and then regretted it as dizziness kicked in. Fighting off Rima had taken every ounce of energy I possessed. Poppy, back in kitten form, jumped on my lap, no worse for the wear, and I began to pet her absentmindedly. A soothing warmth began to return to my body, reenergizing me. "No, if that was the case where are the people and the bartender to at least talk about what happened?"

"I don't know."

"They're all dead," Phillip said in a lazy drawl, just as depleted of energy as I was. He sat on the floor of Erik's living room, back against a wall near the fireplace. "She made the bodies and the blood disappear. No victims, no crime. Even with missing people, none of the evidence leads to her."

Of course, there were no witnesses besides Phillip, Brandon and myself. We wouldn't be enough to prove there was a crime. Our word was strong, but without bodies, there wasn't much to be done. Rima would literally get away with murder.

Rima was still nowhere to be found, and an investigation of her apartment shed no new light. She lived her life like she really was Grace. Her apartment was full of bright colors and stuffed animals. She even had a pet bird. Contact with Lisa showed that Rima had not gone to Baltimore to stay with the elves. Our ally, Francesca, also confirmed that Rima did not come to the Las Vegas demon territory. Not that we were expecting that. After the fall of the demon king, Alister, his territory had been kicked out of the soulmate's inner circle. Francesca's friend now ran the demons of Las Vegas, and she promised to support Francesca, and therefore us, in the fight.

None of this made us safer. My ward over Brandon had only helped against Gedeyon's full control and barely at that. He was still affected by Rima's voice. I realized that I truly had no idea what I was dealing with or how to defend myself.

I looked down at my kitten. "Poppy helped save us. We might have died without her."

Phillip stirred, pointing lazily to the cat. "What in the He-man was that thing? Did you know your cat could transform?"

I shook my head. She'd just been a little kitten who soothed my nerves from time to time. I had admittedly underutilized her and relegated her to more of an emotional support pet. I had figured she made me stronger just by being alive.

Erik looked down at the cat with suspicious eyes. "Yeah,

when you were passed out this cat looked like a freaking lion pacing in front of you. I've never seen that cat do that."

I looked down at Poppy with a slight smile. "Well, we didn't really know what she was when she was submitted for the witch competition all those months ago. She was already dead. Seems I didn't just bring a regular cat back to life. I reanimated a magical cat."

Phillip twisted his lips. "Yeah, we get it. You're a badass. I guess you're even with my griffin."

Faith let out an annoyed sigh. "Yes, the cat is awesome and all but can we get back to Rima. I can't believe I got fooled like that." She sat, yoga style, in Erik's leather recliner chair. "When I find that bitch, I'm going to rip her throat out."

"Well, I hope you don't miss," Phillip began, standing with his hands on his hips like an old man who'd thrown out his back. "Because if you miss, she's going to sing a little ditty and explode your head."

"Raise your hand if you knew these fuckers were invincible?" Charles asked, sitting on my other side on the couch. He looked around the room full of people, his eyes unusually hard.

I hoped he didn't want an answer with that question. None of us did.

I jumped up off of the couch, still holding Poppy, feeling antsy and nervous despite her presence. I wasn't safe, Brandon wasn't safe. Once we regained consciousness, Phillip, myself and anyone with magical warding power surrounded the town in the strongest ward we could find. We ensured that it specifically kept Rima out by using blood from our attack in the pub and hair strands from her apartment. However, I felt little hope that it would do any good.

"I can't just sit here. I need to go check on Brandon," I said, preparing to teleport away.

Erik grabbed my arm. "I'll come, too. Let me drive us

there. We need to discuss what we're going to do with Brandon."

I looked up at him and nodded. There was a deep-seated sadness in his eyes. When he'd gotten to us after the pub, he'd forgotten all carefulness with Brandon from before and grabbed the boy tightly in his arms. There was no confusing things now. Brandon was his, ours to protect and we had to do a better job of it.

We drove back to the pack apartment and walked to Johnson's apartment in silence, the weight of our decision too heavy.

Johnson, seeing our faces at the door, waved us in and ushered us to the kitchen.

"The boy's asleep on the couch. What are you going to do with Brandon?" Johnson asked us. We sat down at his kitchen table.

"You agreed to protect him when the time came," Erik started. "The time has come."

The older man sighed and shook his head. His dark brown eyes under heavily hooded lids seemed weary. He pressed his thin lips tight together and ran a hand through his white hair. "Thing is, I don't think I'm any good at keeping him safe. Phillip was able to snatch that kid right from my hands and bring him straight to that woman. He just used his mind control on me, and I couldn't even try to fight back. And I'm not fit for this fight. I'm 70."

I leaned forward. Johnson was older, but he was far from frail since he was a were. Weres had superior superhuman strength, and like most paranormals, they lived much longer lives than regular humans and were harder to kill. Johnson was still built like the railroad conductor he used to be, tall and broad.

I didn't know if he was just tired from the stress of the impending fight or just nervous. "That's why I'm going to cover you and Brandon in a spell that allows you to resist mind and body control, and hopefully it'll work against Rima's singing, too." I honestly didn't know if it would work, but I was going to throw everything at the wall and see if it stuck at this point.

Johnson nodded slowly. "I know you didn't sign up for this mess, and Brandon imprinting on you came out the blue, but we have to play the hand we're dealt. So, say what you really need to say."

I looked over to Erik, and he looked at me. We'd spoken about it when we first learned what Gedeyon was, and after the day's event, we were certain of what we had to do.

"Amina can't keep him. At least not now," Erik stated, he looked down at his hands resting on the table, and I didn't have to see his face to know this was painful for him. Even though he had moved away from us and was estranged from Brandon, I knew he still considered us his family.

"It's too dangerous. When we win this fight, we'll take him back," I cut in. I said the words. I stuck to what we agreed on in the car, but it didn't mean I felt good about it. Brandon wasn't my child, but he had become family now.

Erik nodded in agreement. "And if we don't make it. You have to keep him. You're good people, and he likes you."

Johnson lifted a shoulder. "Brandon's a hyena like me. He's family. I'll keep him. But I expect you both to win this thing, so he's going back."

I smiled and grabbed Johnson's hand for his comfort as much as my own. "There's something else. We need you to leave town. The soulmates are going to come here. Brandon's a prime target for us, and we don't need him to be so easy to find. Queen Arwa in the Fae Realm agreed to take you in for the time being."

Johnson leaned back in his chair and looked at the both of us with a frown. "You want us to live with the fairies?"

"Only for a while. Look at it as a vacation. Lisa said it was really nice there and although she was attacked by a dark fairy while there, security has since gone up. And if you needed to reach us, Queen Arwa can get in touch with us. And Felix can communicate through realms and will check in regularly."

Johnson sighed with a worried look. "I don't like it, but I understand. When do you want us to go?"

"Tonight. Now," Erik replied in an urgent tone. "We can't wait anymore."

Johnson widened his eyes and shook his head before standing. "This world asks a lot of an old man. Alright, let me go pack a few things."

I let out a shaky breath and rested my forehead on the table. I felt like shit. That beautiful little boy had been through so much already. He just needed some stability, and I wasn't giving it to him.

I wasn't a mother. I never thought I could be in this world. Taking on a traumatized child seemed like a weight I didn't need. And yet Brandon had been one of the most precious things in my life recently. I'd felt better with him. Normal even. Now I was sending him away.

I soon felt Erik's hand on my back.

"Come on, let's say goodbye to the kid," he said in a low voice.

Telling Brandon we were leaving was a heartbreaking process. We waited with him until Bella, a fairy from Arwa's court and friend to Lisa, came and took them away.

A tornado of colorful glitter, or fairy dust as we knew it now to be, filled the room and a woman of average height with loose brown curls appeared. She gave a slight wave at the four of us with a smile before walking over to Brandon, bending to his height. "Hi Brandon, I'm Bella. I'm a friend. Have you ever been to the fairy world?" She asked.

Brandon pressed closer to me and shook his head before burying his head in my arm. "It's really beautiful. We've got all types of fairies and huge treehouses. Oh, and foods and sweets you've never seen. We've got all kinds of pools and hot springs. It's really fun there. You won't want to come back."

Brandon looked up at me with a tear-streaked face.

I forced a smile that felt almost painful. I felt like my heart was stopping. "She's right. Lisa said it was like paradise there. And we will check in on you. You won't be gone long." My voice cracked. God this hurt. His sniffles rang in my ear, and I almost changed my mind about the whole thing. "We just need you safe so that bad lady can't hurt you again. Please, sweetheart, do this for us. Go with Bella and be safe. We'll bring you back just as soon as we can. I swear it."

Johnson got up from his leather recliner chair and walked over to Bella, shaking her hand. "Come on boy; we're going on an adventure. Say goodbye now," he said, glancing over to Brandon.

I stood up from the couch, taking Brandon with me. I kissed his forehead. "We will see you soon, okay? Have lots of fun." Tears began to blur my vision and I willed them not to fall. I didn't even know him a few months ago. Why was this hurting so much?

Brandon wiped his nose with the back of his hand and nodded.

Erik moved closer and patted Brandon lightly on the head. "Be good over there. Don't cause Johnson any problems," he murmured, barely looking at him. I knew he was trying to be stoic, but it was coming off cold.

Brandon looked up at him and then wrapped his arms around Erik's waist. Erik looked over at me, and I saw the faintest glistening in his eyes. Then he looked back down at Brandon and wrapped his arms around the small child.

When Brandon, Johnson and Bella disappeared, I sat back on the couch, motionless. Something in me felt hollow. How had I gone from being unsure about even watching him, while his now deceased mother was missing, to feeling so lonely without him?

Erik sat down beside me. "You should get some rest. It's been a long day for you. I'll stay up. My people are increasing their surveillance presence around the town. And Mae, Bill and Raya moved back in for the time being."

I nodded absentmindedly. "You should go then. I'll lock up here and go stay with Charles."

Erik put an arm over my shoulder. "I have some time before my shift."

I stood up. "I need to pack a few things to go over to Charles' place." I didn't want to be comforted. I just wanted to stay…empty.

Erik stood up as well. "Amina, look at me. I have something to tell you."

I turned and faced him. "What is it?" I asked in an exasperated tone. I was so tired. I couldn't take another negative thing.

He rubbed his forehead, looking just as weary as I felt. "Mae called us to a meeting this morning. She wanted to warn us about the possibility of you and Phillip going bad and that our role as the Six could include subduing you."

I nodded. "I know. Phillip and I went invisible and spied on you."

"You did what?" Erik's eyebrows knitted together in anger.

"You met behind my back to talk about killing me?" I cocked an eyebrow.

Erik dropped his shoulders. "No one was talking about killing you. I wouldn't let that happen."

I turned away from him and headed to the door.

Erik followed.

"If I become a monster that tries to kill innocent children, then maybe I deserve to be killed."

"Don't say that, Mina." Erik grabbed my wrist.

I moved out of his grasp, but even that felt exhausting. "I'm tired, Erik. Let's talk another time."

"Amina."

"What?" I didn't turn around to look at him.

"I…I—"

I paused, waiting. I'd never known Erik to be at a loss for words.

"I should let you rest. I'll lock up here," he finally said.

The hollowness inside me spread and continued out of the apartment. I wanted him to tell me he loved me. I wanted him to say he'd move back in. I got none of those things. Maybe he was building a wall between us. It was possible he'd have to put me to sleep soon. Perhaps he was making it easier on himself by keeping his distance.

I wanted to cry, but I didn't. I had to be strong for what was to come. There was no time for silly emotions. I'd save the impending breakdown for another time. Now I had to prepare for what I was born to do. Save the world.

CHAPTER 7

The next morning I woke up feeling just as raw as I had when I went to sleep so when I got word that Rima and Gedeyon were at the wall I didn't react at first. Maybe I was still in a fog, but after I let the words sink in, I jumped up in a panic.

Gedeyon was mobile. It wasn't just Rima anymore. And they were both here. We had our spell against Rima, but Gedeyon was still a challenge. All I knew was that he was an alpha werehyena who could control other weres in their dreams as well as in reality. He had the power of the evil eye, which I still hadn't mastered.

Our ally in Galway, Liz, an older witch who had trained Phillip and me on our bonding magic, had given us talismans, known as the *Kitab* in Ethiopian, to ward against the evil eye. Now almost everyone wore it. This of course, assumed that the talismans were potent enough against someone as ancient as Gedeyon. Seeing as our wards didn't keep Rima out, it felt kind of foolish to think so.

I teleported, Poppy in tow, from Charles' apartment, along with him, and we reappeared just behind the steel wall surrounding the six square miles of our town. Phillip was already standing there, frozen, face solemn as light snowflakes fell from the cloudy sky, covering the already snow-covered ground.

I shivered, not sure if it was from the cold or my own nerves and fear from the impending battle. I was not ready for this, but I was going to have to pull my strength from somewhere. I wrapped my arms around my puffy coat covered body and tried my best to steady my breathing. It didn't work. I wanted to pass out.

I heard the crunching of snow to my left and saw Erik approach with several members of the pack behind him.

"It's just the two of them. We don't sense anyone nearby. They said they just want to talk right now," he stated, looking at me with eyes that didn't match his words. There was something strong in those light hazel eyes. A deep-seated sadness. He wouldn't look away from me as he continued to walk towards me, his movements unencumbered by the several feet of snow on the ground.

He stopped a foot away from me and lowered his tall body so that his eyes met mine. "If it's just the two of them, it's not worth it for you to go," he said in a low voice. He gently touched the sides of my face with his bare hands, unaffected by the cold. "I want you to stay away from them."

I gave a slight smile, gave Poppy to Charles, and placed my glove covered hands over his. "I'm not here to be protected. You have to stop that. And they won't stay away from me. If they came alone, maybe this is the best time to fight."

He moved closer and kissed me on the lips. "You're right. I'm sorry. You don't need my protection. I love you."

I patted him lightly on the cheek. "I love–"

"Oh my God!" Phillip groaned, tossing his head back. "You aren't a soldier going off to war, leaving your wife to stay at home and write you letters. We're just going to have a conversation with two people."

I frowned. Did he think we were just having a job interview here? This could be it. Our big battle. I for one, did not come to talk. "Who want to kill us. Can't I have a moment to say bye to my mate? Where's your consort? She needs to be close by."

"She is," came a female voice behind us.

I turned and faced Blake. She stood in the snow in a long white belted peacoat. Her platinum blond bob, longer in the front than the back, and fair skin gave her the look of a beautiful snow queen when coupled with the white coat. The only thing that stood out beyond her blue eyes was her signature bright red lips. Her hands were stuffed in her pockets, and she held a comfortable smile on her face. Seemingly unbothered by what lay on the other side of the wall.

"I'm here for you, my friend," she said to Phillip, walking beside him. The vampire's grin widened, and I saw the hint of her sharp vampire fangs. "Might I suggest that we go out? The numbers are on our side."

I tilted my head, contemplating her words. They certainly seemed rational. However, I wasn't foolish enough to think that it was just those two. There could be a cloaking spell hiding more of their followers for all I knew. We had to be cautious and plan this out carefully.

"First let's have a plan. The four of us go out there, and then we talk but as we do Phillip and Amina have to go in for the kill."

Phillip huffed. "They'll be ready for that after what we did to Rima."

Erik swore, rubbing his face with his hands. "Well, we're not going out there to sing kumbaya. We attack, if we're losing, we get out. War has already been declared, so we aren't starting anything." He grabbed my hand. "Let's go."

I looked at him with wide eyes. I wasn't in love with the plan, but I couldn't think of anything better. We knew we weren't giving in, so fighting really was the only way.

Phillip glanced over at me with questioning eyes. "You ready for battle?"

I shrugged. "Ready as I'll ever be. Let's do this."

The four of us held hands, and I whispered the teleporting spell to the other side of the wall, feeling a strange sense of déjà vu from the last time I teleported beyond a town wall to face a not so friendly threat.

When we reappeared, I was surprised to see Gedeyon and Rima standing beside a golden hummer. Where had they gotten such a car? I suppose I wasn't too shocked. I really thought they'd be riding dragons or something just as powerful and magnificent. A large SUV painted gold was not exactly what I thought of when it came to them. Although it was flashy, it also seemed so…pedestrian.

Rima stared at us with a self-confident smile. She was covered in a long, black, fur coat and her long, silky brown hair, hung loose over her shoulders.

To her right stood Gedeyon. He was tall, maybe 6'2, and lean, dressed in a long navy blue peacoat, matching fedora hat covering his short coily black hair, and black slacks were tucked into calf-high black snow boots. His smooth skin was the color of coffee, and slight crinkles around his dark eyes gave him the appearance of being in his mid to late thirties. Of course, he was much, much older. They both were so ancient they were practically coughing up dust. But it didn't show.

"It's so good to see you in person, Amina. You're as beautiful in real life as you were in our dream communications," he said in an accent displaying his Ethiopian origin. He looked over to Phillip. "Good to see you, too. I feel like you both are my children. All grown up. I can sense you're stronger now."

Phillip snorted. "If we're your kids, why'd your mate over there try to kill us?" he asked, tipping his head towards Rima. "That's some Mommy Dearest bullshit."

Rima raised her eyebrows and gave a shocked frown. "Oh, well, I had to defend myself after your mountain lion tried to kill me and let us not forget how you broke my neck. All's forgiven though," she stated, waving a hand dismissively.

I wanted to say something, but I was busy reciting the spell to silence her. Since she was still talking, it was clear it was going to take a while. Phillip also mentioned that it could just stunt her ability to sing, leaving her still able to talk.

I suppose to the onlooker, Phillip and I looked like the monsters. However, she had to know we didn't consider her a victim. Especially not after what she did to Chelsea and Phillip.

"We don't need your forgiveness. With all the shit you did, you deserved it. I'm just mad it didn't work. And I'm sure the families of the people you killed in the restaurant aren't so forgiving," Phillip spat.

Rima gave a one-shoulder shrug. "Who did I kill? Everyone is safe. I just wiped their minds of the whole unpleasant affair and sent them on a little vacation as a reward."

Was anyone actually buying that? Sure, not seeing the bodies made it harder to prove, but when the people never returned, her story was going to start looking like garbage. "Where'd you send them? To heaven? Because I swear I saw someone's head explode."

Rima gave a slight pout. "I hope one day we can work together and become the best of friends."

She was delusional. Obviously, the crazy siren was going to keep the location of the bodies a secret. Gedeyon gave us a patient smile. "I'll apologize on behalf of Rima. She can be very unorthodox in her dealings." He took a step forward, and Blake and Erik moved in front of us.

I frowned. They weren't here to be our bodyguards. I took a step beside Erik.

Don't break your concentration, mi corazon. Phillip's voice boomed in my head. *Let them help us while we do our magic. I won't let them get killed.*

Gedeyon raised his hands and took a step back. "I mean no harm. I regret our initial contact with you, Amina and Phillip. We were too forceful. We tried to control you by fear."

Oh, now he wanted to play nice guy. I wasn't buying it. Phillip and I moved our magic to focus on Gedeyon. We would bind his evil eye and mute his magic as well. Then we'd attack.

"And you tried to kill them," Blake stated, hands on her hips. "You sent a djinn after them, then a dark fairy, phantoms. You put a curse on my Phillip, and you got Amina, and her brother kidnapped and imprisoned. And let's not even talk about what was done to poor Chelsea, who that one possessed and got killed." Blake pointed to Rima but kept her eyes on Gedeyon.

Gedeyon nodded. "Yes, I can only ask for your forgiveness on that. We awoke from our forced slumber and only knew to go back to our old ways. The times have changed so much. We should have changed as well."

I stopped chanting the spell in my mind, Phillip continued. "Not too long ago, you threatened me that we had to either submit or die. Is that what you still want?"

Gedeyon looked over to me, and his eyes gave off a deceptive gentleness. "I won't fool you into believing that we don't want you both. You have a power you know not how to use. We can help guide you."

They kept thinking we were clueless babies. Perhaps that was for the best. It might make it easier for us if they underestimated our knowledge. "Yeah, while you drain us of our soul magic like you did those before us."

Gedeyon lifted his chin and tossed his hand to the side. "A better option, I now realize, is for us to work collaboratively.

We can, in effect, feed each other. We only want to help the world. You can help us do that."

I snorted. "We don't want to help you. We can do good in the world on our own. So maybe you go to your corner of the world, and we'll stay in ours and act like nothing ever happened. All's forgiven." I plastered the sweetest smile I could muster on my lips knowing my offer would be rejected, but wanting to play the part anyway.

Gedeyon displayed his perfect white teeth. "Have you heard the voices yet? The ones telling you to rule. To win?" He paused and looked at me and then Phillip. Neither of us spoke. I remembered the voice during my fight with Melissa, but I darn sure wasn't going to share that with him.

Gedeyon looked down at his coat and brushed the snowflakes off his shoulder, unperturbed by our silence. "Well, if you haven't, you will. You wouldn't be soulmates if you didn't. It'll only get worse, you know. It is the deep-seated desire to control all around you. As soulmates, we have such powers, powers that we are predisposed to use to do something great. We cannot sit by and live average lives. So, you see, it's not our fault that we want to rule. We were made to rule. And so were you. If you don't, your magic will destroy you from the inside out."

Rima nodded with a lazy smile that I wanted to slap off her face. "Our spell on Phillip was only to open him up to his potential, and Amina we needed to contain you so that we could get to you when we were ready."

Now I was more than annoyed. I was livid. Neither Phillip nor I were idiots. We knew exactly why they did what they did. They did not care about us. This best friends act was insulting. We would never have a truce. I'd never forget what they did to Chelsea or how many times they'd tried to kill us. I glared at the siren before speaking. "There is nothing you can say, ever, that will make me side with you. You not only tortured Phillip and tried to kill my ward, but you got my best friend killed. I hope you wither and die." I wanted to spit on her. I was so angry. How dare she act like she was helping us in any way.

She shook her head slowly and tsk-tsked. "I didn't pull the trigger, that was your out of control brother." Her eyes widened in false fear. "Do you want to kill me now? Go ahead and try."

I balled my fists. Oh, I wanted to kill her if I only knew how. Decapitation was still a possibility, but I couldn't figure out how to do that with my magic.

"Rima don't anger her, that doesn't help our cause," Gedeyon replied, looking over to me with those fake sympathetic eyes. "I am sorry about your friend. It was an unfortunate and unintended outcome. Let us offer you something of use. We can cure your sick of this new paranormal illness. Let us do that."

We didn't respond. I could be naïve at times, but stupid I was not. I trusted nothing that came out of his mouth. How were they able to cure the paranormal illness if we couldn't? They weren't even life mages.

Gedeyon looked up at the sky and hunched his shoulders. "It's cold out here. Winter is not my normal climate. How about we go inside and talk more. And save your energy on trying to bind us. It won't work. Others have tried."

"How?" Phillip asked. He momentarily paused, but I picked up the spell.

"I could feel your attempts, Phillip," Rima replied with a bored expression. "I've had to fortify my own wards on you two." She wiggled a hand at us.

"Shit," Phillip muttered.

I poked him in the back. I wasn't giving up. I believed nothing they said. "Keep going," I whispered.

"We aren't inviting you in," Erik stated in a controlled tone. I could feel the magic brimming off of him. His jackal was ready to pounce.

Gedeyon pointed an index finger in the air. "Ah, but we've already been invited in. Many are interested in seeing us cure more people."

"*More* people?" I asked. I still doubted they'd cured anyone at all.

I heard the giant doors within the steel wall slide open behind us. Typically, the doors were invisible to the eye, looking like just another part of the tall steel wall that surrounded the town. However, when opening, a vertical space would form in the wall, and a portion of the steel would recede into another part like a sliding glass door. I turned slightly and saw Carter, and the other leaders of the council and various paranormal groups in town, standing in the entrance. Their faces looked peaceful and welcoming.

"What's going on?" Erik barked to the group.

"I'm afraid this discussion was all just a formality," Gedeyon replied. "Despite your wards, which are quite impressive, your town let us in."

Shock rocked my body as I stared at those I thought were friends with confusion. When had the soulmates gotten to them? Were we being played this whole time?

"What's the meaning of this, Carter?" Erik asked through clenched teeth.

The second in command of the pack, a shapeshifter, was not a member of the Six, but like Ahmed, Azrael, Mae and a few others, he was one of our strongest allies. He supported us and fought alongside us. I'd seen him in battle and never mistook his kindness for weakness. Behind his athletic frame, clean-shaven head and deep brown eyes against a mahogany skin tone was a being who could shift into the stuff of nightmares. However, he was never impulsive or disloyal. If he had changed his mind about our stance on the original soulmates, he would have told us. Or so I thought.

Carter gave us a pained smile. That's the only way I could describe his face. What was happening to him? "We've been thinking," Carter began, "Why enter battle when we can enter a compromise? A mutually beneficial arrangement?" His left eye twitched, and his smile faltered slightly.

Something was off.

"We have the common enemy of this new illness killing us. Gedeyon explained that he has no intention of harming or enslaving us in any way."

Carter was too smart to really believe that. Wasn't he?

"They've had a long time to think about what they did in the past," Paul, a sandy-haired male with a thick build and rosy cheeks replied. He was the head of the orcs and a member of our council. He gave us a full toothed smile that did not reach his eyes. It felt fake and disturbing. "A past, might we all acknowledge that we don't know anything about other than tales. And we all know how stories can exaggerate over time."

"The angels and fae told us about them," I stated, trying to control my rising anger. Had everyone gone stupid? We weren't talking about fairytales. We had first-hand accounts of what the original soulmates and their cohorts were doing, even now, destroying towns that didn't side with them and killing innocent people.

"Those groups have their own motives and are deceitful. You know this," Paul replied.

He sounded like a robot. While it was true that the fae had misled Lisa when she resided in the fae realm, and the angels wiped Felix's mind, among other things, it was all for the greater good. They knew this. An icky worry stabbed at the back of my mind. Nobody sounded like themselves because they weren't themselves. They weren't in control.

"Their deceit was to help us!" Phillip shouted, visibly agitated.

Done with the conversation, the soulmates turned and got in their golden hummer. We stood motionless, possibly all in shock. They slowly drove towards us to enter the town.

If I stopped them, I might have to kill our friends, including Carter. The council and town leaders seemed clear that they wanted the soulmates there. I didn't want to fight our own people. That's what Gedeyon and Rima wanted.

Carter looked over to us with saddened eyes, the eerie smile still on his face. "Give it a chance. We can regroup later. There's no need to risk lives when we can save them."

"Is everything ok?" I knew it wasn't. Nothing was okay, but I needed a shred of hope that what I was thinking wasn't really happening.

He tilted his head, and his eyes widened before us, but he didn't speak.

Erik leaned forward, putting a hand on Carter's shoulder. "Carter?"

Carter blinked his eyes rapidly and looked at us as if he was only now realizing we were there. "Yes, everything's fine," he replied and turned to head inside the town.

The hummer passed us, and Raya gave a little wave. I shot out my hand before I could think and the ground erupted under them. Gedeyon struggled to maintain control of the hummer before it rocked to the side and fell. I smiled at my minor victory. But, of course, it didn't last as the towns-people gathered around and used their various magic to turn the car right side up.

Damn it, our friends really weren't on our side anymore.

"Fuck," Erik whispered, shutting his eyes. "How could we not see this coming?"

Phillip swore and shook his head. "Mind control. That's what that was. They've fucking mind controlled the whole town," he cried with a crack of hysterical laughter.

I'd suspected it, but I wanted to be wrong. I wasn't ready for this particular horror.

"The look in his eyes," Erik began, face blank of emotion except for a small sadness behind his eyes. "It looked like he was trying to fight the control, but he couldn't."

How had we been so blindsided? We were wrong to think we could fight ancient beings. They were more devious and would outwit us. We were fighting an enemy who, just as we began to understand them, would change their methods of operating, leaving us behind again. We were out of our league.

CHAPTER 8

"What are we doing here? We need to fight, or leave," Phillip shouted, pacing back and forth in the living room of my apartment.

We'd all headed there after the arrival of the originals. I sat perched at the end of a dining room chair feeling overwhelmingly lost. Mind controlling the town. How had we not prepared for that? "Did you talk to Mae? What'd she say?"

"She says we can't trust them no matter what they say. We were outmaneuvered here. I say we go and regroup."

"How the hell are they controlling people? I thought that was our mage power, not our soulmate power."

Ahmed, a djinn who used to serve the originals against his will, stood up from his chair in the dining room. The former professor, and our latest ally, was usually dressed in a suit. That day he just wore well fitted gray slacks and a white button-down shirt over his slender frame. His dark brown hair was slicked back, and he sported a neatly trimmed goatee and mustache. His thick eyebrows furrowed together above dark, concerned eyes. "Gedeyon is the oldest were-hyena that we know of, and with his enhanced powers, it's no surprise that he could control weres and shapeshifters. Rima, as a siren, also posses mind control abilities. Not to mention the slew of people they have working for them with control powers."

"I knew we should have used our mind control powers again," Phillip muttered.

"And risked burning people's minds out?" I shot back. We'd done it to a smaller degree with Erik, and I wouldn't do it again. The original soulmates didn't care about our people, but I did.

"Also, I think that leaving would be a wise decision," Ahmed stated. "I myself need to disappear. I have betrayed them, and I can't imagine they would spare me."

"Where will you go?" Phillip asked, stopping his pacing. "How can we reach you?"

Ahmed clasped his hands in front of him, his face a mask of deep concern. "I am not certain where I will go. However, if you need me, send an email. I will do my best to get internet access as often as possible. I will continue to find ways to end these soulmates and gather support. However, if you need me, I will return. I will send word when I settle in someplace." He gave a slight smile that did nothing to reassure us. "Good luck to you all. Trust very few outside of this room." He then dissipated into a dark cloud of smoke.

I turned away from the dust and turned back to the group scattered throughout my living room. "Outside of the Six and Phillip, we can't trust anyone."

"You can trust me," Azrael replied, running a hand through their short dark blond hair cut into an asymmetrical shape. "My only goal is to support the Six and the soulmates." The angel was an androgynous being and preferred that we use non gender specific pronouns when referring to them.

For the first time in my limited exposure to the gothic angel, they looked unsure. Their black eyeliner rimmed blue eyes squinted in concern. "I'm on your side, regardless. But

I'm just not sure my guidance is helpful to you anymore. What you should know is that regardless of how nice Gedeyon is making himself to be, ultimately, they mean to subdue you both. Rima means to kill you. I was told she carved you up, Phillip."

Phillip snorted. "Oh yeah, I'm not confused about her intentions at all."

I looked to Blake, expectantly. I knew the answer, but I had to ask for my own peace of mind. "Well, can we trust you?" I asked.

She huffed and rolled her eyes, placing her hands on her narrow hips. "Are you kidding me? Phillip is my consort, of course, you can. And honestly, it's not just about trust; it's about control. They can take over the minds of our strongest allies against their will."

"We should really consider using our mind control," Phillip offered. "Maybe they won't try to counter it again if they see us step in."

I made a fart noise with my mouth. Phillip was smarter than that. He knew damn well these soulmates wouldn't get run off by our magic. We'd play tug of war with the minds of the townspeople until their brains became scrambled mush. Then we'd be no better than those monsters.

He raised his hands. "Just have to keep throwing it out there. I also prepared a silencing spell a long time ago when I thought Rima was just Grace the siren."

"Why would you do that?"

"Because he's an asshole," Charles replied, face grim. "Except maybe that's a good thing now."

Phillip pointed his finger at Charles with a smirk on his lips. "*Was* an asshole. I *was* an asshole. At the time, I didn't want anyone with mind control abilities threatening my power. As a siren, I knew she could not just kill with her voice but control others, and I didn't want her controlling me. So, if the time came where she did betray me, I wanted to be ready. Of course, I don't remember the damn spell by heart now after my little forced trip to Ireland. However, I have my spells still locked up in a secret location. So, no need to reinvent the wheel here as long as you don't mind it being laced in dark magic."

"Uh, yes! I mind," I said, lifting a hand in the air in a dramatic fashion. If we started using dark magic, we'd be more susceptible to doing evil.

"Well," Felix began, lifting a finger in the air. "Not all dark magic is evil."

"That sentence sounds very wrong," Azrael stated, eyes neutral.

They'd been Felix's guardian angel ever since the half-angel/half-demon had lost his memories. Of course, Felix had only lost his memories because the angels wiped his mind, along with his partner, Francesca Ross. Felix and Francesca had been former hitmen for the demon king, Alister. Knowing the role Felix would have to play in this battle, the angels had decided to steer him in a different direction, separating him from Francesca, who was half dark fae and half-demon. In the end, Felix and Francesca, who still could not regain her memories, had taken out Alister. That was a big win for us because he had been one of the most powerful allies of the originals.

Felix shrugged. "Don't worry, I'm not talking about anything immoral. To break Alister's hold on Fran, we went to that old warlock in the forest Phillip recommended. He was crazy powerful, and not a bad guy. We didn't have to sacrifice a goat or anything. Dark magic can be evil, but what makes it dark is that it pulls on blood, a violent act, sacrifice or the underworld. The warlock just needed my toe to help Fran."

Azrael slapped their forehead and closed their eyes, muttering in a language I didn't understand, but I was pretty sure that I could figure it out. When it came to Fran, nothing was too over the top for Felix. Love is love, I guess?

"Just a toe, you say? Glad it wasn't anything serious," Charles muttered, shaking his head.

Felix nodded. "Exactly."

"Dude, I was being sarcastic."

Sometimes I didn't understand Felix, and it was probably best I didn't.

"Soulmates are powerful, but they aren't all powerful," Azrael declared, hands in their pockets and head hanging as if they were studying the carpeted floor. "Dark magic is strong. However, don't underestimate the power of angelic magic." Azrael peered up at the group, head raised slightly and a glint of silver running through their eyes, giving me a chill. Angels were still highly mysterious. Even more so than the fae. All I knew was that I did not want to fight them. They were a race more ancient than I could comprehend. No, I would never underestimate them.

Phillip snorted and scratched at his scruffy chin. "Oh, I don't doubt angel magic is potent stuff. I'm just thinking we shouldn't knock out all avenues. I mean, the dark magic Felix got could have been worse. To get a spell I thought would be strong enough for Grace, the warlock had to sacrifice a pigeon," Phillip stated.

"I'd rather a bird than a toe," Charles replied.

"You were so afraid of Grace that you got a spell that powerful?" I asked.

"Afraid? No. Paranoid, yes," Phillip replied.

Phillip's paranoia had actually kept him one step ahead of me. It was scary when we weren't friends, but helpful now.

"What about the fae?" Charles leaned against a wall. "Are they strong enough to avoid being controlled?"

I hadn't even considered the fae. Their realm was supposed to be safe from all this fighting. "Oh no," I jumped up, instantly panicked. "We sent Brandon to stay with the fae. If they changed sides on us..."

"I'll reach out to Lisa. She can still make contact with the fae realm," Erik replied before closing his eyes to telepathically reach her.

I rubbed my stomach, pushing back nausea.

Faith began to pace, our agitation probably feeding off each other as the Six bonding magic often did. "What about Hagerstown? Or your friends in Ireland?" Faith asked. "Or our demon allies in Vegas?"

Felix frowned, slowly shaking his head. "You don't think they got to them?"

"It's not like we would know," Phillip muttered. "I'll go teleport to Ireland."

"I'll come with," Blake replied, grabbing his hand as he chanted the teleportation spell.

Charles pushed away from the wall. "I'll go look into Hagerstown."

Faith reached out for him. "Best to go in pairs, man," she said as they teleported away.

Azrael walked over to Felix. "Let's go to Vegas, brother" they said, and they disappeared in a flash of blinding white light.

I looked at Erik. "Lisa's checking for us."

He had to be okay. We couldn't have sent him to danger. "I thought we were keeping him safe. He trusted us."

"I believe he is. It would have been worse to keep him here."

A gust of wind lifted my curly hair off my neck, and I spun around in surprise, taking a step back as I saw a tornado of colorful lights appear. Moments later, Lisa Xu stood before us looking healthy and in good form. She stood barely five feet with delicate features, fair skin, long, straight, black hair, and bright emerald eyes. She was dressed in a hot pink wool coat and above the knee suede boots. Guess living in the elf territory had been treating her well.

She smiled and waved at us. "Hey, guys. I figured I should reply face to face."

"Glad you're safe. What's going on in the fae realm?" I asked, rushing through the pleasantries. I needed to know if Brandon was okay.

Lisa twisted her lips and furrowed her brows in a grimace. "I tried to teleport there, and I couldn't. Queen Arwa mentioned some time ago about closing the doors to her court's portal to protect them from the paranormal illness. This doesn't mean that anything bad happened. She probably just shut it after Brandon came."

Erik rubbed his beard. "She said she would have someone contact us every day to give us status updates on Brandon."

"So, if we don't hear from her today, that means something's wrong," I said before biting at my lower lip as if chewing on my ever-growing fear.

"But remember, time works differently there," Lisa explained. "A day there is like a week here."

"Yeah, but we clarified that we were talking days in the human realm," Erik answered.

Lisa lowered her hands in front of her as if to calm us. "Don't worry, guys. The Seelie Fae are no fans of the soulmates. In all honesty, all fae aren't automatic supporters. It's just that bitch Misandre and her Unseelie court. Most fae would gain nothing by letting the first soulmates run things."

"Have you learned anything since being at Joo-won's?" Erik asked, changing the subject.

Worrying wouldn't do us any good, but my mind could barely focus on anything else.

Lisa leaned forward, brushing a lock of hair behind her ear, revealing dangling earrings. Why was she always dressed like she was about to be photographed? "Yes, apparently they really aren't believers in the first soulmates. They're just betting on the horse they think can win. I was trying to convince Joo-won that we were the ones to beat, but he wasn't falling for it. That's probably because he knew they were going to come here and change the game."

"He didn't tell you?"

Lisa shifted in her stance and tightened her lips together. "He doesn't tell me a lot. Clearly we have some trust issues."

I scratched my head in frustration, completely unsettled, not knowing if Brandon was okay. My mind was a blurry mess. "If you can't change his mind, then maybe it's time for you to come back. It's too dangerous for you to stay there. You don't even know if you'll be able to come back, what with the soulmates being out."

"It's probably safer for you to stay with him," Erik said.

I looked over to him with a glare but kept quiet.

He continued, shoving his hands in his pockets. "He's not hurting you. If you come back, he might. And you aren't confined. You got here just fine."

Phillip reappeared with Blake, throwing his hands in the air. "We went to Dublin, and the whole damn town is vacant. I'm not talking they all moved out, or there was a battle, and everything got destroyed. It's like they just disappeared and left their stuff behind. Everything's intact. Like some damn Roanoke kind of shit."

Blake shivered. "It was creepy, for sure. Then we went to Galway, and it's still standing fine. They've been trying to find out what happened to Dublin, with no luck."

Ed, the leader of the tiny Dublin town that we spent months with when Lisa had banished us, was our friend. He wouldn't just up and leave without telling us.

"I haven't emailed him in a while, so I don't know how long they've been gone," Phillip stated, a look of concern clouding his eyes. "Those damn soulmates are behind this. I know it."

I sat down again, my shoulders slumped. I wasn't going to

be defeatist. As soon as I knew everyone was okay, I would work on another plan to get rid of the soulmates.

Charles reappeared back into our apartment with Faith. "Hagerstown is fine, for now."

Good news, that's what I needed.

A flash of blinding light filled the room, and I shielded my eyes. Soon Azrael and Felix reappeared.

Felix immediately spotted Lisa, and his eyes became as large as saucers. "Lisa!" He cried, walking towards her with arms open wide.

I held up a hand. "Tell us about Vegas."

Felix nodded, reluctantly letting go of Lisa. "Right, well, the place looks brighter. The new leader is actually nice for a demon. Oh, and Fran is doing well. She was planning to come back from her visit there, but now she's not."

I looked at him, waiting for him to continue. Before Felix had gotten his memory back, he was a little scatterbrained, and at times talking to him was a challenge. I had the expectation that once he got his mind back, things would be better, and he'd be this different guy. I'd come to love his quirkiness, so I wasn't too excited about the idea that he would be someone new. However, it turned out that Felix was still the same old guy, just with a better memory.

I blinked my eyes slowly. "And why isn't she coming back?" I asked in as controlled a tone as I could muster.

Felix scratched his head with a giant hand. "They got word that a demon horde is coming to fight them. They think they are some first soulmate supporters come to take them out for not avenging Alister's death. Which is crazy because in the demon world, nobody is loyal. His own people hated him and didn't shed a tear when he died. I was going to go back and fight with them."

"It's not worth the risk," Erik said with a shake of his head. "You could get killed, and we need you safe as part of the Six."

Azrael nodded. "That's what I told this clown, but he's not listening," the angel stated, pointing a thumb at Felix.

Felix snorted. "Damn right, I'm not listening." He stepped forward and tapped his chest. "My future wife is about to battle to the death, and I need to be at her side. I promise I won't die, man."

Erik closed his eyes and sighed. "I don't see how you can make a promise like that. The one thing we have going for us is the Six. Doing things that would put us at risk before we take these old soulmates out is pointless."

Felix twisted his lips in disagreement. "Maybe, but if it were Amina out there, you'd go to her. Don't tell me to leave Francesca to the fates."

Erik paused then gave a slow nod and extended his fist for Felix to tap. "Go support your woman."

Felix smiled and tapped his own fist against Erik's. He gave Lisa a hug, and then turned to the group. "I'll see you all soon."

Faith walked up to him with a deep-set frown. "You aren't saying bye to me. I'm coming with." The two were practically siblings, so I wasn't surprised by her decision.

Azrael patted Felix on the back with a lazy smile. "Ride or die to the end, my friend. Or whatever you kids say nowadays. Except I don't die because I'm an angel, but you know what I mean." They waved their hand in the air.

Faith gave a salute to us as they faded out in Azrael's angel light.

"Don't die!" I shouted as they disappeared. My stomach was so twisted in knots at this point that I thought I was going to throw up. I felt out of control. I needed a plan, and I was at a loss. At this point, getting to them might be challenging without harming our friends, and with the Dublin town missing, I could possibly risk losing those people forever. Yet negotiation seemed futile. "Ahhh!" I screamed, punching the air.

Everyone looked at me, but I ignored my audience.

"Maybe the rest of us should go with Felix," Charles said.

"Right and get ourselves killed? No thanks," Phillip muttered, turning his upper lip up in disapproval.

I held my hands in front of me as if bracing myself for a fall. I was feeling unsteady enough that I could collapse any minute. I needed balance. I needed freaking clarity. "Look, until we figure out our next move, maybe it's good that Felix and Faith are out of town. I have full faith that they'll make it through. Although, we should probably confirm that with Mae."

Charles huffed and rapidly tapped his foot on the hardwood floor. I could barely see his shoe move due to the vampiric speed of his tapping. He was getting nervous or scared. He wasn't the only one. "So what about the rest of us?"

I covered my chin with my hand in thought. "While I don't think we all need to run into battle, I don't think we should stay, either. Lisa goes back to Joo-won, who we know won't hurt her, even if it means defying the soulmates. Plus, we have the binding spell on his two right-hand elves who won't come for us." I'd made that happen, deciding to spare their lives and getting hidden allies instead. "So, the rest of us should get out of town and regroup."

"We can't leave," Erik stated in a frustrated tone.

Phillip clapped his hands together and then pointed at him with both index fingers. He was getting excited, which I knew was a mask for his own fear. He was this close to breaking; I could feel his energy through our bond. I was sure our mutual worry was feeding off of each other. "Oh, please tell me why we need to stay here and have our heads chopped off or our souls ripped out by those deceptive pieces of shit trying to take over our town?"

Erik glared at him and balled his fist at his sides. "Because we need to protect the town. We are their leaders. We can't just abandon them."

This was sounding like déjà vu. After my fight with Phillip a while back, I'd had to flee Silver Spring, but Erik had wanted to stay with the pack to protect them from Seth.

"I don't think they want our help," I stated. I said the words, but it felt hollow to me. I didn't really believe that. I recalled Carter's face. His pained smile. He was fighting through the control.

Erik rubbed his forehead, visibly agitated. "They are being magically manipulated. If we leave, who knows what these soulmates will do? They recruited Seth, a demon, and an Unseelie fairy. Not to mention all of the attacks on you. If a person gets out of line here, who knows what they would do to them. They could make Phillip or even Seth look like teddy bears. At least if we stay, we can fight against them."

"And possibly die," Phillip cried. "Look, I'm not a coward. I just don't like taking unnecessary risks. The people in this town aren't idiots. Well, most of the people in this town aren't idiots. They'll fall in line with the soulmates. Meanwhile, we get the hell out of here, live to fight another day, come up with a new plan, and come back to kick ass."

I wanted to agree with Phillip, but something in me snapped. I didn't want to run. I didn't have a grandmaster plan, but I knew that we had to fight to get our people back to our side. The only way to do that was to stay. "If we run, our people will never respect us, and we'll just be proving that the first soulmates are the better leaders. They won't support us. Erik's right."

Lisa nodded. "I agree. For now, maybe staying is right. If you run off, it'll be hard for me to get Joo-won to support you. He won't see you as strong."

"We aren't!" Phillip shouted, his voice cracking. "At least not now."

I shook my head at him. "Then we keep training. We keep

throwing everything we learn at them. We don't let them stop us from getting better just because they're here. Maybe this is our moment. This is our battle. We don't back down. We fight until we can't." A little hope rose in me at just speaking the words. I was starting to believe, to have hope that we could win. I had to have faith. The original soulmates talked a good game, but they hadn't beaten us yet. There was a reason for that.

Phillip chuckled. "Yeah, good luck with that. You weren't the one bespelled by a psycho body-hopping soulmate," he spat. "She ripped open my chest, and I was too weak to do anything. She had me kidnap a kid and stand there while she tried to make our heads explode." He turned away from us, and Blake put a hand on his back, looking over to us with shocked eyes.

Phillip was scared. I'd never seen fear in him before. It was unsettling. I looked over to Charles and Erik, expecting them to relish in this moment of weakness for Phillip, but was surprised to see no smugness on their faces. Charles lowered his head with a sigh. Erik stood beside me with a deep-seated frown on his face, eyes heavy with thought.

I didn't blame Phillip for his fear, but we had to face it and fight.

I had an idea. And not one I liked. "Let's go talk to them."

Phillip spun around and looked at me. "Are you serious?"

I wished I wasn't. "Yes. We don't know what game they're playing. So, let's learn the rules so we can win."

CHAPTER 9

We could not see Gedeyon or Rima that day. They were too "busy" healing people, which I was still suspicious of. We weren't sure where they were staying that night. Hell, I didn't even know if they needed to sleep. That night the five of us stayed in my two-bedroom apartment, taking shifts for sleep.

Sleep, of course, was fleeting for me. I rotated through researching the weaknesses of sirens and hyenas and boosting my own life magic. I'd break all rules. I'd do mind control on the town if it came to it. I really just needed to know how the soulmates were defeated last time. Maybe I could find out when we met with them.

We got a knock at the door early the next day, instructing us that the soulmates were ready to see us, but only Phillip and me. They refused to speak to us if the others came. It felt like a trap, and I would be going in prepared.

We headed to the council building, a former office that used to house a law firm before the world collapsed. Our friends stayed in the lobby. The soulmates said they couldn't come to the meeting, but they didn't say they couldn't come to the building. I tried to clear my mind of any worries as I walked the hallway to the conference room. We still had not heard from the fae realm, and I hoped it was simply because they did not understand that one day meant human time, not fae time.

The stickiness of fear spread over me again, causing me to grimace and roll my shoulders back. I looked at Phillip, who held a neutral face, chin slightly lifted. If he was scared, he wasn't showing it. He looked every bit the part of being in control, having changed into a deep blue well-fitted suit over a crisp white shirt and matching patterned tie.

I'd taken a chapter from his book and had decided to dress less ready for battle and more ready for business. I wore a boldly colored patterned wrap dress that I could never afford before in the Pre-World. Even ten years later, it wasn't often we needed such clothing luxuries. Lisa had happened upon the dress during a scavenge some time ago. She had been planning to add it to the collection at the boutique she worked in, but instead, she gave it to me as a peace offering for banishing me to Ireland. I gladly accepted it, having no clue when I'd ever have a chance to wear such a beautiful dress, other than a rare date night with Erik.

I paired the dress with simple black stilettos and wore my curly hair back in a low ponytail. We looked like we were going to company negotiations instead of discussing whether we would be living or dying.

The doors to the conference room opened before we had an opportunity to turn the knob, and we stepped through, unfazed by the display of magic.

The space was brightly lit by the unusually sunny day, and all the blinds were rolled up, letting in the sun's rays. We faced the long rectangular oak table, and Gedeyon and Rima sat to the right side of the table at the far end of the room, noticeably leaving the black fabric covered chair at the head of the table vacant.

In between their side and what I assumed was our side on

the left was a large tray with a pitcher of water with lemon and a plate of assorted cookies that I assumed came from the town bakery. I loved that bakery. Their cookies were always so soft and gooey.

I wanted to smash them in Gedeyon and Rima's faces.

They sat there smiling at us, looking like they owned the world. Gedeyon wore a white dashiki and pants set, which sat strikingly against his deep coloring. Rima wore her long hair in a braided crown surrounding her head and a royal blue body-hugging dress ending just below the knees, with an asymmetrical neckline. They looked like regal angels. They were far from it.

"Please sit down," Gedeyon called.

"You don't tell us to sit down. We were going to sit down in *our* conference room, anyway," Phillip grumbled, walking ahead and yanking a chair to sit on.

I looked at him with raised eyebrows and followed, taking a seat next to him. I wanted to tell him to tone it down, but I knew he was nervous enough as it was. If he wanted to come in hot, then I'd let him while I played it cool.

Gedeyon gave him a patient smile, and Rima let out a snort. "Look dear, I think we've upset the children," she said, leaning slightly into Gedeyon.

"You know, now that you don't have an audience, why don't you just come out with what you want," Phillip said, resting his arms on the table.

Gedeyon nodded. "We simply want a collaboration. We've seen the error of our ways in the past. We looked upon the newer soulmates as obstacles, and to a degree, they were. However, if we spared them, perhaps we could have grown a less...resistant empire."

"So, you still want to run things?" I asked. I was already sure of the answer, but I wanted absolute clarity.

"If we don't, who will?"

"How about letting people do their own thing? We aren't

God or whatever you believe in. Our job is just to help and protect. We're public servants, if anything."

"Oh my," Rima said, making a tsk-tsk sound. "Who fed you those lies?"

"Well, obviously, you disagree. And you were punished for it."

"You are so misguided. Those who want to control and manipulate you have told you untruths. Our nature is to rule. You both have felt that. We *are* gods."

I closed my eyes and took in a deep breath. They would not get a rise out of me. I would do my best to talk to them like they were rational beings, but only for so long. "We aren't immortal. We're just tools to help keep the world safe from evil. No one has to tell us that; it's obvious. Our power is about love and connection and respect, not dictatorship, repression, and control. We aren't all-knowing. Our time comes to an end because no one should be in power forever. It makes you less human, and we are, at the core, still humans."

Rima gave a wide yawn before looking to Gedeyon. "She bores me. I told you this would be a waste. We should just kill them and take their power."

Gedeyon tilted his head, studying me before speaking. "You are why we won't lose this time. See, although so much time has passed and the faith of the people has changed, with magic returning, things aren't that different. The people will follow us because they are fearful. They fear disease; they fear the paranormal; they fear the world that they are left with without technology. We must never forget to soothe their fears. That's where we went wrong before. We became the fear that we were supposed to protect them from. If we keep protecting them, they will worship us."

I sat back letting his words sit with me. I'd learned two things just then. One, as a soulmate, it was important that we were looked at as caring leaders, not ruthless dictators, or we'd find ourselves put to sleep like the originals. Two, if we wanted to win back our people, we had to make them see for themselves that Gedeyon and Rima were something to be feared. They hadn't witnessed what we had. We had to make them see.

"We don't need to be worshiped," Phillip cut in.

Gedeyon looked at him, smile still on his face. "You don't have to. Just support our mission. Allow us to draw power from you, if needed, to continue to protect our followers from those who would seek to destroy us and harm our people."

"And just who are your people?" Phillip asked, leaning into the table.

Gedeyon threw his hands out to the side. "The paranormals. We have learned that humans are weak and unreliable. It was the humans that turned their backs on us long ago. Back then, they outnumbered the paranormals. In this new world, they are the minority. If we rid ourselves of them, we will flourish like never before."

I squinted my eyes, not falling for their game. "You brought the Sickness to the humans, didn't you? How? Weren't you still in hibernation for years after magic returned?"

"Ah, you believed we only awoke recently. Not so."

"Our minds came back to life soon after the magic came back," Rima explained. She reached over and grabbed a cookie breaking it in half before taking a mouse of a bite. "Our power was limited then, and our reach was only via telepathy. Our first thought was to end the humans. We were not aware of the magic leaving or returning. We just wanted to reduce the numbers of our greatest enemy. Any remaining would be confined or enslaved."

Gedeyon nodded. "And so, we searched for a being powerful enough to change the world. Our first contact was with those who brought magic back."

"You know how magic returned?" I asked excitedly. If I could get some answers, maybe this meeting wouldn't be a total waste.

"Yes," Rima quickly replied. "And we aren't telling." She pursed her lips and wagged her finger at me like I was a child. "However, once we found them, the steps to bring about the annihilation of humans became a less daunting task. They had access to potent magic. The ability to create disease."

"They found a disease mage?" Phillip asked.

Rima winked at him in the affirmative.

"Why would they do that for you?"

She chuckled. "You assume they had a choice. Even lying in the ground, we were powerful. And the funny thing is, that group didn't all convert to paranormals, so some of them perished by helping us."

I frowned. I really wanted to knock her head off. I was never a violent person, but that might have to change. "How is that funny? They could have brought magic back for altruistic reasons, and you tainted it. You forced a disease mage to use their power to destroy humanity." I shook my head, overwhelmed with sadness. Disease mages were rare. Their power was destructive and ultimately not useful outside of battle. I counted my blessings that I'd never crossed paths with a dark mage.

"Your naiveté is so cute," Rima said in a sing-song voice. "You would paint us as the ultimate evil without even knowing the full truth. Not everyone who helped make this new world was so innocent. We merely took advantage of this situation to better our chances for survival. Your chances for survival. No one loves paranormals. They fear us and hate us. Your human friends will only betray you in the end. While we were behind placing you in that prison, we did not create it. That was the humans."

"Don't pretend to be high and mighty. You've done your

dirt. You're mind-controlling the people of this town, and who knows who else."

Gedeyon poured himself a glass of lemon water. "We don't profess to be innocent. And we are no fools. We won't lose again. We're leaving nothing to chance, so, of course, we have to control the town. It's silly that you didn't maintain that control, Phillip," he said before taking a sip.

"Yeah, well, I was banished, so there was that. By the way, where is the Dublin village?" Phillip barked. A look of pure irritation sat on his face. It was clear he wasn't buying whatever they were selling, and neither was I.

"Safe." Gedeyon perched his elbow on the table and rested his chin on his fist. "There are things that we can do that you still don't even know about. Do you really want to fight us based on lies, or would you rather try to work with us? Let's gain each other's trust, and if you don't like how things are going, you can kill us. Well, you can try to kill us."

I didn't want to join forces with them. While it was possible that the angels and fairies had lied to us, these soulmates had definitely done things to us, not to mention aligned themselves with evil beings well before coming to the table to negotiate. I couldn't forget that, and I had no intention of compromising with them. However, I recognized they were too powerful to fight without a better plan of action. Perhaps the best strategy was simply to play along, learn what we could from them, and then use it in destroying them.

I crossed my arms. "What do you plan to do here?"

Gedeyon smiled. "Heal, guide you, lead the people. Your town seemed a good place to start. And maybe those lost friends of yours can be found."

With our Dublin friends missing and no word from the fae, I had to pace myself if I was going to start my campaign against them. I wanted them blindsided when we defeated them, but I also needed my friends to be okay. "And what exactly do you want from us?"

Rima pointed her index finger in a circular motion at us. "Your cooperation. And for you to bond with us. We can be a powerful foursome. The first joint soulmate pairings ever." She tapped her chin in thought. "Now that I think about it, it could be fun." She gave us a pitiful look. "Sorry for trying to kill you. Especially you, Phillip. I'm a creature of habit, but I was wrong before." She offered a hand to him.

Phillip looked down at it with a frown before reaching outward and shaking her hand. He looked down at their hands, his face a tight grimace of pain.

I pushed my seat back and stood up just as Phillip snatched his hand away and looked at it in confusion. Rima still had a hold over him. We had to find a way to break his connection to her if we were going to beat them.

"Come on, Phillip," I said before looking to the soulmates. "You don't harm the people here; you free their minds, then you'll get your truce."

Gedeyon leaned back in his chair, a small smile sitting on his smug face, but he didn't speak. Neither did Rima. I was sure that meant nothing good, but the fact that they didn't immediately attack us was a good sign, as well.

I began to walk away. I didn't hear Phillip follow me, so I turned partially back, only to see Phillip still seated and gazing at Rima, who was presently giving him a sweet as pie smile.

I rolled my eyes and sighed before marching back and yanking him up by the arm.

CHAPTER 10

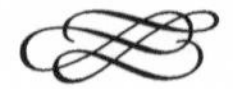

That night there would be a welcoming party for the new "rulers" and their cohorts. Apparently, Misandre, Lorenzo, and Joo-won and company would be parading through our town as well. Our town loved to throw last-minute shindigs for newcomers, and parties for evil beings were no exceptions. Not that anyone was in their right mind to know better.

Although I didn't want to put on a nice outfit again just to fake pleasantries, I believed that tonight could be a good night to put a spotlight on how awful Gedeyon and Rima truly were. Even if I did it indirectly. I knew they were up to no good, and a setting like this would be perfect to have everyone see the real them on display. Even if I had to push a few buttons to do so.

I lay on my bed, not caring if my dark red cocktail dress got wrinkled or not. I patted at my stomach in a vain attempt to beat away the nerves. I did not want to see the red-headed fairy they called Misandre. She kind of scared me. Hell, they all scared me. I was no coward, but I wasn't a fool either. The Ghoul had tried to eat Lisa alive. Misandre and her fae had tried to rip my heart out, and Joo-won sliced into Erik with a magical sword, almost killing him.

In all my years since the world had changed, I'd stayed out of harm's way. Living with my parents, my brother, and a small commune had kept me safe, and probably a tad, okay a lot, sheltered. Then I lost my parents to the Sickness, the supernatural disease killing most non-paranormal humans. After that, we were kidnapped and imprisoned for our paranormal blood. Life pretty much was a long tumble downhill after that with a few breaks in between. Those breaks were meeting our friends. Friends who I dragged into a war I didn't want.

I felt a presence at the doorway, and I looked over to find Erik looking as handsome as ever. The man could wear a ratty shirt and sweats and still look like he should be on the cover of GQ. He was just so damn fine and strong looking. He wasn't Thor, but he was definitely Thor adjacent.

Our relationship had undeniably been tested, but I wasn't willing to give up on us. We would make it to the other side of this whole soulmate foolishness, and we would have the calm life we both deserved, together. I loved him, and he loved me. No soulmates, paranormal illness, or pack groupies would stand in our way.

He looked down at me with a smirk, gazing over the length of my body slowly enough to make a girl blush. When I looked up, I noticed his usual hazel eyes were the amber color of his jackal.

"Full moon coming up?" I asked, leaning up on my elbows.

He nodded without saying anything and stalked–because walking was too tame of a word for how he moved – over to me. He pushed my knees apart with his leg forcing my dress to creep up my thighs. Still not speaking, he stood between my legs and leaned forward, balancing his hands on either side of my arms.

"Can I help you?" I said in a low voice.

Something predatory flashed beneath the surface of those eyes, and I sucked in a breath as he moved closer to me. He rested his forehead against mine for a moment, eyes closing before he moved to my neck. I felt him inhale, sending a shiver through me as his breath tickled my skin.

"Why do you always smell like this?" he finally whispered.

I never stopped loving how he seemed so impressed with the way I smelled. Even with no perfume, he loved the essence that was me, and I loved his. We just fit together so right. How he wasn't really my soulmate, I didn't understand. "What, soap? I didn't want to waste my limited supply of perfume on these people."

He chuckled as he nuzzled his face in the crook of my neck, still sniffing. He gave a playful bite, and I yelped. He didn't break the skin or cause me any serious pain and...I kind of liked it.

"I could stay like this, with you, forever," he moaned.

"Just sniffing me?" I giggled like a teenager, relishing the moment with him despite the stress of the world around us.

"You laugh, but your scent just...does something to me." He nipped at me again, eliciting another cry from me.

"As long as you don't eat me, that's okay."

"No, I don't want to eat you. Well, not the way you're suggesting."

I cocked a brow, feeling a jerk in my core. "Oh, really now?"

He grabbed me by the waist and flipped me so that he was lying back on the bed, and I was resting on top of him. I straddled him between my thighs and kissed his collarbone under his deep blue button down. His hands moved down my back to my bottom, lifting my dress high around my waist before stroking his hands back down to my butt.

Moving from his collarbone to his neck, I licked a pattern over his smooth, hot skin, causing him to tighten his grip on me. I sucked his skin into my mouth, and apparently, that was the golden ticket because he let out a growl that vibrated from his chest into mine. He arched up, and his hardness pressed between my legs. I ground down on him, wanting to feel more. When I bit at his ear lobe, he moved a hand from my bottom and covered my damp opening. I pushed onto his hand a bit like a cat in heat. It had been a while, and although I was clear that sex wouldn't fix anything, I wasn't sure I cared right now.

He pressed against my soft bud in slow, agonizing circles, succeeding in making me more excited. He groaned, and before I could move, he ripped the satin fabric covering my bottom and threw it on the floor.

"I liked those panties," I cracked before moving my mouth to his other ear lobe.

He moved his hand back to my opening to continue his ministrations. "I'll get you more," he replied in a barely audible whisper.

At least, I think that's what he said. I could barely stay coherent as his fingers increased their speed. I pulled back from his ear to release a moan, and he leaned forward and gave a teasing lick of his tongue over a bra covered breast.

I took that as a sign and undid my strapless bra, tossing it in the same direction as my destroyed panties. I pushed down the top of my dress and leaned forward, and this time his tongue lavished my nipples equally, sending me into further exhilaration. His mouth, coupled with his finger work, soon resulted in a flood of explosion from my core, and a cry tore from me. My legs shook as I rode the wave of pleasure before collapsing briefly onto his chest.

However, I didn't allow myself to rest long. My hands went to his belt, almost shaking with more need. He looked down at my hands, and an arrogant smile crossed his lips.

"Why is your belt being difficult?" I grumbled, practically yanking at his waist. This wasn't rocket science but apparently, post-orgasm-Amina didn't have all her brain cells.

Erik gently clasped my hands and brought them to his lips for a light kiss before moving his hands to his belt, eyes on me with such wanton intensity I could have turned into a puddle right there. He undid his pants with ease and then placed his hands behind his back. "Continue."

I chuckled and got off of him, then pulled his pants and briefs down in one go. I then quickly moved back over him before carefully lowering down onto him and beginning a slow grind. His cocky smile left his lips, and he threw his head back, mouth open in his own haze of pleasure. I closed my own eyes as I enjoyed our bond and the feel of him in me.

The connection was almost emotional. I couldn't explain it. Tears dotted the corners of my eyes as I continued to ride for who knows how long. This man was in me, physically, emotionally, psychically. It was too late for anyone else. He was mine, and I was his.

Erik grabbed my lower back and pulled me towards him. I opened my eyes and balanced my hands on his hard chest. He looked up at me with gentle, kind eyes that squeezed my heart. Then something more primal entered them, making his jackal eyes shine brightly before he drove his hips up, repeatedly sending me out of control and again over my peak. He soon followed, holding on to my waist tightly and crying out into almost a howl.

Even after the wave had crashed over us, we remained connected with me lying on his chest, now slick with sweat. I didn't care.

"Let's just stay this way," I whispered, still trying to slow my racing heart.

Erik stroked my hair and kissed the top of my head. "I don't think the world's going to let us do that. But I promise that when this is all over, we'll go on that trip to Costa Rica together, and we can just lie like this for however long we want."

I sighed, still content. "I'd like that."

Just then, we heard a knock at the door.

Erik let out another growl.

"Should we ignore it? Maybe it's just someone trying to sell us something," I cracked.

He gave a hearty laugh. "If only those were the kind of unexpected visitors we got nowadays." We grabbed my face and kissed me hard before slapping me on the rear.

I cried out when I pulled away from him, my body still sensitive. He arched up, face twisted in desire. Clearly, he was still just as sensitive as me. I pointed to his still very present erection. "Perhaps I should be the one to answer the door."

He looked down at himself, then looked over to me with the same jackal eyes. "It's all your fault." He flashed me a wicked grin, and I noticed his elongated canines.

That sight only seemed to excite me, and I crossed my legs in a weak attempt to hold back.

I snapped my bra back on and dug a new pair of panties out of my dresser drawer. "My bad."

The last thing I wanted to do was to answer the door, but ignoring a knock on the door could be the difference between life and death in this world.

I opened the door, fluffing out my hair at the same time.

Mae and Bill stood on the other side dressed to the nines. I'd never seen Mae so done up. She wore a long beaded black gown with three quarter length sleeves. Bill wore a black tuxedo, still rocking his turquoise pendant chain.

"You both look like you're going to walk the red carpet. Is this thing really that nice?" I asked, motioning for them to come in.

"Apparently, we are all to wear our finest garments to impress them," Mae muttered as they walked through.

“Water, tea, a shot of whiskey?” I cracked.

“I’ll take the whiskey,” Bill said with a straight face.

“Coming right up,” Erik said from behind me.

I looked over to him and noticed that he was back to normal. I was a little dismayed he recovered so quickly.

“I’ll have one too,” Mae stated.

I gave her a wide-eyed look.

“It’s been that kind of day, child,” she said in response to my face.

Erik grabbed four shot glasses from the kitchen cabinet before walking to the dining area to a rolling glass serving table we used to house our very limited supply of liquor. He quickly poured us drinks, and we accepted them, clinking glasses before gulping down our drinks.

“So, to what do we owe this visit?” I asked.

“We just wanted to touch base with you,” Mae stated. “I’m sorry I couldn’t prepare you better for their visit. I had no real idea of how everything would begin. I envisioned a large battle, but maybe I was wrong.”

I waved a hand. “Well, feel free to vent. I have a soundproofing spell up so no one can eavesdrop. Why aren’t they trying to kill us anymore? Or even confine us? They’re talking compromise, now.”

Mae rolled her eyes, annoyance covering her elegant face. “Compromise my butt. They are placating you. Don’t believe the hype, as the young folk say.”

“Do kids still say that?” I muttered to Erik, who responded with a shrug.

Mae narrowed her eyes at me. “Don’t be sassy now.”

I gave her a sweet smile, and she shook her head in pretend anger.

“Glad you can keep your humor,” Mae stated. “Listen, this is only the calm before the storm. It is in their nature to control, and they do not compromise. It is their way, period.

As soon as you disagree, they will subdue you. They are too arrogant to admit defeat or allow anyone else to lead."

"I get that, but we aren't strong enough to fight them, at least not without getting others hurt. I can't risk that."

Mae put her glass down on the table. "I know, but all isn't lost. Their strength is still limited. Their advantage is just that they know how much their powers can do and they have fooled their followers, both the good and the bad, to believe that they are still all powerful. Your goal should be to protect the innocents they will surely harm with their self-righteous and deceptive ways. I know you heard otherwise, but for now, you all must stay in town."

"Right, I was thinking we stay and show people how truly evil they are. We could have them talk to people in other locations about what's been done to their towns. Assuming we can do it safely." I paused, just hearing what she'd said. "Wait, you said for now. Are you saying that at some point we should leave?"

Mae sighed. "I hope not, but my visions keep changing. I can't trust my mind like I used to due to this damn sickness. I've seen so many things; I can't tell which way is right and which way is wrong. At least not when it comes to you. The soulmates, I'm very clear on. I also know that if you leave this town, all hell's going to break loose. Now is not the time to run. Just be smart. Stay low until you can't anymore. Keep them on their toes just like they do you. Don't show your full hand."

I rubbed my bare arms and looked around the room, not feeling anymore soothed by Mae's words. Not that she was ever soothing to begin with. "Well, that won't be hard since we don't have much in hand."

Mae patted my shoulder. "I get it, I do. In the meanwhile, there's something you need to do, and you're not going to like it."

~

The party was an exclusive affair with only the powerful people in town attending. Held in Blake's burlesque club, the place was packed. The club was all dark spaces with black walls and floors, and suede and leather furniture. Crystal chandeliers and wall sconces emitted the barest of light. On the walls were framed posters of 40s and 50s pinup girls. To the right was a long stage where one athletic woman in a black sparkly bikini did a balancing act with a huge silver hula hoop. To the left, along the back of the room, was a long retro style bar in front of a glass wall and lit from below the counter. Several guests stood around the bar while bartenders moved behind it, shaking concoctions in mixers. Attendees filled the floor, either standing about or sitting at the small circular tables, and servers carrying silver platters of hor d'oeuvres walked about. The Eurythmics, *Sweet Dreams,* blared from speakers throughout the club. I used to love that song, until now.

The guests of honor had yet to arrive, and I was thankful for that.

"Why is it that darn near every time I dress up, it's for something I don't want to go to?" I muttered, leaning over to Erik.

"It's because we have bad luck, which I'm beginning to think is because Gedeyon put his evil eye on us," Phillip replied, appearing beside me looking dapper in a maroon three-piece suit.

"How have we not put that together before?" I stated before turning to him. I paused and looked him up and down. "You're wearing the same color as me." We looked like a couple at junior prom.

He gave a nonchalant shrug. "Great minds think alike." He leaned past me and gave a wave to Erik. "What up, jackal."

Erik rolled his eyes. "Don't call me that," he replied. He

lifted his head and sniffed the air. He then leaned in front of me, sniffing in Phillip's direction. "Why do you smell like you fell into a vat of vodka?"

Phillip gave an exaggerated nod. "Because I drank… a lot." He turned to face us fully, his hands animated as he spoke. "See, see, I thought if I got a little bit drunk, my mind would be too cloudy for that soulmate bitch to control me."

I gave him a blank stare. "That is so stupid. Why did you even come?"

Blake sauntered over to us dressed in a short, sparkly gold dress. Her platinum hair was slicked back, and her face was done with smoky eyes and nude lips. She came to show off. "I tried to tell him that," she stated, resting a hand on Phillip's shoulder. "He insisted on coming."

Phillip leaned behind me and grabbed a small plate from a server filled with bruschetta. "I was told by Rima that if I didn't come, they would take that as an act of aggression. She's gonna fuck me over tonight, I just know it." He stuffed the food in his mouth without biting.

I crossed my arms and glared over at Blake. "Tell me why you are hosting this thing for them?"

She touched her chest in feigned innocence. "Like I had a choice. If we are supposed to play nice, then how could I say no when it was suggested?"

"Fair point."

"It's a Friday night. I'm losing business by shutting this place down for a party that was not booked."

"How kind of them to take your space."

"I'm assuming this is how things will be from now."

Phillip nodded again. "Yeah, we're their bitches now."

I put up a finger. "I am no one's bitch. And spread the word about how they bully people into doing things for them for free. But on another note, I'm glad we both ran into you. We met with Mae earlier, and she suggested that we do the thing we all know we don't want to do."

Blake clapped her hands. "An orgy? Because I wouldn't be against that," Blake said with a suggestive smile.

I raised my eyebrows and clutched imaginary pearls. "What? No. She suggested we all move in together. Something about watching each other's back and strengthening our bonds. We have a leg up by having not only the Six but additional mates. All that connection just gives us more power boosts even if they're multiple connections with the same people. Gedeyon and Rima aren't stronger than us. They're just a little wiser, is all."

Blake tapped her chin. "I see, I see. So, in a way, you and I are connected?"

"Yes, through Phillip. And through Phillip and I, you are connected to Erik."

"Got it. And we *don't* think an orgy would help strengthen that bond?" She looked from me to Erik, expectedly.

Phillip shook his head. "I am not having sex with Erik. He's taller than me, and he's going to try to make me a bottom, and I can't do it. Also, I'm not gay, so that would present some challenges there."

Erik passed his hand over his face. "Someone put him to bed," he said through gritted teeth.

"Fine, but not you," Phillip replied, pointing at Erik.

Erik leaned towards me. "I don't want to live with these people," he said in a not so soft whisper.

I threw out my hands. "Should we have this conversation again when you aren't so hungry, and he's not so drunk?" I asked Blake.

She shook her head. "No. We get it. We can move into your place. It's the largest. I suppose I can share a bed with Phillip again, unless you want to play swap some nights?"

I opened my mouth to call off the invitation when I noticed a female with long deep red hair come through the entrance. Misandre.

Her hair hung almost to her waist in cascading waves.

She wore an extremely low cut deep green jumpsuit that made her pale skin stand out. She cut her bright pink eyes at us with a glare so hard I fought the urge to step back.

By her side was a handsome bronze toned man of average height with wavy black hair and coal black eyes displaying no white. He wore a black three-piece suit over a toned physique. He looked to us with a smile, exposing two rows of sharp teeth. Yikes.

"Who's that beside the fairy bitch?" Phillip asked.

"I think he's the one they call the Ghoul," I answered with a grimace. A vision of him slicing into Lisa's flesh and eating it popped into my head, making me clutch my stomach.

Phillip tapped his forehead. "Right, right. The one Lisa thought she killed by dismemberment? Is she coming to this? Because that is going to be an awkward reunion."

"Yeah, but everyone's supposed to be in a truce, so they can't touch her."

"It's going to be awkward for a lot of us," Blake muttered, taking a sip of her wine as she eyed an entourage entering the room.

I followed her gaze and saw Lisa, looking beautiful as ever with her long, jet black hair pinned to one side and a body hugging royal blue gown covering her petite frame.

On her left was a tall, tanned man with high cheekbones, full lips, and mesmerizing marble colored eyes. Besides the otherworldly eyes, his pointed ears gave away his lineage.

Joo-won, the Elven king. He bordered between beautiful and handsome, and looked every bit the model with a swimmer's physique covered in a well-tailored navy blue pinstriped suit. His short black hair was sculptured expertly, and he gave off an air of royalty with a tinge of arrogance in his eyes.

Following the pair were Joo-won's right hands. Senna, a woman with smooth mahogany skin, long deep brown hair, and green eyes. She wore a simple black thin strapped camisole style gown. Rows of colorful beaded necklaces encircled her neck. By her side was Yuri, almost albino in completion with stark white hair. He wore a tailored gray suit with a black turtleneck peeking through.

Joo-won looked over to us and began to head our way, the rest moving in sync behind him like a collective of models. I was pretty sure the elves, with their glamour, were even more beautiful than the vampires. Jerks.

Blake let out a sigh and looked away. It wasn't too long ago that she had escaped, staying with Joo-won after we had accused her of being the soulmate. She'd used that time in his presence to learn more about the soulmates, instead of betraying us like I thought she had. In turn, Joo-won had almost killed her. That she was standing her ground gave me even more respect for her.

Joo-won stopped in front of us with a smile on his face. "We meet again. This time under more pleasant circumstances. I do hope all is forgiven? I certainly have moved forward."

"It's better for us to be friends than enemies," I replied with a tight smile. I actually did mean it. Joo-won on our side would do wonders for our stance. It would make people think that maybe something was wrong with the original soulmates if their followers started to switch sides.

"I'm glad you see it that way, Amina."

Clearly, he and I weren't thinking about friendship in the same way. I'd have to change that. "For now," I added before looking at Yuri and Senna, who regarded me with careful expressions. I was fairly sure they had not told their boss they owed me a debt for not killing them.

Joo-won took a step towards me. "You are no match for them. Do as they demand and live," he said in a lowered voice.

I wanted to roll my eyes but kept my face pleasant. I was tired of people not believing us. As my mom used to say, I could show them better than I could tell them. He'd just have to see what we could do just like everyone else. "Do you believe in them?"

"Belief doesn't matter. Only survival. All I can do is maintain what I have. It won't matter how many people you have siding with you. The loss of Alister did nothing. They didn't even really care that I took in Lisa. This is not simply a game of manpower. We're all only cannon fodder." Joo-won looked from me to Phillip. "The two of you don't scare them. Not anymore. They now know your secret."

"What's our secret?" I asked in a tight voice, ready for the insult that was coming.

"You aren't smart." He smiled at us and leaned back.

Lisa huffed, and poked Joo-won in the shoulder. "Don't be an ass. They both are some of the smartest people I know."

Joo-won chuckled. "Then you need to know more people, butterfly."

Burn. Well, he wasn't lying. These beings were all older and wiser, so compared to them, we were just a bunch of ignorant kids. But kids could be geniuses too.

"This fucker is ruining my buzz," Phillip announced and walked away.

"He really has changed," Lisa observed. "The old Phillip would probably have tried to mutilate you."

She wasn't lying. Drunk Phillip made things easier for me.

Joo-won waved an unconcerned hand. "I don't mean to insult my new friends. It's just that a 3-year-old cannot outsmart an adult. You are still learning. They've forgotten more than you know."

I chuckled. His doubt, their doubt would be to our advantage. They were using old rules for an outdated game. "I wouldn't go so far as to call us friends. And I wouldn't count us out of the fight. See, their rules are old and outdated, just like them. We are the fresh new faces who know the lay of the land. We're faster with more energy. Our minds work faster than theirs. We know how to work smarter, not harder."

His grin widened. "Your optimism is delightful."

Asshole.

"Oh, shit," Lisa said, looking behind me.

I turned slightly and saw Lorenzo and Misandre march towards us, a determined scowl on Lorenzo's face.

"I doubt they're coming over just to say hi," Lisa muttered, taking a step back. "I really should have set him on fire."

I turned, blocking Lisa. Erik did the same. I wasn't excited to get into a round two battle with the fairy queen, but I wasn't going to let her hurt my girl, either. I could take her. Okay, I really didn't know that, but if I couldn't beat her ass, we'd be in real trouble.

"Fairy," Lorenzo began as the pair came to stand in front of us. "Glad to see me?"

Lisa huffed. "Well, that's a dumb question. Of course not."

He gave a snort, crossing his arms. "Shall I seek some revenge"?

I took a step towards Lisa. I would kill him if he tried anything, but first, I would make sure everyone knew he was threatening us, and this was the company the soulmates kept.

"Only if you want your head torn off," Erik stated, taking a step forward.

Lorenzo raised an eyebrow. "Do you think you're more powerful than me, jackal? It's been a while since I've tasted were flesh. It might be worth finding out."

Erik unbuttoned his jacket without speaking. Lorenzo laughed and moved around us with inhuman speed. I spun around, and Lisa was now several feet away, clawing at Lorenzo's hand as he raised her off her feet by the neck. He opened his mouth impossibly wide, his sharp teeth looking even more horrifying.

A blur of movement shot towards us and propelled

Lorenzo across the room, causing him to drop Lisa to her knees.

What the hell was going on? Lorenzo and this being, who moved so fast all I could see were shadows of movement, crashed into several tables. The blur jumped back from Lorenzo, and pointed a silver handgun at the ghoul lying on his back on the floor.

I quickly realized that the being was Charles. His eyes were full vampire red now with just a tiny black pupil in the center. He pulled the trigger, and Lorenzo bounced off the floor as a bullet hit his right shoulder.

The other guest stood back, frozen in shock and the music stopped.

In one effortless movement, Lorenzo rose to face Charles. His smile remained. "You think a simple bullet can hurt me?"

Charles gave a lazy smile, eyes lowered, and almost closed. "Nah, not with a simple bullet. But that was no simple bullet." He took a couple of steps back.

Lorenzo's smile suddenly twisted in pain, and he stumbled backward grabbing his shoulder. "What the fuck?"

"See, I kind of specialize in magical technology. And I just shot you with one of my exploding–"

Lorenzo's arm tore away from the socket in an explosion of blood and gore. It barely missed Charles and the other nearby guests ,who cried out in horror. Pieces of Lorenzo's arm fell to the floor, leaving a shredded space where his arm once resided.

Nice. Well, not really nice. It was actually super gross, but one point for our side!

"Motherfucker!" Lorenzo roared before moving towards Charles.

My brother raised his gun and pointed it back at Lorenzo. "Come at me again, and I'll get the other arm. I'm trying to be civil since I don't want to start a war, but if you keep coming after people, I might have to get a little disrespectful."

Lorenzo took another step forward.

Maybe he should have killed the ghoul. Although I wasn't sure, everyone had witnessed him making the first attack, which is what we needed.

"No more fighting!" Boomed a deep female voice from the entrance of the club.

The sound reverberated across the room. The crowd turned and saw Gedeyon and Rima standing like two visions in white. They practically glowed, with Rima dressed in a floor length, one-shoulder, fitted gown, and a complicated braided updo, and Gedeyon in a tailored white suit, looking like a televangelist.

"We are supposed to all be friends now," Rima said, spreading her arms. She gave a peaceful smile and looked around. "Let's allow our past to stay in the past."

Murmurs of agreement could be heard throughout the room.

Rima clapped her hand to gain the crowd's attention. "Please, someone, let's clean this place up again. Lorenzo, go heal in the town infirmary," Rima continued. "Let's get the music back on, enjoy yourselves. We are here to have fun tonight."

On cue, the music returned, and chatter and movement grew. A crowd quickly formed around the first soulmates like they were pop idols.

Lorenzo stomped out of the room with an escort.

Misandre remained, glaring at Lisa, who wisely ignored her.

"I need a drink," I grumbled, walking to the bar. I leaned on the counter next to Phillip and Blake, who were currently downing shots of clear liquid. This was no time to get drunk. "More vodka?"

"It's that kind of night," Phillip replied, slamming the glass down. "If Pastor Gedeyon and Tammy Faye Faker over there start slapping people on the foreheads with God's blessings, I'm out."

"That's kind of hilarious. You're funny when you're tipsy."

I looked back at the soulmates, and grimaced.

Rima patted the cheek of a woman who looked at her like she was Mother Teresa. Gedeyon smiled and shook hands like a presidential elect. What Kool-Aid were these people drinking? Phillip and I had regrown limbs and had come up with a test for the paranormal illness, yet we barely got so much as a head nod from folks.

I took a gulp of my drink and looked around the crowd. I spotted Senna starring at me. She tilted her head to the left and walked down a hallway leading to the bathrooms.

I looked at Erik. "Can you watch my drink? I need to head to the bathroom."

He nodded and took my drink devoid of expression. "Tell me what she says later,"

I gave him a wink, no longer surprised at his perceptiveness.

Once I reached the bathroom, an elegant space with a dimly lit chandelier hanging from above and marbled floors, I found Senna leaning against the bathroom sinks.

"What is it?" I asked, crossing my arms.

"No one's in here, but can you do a soundproofing spell?" She spun her index finger in a circle to signify my spell, I guessed.

I nodded, and recited the quick spell to prevent anyone from hearing us speak.

She clasped her hands in front of her with a nod. "We don't have much time. If I were you two, I'd take my mates and leave town. They don't want to be your friend. They only want your obedience. You want to know how they came into so much power so quickly?"

"The question has crossed my mind."

"Rima has been working her magic from day one in your town, and their magic spreads like a virus. You'll see how it works soon, I'm sure. It's terrifying. The only reason they haven't used you as food yet is because you are more valuable to them alive."

"What do you mean by food?" This was new. If they had a special kind of food supply, maybe we could win by cutting them off.

"It's how they get their strength. They kept poor souls alive, including former soulmates, in the worst of conditions and ate at their souls little by little until they were nothing but husks. Or so the tales from my people go. And I've seen them remove a soul from a body. It's chilling. Rima may have attacked you several times, but she never planned to kill you. She only loves to torment. Gedeyon's way is different, and after Rima, people get a false sense of comfort with him."

"Like good cop, bad cop." If they were eating souls then they had a nice farm of people right here to chomp on. I had to keep an eye on them 24/7 and catch them in the act, before they actually killed someone. I'd also need to find out how exactly they took the souls.

Senna crossed her body with one arm. "But make no mistake about Gedeyon, the outcome will be the same for you. He is kind to you the way a farmer feeds his cattle well. They want you strong, mentally, and physically. They will savor you until you are no more. Soulmates aren't meant to be as powerful as they are, but soulmates aren't supposed to eat souls, either." She looked at me with haunted eyes. "You can't win. You can only run."

I tightened my fists to fight against the fear rising in me. Fear was not my friend in this battle. I had to hear Senna's words without reacting to them. Easier said than done, since it felt like my knees were going to give out any moment. "Why are you telling me this? Why do you care if we survive?"

Her eyes darkened. "You bespelled Yuri and I to support you. If we are to die fighting by your side, make it worth it. Until you are strong enough, you should run."

"How can we power up in enough time to fight soulmates who are thousands of years old?" I had my pets, my mate, the Six, my own magic. Was that enough?

She shrugged. "Eat souls like they do? There are plenty of evil beings out there for you to kill without feeling remorse. Eat the bad souls."

I frowned. I could never do that even if I knew how. The idea of it was monstrous. "I'd feel remorse, regardless."

"You have to be as ruthless as them to win."

That wasn't my specialty. I didn't want to be them. I wanted to be better than them. "There has to be another way. They were taken out before. If we could find that spell, maybe we could win again. Maybe strengthen it, so it doesn't just put them in hibernation but kills them."

Senna scoffed. "Good luck with that." She looked towards the door. "Someone's coming." She looked back at me. "I'll help you search for this spell. I have connections in the fae world, and we've been around a long time. But if things start looking bad for you, get out."

Senna was offering up more information than she was obligated to. I'd bonded her to help in the fight, but she was giving me insider secrets. "Why do you care about us?"

"They will never let Joo-won and our people be free. We will be their henchmen for eternity." She shook her head and scrunched her face, tapping the counter in frustration. "If Joo-won wasn't so powerful, they would have never come to us. Weaker elves are better off than us now. If you promise not to do anything like that, if you defeat the first soulmates, then at least Yuri and I will continue to have your backs regardless of your spell." She turned to the mirror and began to fluff her hair as the door opened behind us.

A woman walked in to use the restroom.

I gave the woman a polite smile as she went into the stall, then proceeded to wash my hands at the sink beside Senna. I looked into the mirror, and Senna looked back at me through our reflections. I gave her a nod, which I hope she took as agreement that I would not do to her what the soulmates were doing to them now. In the mirror I could see her reach over and pat my shoulder, but I could not feel the pressure of her hand. I looked down to my right but didn't see her hand there. I looked up, and she was gone. Instinctively I looked back at the mirror, but that reflection was gone as well. Darn elves and their trickery.

I reluctantly went back to the party. Erik greeted me at the beginning of the hallway for the bathrooms before the space opened up to the club.

He passed me back my drink. "Everything okay?"

I nodded again. "I can fill you in–" I was interrupted by a loud shout near the door.

"Gedeyon! Rima!" shouted an older woman dressed in all black. She had a mix of black and gray hair, and her face held a wide grin and glassy eyes. She looked vaguely familiar. Perhaps a local witch. "I want to thank you for all that you've done! You've healed my son of his sickness."

The crowd, including the soulmates, looked over to the woman with curious eyes.

She threw her hands out to the side. "I've seen the good that you've done, and I thank you. You are both our saviors."

Rima sauntered over to her and touched her face lightly with her fingers. She said something I couldn't hear, and the woman grasped her hand in between her own, kissing her fingers before quickly letting go.

I thought I would vomit from the show.

Rima gave her a slight head nod and then turned from her, blocking the view of the woman. Sudden cries of shock had me moving to get a better view of the woman, and found myself joining in on the horrified screams as we all watched the woman magically slice her own throat with a movement of her index finger, thick blood spurting out.

The music stopped again, but no one close to her moved to assist her as they watched her drop to the ground, a smile still on her face as she bled out. I ran in her direction, tripped over something, and sprawled hands first on the ground. Erik grabbed me, pulled me back up as I looked toward my right.

Rima touched her mouth, her eyes wide. "Oops," she whispered, moving her foot back, the cause of my fall.

I looked back at the woman to find Phillip already there, attempting to heal her. I saw him close the wound in her neck, and the woman began to gulp in air.

"Get her to the hospital," he shouted at a man nearby. The man looked at him with the same dull eyes, not moving. Phillip snapped his fingers. "Now." I could feel the power in his command, and I knew he used magic, not that I blamed him.

I looked over to Rima, ignoring the fact that the music and "festivities" had started again as if no one had just witnessed a woman try to kill herself. "You did this!"

She cocked a brow. "Is that what you saw?"

"You said something to her to make her cut her throat."

"Now, why would I do that?" She touched my shoulder, and I moved away quickly. "Don't be so paranoid, little girl." She walked away, a crowd of fans surrounding her.

I shook my head slowly. "We thought this would be a battle. It's an infiltration, and it happened so expertly, right under our noses."

Not too long ago, the witches had done all they could to protect us from these soulmates. I wondered if they had known back then that all their efforts would be for nothing. How could Mae not have predicted this?

Raya stepped in front of us. She wore her wavy bob with a part down the middle, and she was dressed in a red off the shoulder silk blouse and black women's tuxedo pants. "Gedeyon wants to talk to you, Erik," she said, with the same creepy smile I'd seen on practically everyone here. God, they really had gotten to them all.

Had Rima and Gedeyon really taken over in one night, or had they been slowly controlling minds, a few at a time?

Raya gave me wide, concerned eyes that didn't match her smile. "I get it, you think I've turned on you. I haven't. I still like you both and support Erik. But why does my support of you two and the soulmates have to be mutually exclusive? They've healed sick people of this regressive illness. I'm up next for healing. They can heal you too, Erik. And Mae."

I gave a dry chuckle. "And just like that, you're BFFs? You don't tell us they're coming, and you just invite them into our town?"

Tears welled in her eyes, and she blinked rapidly to keep them at bay. I could see the inner turmoil already in her face. She was struggling against the control as well. However, like Carter, she was losing. "We knew you wouldn't understand. You've been forced to believe, all this time, that these soulmates couldn't be redeemed and came to do us harm. Carter and I didn't even know they were coming until the day of."

Erik took the last gulp of his drink and put it down on a nearby table. "There's no point in continuing this discussion. What's done is done." Erik kissed me on my cheek. "Won't be gone long."

I looked after them, burning with anger. I wasn't mad at Raya. It wasn't her fault. She was being controlled. We'd have to break that control in secrecy and have her and Carter pretend they were still under a mind wipe. I didn't see another way. I couldn't risk them sacrificing themselves like some brainless zombies.

"Amina!" Rima shouted, waving me over. I took in a deep breath and walked over to Rima, who was now perched on a table, her legs folded, and a glass of what appeared to be champagne in her hand. Where had we found champagne? I guess for these soulmates, we could make such a drink accessible.

"Amina!" she exclaimed like we were the best of friends. "I was telling this group all about soulmates and how much I liked you. Champagne?"

I shook my head before taking a sip of the drink I already had in my hand.

"You don't know what you're missing. I procured this from a Wiccan village in the south of France. It's been forever since I've been able to drink or eat. It's not easy coming back to life after sleeping for over 1000 years."

"I can imagine," I replied with innocent eyes. Maybe since she was drinking, she'd be more forthcoming with information. "Just how did you drift off to sleep again?"

She wagged a finger at me with a playful smile. "Why talk about such dreary things? I was just telling them how much I admired you."

Oh, please. "Really?"

She nodded. "Although I deceived you, I really do like you. The way you care about others, even at risk to yourself, is very impressive. So many times, you could have left and never turned back, and yet you always returned to help. You helped those at that paranormal prison; you came back for Phillip when he and I had that misunderstanding–"

"Misunderstanding? Is that what we're calling it now?" I chuckled. "You possessed the body of my best friend and tortured Phillip."

She pouted. "I admit, I do have a lot to atone for."

A few sympathetic murmurs from the group could be heard.

"But, as I've told my new friends here," She waved around to the crowd. "I will put in the work to do right. Just as Phillip did when he returned from Ireland. Life should be about giving and getting second chances. And you are so merciful. I'd hope you'd let me prove to you that I'm a good person. You forgave Phillip for confining you and almost killing you. You befriended Joo-won's people."

I almost choked on my drink, but kept playing it nonchalantly. She couldn't know about my deal with Senna and Yuri, could she? I glanced up at her with careful eyes, but her face didn't give anything away. She may have known of the fight at the cell when we imprisoned Seth.

"Oh, and you fought with Raya, and now you two are pals. You forgave Lisa for banishing you. And Ahmed, didn't he try to kill you?"

Was she comparing herself to these guys? Raya fought me when she was sick, Lisa thought she was doing the right thing, and Ahmed was under their orders because they had his lamp. "Yes, per your orders."

She tilted her head and smiled at me as she took another sip of champagne. "I was so messed up then."

She said it as if talking about her younger days when she was a rebel child. It was only a few months ago, and she was far from a child or a misguided youth.

"By the way, where is Ahmed? I wanted to say hi."

Yeah, right, lady, I thought. She'd say hi by exploding his head for his betrayal. No way were we going to tell her a thing. "I have no clue, and I don't want to know."

She eyed me with a neutral expression I could not read, but her eyes were so cold I had to stifle a shiver.

She shrugged with a laugh. "What shall we do about such naughty children?" She looked over to Phillip, who stood with a slight sway beside Blake, who eyed him with concern. "Phillip, dear, haven't you had enough?"

At the mention of his name Phillip looked up at her. His eyes were glazed over and he seemed barely coherent. How much had he drunk already or was this her mind control?

"What are you my mother now, too?" Phillip slurred, swaying his glass of champagne in the air.

Rima gave him a closed lip smile. "Since you like to drink, how about you come here and drink from me," she said in a sing-song voice.

The crowd around us gave an 'ooh' sound like she had said something worthy. What the hell did she mean, drink from her?

She curled her index finger in a come-hither motion, and Phillip passed Blake his glass before stumbling to Rima, eyes still glistening.

"On your knees, my pet," she sang in a low voice, now pointing to the floor. Without hesitation, Phillip dropped to his knees and looked up to her adoringly.

Crap, she was using her siren magic on him, and as I thought, his drinking liquor wasn't protecting him. And my wards weren't working either, at least not on him. Damn it! How were we supposed to fight the soulmates if Phillip was going to play puppet to her! It wasn't his fault, but it was frustrating.

"Open your mouth," Rima continued before taking a swig of her champagne. She then bent down and poured her drink from her mouth into his.

I waved my hand and shouted a magic freezing word. The whole room paused, including the amber liquid, which fell midway from her mouth into Phillip's. Phillip, the only person unaffected, fell back on his butt and spit out the bit of champagne that had made it into his mouth.

"What the fuck?!" He cried. "This bitch is crazy!" He slid back away from her before standing up.

I nodded. I had had enough of her freak show.

Rima, who was still frozen in a bent over form, moved her eyes upward towards me. No, she wasn't fully frozen, but my power did work! I could hurt them. Suddenly all those hours of practicing and meditating seemed worth it. And my power up with Poppy before heading out felt like the smartest thing I'd done all night.

"Impressive," I heard Gedeyon say behind me.

I spun around and noticed Gedeyon looking at me, but his body was frozen in mid form, his glass halfway to his lips.

"But how long do you think this will last on us? Maybe for these other paranormals, or for humans, a freezing spell can last an hour or more."

"I don't care. It's working now, and that's more than nothing."

"Maybe you two won't be as boring as I thought," Rima replied behind me.

I didn't bother looking at her. I really hated that woman. "Drop your hold over Phillip." I had a leg up now, and I was going to use it.

"I'm sorry, Phillip," Rima stated, straightening up. Shit, she was already slightly mobile now. Well, at least I knew my window of time. When it was time to really attack, I'd have to go for it, no delay. My mind began to spin with possible quick assaults.

"I promise I won't purposefully humiliate you again. I couldn't resist. You're just so much fun to play with. You know how it is. You did the same when you were in power." She giggled. "Remember that guy whose tongue you ripped out?"

"I do," Phillip huffed. "And Amina and I used our magic to heal him. I was under a dark spell. Still am. What's your excuse?"

Rima lifted a brow. "Touché."

I released the room, ready to leave.

A man got on his knees in front of Rima. "I'll drink from you, goddess."

She squealed in delight, and I turned my head before seeing anymore. This was not going to be my life. This party was horrible, but at least I'd come out of it knowing their weaknesses. Things weren't so dismal after all.

CHAPTER 11

It was four a.m. that next morning, and I woke up in a sweaty panic. I'd had a nightmare. Rima had jumped into my body and caused all sorts of hell. Gedeyon had turned into the largest werehyena I'd ever seen. As big as a house. He'd eaten half the town, leaving nothing but a mountain of bones behind.

I felt Erik's comforting presence behind me, his chest against my back and an arm over my waist. I shifted around to face him. His face looked so relaxed and peaceful asleep. I reached up and brushed a thumb across his cheek and smiled. I was a tough woman, but I had to admit I felt better having Erik back in the house.

I moved his arm to his side and then sat up, careful not to wake him. I didn't want to go back to sleep right then, fearful of revisiting my dream and I thought reading a couple of chapters of a book out in the living room might be a good distraction.

I walked down the short hallway, past the closed door where Blake and Phillip were staying, and moved to the living room off to the left. I stopped short when I spotted a figure lying down on the couch covered in a blanket. I leaned forward and narrowed my eyes. Phillip.

I sighed and put my hands on my plaid pajama covered hips. Why was he out there? I was hoping for this space alone.

"What's wrong?" Phillip croaked through the darkness. "The jackal kick you out?"

"No. Did the vampire kick you out?"

Phillip sat up. "No."

"Don't tell me she snores."

"No. Even though she's a living vampire, and that's totally possible. Apparently, *I* snore really loudly when I'm drunk."

I walked closer to him and lit a candle on the coffee table with the snap of my fingers. "So, she *did* kick you out?"

"I left willingly to respect her sleep." He threw his feet to the ground and patted the spot next to him. "I'm actually glad we both have this time together without your bodyguard hovering over us."

I looked at the sofa, but didn't move. This felt like a setup.

Phillip threw his head back. "Don't worry, I won't try anything on you. It would be the ultimate in disrespect to do that in your own home. Plus, I think you'll have your hands full with Blake. Saving her life made you her new best friend, slash girl crush."

I shook my head and went to sit down next to him, folding my legs under my bottom.

"Thank you for having my back at that sham of a party," he said, staring at the lit candle.

"Of course." I felt odd sitting here calmly like this with him like we were old pals. Truth was, ever since I'd met him, we were hardly just relaxed and calm around each other. Maybe for a while in Ireland we were, but that was it. There was always a fight with us. We were either battling each other or saving each other, or trying to plot our next move. I wasn't sure I knew how to relate to this 'normal' Phillip. I didn't even know if I could like a 'normal' Phillip.

Silence rested in the air as I waited for him to say something more. I could feel the tension from my right as he shifted in his seat. Perhaps he was feeling the same as me.

"I'm in love with you."

Nope, no, he was not.

I hung my head and dropped my shoulders. "Phillip."

He held up a hand. "Let me finish. Maybe one day, you'll love me back. Maybe you won't, and you'll go on to marry the Jackal and have lots of furry witch babies, and they can call me Uncle Phil." He laughed at that. "Whatever you decide to do, I just want you to know that I have your back. I'm never going to hurt you or let you down. And if you need me, I'm there. Because I love you and everything that comes with that. You are my heart, *mi corazon*."

I shook my head and grabbed his hand. Dang it, 'normal' Phillip wasn't such a bad guy. "Why are you being so sweet tonight?"

"I'm not a good man."

I raised a brow. Better he said it than me. "What are you talking about?"

"Hear me out. I was, am, under that dark spell, but I'm still a monster. I did those things because I'm a bad guy. The spell just allowed me to do the things that a person isn't supposed to do. You know how, back in the day, when you'd drive on the highway, and some asshole cuts you off? And you think, 'I should just ram my car into his, but I won't because I don't want to fuck up my car.' Well, under this spell, if I didn't have the thoughts to do these bad things, I wouldn't have done them. So, it's still my fault in the end."

"Well, we all have crazy thoughts. It doesn't make us horrible people. I once envisioned running over Latasha Rogers, my sixth-grade nemesis, with a bulldozer. Had I been under that spell, I might have done it."

I heard Phillip snort, and he squeezed my hand. "It's not that simple, Amina. You gave an example from when you were eleven or twelve. You don't think like that now. I got into bad shit when I was younger, especially after the magic returned. Stuff Mae didn't know all about."

I stiffened. What in the hell kind of bad guy was he? "Did you kill or rape anyone?"

"Hell no. But I beat up people, I stole. I was part of a gang."

"A paranormal gang?"

"Yeah. So, you see, it wasn't a stretch for me to be a monster."

I shook my head. "I don't understand why you're telling me all this. I lessened the spell that was on you, and you've been nothing but good. Even if you have those horrible thoughts, you aren't acting on them anymore. Lighten up, Eeyore."

"You say that now until Rima gets me to give her a baby whose soul she can take. I'd rather die before I go there. We're powerful enough to put up a wall between us. If I have to go, you won't be hurt. But, if you have to go, I'll go with you."

I turned to him, confused and no longer tired. "What are you talking about, Phillip? No one is dying. And even if I were to die, why would you die with me? That is so pointless."

Phillip didn't look at me, only kept staring at the lit candle. "Not to me. I don't want to be in a world that you aren't in."

I gently rested my hand on his shoulder. "Stop being so dramatic, Phil."

"Let's face it. The soulmates picked a hellspawn to control. We take out the soulmates, then you and your Six can take me out. That way, we don't have to worry about us ever becoming the next world dominating soulmates."

I looked away from him. His plan, as ugly as it was, made sense, but I was reluctant to even consider it. I was beginning to believe that Phillip was a better man than he'd given himself credit for. "Let's think in the positive, just for shits and giggles."

I got up and grabbed an old comedy movie from our limited Blu-ray and DVD collection. "You need a laugh," I muttered, putting the movie in.

I walked back to the couch, catching Phillip's haunted eyes by the light of the candle. I had to pull him together if we were going to get through this. I already had my own crap to handle, we both couldn't crack under pressure. The world was counting on us.

~

"Wake up, little sleepy heads," sang a female voice. "Aww, don't you both look so cute together."

I opened my eyes, my vision blurry from sleep. The room was still dark, with only the barest light from the early morning sky pouring in from the windows. Blake stood in front of me, her hands on her hips and a smirk on her face. She wore a red lace teddy with a black silk robe over it, but barely covering her body.

I frowned at her. "What the hell are you wearing?" I asked, sitting straight and rubbing the back of my neck, which had apparently been resting at an odd angle on the back of the couch.

"She always dresses like that," Phillip called from the floor in front of the couch. He sat up and rubbed at his eyes.

I tilted my head, still confused. "It's like 10 degrees outside, and you're dressed like a lingerie model."

She grinned at me. "Thank you! As you know, I'm a

vampire, and I don't feel the weather like you do. Plus, I have to stay ready."

"For what?"

She gave me a playful roll of her eyes. "You guys might change your minds about the orgy."

"Oh my God, give it up, lady."

"You're missing out. Sex is natural, and it might take some of the stress off of you."

"I don't think group sex is going to relax me." Especially if I had to get naked around Miss Perfect Body USA, I thought to myself.

"I don't know, Amina, we might want to give it a try," Phillip said with a wiggle of his brows.

"Why didn't I get an invitation to the party?" Erik called as he walked into the living room, clad only in loose plaid pajama pants.

"Jesus, dude, put a shirt on," Phillip muttered, rolling his eyes.

I didn't mind the view of the hard lines of his chest and abs. He leaned back, stretching his arms above his head, and I leaned forward, eyes fixated on the v-shape of his pelvis muscles as more skin exposed itself when he stretched his body. I couldn't help but notice that Blake was unabashedly looking as well.

I snapped my fingers. "Hey, eyes off my boy toy, Blake," I demanded with a face of mock annoyance.

She turned to me and gave a wink. What did that mean? I was going to have to threaten her, I see.

Erik snorted and gave me a quick peck on the lips before perching on the arm of the couch beside me. "So, why is everyone out here? Something happen with the soulmates?"

"No, I just caught Amina and Phil out here sleeping together," Blake said with a shrug before flopping down beside me.

I looked at her with wide angry eyes before turning to

Erik, who gave me an expectant look. "We weren't sleeping together. I got up a few hours ago because I couldn't sleep. Phillip was already out here; we watched a movie and fell asleep. I was on the couch, and Phillip was on the floor."

Erik nodded slowly. "Ok, well, I trust you," he replied, then kissed me on the forehead and headed to the kitchen. "Who wants coffee? I'm making coffee!"

"Is he really fine?" Blake asked in a low voice.

Of course, he wasn't. When it came to Phillip and me, he was never fine. "Yes, put on some clothes."

I walked to the kitchen and stood beside Erik as he looked, rather angrily, at the coffee maker. "So, what did the coffee maker do to you?"

Erik relaxed his face, only slightly. "I have a 10 a.m. pack meeting."

I sighed with a bit of relief that he wasn't angry with me. "You called a meeting?"

He looked at me, his jaw clenching. "No, they did."

I closed my eyes and shook my head. They were already making their next move. "Not good."

He looked back at the coffee maker. "Not good at all."

~

The entire pack squeezed into a former concert venue in town. It was more like a club with black cement floors and dark walls, filled with framed posters and pictures showcasing the history of musicians and bands that had performed there in the past. At the wall opposite from the entrance, stood a grand stage under colorful strobe lights. The last time I'd come here, there was a pre-gathering for the pack's full moon shifting. It's where I met Brandon.

The mood still seemed light, but I could not join in the laughter and small talk filling the room. I had to sway the crowd from Rima and Gedeyon's thrall. Once we reached the base of the steps, Carter appeared from our right. Erik looked at his friend, but didn't speak, his eyes displaying a dead calm.

Carter coughed uncomfortably. "I realize you both are upset that we invited the soulmates in. This wasn't the most ideal situation, but it really is for the best."

Erik didn't reply, and neither did I. Instead, I focused in on Carter's mind, using my magic to wrap around him and wipe away any prior hold. Rima's magic had always proven tough to break, but perhaps because she'd used her gifts over a mass of people instead of concentrating it on only one person like Phillip, the hold wouldn't be as strong.

"Carter, tell us what this is about," I said in a low but commanding voice, forcing my magic out with each word.

Carter stiffened, and his eyes glazed slightly, the typical look of someone under magical influence. I hoped this time it was mine. "People have called for a new vote on who should lead the pack. With Gedeyon here and him being a werehyena, well, we just can't pass up that kind of leadership. He's older than us all. He knows so many things. He can guide us and make us invincible against our enemies."

"*They* are our enemies."

Carter glanced at me, a pained look in his eyes. He was fighting the magic. Mine or Raya's, I couldn't tell, but the struggle was covered all over his face. "They are the enemies. But most people don't see that. They haven't done anything to the rest of the town. They don't care about the news reports of what's happened to other towns. The soulmates have said it's all false news."

Ok, I didn't like what I was hearing, but the fact that Carter was giving me this information meant I still could break through those who were influenced by the soulmates. His pained expression, like he was passing a kidney stone, didn't bode well for whether I could break the hold entirely, though. I clasped my hands together and pursed my lips. I had more questions, and I wouldn't waste this opportunity. "How are they curing people? Their powers aren't healing. They aren't witches, mages, or fae."

Carter adjusted in his stance, squinty his eyes under the lights, but I knew it wasn't related to his eyes. He was still struggling with the opposing holds. I couldn't put him under this much longer, or I'd possibly break him mentally. "I've only seen them hoover their hands over people like you've done."

Where they borrowing power from somewhere? Still, that didn't explain how they had the strength to cure, but I didn't. "So, it's not a potion or spell?"

Carter shook his head slowly, eyes dead.

I bit my lip in thought. "It could be dark magic." Or maybe they were still draining Phillip and I of our power. Since there could only be one strong soulmate pairing at a time, we could be losing all sorts of gifts we didn't know about because Rima and Gedeyon wouldn't stay dead.

Carter raised his hands in surrender. "I think we need to give them a chance to prove themselves. Our people are dying. Even Amina and Phillip can't heal everyone. Only the really strong can even have their symptoms curbed under her magic. But, they can help everyone. Let's give it a shot. Okay?" He gave us the thumbs up before walking away.

And just like that, my hold snapped and went away. I looked around the room. Had Rima seen what I was doing and strengthened her hold on him? I couldn't find her, so I had no idea. Phillip and I were going to have to do the mind control announcements he used to do. Perhaps that would be strong enough to break her hold over everyone without harming their minds.

Erik ran a hand across his face. "We're going to have to mind control everyone, Mina. We're going to have to risk it, or we're going to lose."

I glared at him. "You read my mind?"

"You're practically screaming in your head, and I couldn't shut it out. I am your mate. We're connected. Plus, I know you controlled Carter just now. That was helpful. I hate to admit it."

The room grew quiet, and I looked to the stage to see Gedeyon standing there with Carter, Raya, and two other weres, a man and a woman, who were part of the top five.

"I suppose I should join my pack," Erik muttered before walking up the steps to the side of the platform.

The vote played out just as we expected. It was no surprise Gedeyon won by almost a landslide. The only people who voted for Erik were myself and a couple of the women who had formerly been competing to be a part of his harem.

Gedeyon looked over to Erik with a smile. "You have been a good leader. I think it only right that you be my second. Will you accept the position?" He offered a hand for Erik to shake.

Erik looked at it as if it were contagious.

"It's okay, Erik," Carter said, giving Erik a light slap on the back. "I think this is the perfect compromise. We're all willing to take a step down."

Erik looked at Gedeyon's hand a beat longer, and I thought he might actually slap it out of the way. I knew I wanted to. Instead, he reached out and shook Gedeyon's hand, sans smile.

"I'm glad you're being so agreeable, because we really need you for the fight," Gedeyon stated.

"What fight?" Erik asked.

My question exactly. If Phillip and I were stepping aside, for now, who was there left to fight?

The whites of Gedeyon's eyes brightened, giving him the god-like look that many in this town believed of him. "Our fight against the humans, of course. We must protect the paranormals at all cost, and get rid of what is left of the human population."

"Not all humans are the enemy," Erik replied with gritted teeth.

Gedeyon held his hands out to his side, palms facing up as if he were some messiah. "Humans are the bane of our existence. They are jealous because they are weaker. That jealousy causes them to bring forth terror and violence to our kind. Just as they have done with that serum made from our blood. Do you think they are sitting quietly while we grow in power and numbers? They will not let us flourish without a fight. And we must not underestimate them. What they lack in numbers, they will make up in intelligence and will. We must crush them now or risk our own extinction later."

He was talking about genocide. A race war of sort. I wasn't going to let this happen.

I walked forward. "They are the minority. Just because they don't have gifts, you want to destroy them."

"I am only doing to them what they did to us!" He smiled down at me like I was a little child who didn't understand the world. I'm sure he would have patted my head if I were closer.

The crowd cheered him on as if they had any clue what happened over a thousand years ago. Yeah, we were going to have to do that mind control announcement sooner rather than later.

"They killed all magic, and any paranormals that existed went with it. Do you want to risk your friends and family to find out if you'll make it?" Gedeyon raised his voice, and I fought an urge to step back.

I felt eyes on me, and I looked away. This was a debate I wouldn't win. At least not right now. He had knowledge on his side or, at least, the believability that he knew more than anyone else. And the more I pressed against the new pack leader, the more I would look like an enemy, and I didn't need that right now.

"I concede that I don't know everything, but when we talk about annihilating a group of people, it doesn't make us sound like we're on the right side here. There just has to be a better way."

Gedeyon glared down at me. The look in his eyes was both wise and terrifying. There was something ancient and foreign there that I'd never come across before. "You will come to see, my child; my way is the only way."

A cold fear raced up my spine, but I stood my ground. "Your way failed. I say we try something new." I looked around at the crowd, pushing my mind controlling magic out. "You guys are smarter than this. Don't just take their word for everything. Weigh the risk and listen to reason and to the people you know and trust, which is not him." I pointed to Gedeyon on the stage.

The crowd around me began to murmur with looks of confusion and doubt. A few called out to ask for time to consider starting a war, and a few others even called to avoid fighting and that humans weren't the enemy.

I smiled back at Gedeyon, who looked down at me now with blazing anger. I gave him my teeth before turning and walking out on shaky legs. I wasn't going to bend over and let him ruin this town on my watch. Even if the risk were high.

CHAPTER 12

Almost a week passed, with the original soulmates running things and us undermining them where we could. Phillip and I tried his announcements again, with the focus on giving people back their thought of free will instead of forcing them to think a certain way. That seemed to work, but naturally our access to public announcements were quickly pulled. Rima and Gedeyon started to assert control again, but we began to take it to the streets and hone in on our allies like Carter and Raya. So far, they appeared control free, but I was still cautious.

By the end of week one of the soulmates, I came home after work to find Phillip cooking in my kitchen with Blake sitting on the counter with what looked like a full bottle of blood. It was still weird sharing a place with them, but every night the four of us worked on our bonds, and I had to admit, I was feeling stronger. I should have been more drained with all the magical deprogramming we were doing, but I wasn't. Perhaps Blake and Erik were actually supplementing any depletion we'd gotten from Rima and Gedeyon still being alive?

Phillip turned partially to me and gave a head nod.

"Honey, you're home. How was work? Don't mind us unemployed people, over here."

Blake waved her bottle at me.

It was a Friday evening, she should have been getting ready to go to her club. "Why are you not getting ready for work?"

She snorted. "Didn't you hear? Rima took over my club. Kicked me out. Apparently, I'm being punished for Phillip's little psychic announcement that went out."

I sighed and walked over to her, patting her knee. "I'm sorry. I can go down there and get her to back off. Since I'm able to break the hold, I can get folks to help me kick her out."

Phillip raised a hand and then pointed at me, his back to me at the stove. "And then she'll explode their heads."

Fair point. "Yes, there is that. But I've been working on a sound cancelling spell. She can sing all she wants, but we won't be able to hear it."

"Have you tested it out?"

I pouted, knowing how stupid I was going to sound. "Only on myself."

He dropped his spoon in the pot and rubbed his temples. I didn't have to ask to know that was a movement of frustration.

Blake looked at him with amused eyes and then smiled at me. "Test me. Let's see it work."

I gave her an appreciative head nod ,then I pushed my hands out and whispered the spell of sound canceling. It wasn't one I'd made from scratch. I'd discovered it in a Wiccan website, and I mixed it with a few other spells so that it was really focused on not absorbing mind and body control magic through sound. I'd become more confident in my spell casting abilities after my challenge with Phillip several months ago, so I was hopeful this would work. Since Rima was a soulmate siren, I couldn't just put any old spell on her. She was too powerful for that.

When I was done, I dropped my hands and looked at her expectantly. Then I realized I'd have to order her to do something to test my magic.

"Blake, hop on one foot."

She crossed her eyes. Jumped off the counter and began to hop. My heart sank. Damn it, I really needed that spell to work. Of course, maybe it didn't just work on any control. Maybe it really would only work on sirens.

Blake then bent over, laughing. "I'm just messing with you. You didn't control me. Your spell works."

Phillip looked over to me, chuckling. "You told her to hop on one foot, she hopped on both feet. And people's eyes don't cross when we bespell them."

I huffed and put my hands on my hips. I was glad they were laughing but more glad that my spell actually worked on someone powerful. I looked up at the ceiling, feeling overcome with happiness. "This could really work. Once we confirm Dublin is okay, we will have nothing holding us back. What can Rima do to us without her siren ability? I mean, she'll still have soulmate magic, but so do we." I punched the air in front of me in excitement. I had a win!

Blake did a jig then pointed at me. "Tell me to do something else!"

I tapped my chin. "Blake, kiss Phillip," I commanded with my magic.

She looked over to him, then moved to me, grabbed my face, and kissed me quickly on the lips.

I dropped my mouth open in shock. "I said Phillip."

She rolled her eyes and twisted her lips. "I know you did, but you don't control me!" She gave me a hip bump, grabbed her blood, and danced out of the kitchen.

Phillip chuckled as he went back to stirring the food. "Now we just need to get to Gedeyon. He still has control over all the weres since he's an uber alpha. Even without Rima's magic."

"Yes, but with Rima's power possibly ineffective, we have a bargaining chip."

Just then, the front door opened, and Erik trudged in. I say trudged because he looked like he was a walking zombie. His lids were low, and he dragged his feet.

"Hey," he said, continuing to walk.

I followed him. "Hey, yourself. I have some good news. My sound canceling spell works. We can possibly block out Rima's siren call."

He gave me an unimpressed head nod and kept walking to the bedroom. What the hell?

"What's going on?"

He collapsed on the bed. "I'm sorry, I'm just exhausted." I knew he was. He'd barely been home the past few days. It seemed that crime had risen, and that kept him busy.

Erik closed his eyes. "In the past four days, we've had two suicides, street fighting between paranormal factions, missing persons, and several domestic disputes. I have no idea what's going on, but it's keeping me busy. I just need to rest while I can."

I sat down beside him and rubbed his shoulder. "Anything you need from me? I can give you a power boost."

He shook his head. "You need all the power you can get."

"But I feel like I'm draining you."

He took my hand and kissed my fingers. "Crime is draining me. Never you. And that's exciting about your spell. We needed a win."

I knew he was lying about me draining him. There was no way we could keep taking his energy to strengthen our magic with him not getting enough rest to replenish and still expect him to be full of life. At least Blake could go to sleep or drink blood. Erik was constantly on the go.

His cellphone buzzed, and he sighed before digging in his

pocket to get it. He looked at the text message, sighed again, and sat up. "I have to go; someone reported another missing person."

I frowned. "How many people have gone missing?"

He stood up and rubbed his face. "Ten."

"That's a lot for a town of this size. Could it be that people are just leaving, or if they're kids, running away? Maybe they got tired of all this change in leadership and left." I knew my questions were just me hoping. The alternative was probably the truth, and it meant that we hadn't done what we swore we would. Protect the town.

"Maybe, but most of them were said to be content with living here." More dread filled my gut. "When did this all start?"

He glanced sideways at me. "It's been going on the past few weeks. Which is a lot for a town of this size."

"This is the soulmates."

He gave a slight lift of his shoulders as he headed out of the bedroom with me following. "I'm certainly not ruling them out. I don't believe in coincidences. My only question is, what are they doing with the people?"

"Senna said they ate the souls of the last soulmates. What if they do that to regular people too? I need to go there and find out."

Erik scrunched his face before reaching the front door. "Hell, no."

I knew he was scared for me, but I was here to protect. If people were being kidnapped and in danger, I had to save them. So far, I wasn't doing a good job of protecting our people.

"I'm going to their stupid place, and I'm looking for those people and setting them free. I'm done sitting back. You can come with me."

"We aren't ready to fight them."

Phillip poked his head out of the kitchen. “We fighting soulmates now?”

I nodded, and Erik shook his head. Phillip looked at both of us with narrowed eyes.

I sighed. “We think they’re kidnapping people, and we need to find out and save them. I won’t fight if I can avoid it, however, maybe I can prevent them from doing anymore kidnapping once I know why and how they’re taking people.”

They could take our positions, and we would remain silent, but if they were killing people, I wouldn’t have any choice but to make a stand. I wasn’t without power. If I could win one victory, that might help the greater cause.

CHAPTER 13

The next day we finally paid a visit to the soulmates. Rima and Gedeyon took over several apartments on the penthouse floor of one of the more luxurious apartments in the area. However, they had used magic to completely change the structure of the entire level.

Upon exiting the elevator to see them, we turned right and faced floor to ceiling glass doors framed in golden etchings. I walked closer, and through the doors, I could see the door to the pool area on the left and on the right the doors to the gym. Not where I needed to be.

Upon turning to the left of the elevators, we were faced with thick dark wood, floor-to-ceiling double doors covered in intricate carvings. One door appeared to be African inspired, and the other Indian or Middle Eastern. Heavy knockers hung from the doors. I looked up, expecting cameras directed at us, but there was nothing. There were no guards, either. This was a far cry from the security previously provided to town leaders.

"They certainly aren't concerned with anyone attacking them by surprise," I muttered as I rapped the knocker against the door.

"Why fear ants?" Erik replied.

The door opened, and I expected a butler to appear or no one, in a show of magic. However, Gedeyon appeared, dressed in royal blue slacks and a tailored white embroidered dashiki. He gave us a politician's smile, waving his hand for us to come in.

"What a pleasant surprise. I'm happy you finally came to visit us," he said, opening the door wider for us to walk inside.

Once in, I couldn't help but widen my eyes in surprise as I looked around. As I'd heard, they had completely changed the layout, gutting the six penthouse level apartments to give them one giant-sized apartment.

The hallways were covered in a teal wallpaper that glowed with silver tribal markings and boldly colored artwork.

"Care for a tour?" Gedeyon asked with an amused look, as he stared at my awe-struck face.

Of course, I did; a lay of the land might give me some information I needed to know, such as if someone was being held against their will.

I straightened up. "Please."

Gedeyon led us to our right, where open double doors lead to a gigantic dining room. The space was filled with terra cotta colored walls, a long black, rectangular table, black chairs with silver etchings, shining color gemstone covered plates and silverware, and equally colorful seating in the chairs. Even the ceiling was not forgotten with a mural filled with blues, greens, reds, and orange. Brass and bronze chandeliers and wall sconces lit the room, and patterned rugs covered the floors. It was breathtaking, but I kept my mouth shut.

Beyond the dining room were closets, bathrooms, and the kitchen. There was also a long balcony that was fully decorated and somehow untouched by snow. The whole place was the size of one two bedroom, two bathroom apartment.

We left the space, and went across the hall to the living room. Where the dining room was more of a nod to Rima's lineage, it was clear the living area was all Gedeyon. Floor to ceiling windows wrapped around the open space, decorated with dark wood, brown and beige patterned pillows, throws, and rugs. African artwork and masks hung on walls and sat on the furniture. A black, leather sectional couch faced the one wall in the space which held a fireplace. Additional giraffe and zebra printed seating and pillows also filled the room. Warm lighting hung from the ceiling and emanated from tall architectural lamps. Against another short wall was a mini bar area, complete with a counter and seating. I felt like I was visiting a luxurious hotel in Kenya rather than an apartment in Silver Spring. What was this? Better Homes and Gardens, villain edition?

Gedeyon pointed to a closed door near the fireplace. "Over there is my office. And down the hall are four bedrooms and two lounging areas that connect to the two master bedrooms. What do you think?" he asked, hands on his hips.

"You took out six, two bedroom apartments to make one 4bedroom apartment?" I replied and shrugged. "Seems like a waste of much needed space."

Gedeyon tilted his head back with a chuckle. "I'm actually surprised you didn't do this already. We are soulmates, and we must have residencies worthy of our stature. What we have done is humble compared to the palaces that I have lived in before."

"We're supposed to be of the people. We shouldn't be taking resources. You've even shut off use to the pool and gym!"

Gedeyon looked at me with confused eyes. "It takes nothing for others to use the facilities in our neighboring building. Of course, you have access to our pool and gym here. In fact, if you'd like, you and Phillip may stay in our spare rooms."

"Hard pass," I replied in a dry voice. "Thanks for the tour, but we're actually not here to interview you for Better Homes and Garden, not that that magazine exists anymore."

"Ah," Gedeyon stated, raising an eyebrow. "So why are you here?"

"We have a couple of major investigations going on in town, and we just want to ask you a few questions," Erik answered. I fell back since detective work was more his gig than mine.

"I see. Well, then let me lead you to my study for us to talk." Gedeyon waved his hand towards the right of the room and began to walk. "Shall I call Rima to join us?"

"That would be a good idea."

Gedeyon opened the door to an equally well-designed room with high end furniture and décor. We sat down at his unnecessarily massive oak desk, and he sat back in his equally unnecessarily large chair/throne and closed his eyes. He then quickly opened them.

"She's on her way," he stated.

"I'm here," Rima announced, suddenly appearing behind Erik and me. She walked over to Gedeyon's desk and perched herself at the edge, giving us an unbothered smile.

"What can we clear up for you?" Gedeyon asked.

So many things, but we'd go bite sized.

I opened my mouth to start with the missing people but closed it quickly, remembering that we weren't here to confront them from the start. We wanted to get their guard down a bit and ease into it. At least that was Erik's police tactic.

"We've had a growing epidemic of drug use in town lately, and it's causing a lot of violence," Erik began. "In particular, a magic based drug called Aura. Our former leader was probably on it. It can make people behave primitively and violently."

"Yes, I have heard of this, Aura. It unlocks a very primal part of the brain and gives it more control over the body."

"The prefrontal cortex," Erik cut in.

Rima nodded. "Yes, it magically inflames it. And with some, that inflammation leads to primal violence and behaviors. It's permanent. The infection also spreads through bodily fluids with someone on the drug."

"So, a person who never took Aura can still end up with the same negative side effects of going primal if they had contact with a person on the drug," I surmised. These asshats were behind the drug. I knew it in my bones.

Rima nodded slowly. "And just like that, a drug epidemic becomes a disease outbreak."

"So, you know all about it," I said with twisted lips.

"We know what our scientists have told us," Gedeyon cut in. "We don't know why it affects some the way it does, and not others. We know the side effects aren't related to dosage or power level of the individual. The drug itself, or the magic behind it, is the disease."

"Where did the drugs come from?" Erik asked.

Gedeyon threw out his hands to the side. "Now, why would you think we'd know that?"

Uh, because you were behind the first pandemic that killed half the population? It wasn't a reach. I wasn't falling for it. But, why lie now? If they admitted to their role in the first human infection, then why hide their role in the new paranormal infection? Then again, they didn't care about humans, and they needed us.

Erik leaned back, his eyes cool. "You aren't behind it?" He knew just as I did that these guys were guilty as charged, but he was playing it poker-face cool. That was not my specialty, so I'd let him run with it.

Gedeyon raised a brow. "What would be the purpose?"

"To make yourselves look good when you swoop in and cure people."

Gedeyon turned his lips downward and tilted his head slightly from side to side. "Perhaps. But we aren't behind Aura. We believe it comes from a human and paranormal group that we haven't been able to locate. It's just fortunate for us that we can at least cure people of the negative side effects."

Wait a minute. Cure the side effects? That wasn't the same as curing the disease. I leaned forward in my seat. "Can you cure those who were infected or not? Either by being bitten or taking the drug."

Gedeyon didn't reply, only smiled, and sat back in his seat. I looked to Rima, who was busy studying her nails.

"You said you could help cure those who were infected! You're curing a side effect that can come back. That's no better than what Phillip and I were doing, except we weren't telling them they were cured. Because they're not. People are killing themselves, thinking you're gods."

Although it was a letdown that there still wasn't a cure to the disease, in a way, I was relieved that they weren't able to cure the paranormal disease. It made them seem less powerful.

Gedeyon did his familiar eye brightening thing, but this time I didn't shrink back. So far, he hadn't zapped me with lasers from his eyes, so I figured it was more for show than anything else. "We are not liars. It is our intention to cure those infected once we are fully back to our original selves. However, for now, we are limited to helping those suffering from the primal effect of the drug," Gedeyon replied in a tight voice. "And unlike you, we are able to help more than just the magically strong, so I would suggest you tone down your self-righteousness."

I sat back, biting the inside of my cheek to control my anger. We probably could help weaker paranoramals if they weren't siphoning our power. However, now that I knew the truth and had our power base in our friends, Phillip and I would have to try alleviating others of their symptoms as well. Four could play that healing game.

"Oh, don't look so sad, Amina. Perhaps you, Phillip, Rima, and myself can join together to cure those infected. We need to start working together. We haven't hurt anyone this past week. You owe us our truce."

I remained quiet. Thinking of a reply. Any truce I gave them would be a lie. I wasn't sitting back if I could help it. Yet, without being ready to fight, I'd have to tell them something.

Rima snapped her fingers in front of my face, her upper lip turned up in a sneer. "We are not here in this insignificant town just to run a bar," Rima replied. "We came here for you and were nice enough to give you time, but we have our own requirements that we must tend to."

I leaned away from her. If she snapped her fingers in my face again, I might have to choke her. "Again, what does that mean?"

"What was the other matter that brought you here?" Gedeyon asked, he balanced his chin on his hands, elbows perched on his desk.

If we weren't submitting to them, I'd think they'd want to talk about that. What requirements did they have that our cooperation would affect? We'd defied them every step of the way short of declaring war or attacking them, at least not since Gedeyon had arrived. We had to be a nuisance by now. Why hadn't they attacked us?

Erik cleared his throat, drawing my attention away from my own thoughts. "There has been an increase in the number of missing people in our town."

Rima waved her hand. "That would be expected. You can try to rebuild this world, but there are creatures and magical elements that are not so kind to an industrialized society.

Grounds that can swallow a building whole, monsters that can appear from nothing and kill an entire group. Every time your people leave this city to trade at your malls and shopping centers or visit another town, they are risking their lives in just making the journey. Even within the confines of the towns or trade areas, they cannot be certain that the other individuals will not be untoward. The human and paranormal trafficking ring is alive and well. There could be people here involved."

"So, you're saying that the suspicious increase in disappearances are related to either monsters or human trafficking?" I asked, giving a skeptical look. It wasn't that I doubted those possibilities. It was that I doubted that those options would suddenly increase so dramatically so soon after the soulmate's arrival. I simply didn't believe in coincidences anymore.

Rima shrugged. "Who is to say?"

"So, you have nothing to do with any disappearances?"

She smiled. "Now, we didn't say that." Rima stood up and walked to the door. "Follow me."

This is what we came for. I knew they wouldn't care to hide things. We were insignificant to them and worst case, they'd mind control anyone who did care.

Gedeyon stood up as well, and the four of us headed out of the room, through the living room, and back to the main hallway. She led us to an unassuming door. She pressed on it, and the door slid to the side. Inside reminded me of a salt room in a spa. The walls glowed with golden yellow, reflecting off the salt coverings and what appeared to be heated marble floors. Black stoned lounge seating sat against the walls. A lone male with messy brown hair, relaxed on the smooth stone lounge chair with closed eyes. He looked asleep and did not seem to stir at our presence.

However, it wasn't the room's layout or the sleeping man that held my attention; it was the floating orbs of light. There weren't that many, only five. They looked more like large iridescent bubbles filled with a glowing shapeless mass.

"What are these?" Erik asked, looking up.

"Our requirements," Rima replied as if that explained everything. She waved her hand at the sleeping man. "Come here, Xander, dear."

Xander, who had to be under thirty years of age, at least visually, opened his eyes and stood up. He looked over to Rima with longingly, and walked over to her outstretched hand, grasping it with both of his hands. Rima lightly tapped his cheek with her free hand.

"Your offering will be remembered. Blessings to you in the afterlife." Then she placed her hand over his heart and closed her eyes. A red glow surrounded her hands. Xander threw back his head, and a blinding white light shot from his open mouth, shaking his body. The mass of light swirled above our heads, bouncing against the walls. Soon the light disappeared, and Gedeyon raised his hand in the air and closed it into a fist. A clear enclosure surrounded the light, gathering it closely together until the enclosure became a circle filled with light like the others.

I looked back down to Xander and gasped, seeing only a pile of clothes and a pair of shoes where he once stood. "Where'd he go?" I asked, an icky fear trickling down my spine.

"He's dead," Erik accused, with a deep frown. "You took his soul out and turned him to dust."

"It's much easier to clean up," Rima exclaimed.

I put a hand to my mouth, horrified. "What? That was his soul coming out of his mouth? These are souls in these bubbles?"

Gedeyon lifted his shoulder, unbothered by this nightmare. "Yes."

"You're kidnapping people and ripping their souls out of their bodies?"

Rima sighed and rolled her eyes. "Oh, you are so dramatic. We are inviting people to stay with us, and they are treated like kings and queens before they offer up their souls."

I felt sick inside. They were clouding these people's minds and having them offer their souls up with a smile. They were monsters. Rima tsk-tsked. "Oh, Amina, you look so shocked. Do you think being a ruler comes without sacrifice?"

"It shouldn't come with the sacrifice of innocent people," Erik snarled, a growl in his voice.

"It is the only way for soulmates to survive as long as we have," Gedeyon cut in.

"I thought you became immortal by killing the new soulmates or siphoning our powers," I said, looking away from the pile of clothes and human ashes on the ground. I wanted to run away screaming from this nightmare.

"That prevents us from dying. Taking souls makes us stronger so that we could take out the other soulmates. It gave us the ability to come back when magic returned and reach our allies, even though we weren't mobile." Gedeyon reached his hand up again, and a glowing soul-filled orb floated down. He pressed it into his chest, and it melded into him until it was nothing. For a brief moment, his body glowed with a bright white outline, then it was gone.

I could feel Erik's anger growing beside me, and I felt the same. I grabbed his hand, which was currently in a bald fist, and laced my fingers with his, hoping the contact would steady us both. At the moment, all I could feel was rage.

I knew that Phillip and I were using the energy of our friends to grow strength, almost like vampires, so we weren't far off from this ourselves. However, we weren't killing anyone. We weren't taking souls and leaving husks or empty clothes. Were these the monsters we would become if we didn't put limits on ourselves?

"You should feel privileged that we are even sharing our

secret," Rima added. "Now you know the source of our strength for you to do the same." She gave me a wink. "An even fight might be fun!"

"If you want a fair fight, you'll tell us where our Dublin friends are so we can battle you with no restraint." I'd thought Rima was crazy before, but there was no mistaking it now. Arguing with them almost seemed futile. "You murdered a sixteen-year-old, a pregnant woman, two elderly people, parents, respectable citizens in this community." I recounted the several missing people that Erik had discussed with me.

Gedeyon lifted a brow. "We murdered no one. Everyone came on their own, including the pregnant woman. The teenager was brought by her father as sacrifice. Therefore, you might want to talk to him."

I shook my head and closed my eyes, confused that he thought we were so stupid. "I'm sure every one of those people were mind controlled by you. You are responsible for all of this!" I could feel my voice getting louder, and my hand twitched with anger. I wanted to set them both on fire, but I was sure it would work against us.

Gedeyon sat down on the lounge seating, looking very relaxed as he leaned back on his arms. "Souls bring a different level of strength, the younger, the better, and a pregnant woman is a two for one. Even better." Gedeyon smiled, glancing over to Erik. "I see the anger in your eyes, young jackal. What will you do, attack me?" Gedeyon spread his arms. "You may try."

I squeezed Erik's hand. I didn't have to read his mind to know he would try to attack, and he'd only get himself killed. His were magic practically glowed around him. I'd never felt such energy from him before. It was almost stifling. I was so busy focusing on myself that I didn't stop to realize that the bonding sessions we were doing with Blake and Erik could possibly work in their favor as well. Fighting, at least now, would do nothing to protect the town from these monsters. Not that we were much help.

"We'll tell others what you're doing." I wasn't so sure how effective it would be, but it was worth a shot.

"We'll just wipe their minds. This town is our puppet show," Rima replied with a shrug. She raised her hand, and an orb lowered down from the ceiling toward her. Instinctively, I shot my hand out, and to my relief, the orb paused in the air. Maybe I did have some magic mojo over these guys.

Rima frowned and glared at me. "Let it go," she demanded.

"No," I stated, taking my other free hand and quickly sending all of the orbs to float behind me.

"Do you think this will stop us? You think this town knowing what we're doing is going to prevent us from getting what we need? You don't have enough people to beat our followers who would descend upon this town in a snap of my fingers," Rima stated, snapping her fingers for show. "If you tell the town, it will only make them miserable, because they are powerless to defeat us. They are happy now."

"Except for the people who lose loved ones."

"Well, there is another option," Gedeyon began, seemingly unbothered by the orbs I'd procured. "You and Phillip could finally submit to us and allow us to siphon your strength. It would at the very least lessen our need to take souls, maybe to where we don't need any at all."

Well, that would explain why he didn't care about me stealing the orbs. This was probably all a ploy to get what he really wanted: Phillip and me.

"If you siphon from them, will they be harmed by it?" Erik asked.

I looked sideways at Erik. Was he making the decision for me? Not that we had a better plan, but still I preferred to do the negotiating over my own life.

Rima lifted a shoulder. "They will grow weaker. Their strength can return, but it will take some time. The more we take before they have time to recover, the higher the risk of their death. But you'd be saving your people here."

"So, don't take from us before we have time to recover, and don't kill anyone while you wait. Be patient," I said.

Rima dropped her fake pleasantries and glared at me. "We've been patient enough. No, we will take when we want to, if you agree to this deal. It'll be up to you if anyone else gets hurt."

I sighed and turned my back to them, wrapping my arms carefully around the orbs. "We will think about it. Don't kill another person."

Erik placed a hand on my back.

"We'll think about it," Rima sneered back at us before I teleported us away with the souls.

Yep, we were probably going to have to fight before we were ready. It was time to mobilize.

CHAPTER 14

Before I could focus on our plan of attack, I needed to ensure the safety of the poor souls I'd rescued from the soulmates.

Mae clasped her hands together and peered up at the floating soul orbs in her apartment living room. We'd gone straight from the soulmate's to her place, not sure any location was really safe for the souls.

"And you say they destroy the bodies, so there's no way to return them?" Mae asked.

I nodded, feeling nauseous and numb at the same time. I would never forget Gedeyon eating someone's soul. "If we release them from the orbs, where will their spirits go? I mean, I'm freaking out here that we can even see their souls."

Azrael, who had been quietly studying the orbs, shook their head. "You can only see them because of the orbs. Souls are supposed to be invisible to the human eye if they are not housed in a human vessel."

"So, in heaven, this is what angels look like?" Lisa asked, standing near me and looking up.

We were all standing in the center of Mae and Bill's living

room, looking up at the soul orbs like they were some constellation in a planetarium.

"No, angels look more humanoid."

Lisa placed a hand on her collarbone, her mouth open in awe at the floating souls. "If we go to heaven, will we look like this? I was really hoping we'd be wearing cute white outfits with big feather wings."

I looked over at Lisa and sighed. Leave it to her to focus on the wrong things at the wrong time. "I saw a soul before it was put in an orb."

Azrael looked over to me with curious eyes. "Did you? Well, then perhaps it's because you are a soulmate. You have special sight. Did you see it, Erik?"

Erik shook his head, frowning. "Is this something she and Phillip can do? Take and ingest souls?"

Azrael shrugged. "No other soulmate has ever done such a thing, but it doesn't mean it's not possible. There are other beings that can do such a thing. Demons specifically. They could have gotten the idea from a demon, or even taken in a demonic power that allowed them to do such."

Phillip waved his hand up towards the orbs. "How do we send these souls home?"

"We have to break the orbs, and then I can send them to the realms they are meant to go," Azrael replied before raising a hand in the air. "And before you ask, I cannot break the orbs. These are not heavenly boxes. They are another form of magic. It looks like witchcraft. Strong witchcraft at that."

"Well, that's our specialty," Phillip stated, looking over to me as he held out his hand.

I went to Phillip and gave him my hand, having no clue what he was talking about. "What exactly are we supposed to do?" I asked in a low voice, although I knew everyone could hear me.

"You'll know when you touch them," Mae answered.

Phillip leaned towards me. “Ready to show the people we can fly?” he asked.

“More like levitate,” I replied before taking his other hand and closing my eyes. I took in a deep breath to steady my nerves and clear my head of anything but what I was trying to do.

The room fell quiet around us, and I focused only on breathing in and out. Soon a welcomed warmth spread over me, relaxing every nerve and joint in my body. I yawned, my body feeling heavy as if I’d just neared the end of an hour-long relaxing massage. Soon, I felt the weightlessness similar to the last time Phillip and I had connected on this level. I didn’t have to know that we were floating.

“Shit,” I heard Charles cry.

Other gasps sounded around us.

When I opened my eyes, Phillip and I were floating near the ceiling with the glowing orbs. I looked at him, and he smiled at me, with purple eyes that I knew matched my own now. Apparently, when we got to using our soulmate bond, our eyes went all violet, which I found kind of cool. It made me feel like a superhero, or at least made me look the part.

Without speaking, we released one of our hands, and each touched the side of the same glowing orb. I looked at the bright white mass, ignoring the orb around it until it was all I saw. Moments later ,the orb melted away into a wind of nothingness. The shapeless mass zoomed past us, hitting the wall nearest the patio. Azrael walked over to the area and rose up, touching the mass with both hands. They closed their eyes and mumbled something unintelligible, and the glowing mass imploded, disappearing instantly.

Azrael looked over to us and nodded. “Do another, I’m able to send them home.”

We made quick work of freeing the other souls, and afterwards ,I collapsed on the living room couch, momentarily drained of energy.

"I think we have to take their deal," I said, rubbing my forehead. "They could be stealing more souls as we speak. I know you didn't want this, Mae, but I don't think we have a choice until we kill them."

Phillip, sitting beside me, nodded in agreement. "It's either us or innocent people. What kind of soulmates would we be if we let others die? We'd be no better than Gedeyon and Rima."

"If you give in, you'll make them more powerful," Mae said, taking a step towards us.

"We aren't more important than this town," I began. "We won't die if they drain us. Our souls are too strong for them to take."

Mae's eyebrows gathered together in a frown. "But where will it end? You will just end up the same way as all the other soulmates killed by them before you. This is how they are. You have to be able to make the tough choices to stop them."

"Mae," Phillip started, his voice cracking. "You're asking us to sacrifice innocent people so that we can be safe. It's not right."

I agreed. My conscience wasn't that forgiving to allow me to step back and let people to get murdered.

Azrael walked forward. "It's not right, but unless you have a better option, it might be the only way. The stronger they are, the harder they are to defeat."

"Would you say this if it was someone you knew that they killed?" Phillip asked, sitting upright. "What if Faith's soul was snatched? Mae, what if it was Bill? Or poor little Brandon? Amina said they took the souls of children. No one is exempt."

"You can stop them from taking any more souls. We can keep a trace on them," Mae suggested.

Phillip cried out, clutching his head.

Startled, I turned to face him. "What's wrong?"

He arched his back and kicked the coffee table, still

screaming. I reached out to touch him, but he batted his hand out, knocking my arm out of the way. Jumping up, I looked at the others in confusion.

Bill rushed over to us. "Someone hold him down!" he shouted.

Erik and Charles ran over to us, and Charles pressed an arm against Phillip's kicking legs. Erik ran to the other side and grabbed Phillip's arms, pinning them against the back of the couch.

Bill touched his forehead and closed his eyes. Moments later, he snapped them open. "There's a dark magic inside him. I can feel it, and it's growing, putting pressure on his brain. The more he fights it, the more painful it is."

Not good. "What can we do?"

Bill shook his head. "Either we get that dark magic out, or he has to stop fighting it."

Phillip opened his eyes and wildly looked around. "I can't see!" he cried. "I can't see!"

"We don't have a lot of time," Bill prodded, pulling out a tiny light attached to his key chain in his pocket. He flashed the light in Phillip's eyes, looking at the pupils. "This is moving rapidly. If it keeps up, he won't last long."

"Last long?" I asked. "You mean...?"

Bill gave me a solemn look and nodded.

How had this happened? I couldn't help but blame myself for poking the bear that was the soulmates. This had to be punishment for not giving into them. A reminder that they still had control over us, at least over Phillip. "Well, how do we get the dark magic out? Why is it reacting like this?"

"He didn't fight it before; now he is, probably thanks to your spell. Can you reinforce it?"

I would try my damnedest. I did the only thing I could. Throwing out my hands, I forced my healing magic outward, reciting my spell over and over again. The healing warmth of my magic spread through me, but Phillip still bucked against Erik and Charles in obvious pain.

Azrael appeared at my side and poured their angelic magic onto Phillip. Soon Lisa joined us. Nothing worked.

"We have to break this hold on him," Mae cried, hands on her cheeks as she watched her godson continue to cry out in pain.

"I've tried!" I shouted, on the verge of tears. Phillip was good now. He'd come too far to revert back now.

"Right now, we're on short time," Azrael stated. "Let the magic take him, and we can come up with a fix later. We can't afford to lose either of you. Better he be momentarily bad than dead."

"How do we know we can bring him back if he goes bad again?" Charles asked, leaning further down on Phillip's kicking thighs.

"Amina helped him before. She can do it again."

Everyone looked at me and I gave a confident nod. I really wasn't sure, but I was better off now than I was before. "I'm stronger now, and we have our familiars and mates. I can get him back. It'll just take a little time."

Their faces looked uncertain, but I ignored them and looked to Mae. "What's next?"

Mae dabbed at her eyes. "Phillip, let the magic take you."

"Noo," he cried, through gritted teeth, eyes squeezed shut. "Damn it."

I leaned forward, and held his face between my hands. "If you keep fighting it, you will die. Let's live to see another day."

He opened his eyes in my direction, but his eyes were wide and unfocused. "You have to freeze me, then. Until you can break the spell."

I heard Bill sigh behind me. "We can't really freeze you long term. We don't know if you would survive that. The only beings we know that can live when placed in some form of extended frozen state are the undead and vampires. Even if we put you in a medical coma, you would still age and require medical care."

"Then do that!" Phillip implored. He tried to move a hand upwards under Erik's pressure, so I grabbed it. "Amina, don't hate me, okay?"

"I won't hate you, Phillip. I promise."

He grimaced and tossed his head back, swearing as he bucked against the pain again.

Tears were threatening to appear, and I blinked them back. "Just let go, Phillip. Please. We'll make sure you make it out of this. I promise you."

He hyperventilated for several seconds, and then his body snapped like a rubber band. For a moment, it looked like he wasn't even breathing. Charles and Erik slowly let go of him and stood back.

Then Phillip opened his eyes and looked over to me. His eyes were now focused, and I could tell his vision was restored. That familiar arrogance that I was used to seeing from evil Phillip now shone through, and my heart sank. "I'm sorry, *mi corazon*. You're going to hate me after this," he whispered before disappearing.

~

The one positive thing about living in a small town was that no one stayed hidden for long. So, when Phillip disappeared, finding where he was headed wasn't a huge problem. It didn't take me long to locate Evil Phillip at one of the few restaurants in town. An Irish-style pub frequented by the weres.

He stood in the middle of the pub as still as a statue, his back to us. I walked over to his side and looked up at him. He was looking around the room, face void of any expression.

"What are you looking for?" I asked.

"Someone to kill," he replied matter-of-factly.

I was sure if there were water in my mouth, I would have done a spit-take. "What? Why?"

"It has to be done."

"What? No, Evil Phillip doesn't just randomly kill people. He always has a reason, even if it's a stupid one."

He continued to scan the room, not looking at me. "I need to show them that I'm still in charge. I've been too soft. I let Seth take my spot, and now these other soulmates. The people no longer respect me. I must make an example of someone."

"If you want to make an example out of someone, make it out of Gedeyon or Rima," I implored, grabbing his arm. Fighting them would probably lead to his death, so I was certain my suggestion was foolish, but killing an innocent person was far worse to me.

He looked down at my hand. "Their time will come," he assured me before lifting my hand from his arm and putting it to his lips.

I pulled it back, frowning. I know he wanted me to kill him if he became evil Phillip again, but I was going to have to break a promise. I'd find another way to stop him. "I'm not going to let you hurt anyone. You have to know that."

He gave me a slight smile. "You can't stop me. You were never stronger than me."

I raised an eyebrow. We'd had this argument before and never agreed. "Well, that's bullshit. I would have beat you at your stupid challenge. And, even if, by some magic, I couldn't stop you, do you think you're going to get followers out of fear? It doesn't last. It didn't last with the soulmates either."

"I'll be smarter than them," he replied before walking away. He headed towards a man with red hair cropped close to his head. He was standing at the bar counter with two other gentlemen, laughing and drinking out of a tall glass of beer.

Phillip shot out his hand, and the man bent forward, dropping his glass. His friends jumped back in surprise, looking down at the liquid spread on the floor before looking back up at him as they reached out to his aid.

"What are you doing to him?" I shouted over the rock music currently playing from a nearby jukebox.

"Shutting down his organs," Phillip said with a shrug.

"Stop it!" I called out.

Phillip glanced sideways at me with a cocky smile. "Say please."

Yep, this was the old Phillip I knew and hated. "Please! You asshole."

"Name calling." He gave a shiver. "Just like old times." He balled his hand into a fist, and the man keeled over, falling to his knees. Several people in the bar rushed over to them, crowding around the poor soul. Asking Phillip nicely wasn't going to work. Screw it.

I waved my hand across my body, and the red-headed man rose in the air. With my other hand, I placed a healing ward around him.

"I'll just pick another one," Phillip said in an amused tone.

"No, you won't!" I stated before swiping my hand out and psychically sending him flying across the room. He crumbled to the floor, where I held him down with the force of my body control.

I couldn't break the dark magic over him, and my spell of peace seemed to have run its course. I had to try something different. We were soulmates, bonded by the fates and magic. If I was okay, he had to be okay too. That's how it worked. If I got hurt, he got hurt. Even with our mental blocks up, we could still feel each other. Perhaps having our blocks up, and before that, not opening our bonds, had saved me from being affected by the dark spell. However, it was also probably why I couldn't heal him.

As expected, Phillip was able to easily break the hold I

had over him, and he leaped up, swiping his hand out, sending me flying into the air. I braced for the hit and hovered above him, preventing myself from crashing into a wall. I was getting better at this whole soulmate magic thing. Small victory!

Erik looked above me, helplessly, before glaring down at Phillip, ready to pounce.

"Don't do anything," I called down to him. "I'm going to take care of this

"Ah, feels just like old times, doesn't it, *mi corazon?*" Phillip sighed, brushing imaginary dust off his pale blue button-down shirt.

"You don't have to do this," I said evenly. I wouldn't let him, and I was beginning to understand what I had to do to save him, but I wasn't going to like it.

A millisecond of sadness flashed through Phillip's eyes before filling back up with his typical arrogance. "I did warn you, Amina," Phillip said. "Perhaps you should have let me die."

Phillip continued his murderous spell on the red-headed man who was splayed out on the floor, bleeding from the mouth. The crowd begged for Phillip to stop, but of course, he paid them no attention.

I pushed out both my hands in front of me, pouring my magic through me, and immediately fell. Erik caught me in his arms before I hit the floor.

"We can't let him kill that man," he said through clenched teeth, lowering me to my feet.

"We won't," I shouted before running towards Phillip and wrapping my arms around his waist, his back to me.

"What are you doing?" Phillip asked, attention still focused on killing the man. "If you wanted some alone time, I'm afraid you'll have to wait. Kind of busy teaching the town a lesson. Now, if you want to hold on to me while I do it, then that's fine. Might make your furry boyfriend jealous."

I didn't respond and instead kept holding on and opening my soulmate bond, funneling my magic out. My vision sharpened, and I knew that my eyes were once again purple. I was not tainted by the dark spell, and I would cleanse him of this magic. The magic leaving me felt like my life force rushing out. The last time I felt like that was when I gave blood at the paranormal prison for the power-giving serum. Too much of doing this, and I would pass out or worse.

A human shaped blur ran past me, and I saw it pick up the red headed man and leave the pub.

Phillip cursed, half turning behind him to the door, moving me with him. Erik was gone, and I thanked him internally.

"If you think your jackal stopped me, you're wrong. I'll just find another."

My legs wobbled, and I had to force myself to stand up straighter. I was almost sagging on him.

"Amina?" Phillip yelled. "What are you doing to me?"

"Just giving you a bear hug. Shh, let it happen," I said in a low voice. I could feel the full weight of my body, everything hurt, even my eyelashes. How was that possible? They weighed nothing. My back ached, a dull but persistent pain radiating up and down my spine. My breath caught in my throat as I struggled to fill my lungs with air. What was happening to me?

The movement around me started to fade from my vision, I could barely discern the different voices in the crowd. I blinked my eyes to clear my vision, but it didn't work. Beads of sweat gathered around my neck and hairline, yet I felt cold.

Phillip swung around, and I stumbled. He caught me in his arms, but I didn't budge, feeling entirely too drained to move away.

"Whatever you're doing, stop it. It's hurting you," he said, looking up. Several people in the crowd inched towards us, looks of murderous intent and fear mixed in their eyes. They would kill Phillip and probably me with him. Guilt by association and all that. "Stop!" he commanded, and everyone in the room froze.

"How do you feel?" I slurred.

Phillip looked back down at me. "Strong. Very strong. How do you feel?"

"Like I'm slowly dying."

"That's because you probably are. Stop this."

"You're my soulmate. I can heal you."

"We already know your spell doesn't work."

"I'm not doing my spell. I'm lending you my strength to fight the dark. And heck, if this doesn't work, then at least you'll be the strongest. That's what you always wanted, right?" My eyelids felt like heavyweights, forcing my eyes to close.

Phillip shook me awake. "I don't want power if you die," he said in a lowered voice before lifting me into his arms.

I hung my head on his shoulder, too weak even to lift it upright anymore. It felt like work to even breathe. I had no death wish and didn't want to die. I'd clearly gone too far, but was too exhausted to even heal myself.

"You can't get rid of the spell, Amina."

My mind felt cloudy. I just had to focus on breathing. Slow and steady. I wasn't making myself weak for nothing. I was going to heal his butt if it was the last thing I did, and at this rate, it just might be the last thing I did if I didn't turn this boat around. "Do you still want to kill people...to prove...who's the boss?" I wheezed out.

I felt Phillip shake his head. "No, I don't care about that shit anymore, you know that. I just want you to be safe, and to get these fucking soulmates out of here. I don't want to hurt people."

"Then...don't."

"I won't."

I did a victory dance in my mind, but then got tired from that as well. "Then…my work here…is done."

My sight blurred, but I could make out moving figures beneath my lashes. I could see a tall older man with white hair, Bill. His lips were moving, but I could barely hear him.

"Gone," he said. Well, that's all I could hear him say.

Erik's face appeared in front of me, too, a very worried expression covering him. His lips were moving soundlessly.

Well, that couldn't be right. He was probably talking, but I just couldn't hear him. Why couldn't I hear him? Thinking was a struggle. Thinking took work. I closed my already dropping lids and went slack in Phillip's arms, the last of my energy leaving me.

CHAPTER 15

I stretched my legs, and an instant cramp attacked my left calf. I gritted my teeth and let out a groan. With my eyes still closed, I leaned to my left and massaged my leg, but it didn't help much.

My covering lifted off of my leg, and I soon felt a large cool hand touching my calf. A welcoming numbness soothed away the pain, and my body relaxed.

"How do you feel?" I heard Erik say.

"Cramp," I croaked out. My throat felt raw and dry. I pressed my lips together, feeling my lips were just as dry and cracked. They felt like crumpled paper, and I could only imagine how rough I must have looked.

Erik, at least I thought it was him as my eyes were still closed, rubbed my calf. "Better?"

I nodded, my mind still a bit cloudy, but I quickly remembered the fight in the restaurant. "Phillip! How is he? Did I fix him?"

"Can you open your eyes?" Erik asked, ignoring my question. Why was he ignoring me?

I tried to open my eyes, but my lids felt heavy and sore. My top lashes, stuck to my lower ones, slowly spread apart. I wiped away what felt like little crumbs from my lashes and cleared out the corners of my eyes. My vision was blurry, so I blinked several times until I could focus my sight.

I looked around our bedroom, squinting as the sun's rays peeked through the blinds. Erik looked down at me with tired eyes and disheveled hair.

"How long have I been asleep?" I croaked.

Erik looked towards the hallway. No one appeared, so I assumed someone was coming close. And, as if on cue, a second later, we heard a knock at the apartment door. Erik usually knew someone was at the door before they even knocked with his were hearing.

"And you've been asleep for two days." He then got up and left to answer the door.

What in the hell? Two days?

Erik reappeared with Bill by his side.

"You didn't want to give me a heads up, so I could make myself presentable first?" I muttered before running a hand across my face.

"You look beautiful, young lady," Bill said with a smile.

Phillip popped up behind them, and I sighed. Since he was here, I guess I could say I healed him.

He widened his eyes. "You look…well rested," he said.

I twisted my lips and crossed my arms over my T-shirt, realizing for the first time that I wasn't wearing any of the same clothes that I was wearing at the restaurant. Two days had passed, so that was probably a good thing. I tried not to think about whether someone had bathed me. Even if it was Erik, that was horrifying to me. I had not shaved my legs or my armpits in a week.

Great, I was in a room full of people, looking like a wildebeest.

"Why was I asleep so long?" I asked Bill. "Was it because of the healing?"

He exchanged a quick glance with Erik before looking

back at me. What was with the cryptic behavior? "What you did, young lady, was very brave, but also very foolish."

"I'm his soulmate, wouldn't using our soulmate magic be the obvious fix?"

"Yes, but you aren't all powerful. You still have growing to do, and the magic placed on Phillip was more than you should have handled. Healing him on your own almost killed you." Bill lost his smile and shook his head. "You would have died if it wasn't for the power of Six."

It couldn't be helped. I was scared of Phillip killing that guy. If he killed another innocent man, even while under a spell, there would be no going back for him.

Bill walked over to me and hovered his hands over my head, eyes closed. We all stayed quiet and still as he worked his medical mage powers. I felt a feathery coolness over me briefly as his magic assessed me. Seconds later, he moved his hands away, but said nothing. He opened a satchel I hadn't noticed before at the foot of my bed. He took out a stethoscope and listened to my breathing. He remained silent as he went back into his bag. I looked up at Erik and then Phillip; neither gave a look of emotion, which only worried me.

This was weird. I expected Bill to just give me a clean bill –no pun intended – of health and tell me to stop doing stupid things. As per usual. When I looked back down at his bag, I widened my eyes when I saw him pull out a needle attached to a vile.

"Just need to take a little blood," he said, not looking at me.

I held out my left arm. "Everything okay?" I asked as I watched him stick the needle in my vein.

"Just need to do some checks," he said simply. He capped the vial and took out another small clear container filled with a translucent liquid. I watched him as he poured my blood in the container, closed the lid, and swirled the contents together. He squinted his eyes as liquid became a deep, almost black, purple. He sighed and then packed everything back in his satchel.

"What's the verdict, Doc? Am I not long for this world?" I asked, half kidding and half serious. I gave a dry chuckle, not feeling particularly funny.

He frowned, and stroked his chin. "Did you realize what you were doing when you tried to heal or lend your strength to Phillip?"

I narrowed my eyes. Well, I sure thought I did. "Tried? Did it not work?"

"Well, I'm not trying to kill anyone, anymore so you did something right," Phillip replied, rocking on his heels, hands stuffed in his jeans' pockets.

I raised my hands in the air. "Whoo-hoo! I cured him. One less thing they have over us!"

Bill nodded, not looking as impressed as I expected him to be. "You weakened the spell."

I dropped my shoulders. "So, I only did the same thing as last time, except this time, I almost died. I thought I was getting stronger, not weaker."

Bill gave me a pitying smile. "No Amina, I didn't mean to suggest that. I now believe that last time you only contained the spell. Similar to isolating it and putting a cover over it. This time you actually lessened the spell…by sharing some of his curse."

I dropped my mouth open, shocked to the core. "Are you saying I'm cursed under the same dark spell Phillip is under?"

"A weakened version of it. You essentially took it apart and took some on yourself. Now you both have the curse, but it's much weaker than before."

I wiggled my jaw in thought. I wasn't going to make this a set back. The moral of the story here was that we weakened the curse. "That's a good thing, as it makes it easier to fight against, and perhaps even break. Wait, can Rima control me?"

"I believe that because the curse is weakened ,there are certain effects that are no longer there. Namely, her control over you both."

That was a relief. "Thanks Bill."

"Anytime, young lady. Give me a call if you need me," he said before turning and leaving the room. Erik followed him out.

I looked to Phillip, who raised a hand to shush me before I could even speak. "I know, I know. We're going to have to let them siphon off of us," he said with a resigned sigh. He flopped down on the foot of my bed and leaned his elbows on his thighs. "We can't stop them from taking souls, and we can't protect ourselves. They have us by the balls."

I nodded. "I should probably go over there today. It's already been two days, and I don't want them hurting anyone else."

Phillip waved his hand towards me as if swatting a fly. "No. Relax. They'll be okay."

I narrowed my eyes at him. "What are you talking about? They aren't patient people."

"They got their power up already."

I straightened up. "What? How? Did they kill someone again?"

Phillip shook his head. "They took some from me already," he replied, glancing over at me with a lopsided grin.

"Phillip," was all I could muster to say. I was honestly shocked at his selflessness.

"I couldn't have them hurt anyone. And after what you just did for me, it's the least I could do. Let me handle this."

"You can't do this yourself, Phillip. It can't be good with you, us, trying to keep the evil from taking over. Plus, couldn't you die if they just took from you? We have to share this burden."

"I'm okay right now."

I nodded. "Yeah, and I want to keep it that way. You go down, then I go down, remember?"

"He remembers," Erik stated, walking into the room. He glared at Phillip sitting on my bed, and Phillip successfully ignored him. He titled his head and crossed his arms, eyes still on the other man. Phillip finally looked up at him with a smile and stood up.

I didn't bother commenting on the exchange. Instead, I kicked myself in my mind for not mentioning something to Phillip myself. I really had become too comfortable around him, and I couldn't put the work on Erik to assert proper boundaries. I frowned, suddenly realizing something.

"Wait, you knew about Phillip doing this?" I asked Erik.

He nodded, sitting down on the edge of the bed, close to me. "But, we haven't told anyone else. We already know Mae wouldn't approve, and we don't want to force anyone else to lie to her."

I looked out of the window again. It was so sunny out. I almost believed it would be warm, but we were in the dead of winter. I wanted to fly away and escape. But I couldn't. To leave now would mean allowing these soulmates to continue to kill and eat the souls of those they murdered. The thought sickened me.

"Does it hurt?" I whispered, still gazing out of the window.

"No," Phillip answered. "You get a little dizzy, like you've been spinning around in a chair. You're weak after."

"Do we have to go every day?"

"Yeah. It's quick though. Five minutes for each. I can go today."

"That would be three days in a row. I can't let you do that."

Erik rubbed my leg over the covers. "You're still in recovery, Amina," Erik stated. "Let Phillip take this one today."

Phillip leaned against a wall, and nodded in agreement. "And maybe tomorrow we'll have a plan to get rid of them, and you won't have to do anything."

"What would they do if we just tried to kill them? Like, I don't know, do what you were doing to that guy in the diner. They aren't life mages. They don't have our power."

Phillip chuckled. "Yeah, I tried that."

I looked at him in surprise. "Really? When?"

"Right after the diner thing happened. I really thought you were dying. For a few minutes you weren't even breathing."

I looked at Erik. "Seriously?"

Erik grimaced. "It was touch and go. We didn't know when, or if, you'd wake up."

"I felt guilt and anger," Phillip added. "It seemed I didn't have anything to lose, so I decided to go rogue and kick ass."

Wow, that was so stupid and…touching. "And what happened?"

Phillip shrugged. "Gedeyon did his whole evil eye thing, and I got violently sick. It was a real success."

"I had to save his life," Erik said in a deadpan voice.

Phillip gave a dry laugh. "Yeah, that was fun, he had to carry me out of their place like some damsel in a romance novel. So, in conclusion, by the time I can get my magic going on them, they've already started to melt my brain. I'd forgotten to refresh the siren call canceling spell you developed. So I wasn't thinking."

Erik coughed into his hand. "Well, it was two against one, so that was stupid."

I looked back and forth between both men, my mind racing. Maybe the answer wasn't just in growing stronger but in making the soulmates weaker. That way, if we weren't fully prepared or powered, we'd still have a fighting chance. Suddenly, an idea popped into my head. "What if we mute their magic? Like how Hagerstown does to new guests that come to their town. Or maybe we can put a spell on them that makes them good." I was quite ashamed for not having thought of this before, actually.

Neither man said anything, and I could tell by their expressions that they were contemplating it. I pressed my index fingers to the sides of my head to somehow focus my thoughts. "Yeah, I could work on the spell and get it strengthened with our own soulmate magic and the power of Six. When I go in for my turn tomorrow, I'll try it."

"They could hurt you if it doesn't work," Erik finally said.

"If it doesn't work, they won't know any different. This isn't an attack. They won't feel the magic on them just like we didn't when our magic got muted."

Neither Phillip nor Erik looked convinced.

"Do either of you have a better plan? This is not going to be my life. I'm going to fight!"

CHAPTER 16

How do you mute someone with god-like powers? That was the question of the day. I stayed up all night trying out spells on Erik and Blake. They were both more super-powered now than before, so a regular muting spell was easily broken by Phillip.

I flopped down on the couch, face first, early the next morning, refusing to sleep until I had a solution.

I heard footsteps behind me and turned slightly to see Mae standing there. I turned and sat up. "Sorry, I didn't even hear you come in."

"Phillip, let me in." She sat down next to me as I made room for her. "I had a dream that directed me to an answer I think you've been searching for."

Mae and her visions were always something I wanted to hear. I needed any edge I could get. "Do tell."

"You know, your gift isn't about spell and potion making. You're a life mage. Use that magic, stop fighting it."

I folded my feet up under me, racking my brain regarding how her words could relate to what I needed. "How do I pause their powers without a spell? My magic only allows people to do things."

She gave me an expectant look, and I felt like a fool for not being able to give her an answer. "Isn't using magic doing a thing?"

I widened my eyes in understanding. Yes, it was. "I can make their body stop using magic."

She smiled and patted my cheek.

Could I really magically control a soulmate? I thought back to the party at Blake's place. I actually had, even if briefly. I could reinforce my magic every hour if I had to, but I was in a better place now than I had been.

Mae stood up. "Remember to power up with *all* of your bonds first, honey." She turned and walked towards the door.

I jumped up. "That's it? You're leaving?"

She waved a hand in the air. "I said what I came for. Talk later."

I looked on after she left, and soon Phillip came back from his room. "So, you're going to try to body control a soulmate? We could never work that magic on each other."

I rubbed my chin, still thinking. "Yeah, but they aren't our soulmates. We don't cancel each other out. We know that now. Even if it last, a short while like our mind control magic, that could be enough to make them defenseless."

"What about defeating their crapload of followers?"

I waved my hand. "We'll deal with that later." I was getting excited. I finally had a plan of attack.

I just hoped it worked.

~

I sat in Gedeyon's study the next afternoon fully so powered up I practically glowed. They thought I was there to get siphoned, and I was, but only to block the real plan. The key was for me to mute them before he siphoned me.

Erik was right outside the apartment. Phillip wanted to

come, but he could barely stand up, and I didn't want him going off the plan if his evil curse decided to kick back in because he was too weak to fight it.

The whole thing seemed like a long shot, but it was better than nothing. I really wanted to get the whole affair over with and get the hell out of his apartment. The only thing I could think about now was those floating souls, and an anger simmered in me that threatened to distract. Fortunately, I'd bespelled myself with my own peace of mind spell and used my siren cancelling spell, so I felt like I had enough magical armor on me to get through this.

"Would you like a drink before we begin?" Gedeyon asked.

Was he kidding me? This wasn't a visit to the spa. I shook my head. "No. Where's Rima?"

"Attending to some business at her club."

You mean Blake's club, I thought. That was not good, it was easier for this to work if they were both here. However, I'd keep pushing through. Maybe one at a time would lead to more chance of success.

"You'll have to come back later for her."

If this worked on Gedeyon, I'd have to immediately go to Rima and do the same.

Gedeyon sat down in the chair across from me in front of his desk. "I heard you weren't feeling well. How are you now?"

"I didn't come over here to chat. Let's just get this over with."

"Why make this unpleasant?"

"I'm not donating blood to those in need. This is not fun for me."

He brushed a strand of hair hanging in front of my eye from my face, and I batted his hand away. "The four of us would be good together," he said in a low voice.

If he was trying to be seductive, it wasn't going to work.

Putting aside the fact that I had a wonderful man already, the whole killing of innocent people and eating their souls didn't exactly turn me on me.

"We've had this talk before. Can we move on?" I growled.

He gave a smirk. "Certainly."

I sat upright in my seat and balled my hands into fists, resting them on my thighs. I closed my eyes and began to push my magic out, my mind focusing on nothing but Gedeyon. I couldn't risk ordering him aloud through my words, so instead I focused my thoughts on him. I envisioned his power as a sword, rusting and crumbling then being swept away by the wind.

After several seconds passed, I opened my eyes in confusion. He hadn't started siphoning yet. While that was good, what was he waiting for? Did he know what I was doing?

He raised an eyebrow. "You need to open your mouth. That's where the energy is transferred. What were you expecting?"

I honestly didn't know what to expect. I'd forgotten to ask Phillip exactly what the siphoning entailed.

I parted my lips slightly.

"More."

I opened my mouth a little wider.

"More."

I glared at him. This was worse than going to the dentist. I couldn't help but wonder if he was tricking me now.

He smiled and scooted his chair towards me until our knees were touching. I fought the urge to move away. Instead, I maintained my position as he touched the sides of my face and leaned towards me. I shut my eyes again and continued to force my magic out to surround him and suffocate his powers. If it were a body part, it would be torn away.

Thankfully his lips did not touch mine, but I could feel him doing something. His lips hovered over mine, and I could feel the heat of him on my face and neck. However, that heat contrasted with the chill of cold enclosing my extremities. I shivered, struggling to keep focused.

My head began to feel fuzzy, but I pushed forward past the dizzying cold, and soon it subsided. I could only assume my friends were fortifying my magic through our bonds from afar. We'd helped each other with telepathic magic before, this would be no different.

Minutes passed, and the warmth of Gedeyon's body heat retreated. I slowly opened my eyes to see him sitting back in his seat, looking all too pleased with himself. I had no idea by his expression if my magic had any effect.

"Feeling stronger now?"

He narrowed his eyes at me, and a cold panic hit my spine. Did he know what I was doing? The hope was that if he couldn't siphon from me then I had succeeded and would need to teleport out of there super damn fast.

"It can take a few moments to hit if I'm not particularly starved. However, it's better to get fed before you get too hungry. That way, you don't take much."

I twisted my lips in anger. If he wasn't in need of my services right now, then why the hell had he summoned me? It was clear they were doing more than getting a fix, they were trying to weaken us.

I got up, disappointed I wouldn't be able to find out right away if my magic worked.

"Oh, by the way, whatever spell you were trying to cast, I don't think it took," Gedeyon called.

I momentarily froze. He did know. Only he thought it was a spell.

"You need to stop fighting us, little soulmate. We've been there, done that, bought the T-shirt, as you Americans say. You can think of nothing to defeat us. But it's fun watching you try."

I straightened up and kept walking. He didn't know for sure my magic hadn't worked. He didn't even know what I was trying to do. I decided not to fall for his words and keep hope alive.

Guys! Lisa's voice suddenly rang in my head. *Can you come to my place? Queen Arwa is here.*

What was the fairy queen doing here? She was supposed to be watching her court and, most importantly, Brandon.

~

I rushed into Lisa's 9th floor apartment. It was a distinctively feminine space. Her living room and dining room area was painted a pale blush pink. Her couch was ivory, and black, white, and pink pillows crowded her seating. She had clear coffee, side and dining tables, and chairs. A crystal chandelier hung over her dining table, and a silver vase full of several shades of pink roses sat in the center. Long patterned drapes hung from her balcony doors behind her dining room space.

Currently Blake, and Charles sat on the couch. Phillip and Lisa squished into each other, sitting on a cushioned gray ottoman. Queen Arwa perched on a pale pink chair as elegant as always in a long teal dress with a matching hijab under her golden crown.

"Queen Arwa, what brings you here?" I asked. "How's Brandon?"

"He is fine."

One less stressor down.

"However, you must leave here. Giving the soulmates your energy is not the answer."

Now, this was different than what everyone else was saying to do. "Well, they're killing innocent people, so we can't."

She gave a slight sigh. "I realize what I am asking is not easy, but if they drain you of your power, all hope in stopping them is lost."

"Even if we go on the run, won't they find us since we're all connected as soulmates?" Phillip asked, looking like he'd seen better days.

I should have felt a little bad for stealing all the energy for my encounter with Gedeyon, but I had good reason. I'd have to share a little now that I was back.

Arwa snapped her fingers, and a chill went through my body, causing me to freeze up.

"There, now they can't find you," she said with a satisfied smile.

"Did you just throw some magic on us?" I asked, rubbing my arms as I got up to help Phillip.

"I did. This will sever the connection between the four of you so that they will not know where you are."

"Couldn't you have done that earlier before they found us?" Phillip grumbled.

I placed my hands on his back and pushed some of my power through my fingers into him. Instantly, he started to sit upright. He turned slightly to face me behind him and gave a wink.

"I didn't have the ability at the time, or I certainly would have. To come across magic powerful enough to inhibit the soulmate bond was not easy." Her eyes darkened, and she looked away from the group. Whatever she'd done to power up had to come at a price as most magical upgrades did. "So, you must use this gift wisely. You must leave this place at once."

Phillip threw out his hands in frustration, looking more energized, and I went to sit back down, still feeling pretty okay. "And go where? We don't know who's friends with the first soulmates. And those who aren't, we don't know if they'll be turned by them and give up our location. So, we can live on our own in some abandoned city or off the grid in the countryside, but then we have to worry about all the other monsters out there."

Maybe other monsters wouldn't be too bad.

"We could go to Hagerstown," Lisa offered.

"That would not be a wise decision," said a voice from the foyer area. Except no one was there. A second later, Azrael appeared dressed in their usual dark attire. Well, that was creepy.

"Does no one knock on doors anymore?" Charles grumbled.

"Why isn't it a good decision?" Erik asked, turning to the angel.

Azrael blew out a breath. "Because it's about to be taken over by the first soulmates."

Well, of course, it was. These assholes just didn't stay still. Did they even sleep? "What? How?"

"Seems our friend, Rima's been leading an attack against Hagerstown, and they just lost."

"Why didn't we know this?" Erik thundered, standing up. "Nobody contacted us."

"Maybe all their tech power was cut off," Azrael explained.

"But they still have mages and witches who could have teleported out to get help," I stated.

"So, then, why didn't they?" Felix asked. He looked to Azrael. "How long has the battle been going on?"

"A few days. The town just surrendered today."

Things were falling into place now. "That's probably why Rima wasn't here today for the siphoning," I muttered. "We need to go help them."

"It's too late."

"No, we can kick them out."

Azrael raised an eyebrow. "Like you did here?"

Ouch. That hurt. However, we were in a better place than we had been a few weeks ago. We knew things we didn't know. Tried magic and spells we hadn't before. Hagerstown had done so much for us. They'd help free my friends back at the prison, given us a place to stay, fought beside Lisa when Lorenzo and his ghouls attacked. Now was the moment we'd been leading up to. If we didn't try now, what good were we?

Charles stood up. "Damn it. Teleport us there. We have to see what's going on."

Arwa clasped her hands in front of her with sympathetic eyes. "I would not advise you to do such. You need to stay away from them. You cannot help your friends in Hagerstown now."

I wasn't running anywhere. "I'm going. I'm sorry, Queen Arwa, but we can't abandon our friends."

"If you go there and lose, you can't come back," Azrael said. "They won't just want siphoning anymore if you fight against them. The fighting starts now, and there is no going back."

"What choice do we have? If we leave, though, they'll continue to eat souls. Gedeyon said my spell didn't work."

"And you trust him, why?" Azrael asked with a cocked brow. They studied their nails as if they were the most important things in the world. Our friends were in trouble, and the angel wanted to play games.

"What are you talking about?" Erik said in a low voice. This was his controlled voice when he was getting angry or annoyed, but wanted to appear steady. I preferred the screaming option, but that was just me.

"Just because Gedeyon knew what you were trying to do doesn't mean he was able to stop it from happening," Azrael began, still inspecting their nails. "Of course, he is going to tell you it didn't work. That way, you don't try anything."

"And what about Rima?"

"It's possible she was. They're soulmates, what happens to one can happen to the other."

"If that were true, then I'd have the dark curse like Phillip did." No need telling anyone that I had it now, since that was of my own doing.

"Phillip was cursed before you even met. Before you were bonded."

"So, what," Phillip began, massaging his jaw as he spoke. "This is like some marriage where anything I made prior to the marriage is still mine and mine alone?"

Azrael nodded.

Ok, that made sense. Now would be as good a time to test that as any. "Well, if they have muted powers, maybe we are in a good place to help Hagerstown."

"First, you have to be sure your magic worked. Then you have to be sure it fully worked. For all we know, it was only good for a limited time or just weakened their magic."

I wanted to scream. All the guessing in the world wouldn't tell us anything better than actually fighting them. We had defenses now. If our offense sucked, at least we could get out alive. "Well, we don't have time to wait it out and see if things worked. Our friends in Hagerstown have been under attack, and we need to help them."

"You're making a mistake," Azrael warned.

I shrugged. "What else is new?"

CHAPTER 17

Hagerstown was surrounded by an invisible ward that prevented anyone not already approved from entering. At least, that's the way it was supposed to be. The official entrance to the town, a bank landmarking the start, usually held soldiers, who also walked the perimeter and perched on top of the bank. If you were new and wanted entrance into the town, this was the only way to get in. In theory.

Somehow, Rima and company had bypassed all of that and forced their way into town. Now ghouls stood at the entrance with their fully black eyes and mouth full of sharp teeth. We stood in front of them, having unsuccessfully tried to bypass the new warding and get into town on our own. However, that just meant it was going to take a little longer than expected.

We were getting in.

"Let us in," Faith shouted, stepping up to a blond-haired man well over 6 feet tall. The fight in Vegas had apparently been all but won when we sent word to her and Felix of Hagertown's situation. They both decided to come and help save their supernatural home.

I glanced over to her briefly as I continued to try to wear down the ward. She looked up to his dark eyes showing no sign of fear.

The ghoul smirked at her. "What will you give me to let you in?" he said before licking his lower lip in an attempt to be seductive.

Faith stepped closer to him. "I will give you an ass kicking. That's what I will give you if you don't let me the fuck into my town, you fucking cannibal."

The man grabbed her left arm, and she looked down at it with a smile. Not good…for him. By the crazed look on Faith's face she was going to kill this man, and enjoy doing it.

Felix walked next to Faith, towering over the ghoul. "Let her go if you want to live to see another day," he growled.

The man gave a chuckle. "I'm not afraid of a weak, little woman."

Who still said things like that? Had he learned nothing with Rima and Misandre around him? He deserved to get his ass kicked.

Before I could register what was happening, Faith had grabbed the man by the throat, her eyes fully red. I couldn't see her tattoos since she was bundled up in her winter gear, but I was sure they were glowing, enhancing her strength. The man's eyes bulged as he pulled at her hand, but it was not moving. His face drained of color, and his cheeks hollowed, appearing to age before our eyes. She was using her succubus power to drain his energy. If she didn't stop soon, she would kill him. That was probably the plan.

The other ghouls stepped forward, pointing various weaponry at us. I raised a hand and froze their advances with my magic.

She continued to drain the ghoul until it was just a mummified shell of his former self. She let him go, and he dropped to the ground, still alive but looking very near death's door. It felt more humane just to finish him off completely, but she just turned away from him and faced the frozen guards with vicious eyes and a teeth baring grin. "Who's next? I'm still hungry."

"Who's in charge here now?" I asked the frozen guards, giving them enough moving room to be able to talk. I heard a car pull up behind us, but maintained my attention on the guards.

"I am," came a voice from behind us.

I turned slightly and saw Lorenzo get out of a bright blue sedan. He wore a leather jacket, which couldn't have been enough to keep him warm. Then again, I had no concept of temperature tolerances for ghouls. "So, to what do we owe this visit?"

Oh, he wanted to play dumb today. "We want to get in town and check on our friends after you attacked for no damned reason," I replied, glaring at the ghoul. I wanted to stop his heart so bad, but knew it would only cause more trouble since I didn't know if our friends were alright. It seemed us holding on to our end of the bargain didn't mean the first soulmates would hold to theirs.

"Ah, well, you came just in time to hear our announcement," he replied before heading back to his car. "Let them in. We're meeting in front of the governor's office."

The governor's office was a repurposed business building that the current leader of the government town, Colonel Robinson used. It was a couple of miles into town, and the eight of us teleported there since we came without cars.

Once reappearing at the building, we were surrounded by what looked like most of the town, and hundreds of fae and ghouls. We stood in the middle of the crowd, which faced the front of the tall glass building. I could hear gasps and cries, and figured it was due to everyone being distraught from the fighting and having these thugs take over.

"Shit!" I heard Charles cry from my right.

"I'm going to kill them all," Faith said through clenched teeth on my left.

What were they talking about? I was too short to see anything. "What's going on?" I turned to Erik, whose eyes were focused on the front, his eyes ablaze with anger.

"They killed him. They killed the Colonel," he replied in a tight voice. For the brief time we'd lived in Hagerstown, Erik had got on well with the man, being former military himself. They'd kept in touch even after we left to stay in Silver Spring, and I believed the Colonel was something of a mentor to him. I counted him as an ally.

"What? I can't see anything," I said.

"You don't want to," he replied, still looking ahead.

"I need to." I looked to my right and pushed forward through the crowd. I couldn't just stand there and listen and not see what was going on. It was my fault this happened.

When I reached the front, I stopped, placing a hand over my mouth.

The Colonel's head rested on a makeshift pike. The spear stabbing through his jagged, open neck where it had been sliced from his body. Bits of bloodied flesh and muscle dropped to the top concrete step in front of the doors of the building. His face held a look of horror with wide eyes and a slack, bloodied mouth. This image would haunt my dreams forever.

The Colonel had accepted us into his town and had treated us well. He'd made sure we had a place to stay and employment. He was tough, but astute and thoughtful. Without his assistance, we would not have freed our friends in the paranormal prison. Now, this former military hero was murdered and disrespectfully put on display in the most barbaric of ways.

I stood paralyzed with fury, my mind in chaotic turmoil.

The doors opened and two fae walked out, holding the doors open. Misandre soon appeared with Lorenzo close behind. There was no Rima or Gedeyon insight. Misandre walked over to the Colonel's head and patted it with a smile on her red lips before walking back to the center of the wide steps.

"Listen, everyone!" she shouted. Her voice amplified through the crowds, although I saw no microphone or speakers. "Your old ruler is no more. Defeated by my hands. I am now your new leader. You will follow me if you want to remain alive. You will support and fight for the original soulmates against all foes."

I glanced over to Lorenzo, whose face held the briefest look of surprise. Interesting. Only moments ago, he was telling us he would be running this town. Didn't Misandre have her own court to rule? I guess she'd be using Lorenzo as her eyes and ears here. Not that it would make a difference. Lorenzo and his ghouls would kill and eat these people, and I knew Misandre would allow it. She was an Unseelie or dark fae and no friend to humans. She'd been feeding innocent humans to Lorenzo and his horde in exchange for their help for a while now.

More cries and shouts of disapproval filled the air.

"You killed my son, you bitch!" shouted a female voice.

"You are monsters," came another voice, an older man this time.

Misandre smiled. "If anyone does not like this situation, raise your hand, and we will take care of you. My ghouls would like more treats for their hard work of the past few days."

The crowd went silent as the ghouls grinned with stained teeth, no doubt colored by the eating of dead human flesh. I wouldn't let that happen. Rima and Gedeyon could pretend they were good all they wanted, but they put Misandre in charge, and there was no mistaking that she was pure evil.

Why, of all the cities to attack, they chose Hagerstown, could only be because it would put us further at their mercy.

However, if they were already breaking promises and harming the people we cared about or swore to protect, then we had no reason to continue to bow down to them.

"Now, here are our new rules. They are very simple. The paranormals will serve the first and true soulmates, and by association, me and my people. As for you humans, you will now be our servants to do with as we please. Your lives are in our hands. You are useless, weak beings. Be thankful that we are now giving you purpose. To those that we find as any form of usefulness, you will be rewarded. Fall in line, and you may be lucky enough to secure long lives. In addition, your housing will be relocated, and you will be grouped together. In fact, all beings will be grouped together according to factions."

I heard cries and talking in the crowd. We couldn't allow this to happen to them. Mae was right; we couldn't give in to these monsters. They would never be satisfied, and they would wreak havoc just to please themselves. What good were we if we didn't actually help? We would be a waste. Someone very powerful brought us together to defend humanity. Who were we to think we weren't strong enough for the job?

I thought of our friends in town, Shayla, Henry, Joanie. I thought of all of the children that I used to teach. Had any of them died in this fighting? The town didn't look damaged, at least not in this area, but that didn't mean there wasn't any destruction, unless magic was used to clean it up. I had no doubt that these monsters forced their way in and destroyed a growing and thriving town. I was done playing nice.

A hand touched my shoulder, and I jumped, ready to pounce. Shayla Winans, a powerful witch, and necromancer, along with her boyfriend Henry Butler, leader of the Hagerstown vampires, stood there with solemn faces.

"Sorry to scare you, but we need to talk. Meet me at my place," Shayla stated before turning and walking away.

I mentally shared with the group to reconvene at Shayla's before looking at the stage again as Misandre went on about the new rules for the town.

"Fuck her rules," I muttered before teleporting away.

~

We packed into Shayla and Henry's living room, all of us staring at the couple as they stood in front of their TV relaying the events of the battle.

"They just knocked down our wards. Our wards were strong. You know that, Amina," Shayla said, gesturing to me. Her brown eyes were glistening with tears, and I sat on the couch, shaking my head. I'd never seen her so emotional. She's always seemed so solid and strong.

Henry patted her shoulder, looking down at his feet, I presumed to hide his own emotion. His long black locks hung over his face, and when he finally looked up, his light brown eyes were bloodshot. He looked tired, and his large, muscular frame seemed to curl in, making him look weaker than I was used to seeing him. The jovial spirit he usually possessed was, understandably, gone.

"They came in and just started killing," he began in a cracked voice. "Killing anybody. Elderly people, kids, the weak. They didn't care. And any of the dead we didn't get to first to properly bury or cremate, the ghouls would take to eat."

"How long was the fighting? Azrael told us it'd been a few days," Erik asked, standing near me.

Henry nodded. "Yeah, about three days. They came in the middle of the night. We had guards on duty, of course, but it still was a surprise attack."

"We'd gotten so comfortable here," Shayla said. "Most groups don't attack government towns. Not only are we too large, but if you attack one of our towns, the other government towns are supposed to come and help, so it'd end up being a civil war if some rogue group had enough fighters."

"Why didn't the nearby government towns come and help?" I asked. "There's some in Virginia and in Pennsylvania, right?"

Shayla shrugged. "Yeah, but what good is it if we can't get word out? They cut down our electricity and blocked our ability to teleport out for help. We were cut off. That's why you guys didn't know."

"They isolated you," Erik surmised. "Then they killed your leadership to make you give up hope."

"Yeah," Shayla replied, shaking her head. Her long black braids were held back in a low ponytail, and she wore workout pants and a long sleeve shirt with tennis shoes. She looked just as exhausted as Henry, with equally haunted eyes. "They killed the leader of the weres and the witches. All of our sick in the infirmary a few miles out of town were wiped out."

Phillip swore. It wasn't too long ago that he had started his campaign of good, part of which entailed healing those who were sick and trying to help those suffering from the Sickness, the disease that wiped out most non magical humans, and the illness that was currently inflicting the Paranormals. I'd learned that people in Hagerstown really liked him and that he had done good. By his reaction, I realized that he not only affected others; they affected him.

"I just don't know how they got in," Shayla said, crossing her arms and shaking her head. "There was really potent magic on our wards."

"And not everyone has access to let in people," Henry replied. "There are only a limited few. That's one of the main ways we make sure the infected don't get through. We have to vet everyone."

"Well, that limited few was all they needed," I snarled. "It was our leadership that let the first soulmates and company just waltz right on in. They were enthralled by Rima or Gedeyon's ancient alpha were magic."

"So, you think someone on the inside let them in?" Shayla asked.

Erik rubbed a hand over his growing beard, looking drained. "Possibly someone under their magic. Someone they bespelled some time ago, just for this moment," Erik answered. "These soulmates have been strategizing in ways we haven't thought of. We've been playing defense while they've been playing offense."

"So, if we fell in line, we would have been spared?" Shayla asked.

"No," I quickly replied. "These assholes don't care for humans. Maybe the Paranormals would be okay, but humans are not going to be treated well no matter what. Humans are work-horses and food to them or useless, because they believe that only those with magic matter."

Henry shook his head. "Despite the wards, I thought our town was stronger. We didn't just depend on the wards. We have our own army. They're a mixture of paranormals and humans, and they are effective. You saw what they did in that prison raid. We beat Lorenzo's people before. And Amina, you and Phillip fought off Misandre's people with just regular humans, back when you were in Ireland. We were outnumbered. Our town is large, but not everyone is a fighter. We've got babies, old people, humans with no magic or fighting capabilities. Even with the civilians fighting with the soldiers, we were still down too much."

Was I missing something? He made a good point. There didn't seem to be a lot of ghouls and fae around, yet somehow they had overpowered them. The numbers weren't working out. "What do you mean? When in front of the governor's office, it didn't look like there were more ghouls and fae than humans."

Henry snorted. "Those are just the ones here to keep us in

check. When we were attacked, there were thousands of them."

Shayla nodded. "Our town now has, what, almost 4,000 people? Maybe if we're lucky 3,000 can properly fight. What surrounded our town had to be two times our population. At least, that's what some of our aerial fighters saw. And they weren't just fae and ghouls. They were orcs, and weres, and gremlins, and beasts I've never seen. We saw giant trolls and flying creatures. There were other witches and demons. It was nightmarish. We have children here who've been fortunate enough never to have seen such horrors. How are they going to look at the world and maintain some happiness, or even sanity, knowing that's what's outside our wards? Excuse me, now those things can freely come inside."

I frowned. We never had a clue how many supporters the first soulmates had. We correctly assumed it would be more than just Misandre, Joo-won, and Alister's people. They were just the head lieutenants. Of course, we now had a large following too, or so we hoped. It would be wise for us to assume that the soulmates had gotten to one of our allies. If I wasn't sure before, I knew better now. The numbers were not in our favor. However, I now knew I could turn our allies back on our side. Maybe even turn a few of our foes to follow us like we did with Alister's people.

"I couldn't even raise enough dead to fight them off," Shayla continued. "Since we were cut off from the outside, I couldn't get to gravesites."

"Babe, you wouldn't have had enough energy to make up the numbers in zombies to fight. There were just too many of them. You'd have died trying," Henry stated, rubbing her back.

Shayla's lips tightened into a frown before she spoke again. "Well, I'm going to pool together other necromancers. Other than through the use of black magic, I'm the only one who can raise the dead in town. I have a network of necromancers on our side, and I can find more. I'm going to raise an army to beat out anything these soulmates can muster. I just wish I felt more powerful."

I wouldn't put it past the first to already have necromancers on their proverbial payroll, so they'd be doing the same. However, a thought occurred to me. "I've been boosting my power through my bonds. It's made me and the others more powerful. So far, we've only kept it within the Six and our mates." I placed my hands on my head as I started to hone in on my idea. "What if, as soulmates, we could make others more powerful like they make *us* powerful?"

Erik squinted his eyes, seemingly confused by my logic. "Get me to where you're going with this?"

I wasn't bothered by his straight shooter style. I knew I sounded like I was reaching so hard I should have pulled a muscle. "Soulmates should be good. We aren't just takers getting fat off the riches of the land. That's what Gedeyon and Rima did. But their style of doing things isn't the rule book on what it means to be a soulmate. What if Phillip and I can not only get power, take power but also *give* power? We already know you and Blake are getting stronger, and I did a spell to make you stronger in your fight, Erik."

He grumbled a reply, still sour about my interference or what I liked to call saving his life.

"What if I don't need to do a spell to boost power? I could just push out my magic and boost a bunch of people at once!"

The room looked at me with shocked eyes. Even Phillip looked perplexed. "Let's test that shit out now. No doubt Gedeyon and Rima will be on their way to shut us down. We're going to need that boost right now."

I nodded and grabbed his hand, and I felt our magic flare back and forth between us. I closed my eyes and directed my magic outwards, filling the room with the warming power.

Soon, I heard gasps of delight and a few happy toned cursed words.

I opened my eyes and looked around at the smiling faces. Even Azrael looked amazed. Had I powered up an angel?

"It worked?" I asked, knowing the answer by their faces.

I was met with a chorus of yeses, and I looked back to Phillip, feeling renewed. How had I slugged along all this time thinking I couldn't do anything? I recalled my time first meeting Phillip when he told me to assume no limits until I found them. Yet, all this time we were limiting ourselves when it came to the soulmates.

He grinned at me. "We're going to charge up a town."

"We're going to charge up a fucking town."

CHAPTER 18

We spent the rest of the day powering up small groups. We had to be selective because we hadn't mastered picking and choosing who we powered up. Misandre and Lorenzo and their people were still there, and we absolutely didn't want to enhance them in any way.

Heading back to Shayla's to finally rest, Erik and I walked down a quieter part of the Hagerstown community where housing was less desirable. There was supposed to be a curfew, but I had no intentions of obeying anything from Misandre or Lorenzo.

"I think I should get one more group," I said, swinging his hand as we walked.

I heard a growl rumble from him, and I side eyed him. "What's the problem?"

"I think you should rest before you run out of power. We can't have you on empty."

I winked at him. "Then I have you guys."

He raised a brow, staring down at me. "Then we get out of power. Then it becomes a vicious cyc–" he stopped and quickly spun back around, facing the steps of a house to our left. "Come out of the dark."

I snapped my fingers, and a ball of fire hovered in my palm. I pushed my hand out and found Joo-won sitting on the steps in a relaxed manner, arms resting on the stairs supporting his upper body.

"Creepy, much?" I asked.

He gave me a lazy smile. "I like the effect it has on people."

I twisted my lips. I guess it worked.

Erik took a step forward, but didn't block me as he usually tried to do. I decided to take that as a sign that he was finally realizing I didn't need his protection. "Can we get inside for this little reunion?"

Joo-won looked up at the night sky. "Where is my butterfly?" he asked.

"If by butterfly you mean Lisa, she's busy elsewhere in town," I replied.

"You can't possibly think I came all this way and risk all that I have, just to see you two? When she contacted me, I expected her to be here. Bring her here so that I may see her lovely face."

I frowned. This was news. Why had she contacted him and said anything to us? He was still the enemy.

"I'm here," Lisa announced, appearing beside me.

Joo-won gave her a closed lipped smile before walking up the steps. The doors to the seemingly vacant townhouse opened, and he went inside. "Come, come."

Lisa marched ahead with no concerns.

What was going on?

Once inside, the door closed behind us, and we followed Joo-won down the hallway past a formal living room, dining room, and kitchen until we faced another living area. Yuri and Senna stood in the center of the space lit only by the fire coming from the fireplace. I closed my hand and extinguished my own flame.

"Have a seat," Joo-won offered.

I crossed my arms. "No, we'll stand. Lisa, why did you call him?"

"Senna and Yuri told me about your little deal," Joo-won cut in. He turned his back to us as he faced the fire, warming his bare hands that I knew weren't really cold, seeing as he was sitting out in the cold without gloves in the first place.

I looked to Senna, and she stuck her chin out at me before rolling her eyes.

"So, you went and snitched to your dad, huh? Pathetic," I said in an exaggerated tone.

Yuri cleared his throat. "Actually, it was me who told him." He shrugged, looking far from apologetic. "I cannot lie to my commander."

I glanced over to Joo-won, who was now looking at me expectantly. "Ok, yes, I did entrap your people. Desperate times call for desperate measures. We need support, and I'm taking it anyway I can get it."

"I don't blame you. You need help, I am here to do such."

I raised my eyebrows. "Out of the blue? You're now on our side?"

"Not exactly, but we're beginning to see the deal that we had entered with the soulmates won't last, and my people may be doomed anyway. We received a certain premonition that siding with the first soulmates could later lead to our misfortune."

"So, you'll help us?"

"If by help, you mean neither I nor my people will fight alongside the first soulmates, then, yes. We will remove ourselves entirely from this battle."

"So, you're going to be neutral," Erik stated, looking less elated than I felt.

Damn it. Of course, they wouldn't help us. They were neutral fae at their core.

"It is what we are. But I can give you a bit of information."

"Please share," I said, holding in my disappointment.

"The soulmates have nearly 100,000 followers worldwide."

Erik swore, and I got dizzy for a moment, overwhelmed by the number. I squished the sides of my face with my hands. "How'd they do that?"

Lisa made a pfft nose. "I had more followers than that on my Instagram account back in the day."

I dropped my jaw open and looked at her without speaking. Following some photos on a social media site was not the same as signing up to fight and possibly die for someone.

Senna perched on the arm of the couch. "You can assume that number is not full of die hard followers, but those forced to follow, and it includes families, so not all are fighters," Senna added.

"How can we battle that many people?" I asked.

"The government towns combined could muster enough soldiers, and then if you add in towns in other countries who are willing to support us, then it might not be insurmountable," Erik muttered.

"Would all those people come here to fight?" Lisa asked.

"Doubtful," Joo-won replied. "They'll come in waves. There will be smaller groups attacking towns like this one. They won't come all at once."

"On the plus side, smaller groups would be easier to fight." And control.

Joo-won tipped his head in the affirmative. "Yes. However, now that you know that it is possible to gather enough fighters, does that help? You just have to coordinate better to avoid being isolated."

"How can we beat the witch that broke the wards? She or he is the one I'm really worried about."

Joo-won waved a hand dismissively. "Worrying is a waste of emotion. The witches they have are not more powerful, just more dedicated. They spend hours upon hours breaking and setting up wards. They barely sleep or eat, and they work as collectives. This doesn't mean that they can defeat everything. Just know that they are a nonstop combination. You take out some, and you are automatically stronger. If they take a break, you are stronger."

"Why do they work like robots?" Lisa asked.

Senna sighed and adjusted in her seat. "Because they'll die if they don't. If they fail, the soulmates will kill them and eat their souls. They'll just replace them with other witches."

"Geez, that does not seem like a fun gig."

"The witches they use usually don't have better alternatives. So, you see, the key to fighting those witches is to keep at it. If they break your ward once, just rebuild it. It might take them a week or more to break it down again."

Joo-won nodded before turning back to whatever was interesting in the fire. "If you stop to think about it," he began. "Any time trespassers entered, it was because someone on the inside let us in, it was never the magic of the witches. But there was power in believing it was them. Made you believe you weren't strong enough. So, what's your plan now?"

"Kicking these assholes out of here," I replied. "Are you sure you won't reconsider joining us?"

He clasped his hands behind his back, standing taller. "Me remaining neutral is help enough."

Erik took a step forward, moving his hand towards the elves. "You could make the difference in our numbers."

Joo-won gave a thoughtful nod. "Be that as it may, I cannot intervene. We should have stayed strong and avoided this fight from the beginning. I was concerned about my people, but Arwa agreed to house them for now. I am already regretful of my role thus far. Including the harm to you."

Erik gave him a curt nod and stood back. If he wasn't willing to press the point, then I supposed the debate was over. We wouldn't have Joo-won's support.

A knock at the door disturbed our conversation.

"Who is that?" Lisa whispered, crouching down as if whoever was outside could see her.

Joo-won turned in the direction of the front door, his face its usual mask of non-emotion. "Someone powerful that we did not call," Joo-won replied. "I have bespelled this place to look vacant."

I held my breath. Please, don't be the soulmates. I was not ready for that fight after spreading my energy all over town.

Erik walked back down the hallway towards the door, his head tilted up as he sniffed the air. I opened my mouth to speak, and then closed it as I watched him go to the door and look through the peephole before quickly opening the door.

Ahmed stepped through, and Erik closed the door behind him.

"Ahmed!" I cried, unusually happy to see him. It had not been that long, but seeing any of our allies in these times gave me some form of comfort.

"Amina," he said with a head nod and a less excited tone. "I am glad you are safe."

Always the calm and in control man, I guess I shouldn't be surprised that he didn't jump up and down all giddy upon seeing me. I wasn't embarrassed by his lackluster response. Well, maybe a little. "How'd you find us?"

"Queen Arwa, then Phillip."

Looks like Arwa had been very busy, and I was super thankful for that.

"What are you doing here?"

"Giving my assistance." He looked to Joo-won, and for the first time, I saw his perfect demeanor collapse. His face set in a deep scowl, teeth bared in distaste.

"Djinn," Joo-won replied with a smile.

"You dare address me in that manner after all that you've done!" Ahmed said in a raised voice. "You steal my lamp, forcing me to serve those insane people and do despicable things."

Joo-won lifted his shoulders. "My bad," he replied. He looked at me. "Is that the way you say it?"

Why'd he think I was the gatekeeper of outdated slang? I leaned back slightly, ready to come back with some witty retort, but Ahmed beat me to it.

"My bad?" he shouted. "After all that you have done, the only thing you can say is 'my bad'? Why, you degenerate thief!" He pointed an index finger in the air. "How dare you! Do not trust this elf. He is of the worst kind!"

Yuri took a step forward, ready to defend his leader, but Joo-won raised a hand. "You are right to be upset with me, Ahmed," Joo-won stated. "Procuring is my specialty, but I apologize for the harm that this all has caused you. Please accept my humble apology."

Lisa clasped her hands together to her cheek and smiled at Joo-won as if he had just given the world's best motivational speech. It wasn't that impressive.

Ahmed looked confused for a moment before he regained his composure and looked away. "Arwa told me that she is able to disguise the soulmates so that they cannot be located by the first. It's time for you all to leave and go formulate an actual plan. You should ensure anyone with you is untraceable as well. I have a place you may go."

"Where?" Lisa asked.

Ahmed looked over to Joo-won, who raised an eyebrow. "Do you want me to leave?" the Elven king asked.

Ahmed looked away and brushed a piece of lint off of his dark grey suit. "I do not think it wise to reveal a possible hiding place to the other side."

"He's supposed to be neutral now," Lisa explained.

Ahmed gave her a condescending look, head slightly lowered. "Not the same as being on our side, my dear."

Joo-won put up a hand in surrender. "He is right. Although I have no plans to betray you, I understand your position."

"You sure we can't persuade you to actually join our side?" I asked him. I had to give one last effort before he left. I couldn't shake the feeling that we needed him to win this. "We could really use your help. And if the first soulmates come for you or your people, we could protect you."

He tilted his head slightly towards me. "Very kind of you, Amina. However, we do best by remaining neutral in such affairs," Joo-won replied before looking over to Lisa. "You know how to reach me."

He then snapped his fingers and disappeared, Senna and Yuri following closely behind.

Ahmed cleared his throat and stuck his chin out. "Now that the criminal is gone," Ahmed began. "I have an acquaintance in New York City. A vampire who is on our side. He's a bit...flamboyant, but I assure you he takes his leadership role in his commune very seriously."

Erik shifted his stance beside me, and I could feel restless energy emanating from him. I didn't have to guess that he hated our predicament. The loss, the helplessness, the fear. "What do you mean by flamboyant?"

"He was a pop star in the Pre-World."

"Oh my God, who?" Lisa asked, putting a hand on her chest.

"Niles Davies."

Lisa jumped up and down. "Oh, my god, I'm going to scream."

Ahmed frowned, clearly worried about her excitement. "I would caution you not to."

"I'm not. I'm not. I'm cool." Lisa waved a hand in front of her face. "I have been a fan of his since I was 13, and he was part of that boy band Total Package. Remember them, Mina?"

I nodded. I very clearly remembered them. I was just as much a fangirl as her at the time. I'd even memorized the steps to one of their music videos.

"Niles was always my favorite. Wasn't he yours?"

I shrugged, not looking over at Erik, who I was sure was giving me a horrified look. Actually Niles, although the lead singer, was not my favorite. There was the second lead, Devin Hesters, who I preferred, but no one needed to know that now.

"How'd you meet Niles? Did you grant him three wishes?" I cracked.

Ahmed was not as amused and gave me a deadpan face.

"Sorry." I coughed and straightened up. "Well, let's kick these assholes out of town and then get out ourselves."

"How?" Lisa asked.

I clapped my hands together. I was feeling renewed and even hopeful. I wasn't sure I could win the war, but I was feeling pretty good about winning this battle. "Let's start with breaking the magic that's trapping people in and cutting off communication."

It was time to fight.

CHAPTER 19

We took Joo-won's advice and kept working on the ward nonstop. It took all night with rotational work, but we broke the magic keeping the town isolated. I'd like to think it was my power boost to the local witches that helped give us the combined strength to finally get the ward down.

At the same time, Charles got the power up, and the cavalry from other government towns showed up soon after. With the added numbers, we began our fight to kick the ghouls out.

The witches, with our help, drew up a spell to keep out any possible trespassers and then added a spell to make the town invisible, much like Joo-won had done with his part of town in Baltimore. This way, Misandre and Lorenzo were unable to bring in any reinforcements. Phillip and I also tried a removal spell that worked like a ward. Only instead of keeping people out, it kicked people out. So far, it hadn't worked, but we were still hopeful.

Of course, the fighting was as chaotic as I expected. The ghouls were many, but they were not hard to fight, and even the few dark fae in town were not as formidable as I was used to encountering.

I thought this might lead to the big battle, but a full day of fighting passed, and there were still no soulmates. Did they not care that their cohorts were being attacked, or was this their selfish nature coming to light?

It seemed my question would soon be answered because the next day, Rima appeared.

~

I dragged my way to the entrance of town the morning she arrived, going off the last reserves of my energy.

A ghoul jumped in my path from who knows where, a spear in his hand, which he jutted forward in an attempt to stab me.

I say attempt because I was able to respond quickly. I spun my finger counterclockwise, and the ghoul's eyes rolled back into his head ,and he dropped to the ground.

"What'd you do?" Erik asked in a quiet voice, his face a mask of surprise.

"Stopped his heart. He's dead," I said in an even tone. I'd just killed someone. Even if he was a ghoul about to do something evil, killing still wasn't an easy task. "I wish it was that easy to kill all the bad guys all at once. Especially this bitch."

"I've never seen you fight that way," he replied, relaxing his face from the temporary surprise.

I paused in my stride, a thought just hitting me. It didn't hurt. My magic didn't hurt. Anytime I killed someone directly with my life mage magic, I'd always feel a full body pain, and the stronger they were to kill, the more painful it became. I once was briefly paralyzed after killing a powerful, super-powered human. Even if that ghoul wasn't that strong, it still should have hurt. Perhaps I wasn't affected because I was stronger now, especially so after bonding with Phillip and getting boosts all over the place. However, I couldn't ignore the thought that now being under a dark spell had made my body less adverse, to killing. I wondered if it would hurt to kill someone at a higher power level.

Maybe it was time to find out.

Rima stood at the entrance to the town dressed in a white fur coat with white tights and white snow boots. Guess she wasn't afraid of getting dirty. I was dressed in my usual dark colors because wearing anything light nowadays seemed futile if we wanted to stay clean. I was ready for her now. I'd been busy these past few days, and I was ready for anything she tried. Well, sort of ready. In my mind, I was ready, and that was half the battle.

The town was still under attack, and nothing paused with Rima's appearance. If anything, she was an annoying distraction to my clearing out the bad guys.

Rima looked at the dead ghoul, then up at me. She gave me a closed-lipped smile and a nod as if impressed before smugly tapping on our new and improved invisible ward with a finger. It did not break. "I think my witches can break this in a few days," she said. "This was just a waste of time, don't you think? And now you've made us very angry."

I snorted. "Like I give a shit," I scoffed, arms crossed. I wasn't going to take chances that our wards were perfect. We were making it a prime focal point, taking out the witches who served the soulmates. We left nothing to chance.

Rima's eyes darkened, and she whistled. "Look who's gotten all big and bold after being away from home for a little bit. Aren't you worried about the poor souls you left behind?"

Of course, I was worried, but we were in a damned if you did, damned if you don't scenario. I couldn't become overwhelmed with so many fires. I finally understood that I needed to focus on one fire at a time if I was going to make any leeway.

Phillip appeared beside me, looking a bit battered and bruised. Had he even used any magic to fight? "You're not taking this town. You aren't taking any of us, anymore."

Rima pouted. "Phil, why are you being so mean? Come here."

He gave her the middle finger. "No."

She frowned. "I said, come here, Phillip."

He tilted his head. "And I said hell no, lady."

She leaned back, raising a brow. I could see flames of anger in her eyes. Seems I really had weakened the dark spell on Phillip, and now neither of us would be controlled by Rima.

"I see. Well, continue to play your games. I shall go back to Silver Spring and eat all of your friends."

"Go ahead."

I leaned into Phillip. "What are you doing?" I asked through clenched teeth.

He hovered a hand over his mouth. "Calling her bluff. Maybe your magic actually worked. Let's egg her on so we can test it out."

He had a point. There would be no way to tell if anything worked if she didn't try.

Rima squinted her eyes and slapped the ward with both hands. "Why are you so sure of yourselves?"

Phillip crossed his arms, looking a bit too cocky for his own good. "We muted your magic."

She laughed, actually tossing her head back like it was the funniest thing in the world. Her laughter soon died down, and she opened her mouth to sing her alien song. Her high notes lifted in the air and surrounded us, but nothing happened. My eyes widened with excitement right before several ghouls and fae exploded around us, coating us in a spray of blood.

I dropped my mouth open, momentarily stunned.

Phillip wiped blood from his forehead. "Well, I may have misjudged some things."

Erik rolled his shoulders back, grimacing. "You fucking think?"

I smeared the blood from my face. "We do know that everyone we got a chance to put the sound canceling spell on is still fine."

Rima cackled and pointed at us. "But your magic muting is no good."

Well, maybe not for her since I didn't get to do the magic directly on her, just Gedeyon. I sucked in a breath to regain my nerves. "It could be just you. If Gedeyon could fight, you'd think he'd be here too. And if he's down for the count, then you probably don't have the power to eat souls."

Her laughter died down, and she tightened her lips, not speaking. Perhaps I was right. If one soulmate was powerless, the other soulmate could not use their soulmate magic. So, Rima would just be relegated to her siren call. I was risking a lot of lives on that hope.

"You cannot hide here forever," Rima spat, her eyes blazing with anger. "We will break your wards and set this town on fire. Then where will you run?"

They would try to destroy Hagerstown, but there were witches on our side that would be on rotational duty. Azrael and Queen Arwa had also brought in some fae and angels to strengthen our wards.

"Don't worry about where we go!" Phillip shouted. "Just take your flunkies and leave." Phillip raised his hand in the air and swiped it towards Rima.

Nothing happened.

She stomped a foot. "What are you doing?"

We were unnerving her. This was good.

Phillip smiled. "Wait for it..."

Moments later, we heard cries from a distance. Soon it

became so loud we could hear them above us. I looked up to see Lorenzo, Misandre, and several ghouls flying backwards towards the ward, screaming in anger and fear.

I smiled. It took some time, but it looked like the outcasting spell was finally taking effect. Our magic wasn't useless after all. It just took a long time.

I leaned towards Phillip. "How'd you know it was going to work at that moment?"

He put a hand in front of his face, eyes still on Rima. "I had no damn idea. Woulda been embarrassed as hell. But the fates are finally on our side. And I'm sending additional cohorts out of here too, so make room!" He shouted the last sentence.

I waved goodbye at them as they dropped to the ground in front of Rima, who jumped back in shock.

She looked down at Misandre and the others, rage filling her eyes. Throwing her head back, she let out an ear-piercing screech.

Before our eyes, every ghoul and fae in the surrounding area exploded. Black blood and gore splattered the shocked faces of Misandre and Lorenzo. I could only assume they were alive because Rima knew how to be selective with her magic. Rima, of course, remained clean with not a drop of blood hitting her fur.

She lowered her head and glared at Misandre and Lorenzo. "Fail me again, and next time it will be you who dies," she spat before looking back up towards us, her eyes crazed with anger. "We have been too nice, but that is now over. I will eat your souls and the souls of everyone you love, including your little boy, Brandon. You better pray no one leaves this town because as soon as they do, I will snatch their bodies, come inside and gut this place from the inside out. You are stupid children who have made a costly mistake." She then disappeared, taking Misandre and Lorenzo with her.

"Bye, bitch," Phillip said to the empty space they once occupied. He didn't look scared, but I was.

A cold streak of fear rose up my spine, dampening my spirits. I was doing better at psyching myself up, but they did a great job at truly scaring me.

~

We didn't waste time after Rima left. We immediately headed to New York to meet Ahmed's allies and work on our final plan of attack. I wanted to stay in Hagerstown after Rima's threat, but knew we needed to remove them from the fight. They were battle weary enough.

New York City wasn't as totally inhabitable as I thought. Although there were several unsafe pockets, there were still areas booming with life and fully equipped to beat back any creatures threatening to destroy their communities.

We teleported as a group to Manhattan, where Ahmed's friend resided. It was the six of us plus Phillip, Ahmed, Blake, and Azrael. Oh, and Gary, Poppy and Felix's dog, Dexter. No way were we leaving our pets to get killed back at home.

"Where exactly is this guy supposed to be?" I asked, looking around. I held Poppy's pet carrier tightly as she meowed her displeasure to anyone who would listen. I figured she was cold, and very uncomfortable swinging in the air. Not to mention the teleportation probably rattled her.

Ahmed wasn't sure of the exact vicinity of Nile's community; he just knew it was in Manhattan. So far, I was hoping it wasn't where we were currently located, which was an abandoned street full of crumbled buildings. There were no signs of human life for miles around. The streets were covered in several feet of snow, which would have been pretty if not for the empty buildings giving the area an ominous feeling.

"I sent him an email, and he told us to meet him here. He can be a bit paranoid, especially after hearing about these soulmates. Apparently, their reputation precedes them," Ahmed replied with a patient stance.

I didn't like being out in the open. It felt way too vulnerable.

"Where the hell is he?" Faith cried, doing a two step in the snowy street as she rubbed her gloved hands together. "It's colder than a witch's titty, as my granddad used to say."

I raised my eyebrows and giggled. "I've never gotten any complaints before about them being cold." It was a lame joke, but it did calm my nerves.

"I can vouch for that," Erik smirked, giving me a sideways glance.

I looked away and smiled. Erik wasn't the most humorous man, but when he did venture to joke or an act of goofiness, it made him all the more precious to me.

"Please don't talk about my sister's boobs. I swear I will throw up right here," Charles grumbled with a glare in our direction. "And it won't make any difference since this city already looks like shit."

"I didn't need to know all of that, either," Phillip muttered with a grimace.

The ground suddenly shook, and I stumbled forward. Erik reached out and grabbed my upper arm, steadying me with one hand.

"Is this an earthquake? Are there earthquakes in New York now?" Felix asked, throwing his hands out to the side to balance himself.

Anything was possible, certainly. Ever since magic returned, our environment was no longer predictable, at least not based on the standards of ten years ago.

Erik sniffed the air. "Not an earthquake."

Azrael looked up to the sky and then shot straight upwards, hovering high above us. Seconds later, the angel returned to the ground. "Not an earthquake," they agreed. "There are people riding a dinosaur headed our way."

I'd have to hear that again. "Come again?"

Azrael nodded in understanding. "There are several people riding what appears to be a brachiosaurus with large wings on their way here."

My mouth dropped open, dumbfounded. "Awesome." I looked over to Ahmed, who appeared unfazed.

"That would be him," he replied simply, hands clasped behind his back.

"I thought dinosaurs were extinct?" Felix asked, looking around at us with a confused face. "Did magic bring them back?"

Dexter, the golden retriever, barked and pulled at her leash, looking to escape. I didn't blame her as I strengthened my core to steady myself against what felt like an approaching stampede.

Poppy wasn't doing much better as she meowed loudly in her crate while Gary, the griffin, roared and flapped his wings as he ran around in circles.

"What are we talking about here?" Phillip shouted with raised brows. "I never heard of a brachiosaurus with wings."

"So, what is that then?" Charles asked, pointing in the direction behind Phillip.

We all looked his way. I brought a hand to my mouth in confused shock. It certainly kind of looked like a dinosaur. It was over 30 feet tall, except it was a splotchy purple and had long, scaled black wings and a horn on top of its head.

"That's not Barney," I whispered through my fingers.

Phillip stumbled back, falling in the thick snow.

"Well, that just seems excessive," Blake said, but she moved a little behind Charles. "He couldn't have taken a car or teleported?"

"Maybe he didn't have access to gas. It isn't super accessible now. And maybe he didn't have a witch on tap to get him an electric car," Lisa surmised, taking careful steps back.

"I feel like a horse, bike, or his own two feet could work," I suggested. Then again, where was the fun in that?

We all moved back as the dinosaur creature reached us.

"How is this being discreet?" Erik shouted, his hands balled into tight fists at his sides. "We're supposed to go into hiding, and this guy is showboating like some sort of asshat."

"My friend, relax!" said a man right before he slid down the tail of the beast and landed on his feet. He threw his hands in the air, and his accomplices gave whistles and claps like he just struck a perfect gymnastic landing.

Seeing him up close, I quickly realized it was the former pop star, Niles Davis. He looked every bit the rock star he once was. He had short blond, white highlighted hair that was perfectly styled. His eyes were the color of rubies beneath long, thick lashes. His skin was pale and shimmering. Like actual fine glitter or mica covered every inch of him. Well, the parts that I could see beneath his ankle length furry rainbow coat, which he wore open to expose a fitted white sweater with a deep V neckline and tight, black leather pants.

He looked to Erik with a 1000-watt, dimpled smile. "I'm only showing what arsenal I have up my sleeves. You stay with me, and you'll be well defended. Milo is just one of my warriors." He patted the leg of the beast before heading to us.

He held his arms open as he walked over to Ahmed. "My friend. Long time no see. I'm glad you've made it out well." They embraced in a hug as I turned slightly to eye his companions. They were all appropriately dressed for the winter, gazing at Niles with loving faces like obsessed fans, which they probably were.

Niles turned to the rest of us. "I'm very happy to meet you all. You're doing good work. I've been reading up on you on the internet," he stated, twirling a finger in our direction.

We'd made the news?

"Those first soulmates are scum, and I'm down to do anything to help the cause. Sorry for all the pomp and circumstance, but it's kinda who I am."

"I wanted to have your babies when I was younger," Lisa blurted out with glazed eyes.

He looked over to her and winked. "It's not too late."

Lisa giggled, putting her hands to her already reddening cheeks.

Faith fake gagged. "Eww, Lisa!" Faith exclaimed. "Thanks for stomping in with that thing." She pointed to the beast in disdain. "But can we get out of this cold and then do flirts, introductions, and an explanation of Barney?"

Niles made a gun symbol with his hand towards Faith and made a gunshot noise with his mouth. "Got it. And Milo is a beast. Not exactly sure what kind he is, but we found him in the water near the statue of liberty. Now he's my best bud." He clapped his hands and looked at us all. "Ok, now that I know you are all who you say you are, let me show you my town. You're gonna love it."

CHAPTER 20

Niles took us to a thriving section of Manhattan that was once the luxury district. Several streets surrounding the high-rise apartment where Niles resided were clean and active, as if there were no abandoned and destroyed areas further out. As with most areas, it was surrounded by a protective ward that not only prevented anyone not allowed from coming in, but also made the community invisible, much like Joo-won's area in Baltimore.

Behind the invisible veil were apartments, boutiques, restaurants, bars, an organic grocery store, a school, and on it went. Was Niles really the leader of all this? He didn't seem like the type to run a town.

He led us into his high rise, a glistening building consisting of sparkling windows on all sides, a wine cellar, gym, spa, rooftop pool and outdoor lounging area, library, restaurant, theater and party room. It was its own self-contained living space. I couldn't even fathom what it must have cost in the Pre-World, especially in this section of town.

"We've got a few spare apartments in my building if you want to stay here. How many do you need? We already have several prepared." Niles asked, walking us through the brightly lit entrance area filled with elegant seating, flat screen TVs, artwork, and a coffee and tea section. A woman at the concierge desk waved when she saw us, and Niles blew her a kiss.

"We could do two to an apartment comfortably, but work with less space if that's the only option," Erik replied, looking up at the ceiling and corners as if expecting something, or someone, to jump out at him. It was more likely that he was looking for surveillance.

"Not a problem, man." Niles looked back at the woman. "Hey, Gina, can you get someone to show our guests to their rooms so they can get situated?"

She nodded and got on the phone.

"Why do you glow?" Charles asked Niles with narrowed eyes.

Niles threw out his hands. "Magic. People like the idea of glitter vampires ever since those books came out. I just capitalized on it since actually becoming one. It increased my fan base. It's a gimmick, sure, but it works." He put his hands on his waist. "Now, might I suggest we give you a bit of a makeover."

"I don't want any highlights, man," Felix said, shaking his head.

Niles chuckled. "I'm suggesting something a bit more drastic than that. Although our people here and in the neighboring areas are our allies, there's no need causing a commotion or taking a risk. Ahmed mentioned that you needed to be in disguise. I think we should glamour you. I have a few fae here who can do it, along with you, Lisa."

Lisa rubbed her cheek in thought. "Oh, the possibilities, this could be so much fun!"

As long as it was temporary, I'd give it a go. We were just laying low until we were ready for our full attack, which would be sooner rather than later.

A man with long brown hair and a perfectly contoured

face appeared from the direction of the elevators.

Niles patted him on the shoulder. "Max, can you show our guests to their rooms?" He looked at us again. "I'll call my Fae, and they'll meet you on the guest floor. They'll be able to find you. Then, when you're all shiny and new, we can all meet at the restaurant in this building at 8."

I stepped forward. "Actually, I was hoping we could chat."

He touched my shoulder. "Amina, relax. You're safe now. We are honored to have you here." He smiled again, but it wasn't his fake Hollywood smile. It seemed genuine. "I know you don't know me beyond the songs I sang in the past, and I've heard about what you've been through. A lot of people have, from the internet. Enjoy today and tonight. We can talk strategy tomorrow."

I raised an eyebrow. "You're really going to help us fight?" I had assumed he was just helping us hideout and buy time until we figured out how to attack, but I had no expectations that he would fight alongside us.

He moved his hand away and opened his arms wide. "Of course! We're all going to help."

"Everyone?"

"Everyone able-bodied will. I don't think you know how many fans you have."

He was right. I didn't. "Fans?"

He gave another Hollywood wink. "You're a star, baby."

~

"Any preferences on what you want to look like?" Lisa asked me as we gathered in one of the guest apartments.

I shrugged, feeling awkward about it all. I never thought I was a supermodel, but I never considered looking like someone else, just a better version of me. "I don't care if you make me look like a man. This is weird."

She raised her eyebrows as her mouth dropped open. "Okay."

I threw out a hand. "I was just kidding. Please don't make me look like a man."

She smirked, and snapped both her fingers. An ice-cold tingle spread throughout my body, and I shivered. It felt like I was inside a freezer. When my body began to thaw back to normal, I straightened up.

"Are you done?"

Lisa smiled and nodded before moving on to Phillip.

I raced to the bathroom and looked in the mirror. I was no longer Amina. Instead, I was a tall, slightly less curvy woman with a complexion a couple of shades lighter than my own, long, honey-blond hair and light brown eyes. I looked like freaking Beyonce.

When I went back to the living room, I stood very confused as I looked at the strangers in front of me. Lisa and the other Fae were currently working on Blake, Charles, and Azrael. Ahmed walked up beside me, still his same old self. As a djinn, he had the power to do his own glamour, so he wouldn't need the others to help.

"Who is who?" I asked him.

Ahmed pointed to a tall, pale skinned man with shoulder length red hair. "Erik." He pointed to a woman with an athletic frame and a head of loose blond curls. "Faith." He moved his hand towards a man of average height with tanned skin, a buzz cut, and beard. "Felix." Finally, he pointed to a dark skinned man with long black locks. "Phillip."

"This is kind of freaky," I observed.

Ahmed nodded. "Indeed."

I turned slightly to him, and then jumped back as he looked at me with a smile from a foreign face. He was a few shades darker with a bald head.

"Thanks for the warning," I muttered.

Ahmed gave a slight shrug.

"Hey sis, I got to keep my mohawk, but it's bigger!" said a dark-skinned man with a blond curly mohawk and the voice of my brother.

A woman with a black pixie cut shook her head. Blake?

"I approve of this," said an androgynous looking person with tousled purple hair and the voice of Azrael.

"We're ready for our fashion shoot," Lisa said before snapping her fingers. Seconds later, a tall woman with pink hair cut into a short bob with bangs, looked back at us.

I suddenly thought of something. "Erik!" I cried to the red headed stranger already at the door. "You can't change into a jackal, or that'll give us away."

He nodded. "My were form is glamoured, too. I'll be a panther."

I surveyed the room again and sighed. This would hopefully buy us time, but I doubted much. We'd pissed off Rima, and she would make sure they got revenge. We just needed to end them before they had a chance.

~

"Is everyone looking at us, or you?" I asked Niles as we sat at a long rectangular table in the restaurant.

I'd never seen a restaurant in an apartment before. The place was really like a luxury hotel. The apartments put our best places in Silver Spring to shame. I couldn't even say I'd ever stayed in hotels this nice back in the Pre-World.

"Both, perhaps," Niles shrugged, sitting across from me, before taking a sip of something red that could have been blood. "You're new faces. That always attracts attention. If they knew who you really were, they'd be surrounding us."

"You said we had fans?"

He nodded, relaxing back in his chair. "Yes, you're all over the internet. I'm surprised you didn't know."

"Been kind of busy." I looked over to Erik beside me. "Did you know?"

He raised his eyebrows. "I'd heard things."

"We knew," Charles cut in, sitting further down the table. "We didn't tell you because we didn't want to stress you out. And unstable Mabel over there," he tilted his head across the table towards Phillip, "might freak out."

Phillip scoffed. "Unstable Mabel? I've just been going through some hard times, have a little compassion." He flipped his long locks over his shoulder.

It was so weird looking at the new Phillip. It was weird looking at everyone. I had to stop myself from frowning.

"The point is," Charles continued. "People appreciate all the good work you both are doing healing and powering up towns that were off the grid. You're like Oprah or something. Except no one knows what you look like."

That was good to hear. I hoped that made getting more allies easier.

"So, how did you come to be running this place?" Erik asked, leaning his elbows on the table. He kept looking around the restaurant with suspicious eyes. I could tell he wasn't comfortable with all this attention. Neither was I.

We were supposed to be on the run, not on display. It felt too exposed, and although Ahmed trusted Niles, I wasn't sure I did. Just because he was a former celebrity didn't make him a good guy, despite all his praise of us. If we began to look like we couldn't defeat the original soulmates, they might turn on us for self-preservation.

Niles sat back in his seat, tossing back an elbow. "When the magic came, I was on stage performing on a late night show for my album. Things went dark, and then next thing I knew, I wanted to bite people's necks." He gave out a chuckle, and I swear I heard a group of girls swoon behind me. "I'm not going to lie, the first couple of years were rough, but then I found my niche; a group of fans who wanted to be around me. Men and women. They pampered me, donated blood when I needed it. It was great. But then I realized I couldn't just sing and give people a nice time in the bedroom as my only contribution."

How very mature of him.

"I needed to pull my weight and take advantage of my situation. So, I decided to make something of this town again, or at least this small part of the town. My mom was a mayor back in Dallas, so I tried to channel her leadership qualities. I got fighters, doctors, handymen. Just kept collecting people with good spirits and abilities, whether they were regular humans or not."

"But what made them want to follow?" Erik pressed.

"Is what you're really asking me is whether I used my vampire magic on people to get them to follow me?"

Erik kept a blank face. "Is it so shocking a question?"

Niles waved a hand. "No, my dude. But celebrities have been voted into running things before. I honestly just surrounded myself with the right people. Behind all the rock star image, I'm not an idiot. And the glitter is part of the image. It doesn't mean I'm some guy who can't get my hands dirty." He waved two hands over his chest. "I'm in shape. I train all the time. I can defend these people, and ultimately, that's what matters." He gave a grin, showing his long vampire incisors.

The guy was definitely in shape, and he had obviously proven himself to all of the people in this town. Vampires, to my knowledge, couldn't glamour that many people.

A waitress came back to see how everything was, and instead of giving googly eyes to Nile as she had earlier, she gave an extra special grin to Erik. I had to practically scream to get her attention for some water. Even with his new look, he was still stupidly handsome. Why hadn't the fae who worked on him made him look like a troll? He went from hot brunette to hot redhead.

"We're good now, thanks," I said curtly, wanting to shoo her away.

She didn't look at me as she backed away, only gazed between Niles and Erik as she got farther and farther. She walked over to another waitress, and the two of them whispered to each other and giggled as they snuck looks at them.

I looked at Erik, who appeared totally oblivious to it all. Of course.

Niles chuckled, and I knew he was finding my reaction totally amusing. Glad someone was enjoying themselves.

I rolled my eyes. "So how many people are in your town?" I asked, trying my best to move past my growing annoyance.

"Not as many as you think. We are actually a collection of communities that are working together. There are only about 1,500 people under my leadership, but we share resources with about four other communities in this area. Those communities are much larger. And all the communities agree that we're team new soulmates. Well, one leader might have to be swayed, but I'm sure you can do it." He gave me a wink before dipping a French fry in ketchup. "I didn't glamour anyone. I'm just, not to toot my own horn, charismatic."

Some of the evilest people were charismatic. I wasn't going to get comfortable here anytime soon. Rima's threat had scared the snot out of me, and I didn't think I could ever be completely trusting until both she and Gedeyon were dead.

~

I looked up at the ceiling that evening in the bedroom of my guest apartment, Erik sitting at the edge of the bed and kicking his shoes off. "Did you get any word from Silver Spring regarding whether any souls have been taken?"

Erik scratched his beard, scrunching his face. "No. The town's cut off. Just like Hagerstown."

"Maybe we should sneak back and check things out."

"No, too much of a risk. We got Mae and Bill out. Carter and Raya stayed back."

I perched on my elbows and looked down at him, an unsettling feeling in my stomach. "I'm not going to sleep until I have a plan. I'm thinking we all power-up, contact our allies, and march into town. If my magic muting spell worked, we can't risk losing this opportunity. It could wear off. Or they could find a spell to break my magic."

He glanced over at me, balancing back on his arms. "You think we're ready? I feel like we still haven't reached our maximum bond. Just in my gut."

Amina, why are you running from me, Gedeyon's voice boomed in my head.

Erik's reply was drowned out in my head, and I sat up, looking around the room. It felt like Gedeyon was right behind me. We weren't traceable by the soulmates, thanks to Arwa's magic, but that didn't mean they couldn't communicate with us.

I stayed completely still as if my lack of movement would make him go away.

"Amina, everything okay?" Erik asked in a careful voice.

I didn't respond, still listening out for Gedeyon.

You'll just make things worse for you in the end, Gedeyon continued. *But fine, rest for now. When we find you, it will not be good for you. We tried hard to be kind, but it seems you don't like kindness. You're not as smart as I believed you to be.*

I balled my hands into fists, willing him away. "How does it feel being powerless?"

He chuckled in my mind. You didn't take my powers. You just made a minor dent. Nothing we can't move past.

What did that mean? What kind of dent did I make?

Something worked, but I knew he wouldn't be giving up that information.

You'll kill your friends. You do know that, right? You won't stay the way you are. It is inevitable. They will stand in your way, and you will have no choice. Is that what you want?

"I just want you to go. I'm not scared of you anymore. And you know it."

Your continued stupidity will be your demise. I could help you. I could help you both. Tell me where you are. I won't even harm your friends. You cannot win this.

"Get out of my head!" I squeezed my eyes shut and began chanting a blocking spell. I'd put one up before, but it had to be strengthened.

Gedeyon laughed in my mind. *I will never leave you alone. You are my child.*

He suddenly appeared before me, causing me to scramble back, smacking against the wall. I swung my hand out, and he grabbed my wrist and steadied me. He began to blur before my eyes, his outline vanishing until all I saw was Erik in front of me, holding my wrist. He looked at me with wide concerned eyes.

"Amina?" he asked.

I looked around the room and wrenched free of Erik. "Gedeyon was just here. He was talking to me through telepathy. They found us."

"I don't think they did. He's just messing with you."

I turned to glare at him. "How do you know that? Do you really want to take that chance? That leader who isn't sure about us could have let them into town."

He tilted his head and narrowed his eyes, looking at me as if he were thoroughly confused. He probably thought I was crazy, which only pissed me off further. "We added our own wards, remember? If someone tries to break in that we don't know about we'd feel it. And we're all taking shifts to stay alert. Azrael's on alert now."

I pursed my lips trying to contain my anger. Panic threatened to overtake me, but I'd done the work to calm myself. I wasn't going to fall apart in a heap now. My panic attacks were a part of my life, but they would no longer rule me. I closed my eyes, inhaled a deep breath, counted to ten, and let out the air before speaking. "I know the plan, Erik. It doesn't mean it's full proof. I know what I heard."

Erik took a step towards me. "Don't let him get in your head. We're so close now."

I closed my eyes. I didn't hear any more from Gedeyon, but it didn't mean that my blocking spell worked. Erik didn't believe me. Fine, he didn't have to. I knew what I heard and saw.

"Amina, just rest. I can stay up."

I waved him away and went to stand by the window, looking out at the snow falling onto the street. I hugged myself, still shaken from Gedeyon's visit, but I was in control. "If you want to stay here, that's fine. But I think Phillip and I are going to have to leave. It's too dangerous for us to be around you all. Whether you believe me or not, Gedeyon is getting closer, and I can't risk him controlling us and hurting you all."

Erik gave me a pained look, and I tried my best not to be affected by it. "Why do you always want to leave me?"

"You should talk, Mr. I'm-going-to-go-live-in-the-woods."

"That was different."

I sucked my teeth. "Of course, it is. You're always right."

I heard him walk closer to me. "I'm not always right."

"Then listen to me for once." The control I thought I had on my emotions was threatening to break. I was getting agitated, and I felt like fighting. I wanted to hurt someone. I wanted to hurt him. He didn't believe me. He thought I was stupid and naïve, just as he did when we first met.

Erik stood beside me and sighed. "I listen to you, always.

I'm just saying let's not run off until we have a plan of where we are going. We are more vulnerable out there alone."

I wanted to say something about him not feeling too vulnerable when he was living alone in the damn woods, but I'd said enough on that. Instead, I moved away from him and sat on the edge of the bed. Poppy came out from under the bed and rubbed her head against my leg.

Erik crouched down in front of me and searched my eyes. "Why are you mad at me?"

I shook my head and picked at a loose thread on the bed. I was mad, and I couldn't figure out why. I just knew I wanted to yell and make someone else angry besides me.

"Everywhere we go, women fawn over you. It's annoying. Even in this glamoured state, they love you."

Erik lightly plucked my kneecap. "How many places have you and I gone?" He grinned at me, but I rolled my eyes, not feeling playful. "We've only been to Hagerstown, Silver Spring, and here."

"So, that's enough. I've had to fight on two occasions because of you."

"Now you're making me feel guilty."

I stuck my chin out. "Good."

He stood up and rubbed at his eyes, looking suddenly weary. "But, you know, it's not like you don't have a soulmate I have to sit back and tolerate. And unlike you, I don't have any feelings for those other women."

I froze, and looked at him with raised brows. "I don't have feelings for Phillip."

He moved his hands away from his face and twisted his lips. "Lie to yourself, but don't lie to me. I've seen how you look at him. When he was hurt, you seemed broken."

I looked away from his heavy gaze and down at my fingers to avoid those accusatory eyes. He was wrong, but I knew he wouldn't believe my words. "Phillip was hurting. He's my friend."

"I'm just a barrier for you two. Don't feel obligated to stay with me just because we got together first."

Where the hell was this coming from? "Do you really think I'm with you out of some sense of obligation? You should know better than that."

"Then if I said to stay away from him after all this is over, would you?"

I glanced up at him, confused. Would I? Could I? I'd gone from liking Phillip to hating him to liking him again. However, it wasn't romantic this time. Erik had to know that. This line of questioning didn't seem like him. He was usually so confident. Of course, I'd started it all by talking about his fangirls, so we were both being silly tonight.

"I'm not sure that's a fair thing to ask of me, Erik."

Erik snorted, and stepped away. "Of course not. I just have to sit back and wait until one day..."

I raised a brow. "One day, what?"

He looked down at me with dead eyes. "One day you run off with him. Let's face it. You and I are just biding time."

I tilted my head and frowned. "Whoa, where is this coming from?"

He shrugged. "It's what I think. It's what everyone thinks." Who the hell was everyone? Had the others been talking about more than just putting Phillip and me down if we got out of hand?

"Is that so. Well, if you think that, then why are you with me?"

"Maybe I'm just trying not to rock the boat until after this is all over. We have enough to stress about."

My heart could have fallen out of my chest. He was basically saying he was with me to appease me so I'd stay focused on the mission. What kind of weak woman did he think I was? Had he always been thinking this?

"I can't believe you just said that. You're a real asshole;

you know that? Don't do me any favors by staying with me. I'll make it out all right," I sneered.

"Of course, you will, you'll have Phillip!"

"And you'll have your harem of women."

Erik ran his hand through his red mane, seeming puzzled when his hands weren't immediately freed, clearly forgetting he had long hair now. "Woman, for the last time, I–"

There was a knock at the door. I jumped up to answer it, but Erik whizzed by me and looked through the peephole of the front door.

"Of course," he grumbled before opening the door. "What do you want?"

Phillip leaned back with wide eyes. "What did I do?"

"Breathe," Erik spat, walking away from the door.

"Ignore him," I said to Phillip, waving him in.

Phillip cautiously walked into the apartment, looking between Erik and me. "Lover's quarrel?"

Erik growled, but didn't speak.

"What's going on, Phillip? I asked, crossing my arms.

"Seeing as we have a bit of downtime, I was reminded again that our friends in Ireland are still missing. We need to find them."

"I agree, but how can we do that?"

"Niles has some powerful witches here. Maybe they can help us tap into our bond to find them. I'm not sure they're stronger than our witches, but it's worth a try. Might be easier now that we know how to power boost."

"Of course, you want to bond," Erik said, hanging his head to the side.

Of course, were his favorite words tonight. Seems he expected everything.

I placed a hand over my eyes and tilted my head back. "Phillip, we already tried that, and it didn't work. I really don't think these witches are any stronger."

"Well, we didn't try to reach Liz. We already know Mae

connected with her when we were banished via telepathic dreams."

"And Mae was unable to reach her this time around. What are you getting at?" Erik spat.

Phillip let out a breath and crossed his eyes, looking as if he was trying his best to hold in his annoyance. "We didn't use our soulmate magic to connect with her. I don't know if we really can, but it's something we haven't tried before."

I ran my hand from my eyes to my cheek, thinking. "It's worth a try."

"Great." Phillip grabbed my hand, and before I could say anything ,Erik yanked it away. Phillip gave him an incredulous look, face twisted in angry confusion. "What is wrong with you, man?"

Erik's eyes blazed with equal anger, his jackal eyes glowing from within. "You don't need to touch her to connect."

Phillip snorted. "Uh, actually I do, and you know that. What the hell is going on with you?"

Erik pointed at him. "I don't like the fact that you're always around her. You'll find any reason you can to touch her. She's always coming to your rescue like you're some damn damsel in distress. Let her rest for a fucking minute."

Phillip gave him an icy grin and looked away. "I don't know if it's that time of the month for you or something, but you need to calm down. Amina's my mate, and I will always be around. If you can't man up and handle it, then step aside."

Jesus, why? I rubbed my temples. "Phillip, please don't poke the bear, jackal, panther."

However, it was too late. Erik stepped forward and shoved Phillip in the chest. "I'll show you what manning up looks like." His jackal incisors lengthened, protruding from his mouth.

Phillip looked down at his chest and then up at Erik. He stepped forward, a frown on his face. "Do something then."

I threw my hands out. What was wrong with these guys? What was with all the show of testosterone? This wasn't like them at all. I knew I'd set the course of the night with my own foul attitude, which I still couldn't shake, but I didn't mean for it to transfer on to Erik and then Phillip.

"Both of you settle down. Neither of you has to prove anything."

Erik threw a hand out in front of my face. "It's not about you, Amina. Stay out of it," he replied, still glaring at Phillip.

I looked at his hand thoroughly perplexed. Had he tried to dismiss me like some peon? Ok, well maybe he had just lost his mind. "I beg to differ." I moved his hand out of the way.

"Settle down, *mi corazon*," Phillip began. "You're cute and all, but it's about more than you. Erik's been a dick since day one. So, I'm about to teach him some manners."

Erik made a come here motion with his hands. "Please, go ahead and teach me some manners."

Phillip touched my shoulder and gave me a patient smile. "*Mi corazon,* step back. I don't want you to get hurt."

"I'm sick of you calling her that!" Erik shouted before punching Phillip in the face.

I gasped as Phillip stumbled back. He touched his lip and looked down at the blood that covered his fingers in disbelief. He looked back up at Erik and tackled him to the ground. The two wrestled on the floor, punching and kicking at each other like some UFC fighters from the Preworld.

How the hell had we gotten here? Something was very wrong.

I threw my hands up in the air, and both men separated and flew against opposite walls.

They struggled against my magic, kicking their legs in the air and attempting to push from the wall.

"I don't know what's gotten into all of us, but we *cannot* fight each other," I shouted.

"He started it," Phillip cried.

"What are you, ten?" Erik shouted back.

"Erik," I began, "You can't fight Phillip. If you're mad at me, then be mad at me. I know that I've put you in some awkward situations with Phillip."

"It's not like he hasn't done the same to you," Phillip countered.

I gave an exasperated sigh. Suddenly, I was feeling very tired. "Really, Phillip?"

"Truth hurts," he muttered with a shrug.

Erik shook his head and grimaced. "You know, I don't have to put up with this shit, Amina."

"Then don't," Phillip cut in, attempting to lean forward. "Go get one of your groupies or one of Seth's surviving left-overs and live happily ever after."

"Phillip, shut up." I narrowed my eyes at Erik. "You're right, Erik. You don't have to put up with any of this. I'm sure you're regretting ever making me your mate. And quite honestly, right now, I am too."

I released my magical hold over both of them, and they tumbled to the floor. "I don't need this shit right now. There are people trying to kill me and our friends. Both of you check your egos. Now, I'm going with Phillip to try to conjure Liz, and then I'm going to stay with Lisa for the night. Watch my cat."

I walked to the front door and flung it open, Phillip trailing behind me. I half expected Erik to say something to make it better, but he didn't. Maybe he wanted me gone. Maybe he really was tired of the whole soulmate pseudo-love triangle. I wouldn't blame him if he was over it all. I certainly was.

The worst part was, I didn't have time to focus on making it better. I had a missing town to find.

CHAPTER 21

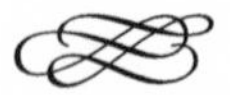

We'd tried all night to connect to Liz to no avail, and I did as I said, crashing in Lisa's room with a heavy heart. That night, I'd done something I hadn't done in a long time. I cried myself to sleep. Stress, fear, exhaustion, worry. It all came tumbling together in my mind, and no meditative breathing would help. Therefore, when I got word that Liz was in Phillip's room the next day, I almost tripped running from Lisa's room to Phillip's place.

She must have seen my look of exhaustion mixed with gratefulness, because she didn't say a word as she opened her arms to embrace me in a tight hug. The older woman looked regal as ever, with her long white hair hung in a braid down her back.

"I'm glad you're okay," I stated, finally released from her embrace.

"Yes, yes, I'm quite well," Liz replied, smiling at the others. Phillip, Blake, and Azrael were all seated comfortably in the living room. How long had she been here?

"How did you get in, by the way?"

She clasped her hands together. "I waited patiently in the vicinity that you alerted me to in your message. Someone eventually showed up. Then they had Ahmed validate that I was good. He told me to tell you he was gathering the others, by the way."

He was always the efficient one. "I'm sorry to get right to it, but do you know what happened to the Dublin town?"

She smiled. "Yes, I do. A seer friend had a premonition that the first soulmates would attempt to come for your allies. We had no idea when and we definitely didn't know they'd be showing up at your door so soon, or at all. However, I decided that the best thing to do would be to hide the town."

"Hide it? Like, make it invisible like this place?"

She wagged a finger in front of her, like an instructor. "Not exactly. I, along with some other powerful allies, relocated it."

"Oh, so you moved everyone out of town to some hiding place?"

Liz's eyes twinkled. "In a sense." She was being coy with us. "Let's just say that the town is still together and you won't be able to find them, as I'm sure you know by now. Even if you try a location spell. Sorry we had to deceive you earlier but it was for the best."

I hugged myself feeling a bit relieved. Our Dublin friends were safe, Brandon was safe, and Hagerstown was safe. We just had to check in on Silver Spring. However, for now, I would be happy with just this bit of good news. I needed something.

"Tell Ed when I see him, I'm going to kick his ass for not telling us he was leaving," Phillip growled, crossing his arms as if he were upset, but his lips were turned slightly up, and I was sure he was as relieved as me.

Liz walked to the couch and sat down. "Ah, overseas teleporting takes a lot of an old lady," she said. She patted the seat next to her and tilted her head for me to sit beside her.

I did as she nonverbally requested, still feeling a bit

soothed by her presence. The others, sans Erik still, arrived and took seats around the living area. We then began to recap all that had happened since the original soulmates' arrival.

When Erik finally arrived, I stiffened and looked away, unable to meet his eyes. I looked to Liz, who met my eyes with a curious face. She tapped her chin and looked around the room, studying us.

"How's the bonding coming along with everyone? Now more than ever, we all must be strong together."

We all averted our eyes from her, looking at every possible uninteresting part of the room instead. I found a nice bottom of the bookshelf to occupy my eyes. I didn't want to tell her that the bonding had come to a halt last night due to a silly argument. It felt like a setback, and I didn't understand why I was feeling this way.

"That good, huh? Erik, are you bonding well with the Six and your mate?"

I held a breath, looking down at my hands, which were currently tightly clasped in my lap. What would he say? If it was something hurtful, I might lunge at him and punch him in the stomach, or run out of the room crying. I was feeling a bit unstable right now, so it was anyone's game.

"It's going fine," he answered simply, sitting down at the dining room table adjoining the living room space.

"Amina?" Liz pried.

"Fine, everything's fine," I squeaked out.

She pursed her lips and looked to Phillip. "Well?"

He raised his brows and shoved his hands in his pockets. "Things are going fantastically." He gave her a cheesy TV host smile.

Liz lowered her thin brows. She was clearly not buying what we were selling. "You all are lying to me. Why is that?"

No one spoke. Liz put her hands on her hips and looked

around the room before her eyes settled on Felix. "Young man!"

He pointed to himself. "Me?"

"Yes, dearie."

Felix looked around the room with quizzical eyes and a smile. He looked like he was wondering if he was being set up for a trap, but none of us gave anything away, including Azrael who sat on the floor near the floor to ceiling window looking very amused.

Liz went on. "How are you all bonding? Are you closer than ever now?"

He cleared his throat. Felix was freaking George Washington. He couldn't lie even if you paid him. "Well, for the most part, yes. I mean, we have a few arguments here and there. Like Faith is being a pain about me helping my future wife back in Nevada."

"Are you kidding me?" Faith cried, throwing her hands in the air. "Thanks for throwing me under the bus, butthead. I am just concerned that you are so busy helping someone else that you are neglecting the greater mission, which is to bond with us as Liz is saying." She batted her eyelashes in the most girlish way I had ever seen from her. It screamed fake and not to be trusted.

More importantly, I had no clue Faith and Felix were fighting this bad. I took cold comfort knowing I wasn't the only one currently set on angry.

Liz lifted her chin and looked around the room, but I couldn't get a read on her. "So, the answer is no. You are not getting along, and everything certainly isn't fine. I can feel the negative energy just simmering in the air." Liz waved a hand in front of her face. "I can barely breathe."

Well, wait, who else in the group was a mess? Five out of eight was enough.

Charles raised a hand, leaning on the counter to the open

kitchen with a short glass of brown liquid. "Well, I'll give you a recap."

"Soda?" I asked.

He waved the drink towards me. "Whiskey. Anyway," he said loudly before I could judge him in a motherly tone. "You see, Felix and Faith's issue. Lisa, Blake, and I have a situationship." Lisa let out a loud sigh, but Charles went on. "Erik, Phillip, and Amina also have a triangle thing going on along with Erik's fake sister-wives."

Liz reared back with raised brows. "Anything else?"

Yes, there was something else. Something that had been nagging at the back of my mind for a while now, which I was avoiding bringing up with the group, but no time was better than the present.

"Yes," I started, crossing my arms. "No one really trusts Phillip and I."

The room filled with objections, but I shook my head. "We heard you and Mae talking about not trusting us and taking us out if we got like the original soulmates."

"We would never do that, sis," Charles interjected.

I shrugged. "Maybe you should."

Phillip lifted a finger and leaned towards me. "Say what, now?" he questioned.

"If we look like we're becoming some murderous egomaniacs, we could be really hard to fight if you wait around. Get us when we're still newbies. I don't want to be like them. Eating souls and conquering people."

"I'm not certain I agree with your proposal," Phillip said, straightening up. "I don't want to die, and if you all are going to plot and scheme behind me, don't think I'm going to roll over. That goes for you too, Blake."

"I haven't talked about killing you, sweetheart," Blake replied with wide eyes. "I have your back all the way."

Liz was now standing and looked seriously annoyed with us. "Alright, dearies!" she shouted. "All this bickering will simply not do. Your power, in part, comes from your friendship and bonding. This arguing isn't helping. I think I know what's going on." She waved her hands in front of her and closed her eyes, and we all remained silent for several seconds. When she opened her eyes again, a look of concern filled her eyes. "I felt a darkness when you all arrived, but I assumed it was due to Phillip's dark spell. However, it felt way too potent, and I knew that Amina had dampened that spell. Now I know better. You all are wrapped in the evil eye."

The evil eye? How could it – Gedeyon. He had probably put the curse of the evil eye on us at some point before we left town, and it had simmered in us until now or even lay dormant until he activated it after our escape. Perfect timing for him. They were always one step ahead of us.

"You think Gedeyon did this?" Erik asked, crossing his arms.

Liz nodded. "Very few beings have the power of the evil eye and can control it in the way that he can. It would make the most sense for it to be him."

"He contacted me last night through his astral projection magic. After that, everything went really south." I was livid. I was riding such a high and didn't even know he was setting another trap for me. However, at least we knew before the proverbial shit really hit the fan.

"I'm sure it wasn't a coincidence."

Faith stomped a foot and swore. "This is so petty," Faith grumbled. "He's making us argue like a bunch of teenagers in an old TV drama. He's some big bad, powerful guy, and that's how he's going to exert his power?"

Liz shook her head as she sat back down next to me. "Oh, I'm sure he's doing much more than that, dearie. This is just an extra bit of insurance, I suppose, and it's working as far as I can see. It's certainly sidetracking you. The worst thing the lot of you can do is split up, and your curse is only going to get worse as time goes on."

"What could happen?" Erik asked. He looked exhausted. I wondered if he slept any after I left last night. Maybe he still cared.

"Many things," Liz replied, interrupting my thoughts. "You hate each other and refuse to work together to use your powers to defeat the soulmates. Or even worse, you use your powers to destroy each other."

"Could we really hurt each other?" Lisa asked in a quiet voice, wringing her fingers together. She looked genuinely worried, and I didn't blame her.

"Of course, you can." Liz looked over to her with a sympathetic smile. "None of us, including you, are all powerful. We are all at risk of darkness taking over, and the evil eye can bring misfortune your way."

"It's been doing that already, hasn't it?" I said, looking down at my feet. "We've been run out of our positions and our home, and Hagerstown was attacked. We need to leave here, if that's the case. It's too dangerous for the people living here. Even if we are hidden, it's not enough."

"Well, now we have to get rid of that evil eye." Liz smiled, but her smiles didn't always mean good things. I was coming to understand they were her attempts to put us at ease for something difficult or unpleasant. I was betting the cure for the evil eye would be both.

CHAPTER 22

"There are a few things we could try," Liz explained. "However, realizing that Gedeyon is ancient, and therefore powerful, it might not be easy."

Surprise, surprise.

"Some people cure the evil eye with mirrors, touch, an egg, hand gestures, or even charms. I've never seen so many people affected by it at once, and I've only actually cured it one time, about four years ago. It was my first and only case. Ireland doesn't get a lot of evil eye curses. However, I think your bonds might make this more successful if we use that to our advantage." She clapped her hands together. "Ok, let's begin!"

Liz had Azrael grab a large floor to ceiling mirror and place it against the living room wall. "Right, have a seat on the floor in a circle in front of the mirror, dearies," she ordered. "Grab hands to form a link."

Ahmed and Azrael stood to the side, Liz having determined that they were unaffected. We'd cleared out the center of the living room, I grabbed Charles' hand, and Lisa grabbed the other. I tried not to notice that Erik had grabbed the hands of Blake and Felix.

Was he still mad at me? We were all cursed. This wasn't us. I had to keep telling myself that. At least, I hoped it was the truth.

"Clear your mind of negative thoughts and feelings," Liz went on, standing in the middle of our circle.

Easier said than done, but I tried. I thought of my mom and dad. I wished they had survived the Sickness, but the memories that I had of them were good ones, and I could narrow my energy on those thoughts, pushing away my inner turmoil about Erik for the time being.

"Close your eyes."

We did as we were told, and seconds later, I heard her mutter unintelligible words. I felt a slight wind like she was flinging her hands in the air. I'd have to ask her about the gestures and words she was using for future reference. Minutes passed, and I soon felt her cool hand on my forehead as she continued to chant. She moved past me and on to Charles, where I assumed she did the same with him.

I didn't feel any better, just a little silly. However, I kept my mind on my family to push away the intruding doubt. In this particular memory, we were all on vacation to Myrtle beach, dining al fresco at my dad's favorite seafood spot. Charles and I were maybe 14 and 15 at the time and were begging our parents to let us walk the boardwalk after dinner, to which they ultimately agreed. We would then spend the earlier part of that night going to arcades and a haunted house. I didn't hang much with my younger brother socially during high school. I was too cool for such things, of course, but that weekend was one of my best weekends with him to this day.

I smiled and gave Charles' hand a light squeeze, which he did not return.

"No, no, no. This simply will not do," Liz cried.

I opened my eyes and looked up at her as she threw her

hands up and sighed. "If you're going to connect, it must be meaningful."

"Connecting?" I asked. "I thought we were just curing ourselves of the evil eye."

"Yes, yes, dearie, that's all part of it. But this is not your basic evil eye. It is much more potent. I am powerful, but I have my limits. You all must pull from your own inner strength, and I don't mean the physical. Use your bonds. That's why I ask you to clear your mind of all negative thoughts."

I thought I'd done just that. I was in a good space.

"Amina, are you mad at Lisa?"

I'd gotten over any anger I had at Lisa some time ago. Turns out, sending me to Ireland was the right thing to do. "No. We're good now."

Liz rubbed her temple, closing her eyes, and rested the back of her free hand on her hip. "Then why are you holding her hand, sweetie?"

Because she was one of the few people in the circle I wasn't pissed at, or awkward with, right now. Somehow I didn't feel like that was the answer Liz would want to hear, so I kept my lips pressed tightly together.

"All of you are playing it safe. You won't fully heal if you don't address the negative energy between you. You lot, in particular, have been cursed. And you've been cursed with a purpose. It was foolish of me to think I could do this all on my own when I have the Six and two mate pairings right here." She looked back at Ahmed and Azrael. "Also, I will need the lovely angel and djinn to stand beside me to assist. I am a wee bit knackered, but I am going to persevere, and I'll be needing your energy." She looked around at us again. "Right then, you," she pointed to Erik. "Come hold Amina's free hand." Erik got up and moved towards me. He grabbed my hand without so much as a glance. It felt unusually cold.

"And Phillip, you grab Erik's hand."

Phillip leaned back with wide eyes.

"Today, dearie. Let's move." She waved him over.

Erik growled.

Phillip paused. "I'm not walking towards anything that growls."

Liz looked to Erik in disapproval, her lips pursed together. "Young man, move past your anger, for now, so that I may do my job. I really shouldn't have to say this, but no growling, please."

Erik rolled his eyes, but made no more noise.

Liz gave him an appreciative smile before looking at Charles. "You, go hold Phillip's hand." She pointed to Blake. "Hold Amina's and Lisa's hands. Faith, you hold Lisa's hand, and Felix, you hold Faith's and Charles' hands."

Charles cleared his throat. "Excuse me ma'am. Uhm, shouldn't I be holding Lisa's hands since we aren't on the best of terms?"

Liz chuckled. "Oh no, sweetie, what is going on with you, to my understanding, is beyond the reach of the evil eye. That you must work out on your own. Just as Amina and Phillip must work their matters out on their own." She gave me a wink.

I decided the fact that Erik and I were made to hold hands meant that she believed our current tense situation was more the curse than actual feelings, and that gave me a little peace.

"Alright dearies, let's begin again. Ahmed mirror my hand movements and gestures, and Azrael, say a Christian prayer. I will not leave until I cure these lovely, but foolish children."

~

The whole endeavor took an hour, and Liz determined that she felt less darkness radiating from us, but that the next day would give us a better sign. She mentioned something about needing oil and water to test us.

I looked around the room and saw Felix picking Faith up in a giant bear hug. Charles gave Phillip an appreciative handshake. Blake and Lisa looked at each other with less annoyance than usual. Only Erik and I stood awkwardly next to each other like strangers.

I cleared my throat. Someone had to break this silence. "Feeling like becoming BFFs with Phillip now?" I said in a joking manner, hoping he would take the olive branch.

He snorted. "Oh yeah, we'll go get friendship bracelets with the half heart charms. Don't be jealous, okay?"

I looked up at him, and he gave me a slight smile before tilting his head towards the front of the apartment. "Let's go back to our place."

We excused ourselves and walked back to our temporary apartment in silence. Once there, Erik led me to the couch, so I sat down.

"Did you sleep well last night?" I asked, stifling the sarcasm in my voice.

"Of course not." He glared at me then looked away. "The love of my life wasn't with me. How could I be happy?"

I smiled at that. Even though I now knew Gedeyon was behind our argument, it didn't mean it didn't hurt. I took cold comfort in knowing that he was in pain because of our fight too.

He tapped his knee lightly against the side of mine. "I'm sorry, Amina."

I nodded. "I'm sorry, too. I know you're in an awkward situation with this soulmate thing."

"I can say the same for you, with me being alpha over the pack."

And ridiculously good-looking so that you attract a female fanbase everywhere you go. I didn't add that part as I didn't think it would move the conversation anywhere positive.

I grabbed his right hand. It felt warmer this time. "I don't like fighting with you, Erik. It hurts my heart." I looked down at our hands. I felt corny as soon as I said that, but it was true. I loved him, and as much as I wanted to fight against it, I needed him.

He gave me a pained look. "What am I going to do with you when you say things like that?" He pulled me to him and kissed my forehead.

"Can we just forget yesterday and move forward?" I leaned my head on his shoulder.

"I don't think we can, Mina." His voice sounded heavy and sad. It scared me.

I sat upright and looked at him, but didn't speak. His eyes looked tired, but there was something haunting in them. I'd never seen that look before. The sides of his mouth turned down, and for a moment, I thought he might cry. Something broke in my heart.

"What's going on?" I touched his arm, wanting him to look at me, but he didn't.

"Mina, we should end this."

My heart stopped for a moment. At least it felt like it. Dizziness overtook me, and I moved away from him. Was Gedeyon's evil eye still hovering over us now? "I don't understand."

"I think we should break it off, just for now. Until this soulmate business is settled. You and Phillip need to focus on your bond…and your feelings."

"I don't–"

"You do." Erik glanced down at me with lowered lids. "I see how you care for him. That day at the restaurant–"

"He was in trouble."

"Then at the hotel."

"When he was chained up and almost died? You can't blame me for that."

Erik shook his head, biting his lower lip. "I can't blame you for any of it. You've been honest about everything. Which is why I know what I'm suggesting is right. I'm in the way."

"Erik–"

He raised a hand to stop me. "Let me finish. The two of you are meant to do good together. Blake and I are distractions. At least right now. It makes sense now why Lisa had to send you both away back then. We will keep doing what we're meant to do but our relationship can't interfere with your soulmate bond."

I balled my hands into tight fists. Losing Erik was not how I wanted this to go. "This isn't what I want."

"It's not what I want either, Mina. But we have to look beyond our needs."

I shoved him in the shoulder and moved to get up, but he grabbed my wrist and pulled me to him.

"Let me go. That's what you want. You want to see other people, then just say that. Don't give me this bullshit about breaking up for the greater good."

Erik moved to face me, placing both of his hands gently on the side of my face. I'd read it right, his eyes were watering this time. I don't think I'd ever seen him cry before. It scared me. "I don't want anyone else. This is killing me inside. I love you, Amina. Don't ever doubt that."

"I hate you for doing this."

He rested his forehead on mine. "I'm sorry. I'm sorry."

"Don't do this to us. Loving you and being a soulmate aren't mutually exclusive."

Erik scooted closer to me. "I know, but if I don't let you go, I'll never forgive myself. Especially if we don't win this.

You have to know this is killing me, Amina. Every time I see you look at Phillip or hear about the soulmates, it tears at my heart. But you aren't meant to be just mine." He grabbed my hand and brought it to his lips, kissing the knuckle.

I snatched it away and quickly got up to walk to the bedroom, the ever-present feeling of exhaustion still with me. I collapsed on the bed, still fighting to hold in the tears threatening to betray me.

I soon heard Erik come into the bedroom, and he lay beside me, pulling me into his arms. I stiffened. He just held me tighter to him, and eventually I relaxed my shoulders, unable to fight any longer with the little energy I did have left. "There was a time when you accused me of always wanting to run from you. Even if it was for the greater good. How's this any different?"

"It's not." I felt the hurt in his voice in just those two words, but it didn't make things better.

"Do you think by holding me, it'll make me hate you less?"

I felt him pull me closer as he tapped his chin to the back of my head. "Don't hate me. Please."

I stiffened. Had he ever said please to me before? I couldn't recall. He was a prideful man, but not in a way that made him weak. I was in pain as well, but I knew, deep down, that he wasn't doing this in a cowardly attempt to make breaking up with me less his fault. I honestly didn't believe he planned to go running after the line of women who wanted a shot with him. And yet, none of this made me happier.

I wanted to turn to see his face, to see the love still there, but he held me still.

"I want to see you."

"No. Just...just let me hold you just like this for a while. I know that I'm being selfish."

I relaxed again and closed my eyes. We sat in silence for a long while, my mind numb with too many emotions. It felt wasteful to be so caught up in my feelings at a time like this. I should have been with the others strategizing on how to defeat the soulmates. Not that we had any ideas so far.

"Spend every waking moment with him, after today. Don't worry about me. I want us to win this. I want you strong." He kissed the back of my head. "And then, after all of this, I want you to come back to me."

I sighed. If we survived the fight, coming back to him would be the easy part. The hard part was now.

CHAPTER 23

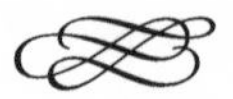

I stood in a field of wildflowers reaching far and wide all around me. A rainbow of colors spread across a green plain underneath a sunlight sky. I closed my eyes and smiled, spreading my arms out as I felt the heat of the sun's rays touch my skin. It was so warm and peaceful here. I heard the slight music of birds chirping and the hum of cicadas far off. No other sounds of life surrounded me. It was just me and nature, and I let the peace wash right over me.

"Beautiful, isn't it," came a female voice interrupting me.

I opened my eyes and saw a woman standing several feet away from me. She was young, perhaps her early twenties, with freckled, alabaster skin and waist length reddish blond hair underneath a crown of wildflowers. She wore a long white slip dress and nothing else. She gave me a smile, and her green eyes betrayed an age much older than her face.

"Hi, Amina. I'm Tilda," she said in an accent I couldn't quite place. It sounded very northern European. Perhaps Swedish or Icelandic?

"Hi. Do I know you?" I asked.

She shook her head, keeping the smile on her face. "No,

but we know you." She looked at a man who stood beside her with the same gentle smile.

Had he been there before? How had I not noticed him? He was a thin Asian man with shoulder-length black hair and light brown eyes behind thin, wire-rimmed glasses. He looked just as young as Tilda and was dressed in what appeared to be traditional ancient Japanese attire. He bowed his head and touched his chest. "It is a pleasure to meet you. I am Riku."

"What are we doing here?" Phillip said, suddenly appearing beside me.

I jumped slightly. Suddenly my peaceful field was becoming too crowded.

"This is the first time any of us have ever been able to reach others," Tilda began. "We are so happy that it has finally worked. Maybe the both of you can make the difference that is so desperately needed."

Us? We? "I'm very confused." This had to be a dream, but maybe it was a telepathic dream like I'd had with Phillip, Erik, and Gedeyon in the past. Who were these people? I really didn't need to make *any* new friends now. I had a world to try to save.

"Our apologies," Riku said, placing his hands behind his back. "We are soulmates from long before you."

Tilda nodded, resting a hand on Riku's shoulder. "We did not survive together long before Gedeyon and Rima murdered us. As they did so many others. You must be pretty powerful for us to be able to speak to you in the dreamscape. Well done."

"You survived longer than us together," said another voice. A man with deep blue eyes and tanned skin appeared to our right. His head was full of wavy brown hair, and he appeared to be in his early thirties. He wore regal attire similar to what I'd seen in movies set in the time of princes and princesses with knights and kingdoms. "I am Federico." He sounded Italian, but

I couldn't be sure. I was one part overwhelmed, and one part sure this was all a dream and that it didn't matter much.

Another man appeared beside him. He looked less than friendly with a scowl set on his face. He appeared to be Native American with long silky black hair hanging down his back. He crossed his arms and let out a heavy sigh.

Federico waved a hand towards him. "This grouch is named Ahanu, which means he laughs. Quite ironic since he rarely does such. I had the absolute pleasure of having him as my soulmate. I say that, too, with full irony."

Ahanu glared at him but did not speak.

What was happening? I looked to Phillip, who looked at the other soulmates with a face full of confusion.

"Hi," said another person behind us. I turned around to see a woman with closely cropped black curls, deep mahogany skin, and sharp cheekbones. She had large brown eyes and wore a white asymmetrical slip dress. "I am Ife." She looked to a man who suddenly materialized next to her. He was tall with short black hair and honey colored eyes. I couldn't narrow in on his origin, but he appeared to be of South American descent.

"I am Playcdo," he announced with a nod of his head.

Ife looked back at us. "We survived the longest, but that's only because we stayed apart most of our lives," she explained in a heavy African accent. I wasn't traveled enough to know where her accent originated from, but based on her features, she appeared West African.

"We were the youngest to die," said a very young voice on our left.

I turned to see two rosy cheeked, small children, no more than ten, standing side by side. A girl with light brown coloring and thick chestnut colored hair, and a boy with fair skin and short blond hair.

The girl waved at us. "I'm Naeemah."

"I'm Duncan," said the boy, who proceeded to blush and look away from us.

"What is this? Soulmates anonymous?" Phillip whispered through clenched teeth.

I elbowed him. We were here for a reason, and I needed to figure it out. I spun around, waiting for another pairing of soulmates to appear, but no other did.

Federico scratched behind his ear as he peered at us in thought. "I assume you've done so well because you remained together? One advantage of being born during the time of no magic, your soulmate auras were hidden. That and the original soulmates were no more. One thing you did that we could not do was grow in strength. We didn't have the time or the protection to even train and practice enough. How'd you do it?"

I gave a proud smile, realizing how blessed we were to have such a strong circle around us. Perhaps I took for granted that other soulmates weren't in such advantageous situations. "We have additional mates and powerful allies that kept growing. We shared our powers, and then others grew powers."

Riku gave a slow nod. "One thing we never got to do much of; sharing the bond. It took us a while to figure out that part of our gift was to be giving. Not to horde power. That is the true strength of a soulmate."

"We've been wanting for a long time now to speak with future soulmates," Tilda began. "We wanted to warn them about Gedeyon and Rima, but we never could. And the death toll kept rising. Until one day, humans were finally able to suppress them."

"Do you know how they did that?" I asked, taking a step forward.

"The sleeping spell!" Duncan called behind me.

I turned to him slightly and smiled. Something about him

reminded me a little of Brandon, and my heart ached a little at not being able to see him.

"They put them to sleep, but then they woke up when the magic came back," he explained further with a serious face.

"So, do we get rid of magic to put them back to sleep?"

"That is one option, but the least desirable one," Riku replied. "Magic returning makes the spell more susceptible to being broken, as we have seen. However, your strength can make it stronger."

Phillip snorted. "We can't beat these guys. They're out there eating souls, and who knows what else."

"Just by existing, they are draining you. There should really only be one soulmate pairing at a time," Playcdo surmised. "But now you are no longer at a disadvantage." Playcdo smiled. "You have us. Never before has a soulmate pairing had the wisdom of the past soulmates to guide them."

A thought entered my head. "Didn't the soulmates eat the souls of the past soulmates they killed? How are you able to reach us?"

"It is only because you have weakened them a bit that we may talk to you," Ife explained. She grinned and clasped her hands in front of her. "Our soulmate sisters and brothers who survived after the subduing of the first soulmates were able to reach out to us in the afterlife and build this bridge so that we may connect with you. That was only possible because magic returned."

"Can't they help you and the other victims eaten by the soulmates get released to the after world?"

Ife shook her head. "No, but you can."

I frowned. "How?"

"By killing Gedeyon and Rima," Federico yelled in an animated voice as he bent back and waved an arm in the air. He then tapped his chest and stood erect. "We will give you the sleeping spell and all our knowledge. The soulmates have been asleep for many centuries. They aren't as smart as us who have been in limbo watching the world all these years."

Excitement grew in me. This was an unexpected gain.

Tilda put up an index finger as if she was about to make a point. "And when Liz and the others helped heal you of the evil-eye, they strengthened your weakening bonds and your dwindling soulmate magic. It also helped us reach you now."

"Then why do we still feel weak?" Phillip asked.

Phillip blew out a breath and crossed his arms. "Okay, so we go back to Silver Spring and use the sleeping spell you're going to give us, and everything will be okay?"

This time Ahanu, who'd been stony silent all this time, snorted. "Do not think they won't be ready for that spell. You can't fight the soulmates with the same methods. If you use that spell be prepared that it won't work."

Federico chuckled and slapped him on the back. "That's the spirit, Hanny," he said. "Give our one chance at freedom all the hope they need to be confident in their fight."

"That is not my name!"

Federico looked around, rolling his eyes. "He's such a delight. Why couldn't I be mated to someone more pleasant."

"He isn't wrong," Ife countered with a patient smile. "Where we have all failed in the past is that we insisted on fighting the soulmates evenly. They did not care about such rules."

Riku removed his glasses and began to clean them with a cloth from his pocket. I wasn't sure if in this dream state glasses got dirty. It was more than likely a force of habit for him, and sometimes habits were more calming rituals than physical needs. "We know that Gedeyon and Rima are more powerful than you since they have our souls and countless others to make them stronger," Riku explained. "We know you have the power of the Six to support you, but that is not your own power. It is support for battle."

"We also have our mates," Phillip countered. "That will strengthen us."

"That will be of use. However, what–"

"What we are saying is that you must fight them differently," Ahanu growled. He pounded his fist into his open hand. "You must crush them using your own magic. Something they don't have. He is a werehyena with the evil eye, and she is a siren. They are the strongest soulmates."

"Tell them something they don't know," Federico sighed, rolling his eyes.

Ahanu glared at him. "Anyway, as I was saying before, I was so rudely interrupted."

"Actually, I was the one who was rudely interrupted," Riku said in a low voice, pushing his spectacles up the bridge of his nose.

Ahanu turned to him. "Sorry. We may not have another chance to talk to them again, and I got too impatient." Ahanu turned back to us, his face still solemn. "You two are life mages. Fight with your own strengths. Do not try to match theirs."

What did that mean? "Maybe it's because I'm a little tired, but I'm not following."

"It is exactly as I said. Where is the confusion!" Ahanu demanded.

Federico patted his partner's shoulder. "What the angry man means is that you use your actual gift in addition to your soulmate magic."

"Time's running out," Naeemah cried in a small voice.

What was she talking about? Did we only have a short time to speak with them? That wouldn't surprise me since this was not something they were ordinarily able to do.

"Life mages are rare," Tilda went on. "This is the perfect time to finally defeat them. You are the perfect soulmates to do this." She looked to Naeemah, who looked around at us with pleading eyes. "We must go. I think our doorway is closing. When you awaken, you will know the sleeping spell. But as Ahanu has stated, don't rest on that being the only answer. Focus on your own gifts. You can win this. We have faith in you, and we will do all that we can to help you." She began to fade from our sight along with the other mates.

Phillip pushed out a hand towards Tilda. "Wait, we have more questions!"

Riku bowed but said no more.

I spun around to look for the other soulmates; only they were all becoming more translucent before our eyes as well until they too disappeared.

I looked at Phillip, and he looked back at me, speechless. I grinned at him, confidence brewing in my soul. I felt like it was the eve of a major exam, and I had just studied everything there was to know about the subject. We were ready, and I needed him to feel that too.

He narrowed his eyes at me, and then a moment later, his look of concern changed into a grin as well. "Let's do this."

Fuck yeah.

CHAPTER 24

When I opened my eyes, it was still light out and the nightstand clock showed 12:30 p.m. I turned over and saw emptiness beside me. Erik had left.

I closed my eyes again and let the pain wash over me. I tried to tell myself that it wouldn't be for long, but an irritation gnawed at me. I took the world's best shower in that luxury apartment and got dressed when I heard a knock at the door.

I looked through the peephole and saw Phillip standing there. I opened the door.

"You broke up," Phillip replied.

I stared at him in open-mouthed surprise. Was he reading my mind? I know we were opening our bonds but still. "Hey, how are you?"

He walked in uninvited. "Erik told me about an hour ago. I'm sorry, do you want a hug?" He opened his arms, and I swatted him away, closing the door behind him. "He thinks you and I are meant to be. I've been saying that."

I frowned. Erik had gotten up and went to Phillip? Why? Did he honestly believe telling Phillip would make us a couple? As if my thoughts and opinions wouldn't play a role.

"That's some bullshit."

"He was just giving me his blessing."

"Even more bullshit."

Phillip shrugged. "I think he's an idiot, but that's nothing new." He gave me sympathetic eyes, and I wondered what he really thought of my current single status. However, he didn't ask, which was quite unlike him. How had that conversation really gone?

"So, why are you here? I'm not going to run to you just because Erik and I broke up."

Phillip stuffed his hands in his pockets. "I know. He was just really weird about it, telling me to take care of you and to make it all worth it. I don't know. Then he said he was going somewhere and not to worry. That he'd be back in time for the battle."

I scrunched my face in confusion. He was running off again? And had we picked a time for the battle, and I forgot? What in the hell was going on with this guy? I didn't have time for disappearing acts right now. We were supposed to stick together.

Phillip walked into the kitchen and opened the refrigerator, foolishly expecting there to be food. He quickly closed it. "Did you tell him about the dream? I'm assuming you had the same dream as me, and it wasn't just some normal sleep dream. I fell asleep on the couch. One minute I was talking to Ahmed, and the next thing, I was off to dreamland like someone put a sleeping spell on me."

I nodded, leaning against the wall. "I had the dream, and he was gone when I woke up, so he doesn't know. Maybe I inadvertently pulled you into my dream when I fell asleep. If I can even do that. Speaking of the dream, I think we need to just go full force now."

Phillip cocked an eyebrow. "Maybe I forgot something from the dream, but they didn't exactly tell us what to do."

"The past soulmates told us to use our own gifts." I had

been thinking about it all while in the shower, and it hit me like a great big epiphany. "The soulmates haven't been using soulmate magic on us. We know that magic is really an amplifier for the gifts we already possess. We aren't immune to their gifts since they're so powerful, but maybe they won't be immune to our magic either. Not the witch magic but the life mage magic. We know that freezing them worked, just not completely, but it's something. And at the time, I was the only one who tried it and with no mates or Six to further strengthen it. We also don't know for sure that they aren't able to eat souls anymore."

Phillip squinted his eyes and rubbed his chin. "Okay, I'm hearing you. Go on."

I pushed away from the wall and began to pace as my thoughts rushed out of my mouth. "Rima just uses her siren magic on us. Gedeyon gave us the evil eye. Everything else they've thrown at us has been from their followers."

"We never used our full life mage magic on them together."

I nodded excitedly. "Because we assumed it wouldn't work since our regular witch spells and individual magic was ineffective. If we focus all our strength and power on our particular life mage magic, we might be able to do some real damage. Building our bond and being able to get energy from others is great, but what good is that boost if we don't do the very thing that particular magic exists to do?"

Phillip looked up at the ceiling, crossing his wrists on his head and eyes growing large with excitement. "If we use all our resources to heighten our power like they do, then–"

"We'd be formidable," I cut in. "The past soulmates were right. We have something they didn't have; our friends. They can power us up." I threw my arms up as if I'd just won the lotto.

I heard a pounding at my door. It was probably one of the others telling us to get a move on.

I opened the door and faced Charles.

"We got trouble," he announced.

Damn it! "What do you mean by trouble?"

"Apparently, Misandre and a small army are wandering close to town. Niles and the other towns are sending some of their soldiers to get rid of them." He looked over at Phillip, raised a brow, but didn't say anything.

How convenient. It was time to get rid of that fae bitch once and for all. "Why aren't they just staying low? The communes are invisible."

Charles lifted a shoulder. "No clue, but a bigger question is, how did the soulmates know we were in New York? And we're all glamoured up. Only a few people have seen our real faces."

"Well, I guess we can ask our old friend, Misandre."

~

Unlike our battles in Ireland, this wasn't a massive event. The army was, like Charles said, small but still formidable. We positioned ourselves in a littered alley several blocks from Niles' town. I peeked around the corner of an abandoned building and stared at the small demon, fae, and ghoul horde standing in the middle of the street. Mixed within the ghouls were several beasts, maybe five, with glowing red eyes, large sharp teeth, and black scaly skin adorned with two horns on their heads.

No one had engaged with them yet. Instead, the local town soldiers were scattered around the perimeter of the area in abandoned buildings and behind vacant cars as they observed the intruders.

"Where are the soulmates!" shouted Misandre, standing between two demons. At least that's what they appeared to be.

The demons, a man and woman, had cold faces and red

eyes to match the beasts. Their hair was cut in a short buzz cut, and they were tall, over six feet. "I will bring no harm to your town if you give me what I want. I have on good authority that the new soulmates, Amina and Phillip, are in this area. Bring them to me."

Silence. How had she found us? Had someone in one of the neighborhoods given us away?

Misandre gave a bored sigh and nodded to the two by her side. "Ok, let's do things the hard way then."

The demon twins walked forward, moving past a beast who stood hunched forward like a grotesque statue. They knelt to the ground and touched the street. Moments later, the ground shook, knocking me off my feet. I steadied myself against the brick wall and watched in horror as the street before us broke apart, sending street lights and cars into the earth.

A rumbling shake added to the magic made earthquake, and we soon found Niles and his dinosaur beast galloping down the street. He paused his beast right before the circle of monsters and Misandre. Several town's people also appeared, surrounding the demon group.

"Whatever you're looking for, we don't have it!" Niles shouted.

Misandre chuckled, her pink eyes glowing. "I know that to be a lie. Give us the soulmates, and we won't destroy your town."

Niles smiled. "This isn't my town. It's a bunch of rundown buildings overtaken by plant life. Destroy away."

"Is that your final answer?"

Niles gave a slow nod, his fangs dropping.

"Very well." Misandre clapped her hands. A spark of light appeared between her fingers before quickly dying out.

What happened next made me fall to my knees.

Water gushed out of the townspeople from their mouths, nose, pores. They stood shaking in a unified terror as the water rushed out of them. Misandre was a water fae, so it was no surprise that she could even control the water inside our bodies. Water from the people poured into the air to form a large pool of floating water.

Soon after, shots were fired towards the evil horde from various angles, however, no other people ran out. If she could do that with one clap, we'd have to think strategically. A ward would protect but it wouldn't mean we could attack. I'd wished Niles' people had waited on us before coming out here. They didn't know what they were up against. Their lives were important, and I didn't want them sacrificing themselves to protect us when we were fully capable.

"We have to help them. If she keeps doing this, they'll die," I said, getting up.

Niles had jumped off his beast and attacked our foes while his beast aided him by stomping on them.

I pushed out my hand and closed my eyes, focusing my mind's eye on the poor suffering fighters on the ground, and pushed a ward over them with a whispering of a spell, amplifying the ward's reach with my magic. The pouring water instantly stopped, and the town's people fell to the ground, severely dehydrated.

When I opened my eyes, I turned to Azrael and Lisa. "Can you teleport the injured out of there quickly? Phillip and I will ward you as you go so you don't get shot."

Lisa grimaced, but nodded her head in agreement.

"The rest of us will focus on getting at Misandre," Phillip stated beside me.

I shook my head. Now he wanted to play hero. "Don't go out there. Wait for us to come back to shield you."

Ahmed stepped forward. "I can ward them."

I looked around at the group. "Well, let's jump in the fire then."

Teleporting into the fighting was pure madness. More of the town's people appeared, except they must have been warded now because Misandre's magic wasn't working. Thankfully.

Niles charged his beast at the demons, but they were now shielded by an invisible wall. In the chaos, only a few of the beasts were killed. A protection shield was put up only recently, and I assumed Misandre's water magic only worked with the shield down.

Fighters ran up to the shield and focused on weakening the magic as we teleported the injured back into the confines of Niles' town for healing. When we were finished, I returned to the fighting. The shield was now down, but I couldn't tell if it was because we'd broken the ward or if the demons had dropped it themselves.

What I did know, was that there was what looked like a large black circle was growing towards the fighting. A fighter stepped back into the circle and fell in.

What in the entire hell?

The circle widened, getting closer to Charles. The buzz cut demons had their hands over it from the farthest edge, and I was very certain they were behind this moving pit.

"Charles, watch out for the circle!" I shouted, running towards him.

Charles jumped forward without looking back and then turned slightly towards it.

"It's a hell circle," Azrael shouted. "Keep away from it. It'll send you to the underworld." They pointed to Felix, who stood nearby, pushing a beast away with his forearm as it tried to chomp at his face. "Help me close this circle."

"Sure," Felix shouted before slapping the beast on the forehead with his "death touch." The beast immediately dropped dead to the ground. Felix turned and raced to Azrael.

The demons were indeed nasty foes. They could open a gate to hell, all without breaking a sweat. Harrod, their king, was probably much worse, and it was curious that he had not bothered to come here. Why they'd chosen to put Misandre in charge was even more curious. I wondered if we finally got rid of her, would the rest of her soldiers fall back?

"We have to kill her," I told Phillip, who was standing beside me.

"Most of the demons are dead so that might not be too hard- oh, hell no," Phillip cried.

I turned to him and then followed his gaze back to the hole where hordes of demons were currently crawling out.

I looked back to Misandre, who was now in the midst of the fighting with an insane smile on her face as she electrocuted those around her with her dark fae magic.

The few who were not fighting the buzz cuts refocused their attention on the newly arriving demons. I had no clue how many demons lived in hell, but I was betting there were a lot more of them than us. We had to close that gate or kill the buzz cuts to stop the gate, and there was no time to waste.

I grabbed Phillip's hand, and we walked towards the fighting with the buzz cuts. "It's time to kill them."

"Let's make it quick," he replied.

Once we were close enough, we concentrated on the demon fighters, pushing our life magic out through our hands. The buzz cuts stopped mid-fight and froze. I could see a look of confusion cross their faces, but they could not move their bodies. Glad to see our body control magic was still working, though it didn't kill them. I then punched a fist out, and one of the buzzcuts dropped to his knees, clutching at his stomach. He coughed, and a spray of blood coated the snow. I twisted my fist and his eyes crossed, and I psychically jumbled his organs in his body like a juggler. He fell face forward in the ground.

While I did that Niles punched a clawed hand through the chest of the female buzzcut, ending her.

Misandre, looking around at her losing battle, and then

violently shook. Lightning bolts surrounded her, and I saw smoke rise from her body. She lifted in the air, her body swaying, but still shaking. Lisa appeared under her, magic pouring from her body. Her temporary pink hair whipped wildly around her face, which held an uncharacteristically determined expression.

"You bitch!" spat the fae queen. She struggled to lift her arms, but Lisa's magic proved too strong.

Lisa opened her arms wide, then brought her hands together, and the thickest bolt of lightning I'd ever seen in my entire life shot through Misandre, leaving a hole the size of a bowling ball through her torso. Another bolt turned her head into so much gore and matter that my stomach lurched in surprise. Ok, it looked like our power boosts to our friends was going to good use!

Lisa dropped her hands, and the headless body fell to the ground. Phillip moved forward and set it on fire with his magic. "About damn time we got rid of her," he said.

Lisa gave him a nod of appreciation as she swayed slightly in the snow. "I don't feel so good," she said in a tiny voice before tipping backward.

A blur of movement caught her before she hit the ground. I felt him before I even knew who it was. Charles to the rescue. Now that was new. Was I able to tell my friends apart just by how their energy felt to me?

Lisa looked up at my brother with lazy eyes. "Take me to the spa!"

He smiled and carried her in his arms as he moved her out of harm's way.

Phillip moved in closer to me, looking around. "There's no way Gedeyon and Rima don't know we're the soulmates. This was all a test to get us out in the open."

I looked at the hole and saw that Azrael and Felix had closed the demon circle. There was now a scattering of demons left to fight, and we picked them off quickly, though not without some casualties of our own.

"We've got to leave, now, before the soulmates come here," I yelled. I looked at Niles. "This was just the beginning. If they bring their forces here, we won't be ready, and more of your people will be killed." The fight had to be in Silver Spring. That's where our allies were headed. Home was where our greatest advantage lay.

Niles shook his head, seemingly confused. "But you can freeze them like you did with those others. That was incredible. I knew you were special." He turned to Azrael and Felix. "And you two, to close a hell gate so quickly, and without a spell, that was amazing. You all are formidable."

I shrugged, feeling modest and tired at the same time. I didn't want the praise. I felt guilty he'd had to fight in the first place. "Thanks, but the soulmates are different. We really have to head back to Silver Spring. Since the soulmates didn't show up here, it's probably safe to say they're still there."

Niles lifted a hand as he petted the leg of his beast with his other hand. "We'll join you."

I gave him a thankful smile, appreciating the additional help. I glanced over to Liz, who was headed our way. I was glad she hadn't left yet.

She put her hand out before I could speak. "No worries, dearie, I'll go bring the Irish cavalry to your home."

I gave her a curt nod and turned to the others. "Azrael, time to get the angels. Felix, your demon friends and Lisa–"

She clapped her hands, a confetti of colors surrounding her. "I'll get the fae. See ya on the field," she said before disappearing.

I looked around for the rest of my friends. I spotted Faith helping an injured person stand. "Faith, can you get to Hagerstown quick and get them to Silver Spring?"

Another townsperson assisted her with the injured soul

as she glanced over to me. “Sure thing, boss lady. I’ll get a witch to teleport me.” She winked at me before turning away.

Boss lady? I wanted to argue that title but figured now was not the time, and for all intents and purposes, I was leading this show with Phillip by my side. I knew we could win and I knew how to do it, time to lead the way.

Before teleporting to fight, Phillip grabbed Ahmed by the arm. Charles, Blake, and I remained by his side before teleporting home as a group. What was Phillip up to now?

Ahmed looked down at his arm that Phillip currently held, then back up at Phillip with questioning eyes. “Everything well?” he asked in a careful voice.

Phillip quickly let go of his arm. “Sorry.” He cleared his throat and raised his chin. “I have something I thought you might want back.” He opened his hand, and Ahmed’s small djinn lamp appeared in his grasp. He pushed it out towards Ahmed.

Ahmed looked at the lamp with the colorful etched-glass lampshade and a brass base. He wordlessly took it and studied it in his hand before looking back at us with tearful eyes. I rarely saw Ahmed exhibit any emotion, other than rage at Joo-won for stealing the lamp in the first place. Therefore, to see him now look so emotional was making me get all teary inside. I underestimated how meaningful that lamp was to Ahmed.

“Thank you,” he said in a tight voice before disappearing in a cloud of smoke to go mobilize our other supporters.

Charles moved forward and patted Phillip on the back. “Well, guess there’s hope for you yet, my man.”

Phillip nodded and shoved his hands in his pockets. “I expected more of a response than that. Like maybe a hug. He was kind of ungrateful.”

I rolled my eyes and grabbed his hand to teleport. “Please, stop while we all still like you. We’ve got some ass to go kick.”

Phillip straightened up. “I’m ready to hopefully not die.”

“There’s the spirit.”

Gedeyon and Rima were powerful, and they had their allies. However, they didn’t share. I was hoping that spreading our gifts to our friends and supporters would be the key to winning this war.

CHAPTER 25

A group of us stood a mile out from the town, shivering in the cold in huddles. Charles walked over to me. "What's the plan, sis?"

I didn't expect to be leading this battle. I'd thought Erik would, or at least he'd be at my side. Without him, it didn't feel like we were ready. Seriously, where was he? I was starting to get beyond pissed off.

Out of the Six, it was just Charles and me currently. Just how it had been in the beginning. Something nostalgic and sad washed over me. I grabbed his hand and gave it a squeeze.

Charles narrowed his eyes in concern. "We can wait for the others to get here."

"Attacking in waves is best. They don't need to know how many people we have." Honestly, *I* didn't even know how many people we had.

"Maybe you shouldn't be at the front line, though. We should save you both."

Phillip walked forward. "We should go first." There was a steely look to his eyes, and his jaw tightened. "This war is about us two, and we're finally at our strongest now. We take Gedeyon and Rima down, and no one needs to fight. The war will be won. If it feels like we're weakening, then the Six jump in. If they bring in their followers, then we bring in our allies. Does that sound like a plan?" He looked down at me, and his eyes softened as he offered his hand to me.

I smiled. Not because I was happy, but because I was scared out of mind, and I had to fight back my fear. Fake it till you make it, right? This could be the end for us, but we'd go down fighting.

I turned back to our new friends. "Phillip and I are going. Charles is going to be our communicator when we need back up. Thank you all for–"

"Wait a bloody minute!" shouted a familiar voice.

The crowd in front of me began to divide, and I soon saw Ed pushing past people with Mercy close behind him. My heart leaped, and I ran to the pair, embracing them both in a tight hug.

"You've got this, darlin," Ed whispered in my ear, and I fought my darnedest not to cry.

Mercy squeezed my hands and gave me a wide grin. "This is going to be fun," she squealed.

I snorted, same old Mercy. "It's not, but okay." She was a badass, but a slightly crazy one. "I'm hoping that Phillip and I can take care of this, and there is nothing for you to do."

She pouted. "Well, that's no fun." She looked over to Phillip with hopeful eyes. "Kiss for good luck?"

Phillip rolled his eyes, but then smiled. He walked up to her, cupped her face in his hands, and gave her a slow, deep kiss that made even Ed cough and look away, embarrassed. I raised my eyebrows and looked down at my boots. When he pulled away, Mercy looked dazed and dreamy-eyed. She'd be holding onto that for a while.

"Well done, friend," Ed whispered to him with a slight push of his elbow into Phillip's side.

I grinned up at him but didn't comment on his kiss. "We ready?" I asked Phillip, offering my hand this time.

He grabbed my hand, then closed his eyes, and I followed suit. I breathed in deeply, then let out a breath before opening my eyes again. I looked back at Phillip. His eyes were now purple, and I was sure my own eyes matched. We were bonded and as powered up as we could be.

It was time to go.

~

We reappeared inside the city in the center of the entertainment row. It was where most of the town gatherings occurred, and it just seemed like the right place to be. I was a little surprised that we didn't have to break a ward to get in, but then again, the soulmates wanted us. They weren't trying to keep us out. They were trying to keep us in. I wouldn't be surprised if we'd have to break a ward to leave. However, if we were leaving, it would be because the original soulmates were dead. We weren't retreating anymore.

I was getting ahead of myself, though. I needed to think about the now. "Should we just go to their penthouse and knock on the door?" I asked, looking around. The town seemed eerily quiet. Granted, it was freezing cold, and a weekday morning, but we still should have seen some people going in and out of buildings and cars on the street. In a way, I was happy about that. It meant no innocent people would get caught in the crossfire.

"Looking for us?" Gedeyon called behind me.

I spun around, my heart suddenly pounding as if it were trying to escape my chest. Gedeyon and Rima stood in the middle of the street, looking very confident and relaxed. I was fine if they were cocky. They didn't know our power level, and that would work to our advantage. There would be no talking things out and trying to compromise. We were well beyond that. I needed them dead. There was no place for them here anymore.

"Here to negotiate?" Rima asked in a catty, sing-song voice.

I wasn't here for the chit-chat. Time for some action. I whispered a conjuring spell and materialized a knife in my hand, and floated it over to Rima. "Slit your throat," I said in a measured voice. "With the knife."

She frowned and looked at the floating knife. At first, she did nothing, but then her fingers moved slightly. She soon slowly raised her arm and reached out for the knife. Her hand shook in resistance before she finally grasped the knife. She placed it to her neck. I could see that her eyes were now wide with horror.

"You're not going to do anything," Phillip said to the male soulmate.

Gedeyon remained still, but I saw his eyes narrow and jaw clench. He wanted to move, but he couldn't.

Gedeyon glanced sideways at Rima, who still struggled to keep the knife from her throat. I knew she'd be strong and that it would take effort to control her. I couldn't give up now.

He looked back at me. "Bring them out now," Gedeyon shouted, looking to his left. I saw him slowly began to move his arms, breaking free of our freezing.

What was going on now?

Six people headed to us from farther up the street. Four in the middle between two swords holding people situated on either side. In the captured group was a curly haired brunette, Bella. But she wasn't who I was focusing on. My knees weakened.

Brandon.

He stood next to Bella with a tear streaked face, and I

momentarily wavered in my control over Rima's body, and she instantly dropped the knife. How had they gotten him?

"How?" I croaked out.

"We have friends in more places than you know," Gedeyon replied.

"Where's Queen Arwa?"

"She's hurt," Bella cried, a look of fear in her eyes.

"Shall we make more people hurt?" Gedeyon asked, his lips turned up in a smile. He lifted a hand, and Brandon gave an ear-splitting scream.

He fell to the ground, and I watched in horror as his body began to slowly contort. Bones broke, muscle strength and hair, nails, and teeth grew. And through it all, Brandon cried . He sobbed so hard he wretched. The shifting was taking much longer than it should have. Gedeyon was prolonging this and making it more painful.

I walked forward. "He's just a child! Stop it!"

I looked back to Brandon, who was still mid-shift, his body deformed. He wasn't yet hyena, but no longer human. His cries were now horrific moans that felt inhuman and tortured. His eyes, still human, were blurred behind tears. He was just a child.

"Change him back!" I demanded of Gedeyon.

He chuckled. "I don't think so. See, sometimes we have to learn lessons the hard way. And sometimes, the hard way becomes permanent. This will be Brandon's form for good now. And if he can survive, every time you look at him, you'll remember what happens when you go against me, and you will blame yourself for as long as you live."

Phillip grabbed my hand, and we teleported in front of Brandon. A sword-wielding woman pointed her weapon at us, and Phillip snapped his fingers, making the sword disappear. I dropped to my knees and placed my hands over Brandon, attempting to heal him as he continued to whimper. Seconds passed, and nothing changed.

I heard Gedeyon's footsteps approach us. "Nothing will change. Your healing won't trump my power over weres."

I could barely see as tears filled my eyes, but I wouldn't give up. "Help me," I whispered to Phillip.

"I have been," he said in a tight voice.

"Me too," Bella whispered.

Gedeyon was right. We couldn't heal the boy. However, he couldn't stay this way. His form wouldn't even allow him to walk, let alone talk. He'd be in constant pain forever. He couldn't survive this way.

"Fix him, damn it!" I screamed.

Rima tsk-tsked. "It's your own fault. You foolishly thought you could outwit us. Now, this poor child has to pay because of you."

I shook with anger. I wanted to rip her throat out. I wanted to rip Gedeyon's heart out, over and over again. Set them both on fire. They would not win. I would kill them. I would kill them. I would kill!

A flash of something with light brown fur sped in front of us. It grabbed Brandon, disappearing. A sword-carrying guard stood open-mouthed as the contents of his stomach emptied through a large hole in his stomach. I knew that energetic blur.

Erik. Finally.

I looked up to Bella. "Go!" I cried.

She quickly disappeared into a wind of confetti.

Only the guard near Phillip remained. "Run your head into that building," Phillip ordered, tilting his head to a nearby brick wall. The guard immediately obeyed and smashed his head into the wall repeatedly until she crumbled to the ground.

He's safe. Erik said in my mind.

I knew it was him. *How'd you know?*

Arwa contacted Lisa to say they were under attack earlier today. I went to get him, but didn't want you to hesitate from what had to be done. I asked Lisa to stay to not draw suspicion. I'm sorry I wasn't able to get to Brandon sooner. He was gone when Lisa got me to the realm.

I can't heal him.

We will figure it out. I won't let him suffer.

I thought of his daughter, who he had to kill when she was stuck midform and loupe. *Don't kill–*

Focus. Kill them.

A loud cry that seemed to echo and amplify broke my telepathy with Erik. Although it wouldn't kill me, Rima was belting out a high-pitched noise that threatened to blow my eardrums. Her voice was soon joined by Gedeyon, who gave a thunderous hyena cackle. Moments later, I heard the movement of several feet along with animal cries and human roars. Their backup was coming.

"We're about to be outnumbered," Phillip said, looking around as the impending noises soon grew louder. "Where are the others? Was that Erik that took Brandon? Is he bringing help? We can't fight the soulmates and all of these guys."

"We won't have to," I replied confidently. I whispered the teleportation spell, grabbing Phillip's hand.

We reappeared just outside of town. I wasn't running away, I was taking the fighting from inside our town near innocent people.

The growing sounds of an army was soon accompanied by the appearance of various beings. From the corner of my eyes, I could see us surrounded by demons, dark fae, vampires, ghouls, and weres. There were beasts of varying sizes that I'd never seen before. This was clearly not the calvary coming to help us. And there were many of them. At least a hundred.

Phillip pushed out his hands. "Inferno!" he shouted. At least half the army burst into flames.

I looked to the rest, balling my fists and focusing my

powers on stopping their hearts. Half of the soldiers collapsed to the ground, dead.

"You want to kill each other," Phillip powered out, and soon the army turned on each other.

If soulmates thought we would be weakened by this, they were wrong. The one thing they hadn't planned for was our shared power boosting. While it wasn't an endless supply, as we shared and received energy through our mates and the Six, we would remain strong for quite some time. At least that was the plan. Phillip drew an invisible circle around us, providing a temporary invisible shield. It was a good thing because Gedeyon and Rima appeared in front of us, separated only by the ward. Gedeyon raised a hand at us, his index and middle fingers separated and curved down. Seconds later, a sudden sickness overtook us. I turned to vomit, and Phillip did the same, projectile vomiting against the ward. The green-yellowish mess slid down the clear wall, and I grimaced as I wiped my face. With the ward they couldn't touch us, but it seemed their magic was strong enough to get through.

"He's using the evil eye on us," I spat out just before I vomited again. I felt like my stomach was in literal knots. This was not the way I wanted to die. I whispered the spell of mirror magic. Whatever was done to us would be done to him.

Gedeyon immediately vomited and dropped his hand, releasing us from the evil eye. I sighed, rubbing my stomach. I had no idea how long that magic would work on him. Things seem to be so temporary when it came to any upper hand we had with the soulmates.

And, as if to show how my negative thinking could make things happen, Rima let out a high-pitched scream and shattered our ward in one note. I felt the wind from the force of her sound brush over us, and I stumbled back. So much for our win.

"Shit!" Phillip cried.

I looked to my right and saw another wave of evil fighters storming our way, except this wave was ten times the size of the one before. We couldn't take this many on. Where the hell were our people?

The ground shook, and I steadied myself. What was this now?

"Please tell me that shaking is coming from Niles and his beast," Phillip said, throwing his hands out to steady himself.

Something the size of a house raced towards us from our right with a person riding on top of it. It was not Niles.

Lorenzo.

Damn it, I'd hoped he would have disappeared after we got rid of Misandre. I wanted to pull my hair out. Where were the others? Were we being set up to die?

Rima continued to sing, and this time, I wasn't immune to her voice. Had she broken my magic that quickly? We knew my spell worked, but we never stuck around long enough to see how long it lasted. I guess we knew now, at least, when it came to Rima's siren call.

Intense pressure gripped the sides of my head, my vision blurry. I wanted to bang my head against the wall like the woman from before. The pain was nauseating. Well, this was just fitting. If we had to fall, why not go all the way down.

A large flap of wings sounded above us. I looked up, ready to expect the worse, but almost passed out with relief when I saw Gary flying down towards the original soulmates. I then heard the loud shouts of battle cries, and I turned to our left. I could have cried from joy.

Erik, not yet in his were form, raced towards us with several other weres behind him. Faith, Blake, and Henry came behind them with another group of vampire warriors. I spotted Shayla behind them, surrounded by hordes of oddly running humans. They stumbled forward, like toddlers just learning to walk.

Zombies.

Shayla had mastered controlling a mass of freaking zombies. Hells, yeah!

Beyond them, I could see Charles rush through with mages and wizards, alongside beasts of varying sizes. They were either animals the witches controlled or their familiars. I could have passed out from gratitude, but I wouldn't because that would get me killed.

What looked like a large mountain lion but gray with white paws pushed through the crowd, eyes laser-focused on me. Poppy. A ghoul jumped on her back, and the creature shook it off before taking a chunk out of its head, killing it instantly. My familiar continued to race towards us, locking eyes with me.

"Little help here," Phillip called. "Don't mind me, just trying to put up a new ward."

I nodded absentmindedly before looking back to my right at the large mass of fighters from both sides currently doing battle in front of us. I could see Felix now with Francesca by his side and an army of demons beside them with angels hovering above them and Azrael. Off in the distance, I saw Seelie Fae and Lisa. Then there were Niles and his beasts, Ed and Mercy. We were all here. Fighting. We had to win.

Something bumped into my back, and I stumbled forward. I spun around, ready for attack, and there stood Poppy, sitting in front of me.

Philip glanced towards me, frowning. "The ward is still up. Did your cat get through?"

I nodded, staring at the beast. It began to purr and bumped its head against my arm.

"How'd you get in?" I asked it, slowly raising my hand to pet it. Once my hand touched its massive head, the animal began to purr louder, and a rejuvenating wind passed through me. Suddenly things became much clearer.

I looked back to Rima and Gedeyon, who were successfully fighting off our attackers. While thankful for their help, I was saddened by the loss of so many, just to help us.

Before Gedeyon could swipe out a clawed hand at a zombie, I lifted him in the air and swiped my hand up and down like I was cleaning a chalkboard. Gedeyon's body flung up and down on the ground like a rag doll until he burst into the largest werehyena I'd ever seen.

He was huge, much bigger than Erik. Maybe eight or nine feet tall, with broad shoulders, muscled limbs, and demonic glowing eyes. If he bit me, I'd be torn in half.

He turned his large body towards us and began to walk in our direction, batting away our fighters like flies.

Erik raced towards him, but Lorenzo jumped from his large beast onto the ground. Erik tackled him to the ground, however, Lorenzo quickly overpowered him. How?

I looked beyond them and saw another buzz cut demon walking forward, hand outstretched. How many buzz cuts did this Herrod guy have?

I looked back at Erik. He collapsed on the ground, his body arching in pain. Blood poured from his mouth, nose, and eyes. The demon was killing him from the inside.

He was going to die if I didn't get to him.

"I need you to focus on the werehyena and siren coming our way, *mi corazon*," Phillip said through gritted teeth as he struggled to maintain our ward.

I looked at Erik and then back at the soulmates, feeling panicked. I couldn't risk the greater good for one person. But he was one very important person, at least to me. "I have to help him."

"You can't split your power to do that; they're too powerful."

"I can't let him die."

"You don't have a choice. You save him, and we'll all die."

I looked over to Erik, willing anyone around him to help, but there was no one. His body began to convulse. I looked back to Rima and Gedeyon, who were now outside our ward. The werehyena pounded against it like a wild animal. Horrific rage filled his eyes. Rima circled around us, moving her lips, but no words came out. This ward wasn't going to hold up with the two of them.

A barely visible crack appeared in our ward.

I had to make an impossible choice, and it made me sick.

CHAPTER 26

"Stop!" Phillip commanded as I pushed my power through to him.

Gedeyon and Rima froze in mid action.

"This ward won't last long," I said, glancing back over to Erik, who was now on his knees, looking near death. He was pale and seemed to have aged beyond my eyes.

"It'll last even shorter if you help him."

I shook my head, baring my teeth. "Then we'll have to run if it breaks."

I moved my hand towards Erik, but Lisa suddenly appeared in front of buzz cut and Lorenzo with raised hands. A strong gust of wind swirled around Lorenzo and the demon, lifting them high in the air. A witch I recognized from Hagerstown raced to Erik's side and began to heal him.

Phillip made a grunting noise, drawing my attention back to him. He was beginning to sweat, and so was I. It felt like we were pushing against a brick wall to keep our ward up. "Look at that, you wait a bit, and things work out," Phillip muttered. Now, if they could only come over here and help us.

I heard Lisa scream, and I looked away. She was now on

the ground, underneath a humanoid creature the color of silver with limbs that looked more like branches than arms and legs. Fae and a dark one at that.

Currently, the fae was clawing into Lisa's right arm. She screamed in pain as she struggled to push the creature off of her while maintaining control of her magic.

I wanted to help her, but I couldn't. I tore my gaze from her back to the ward. Gedeyon was practically windmilling his arms now against the ward. He would slice us to pieces if he got through.

"Shit. He came after all," Phillip exclaimed.

I frowned and looked around, still trying to keep my attention on holding up the ward. "Who's here?" My eyes fell back on Lisa, but this time she wasn't alone.

Joo-won sliced the head off of the fae with a glowing blue sword in one swipe. Senna and Yuri appeared at his side, before taking off to fight. Countless other elves appeared throughout the fighting. Joo-won had decided to fight on our side after all. A renewed faith grew in me.

Phillip swore, and I turned my attention back to our own fight. The crowd around our protective bubble was beginning to grow, and they were not friendly. I could no longer see anyone beyond the sea of faces. The ward between them and us was growing weaker. I could feel it. Where the hell had Gedeyon gone? Not having eyes on him made me nervous.

"With this many beings pushing against the ward, I don't know if we can keep it up," Phillip said, visibly straining as the veins on his neck stood out.

I wasn't feeling any different then a dizziness racked my head, causing me to tilt sideways.

"Don't you pass out on me," Phillip said.

I rolled my shoulders back. "I'm cool. Just lost my footing."

I looked at Rima's eyes, a joyful glee sparking in them as

she continued to sing in an attempt to break our ward. I'd reinforced my spell again, and it protected us again for a limited time. That didn't mean that her followers couldn't still do us damage.

"When this thing cracks, we have to set this horde on fire. Our fire magic won't work with the ward up," I stated.

Giant Poppy growled beside me as if understanding. She looked very concerned about our predicament, swiping and hissing in circles. I couldn't even see Gedeyon anymore; he had faded into the crowd. Not good. I looked for Rima again as well, but she too was suddenly missing in action.

"Drop the ward and set them on fire, that'll help with the pressure on the ward," I directed.

I was already beginning to feel weak from using my magic to kill so many. I shut my eyes and psychically reached out for any of the Six. I settled on the familiar warmth of my brother, marveling at how I could now tell energy apart. However, I couldn't focus on that for too long. I tapped into his energy, just a tiny bit, and powered up. I wished our allies were closer; then I could pull energy from more than one source, which would require less draining of one person.

Gedeyon appeared to our left and raced towards us like a demon possessed.

"Stop," Phillip and I commanded in unison.

Gedeyon paused, but only for a moment. His body soon began to move again, pushing slowly towards us like he was trudging through thick mud.

So we couldn't stop him totally, but at least we could slow him down. That would give us an edge.

A shadow fell over us again, and I looked up to see a flying beast zoom down towards us. Gary flew up and caught the smaller beast in midair, wringing its neck with his beak.

Poppy's growling grabbed my attention, and I turned my head in time to see a horde of zombies of varying stages of decay scramble towards us. Did the soulmates have a necromancer as well? Where was Shayla?

As if on cue, Shayla emerged within the mass of zombies. She walked slower, her head lower, but her eyes were directed towards us, and there was a hint of a smile on her lips.

Not good.

"That's not Shayla," I said, my throat tight.

"Huh?" Phillip questioned, eyes still on Gedeyon. "I think he's warded. I tried to attack him with my magic, but besides the stop spell, nothing else comes close to working."

Ok, we had to multitask here. I could leave Phillip to Gedeyon for a few minutes, but I had to get rid of Rima now.

Felix! I shouted in my head.

Everything good, little mama? Felix telepathically replied.

Not at all. Rima has possessed Shayla. Get an angel to exorcise her out pronto. I'm to the west of the town entrance near the old bank.

On it!

I dropped to the snow-covered ground and began to shake the earth around me. The zombies slowed their run, in addition to other beasts and demons racing our way. Our allies and friends also stumbled but did not stop their fighting around us.

"Freeze!" I shouted to the zombies, but they didn't stop moving. I paused for a moment to think. What was going on? These were one of the weakest paranormals. I should have been able to easily command them. Then it hit me. Of course, they wouldn't listen to me. They were dead, and I couldn't control anything not living. I didn't want to kill them, we needed the numbers, but as long as Rima controlled them, they would be a threat to us. I couldn't be indecisive for long. Phillip needed my aid.

I pushed out magic, sending the first row of zombies flying several yards back. I did the same with the next row and the next until I saw Shayla. I didn't want to kill her, but if I harmed her and she let go control of the zombies, the zombies would go free, and then we'd have an even bigger worry on our hands. No, she had to maintain control.

"Rima!" I shouted, pushing my magic through my voice. "Have the zombies attack your allies."

Rima's face was a mix of anger and confusion as she struggled against my mind control magic. However, my power won the fight because the zombies began to change directions and stumble towards the original soulmate fighters under her navigation. Rima turned back to me and then dropped to the ground, eyes closed. She had probably vacated Shayla's body upon losing control. While I was happy she was no longer in my friend, that made me concerned because I had no idea where she was now. Also, the roaming zombies were now without a conductor. They were now free to attack everyone.

Movement caught my attention from above, and I looked up to see a being with mesmerizing white wings appeared above the remaining horde.

Azrael.

Having spotted Shayla, they zoomed down and became lost in the mass. Moments later, the zombies stopped running and froze in unison. Shayla and Azrael walked past the zombies, Azrael supporting Shayla by the arm. My friend looked dazed and confused, but she had to maintain coherence. She had a mass of zombies to direct.

Azrael nodded over at me, and I smiled, assured that they would keep close to Shayla. Although Rima couldn't reenter her, it didn't mean Shayla wouldn't be a target since she commanded so many fighters on our side.

I turned back to Gedeyon, who was still pushing towards us, but a rush of movement caught my peripheral vision to my right; weres were racing towards us. Gedeyon was calling his cavalry over.

Thankfully, Erik and our allies cut into the crowd of weres. I sighed in relief, but my elation was short lived. To my left, another group, this time demons, came charging at us. I spun around, and there was Rima, back in her regular "Grace" form. She opened her mouth and began to sing again. I was still deaf to her voice, however, aside from Phillip and me, no one else was immune anymore.

Her voice seemed to carry even farther than any other time I've witnessed. Had she caught on to how Phillip and I powered up and learned to do it herself? That was our edge, it would not be good if they could do the same. They would drain their followers fully. The only positive with that is that they'd kill their people, which would mean fewer numbers to fight. However, it would also mean fighting overpowered soulmates.

The fighting in the vicinity closest to us quieted as both sides stopped and turned towards Phillip and me. Even Erik, Blake, and Felix, who were nearest us, turned. They were all under the direction of Rima now and were slowly advancing on us. This was going to get ugly. I wished my siren canceling spell had lasted longer, but there was no point in kicking myself now about it.

"Our ward isn't going to hold against them," Phillip said in a quiet voice. His face was tight with something I rarely saw from him, fear. "We can...we can set fire–"

"No!" I shouted, my fists balling in anger. "We aren't killing our friends or any innocent people. I can't believe you!" Something played at the edges of my mind. I was getting an idea. "I've been studying sirens ever since I found out Rima was one. Technically, they only listen to her because her voice makes them love her. It's why legends had sirens luring sailors to their death. They heard the voice and fell in love, sailing to where they hoped the owner of that voice resided. Rima can affect a person with just her voice, but she can also control them to do her bidding."

"We can control as well," Phillip added, still pushing his power out against Gedeyon, who still marched towards us.

"Yes, but we can't counter her control. It would scramble the brain of the controlled."

I began strengthening our ward to buy us time until we were ready with a fight. The idea was forming. I could feel it. The soulmates in our dream had said to focus on using our own magic. What if we didn't try to be stronger than them, just smarter? "Here, it will be a tug of war with Rima. She won't let go. It would drive everyone mad. No, we have to do something different. We have to boost her control. Instead of fighting what she's doing, let's enhance it to the point that it hurts her. Too much of a good thing and all that."

Phillip frowned and shook his head angrily. "That makes no damn sense. You want to make her control stronger? Won't that make them more loyal and harder to get back?"

"Yes, but it might work to our benefit." I smiled in spite of the current situation. "I read that a siren's call makes a person love her and the control comes because the victim will want to do whatever the siren wants in order to please them. The key is that they are in love with the siren. Let's capitalize on that love by making it deadly. Obsessive. Fatal attraction like. We use our mind control magic to our advantage."

Phillip looked over to me, his mouth opened and one eyebrow raised. "That's the craziest idea I've ever heard of. Let's do it." He looked at our familiars. "Watch our backs, Gary and Poppy." The animals seemed to understand and looked around at our encroaching fighters. "The prior soulmates did say to use our own gifts instead of trying to one up them."

"Yep." I grabbed his hand and squeezed it. "Love Rima!" I called out to the crowd, throwing magic into my voice, which also raised my volume. "You love her so much you want to touch her."

"You want a piece of her for yourself," Phillip shouted.

Our voices echoed just as Rima's had as if amplified. We kept repeating our words, and little by little the crowd turned to face Rima, their eyes filling with adoration and love. They slowly walked over to her, arms outreached.

"Love, Love, Love," the crowd chanted.

Rima took a step back, eyes wide with fear, but she was surrounded.

Gedeyon roared, and his alpha control trumped our magic over the weres. This was fine, they were only a fraction of the fighters. Our side could handle them.

Gedeyon moved from his path towards us and attempted to force his way to Rima, but he was too far. "Protect her!" He shouted in a bass heavy immune voice.

The weres moved upon the crowd, slicing and biting and hitting. The enamored beings did nothing to defend themselves. They only continued on as if the weres were a minor irritant, ignoring their injuries. However, it didn't matter, there were not enough weres to stop the crowd.

"Love her!" I shouted again. "Take a piece of her for yourself, to keep forever and ever!"

Rima stopped singing now, and I could no longer see her in the crowd. We were no longer boosting her magic. Instead, we were controlling them with our own magic, Rima having given up once she saw her own magic turn on her.

"She's going to body-hop," Phillip declared.

"No, she's not," I growled. "Rima, you are going to stay in your body. You like it there."

Guys, send me all the power you can muster. I need to make sure Rima doesn't leave her body! I called out to my friends.

They quickly replied in the affirmative, and I felt Poppy butt her head against my hip. Their power surged through me. My body buzzed with energy. Somewhere far off in my mind, I wondered if I was draining them, but I allowed myself to push the thought away. I needed their strength for now.

"I'm warding the area to limit her moves," Phillip added.

Good. That would be our added insurance. It was time we started thinking ahead in this fight. No one would be getting in or out. I could only hope that it wasn't too late and that we were able to keep her trapped inside.

An ear-piercing scream interrupted my thoughts, and I grimaced as I heard Rima cry out for help as the stomach churning sounds of breaking bones and slick organs reached my ears. Through a crack in the crowd, I spotted a torn limb covered in cloth that looked very much like the clothing she'd been wearing. A leg was tossed in the air, and a winged demon swooped down to steal it away, holding it close like a teddy bear.

Her cries abruptly died, although the chants of the crowd continued.

Phillip walked forward through the crowd. "Okay, you got a piece, now move out the way!" Phillip yelled. "Let me see what's left!"

I followed him. We needed proof that she was gone. Although her dead body wouldn't mean we got her if she was able to body-hop. The chanting ceased, and the crowd dispersed, looking down at their fought for pieces of Rima in their hands. Others who had not gotten a piece, scooped at a bloody pool in the snow, the leftover scraps of the female soulmate, which were not much. Still, others fought over limbs for their own piece. The crowd bumped into the wall of my surrounding ward, looking up from their Rima pieces in confusion. The scene was both disturbing and nauseating.

I looked around, trying to feel for her energy. I should know if she was near. "I'm not letting them out until I know she didn't body-hop. Process of elimination."

Phillip let out a disgusted sigh and dropped his shoulders. "I can't tell. It's a mess out here."

A deep, guttural roar pierced our ears, causing me to cover them. I looked over to Gedeyon, who had dropped to his knees in the snow. His frame shifted and became human again, his magic covering him in clothes.

Phillip leaned over to me. "I think she's dead," he whispered, covering his mouth with his hand. "Either that or give that guy an Oscar, right now."

Gedeyon really did look upset. He pushed his hands into the snow, his shoulders hunched forward as he wept. Maybe she really was gone.

Good.

I turned back to the crowd and opened my mouth to release them of the spell, but Phillip spoke up first.

"You're free of your devotion to Rima, but now you hate Gedeyon, the crying bastard in the snow!" Phillip shouted, pointing to Gedeyon, continuing our mind control magic. "You want his ass dead as much as we do."

The crowd looked down at their Rima pieces in disgust and dropped the parts before turning towards Gedeyon and stalking him. The weres raced in front of the soulmate, protectively. Even more of his followers, who had been fighting outside of Rima's vocal reach, moved forward.

I dropped the ward to allow more of our allies to join and take care of the opposition.

Gedeyon stood up slowly, face now devoid of emotion. "You have no idea what you are doing."

Phillip shifted in his stance and crossed his arms, clearly feeling more confident. "Oh, I think we do," Phillip said with a smirk. "We killed your mate. Now it's time for you to go."

Gedeyon punched his fist out, and Phillip flew back beyond my eyesight.

I turned back to Gedeyon, who was now in front of me. This was it. The battle to end it all. I had to maintain courage and face him. Alone, at least until I could find Phillip.

The world around us was quiet, though the fighting

remained. It felt like I was watching a television show on mute. Was it magic or my mind? "Where'd you send him?"

Gedeyon tilted his head and looked at me with something unsettling behind his eyes. There was a storm of instability there, and I took another step back. "Rima was a good soulmate, but she was always so challenging. I like your style. Join me." He offered me his hand. "With my wisdom and your power, we could be the greatest pairing the world has ever seen."

I looked at his hand in disgust. "After all that you've done. What you've done to Brandon... Do you think I would ever side with you? You have nothing I want."

Gedeyon lowered his hand and sighed. "What I did to Brandon was regrettable, but I had to get you to reconsider. If you'd only listened in the beginning. Ah, well, I might be persuaded to change him back."

He was blaming what happened on me? I kept my mouth shut. He was baiting me. Buying time. He was losing the battle. I had the edge.

I conjured a ball of fire in my hand and tossed it at him. He blocked it with his arm, and the fire went out in smoke.

At the same time, a sudden burning spread on my own arm and just as quickly resided to a stinging. What in the world?

Gedeyon remained still, looking at me with cold, dead eyes.

I pushed my hands out, forcing all the magic I could conjure against him. Blood poured from his eyes, nose, mouth, and ears. Gedeyon stumbled back, but I couldn't see much more of him as my own blood was clouding my eyes. I wiped at my face, confused. How did this happen? Was he able to use witchcraft as well? Did he have a mirror spell too?

"Desperate times call for desperate measures," Gedeyon shrugged, spitting out blood. "We are bonded by magic. If you want to know how, stop the blood magic."

I lowered my hands midway, my magic stopping. I'd let him talk while I figured out how to kill him.

Gedeyon smiled. With the blood covering his face and his eyes glowing, he looked like a horrifying demon. "Through our dream communication and our meetings, we connected. Just as you and Phillip did, and just as Rima was connecting with Phillip. Sadly, her way did not work, but our bond is still strong. So, you see, you can't kill me without killing yourself."

If we were connected, I couldn't win without dying myself. Panic threatened to swell in my chest, but I pushed it away. I was in full control now, and I would not let Gedeyon scare me ever again. I was powerful.

But I still needed answers. "Is that why you didn't die when Rima died? Was it because of our bond?"

Gedeyon threw out his hands to the side in what I could only take as a yes. I thought about that for a moment. This meant that Phillip wouldn't die if I died. I could take out Gedeyon and end this, and he would be unharmed. However, I would die as well. The others would be upset with me, but they wouldn't know why. They'd just think we both died in battle. I didn't want to die, but I didn't see any other way. My vision clouded as my mind tried to focus on my fatal decision.

As if sensing my thoughts, Gedeyon put his hands down and gave me a gentle smile. "Don't be a martyr, Amina. You are better than that. Think of all the good we can do together. We could heal your Brandon. Heal your brother of his addiction. Work on that ever present fear you have that sometimes cripples you." He gave a slight shrug. "Maybe even heal the world of both sicknesses. You are more powerful than Rima was with your Six and alpha mate. With the two of us, no one would ever have to suffer again. And you would not have to worry about me since we would be mates. If you want to save the world, I can do that with you. We know what's best, after all. We can do what's right. With your youthful ideas and my ancient wisdom, it is the best of both worlds."

It all sounded great, but I wasn't that naïve. Not any longer. He was lying, and I would never be able to control him. I would just be delaying the inevitable decision.

He tilted his bed back and crossed his arms. "If you kill me and yourself, your friends and family will suffer. Your mate, Erik, would die without your connection. Think of your brother. How would he feel if he knew you could live and heal and chose instead to die, selfishly."

I looked around our warded bubble and saw my friends surrounding me. They were fighting for the world. For me. How could I let them down? But would giving in to Gedeyon be letting them down, or would killing him and dying?

I looked back at Gedeyon, maintaining my calm although my insides were threatening to suffocate me. I wasn't sure I was even breathing anymore. "I would never be able to control you."

Gedeyon lifted an eyebrow. "Nor I you. Amina, you are not a hero. You are a god. Do you know the hardest part about ruling? You can never please all of the people, all of the time. To some people, you will be their savior, and to others, you will be their nightmare. Whichever side wins is the side that tells your story. Which is why you never want to die. You want to be your own narrator. Ruling is not easy, but it is a necessity. You can't remain an angel." He snorted. "The angels aren't even so angelic. And there is still darkness in you. You foolishly took on part of that curse from Phillip, but I can help you rid yourself of it. I can cure you of your self-doubt and those panic attacks. Think of the greater good."

He did make it sound quite lovely. A paradise where we could heal the world and make it peaceful and illness free. Was it possible to rehabilitate someone as powerful as Gedeyon? I had no idea. Was it worth the risk? Would he lie and turn on me? Just because we would be soulmates didn't mean we'd be on the same page. Phillip had shown me that. I had no ability to stop the bad that he did without a fight. Gedeyon wasn't a life mage, but he had massive power with his ability to control all weres. All the good he promised could never happen with him, and I'd be the fool who let this monster go. On the other hand, if I died, the others would survive. Yes, they'd be sad. But they'd be alive, and maybe someone, perhaps Phillip, could heal Brandon.

I straightened up in my stance. The risk was too great. I couldn't let my selfishness and fear, even if it was love for my family and friends, put the world in danger. Ed and his town folk, Hagerstown, Niles and his people, the angels, Fae, even Joo-won and the elves, were not fighting just to have Gedeyon survive because I was afraid to die. They were risking their lives for me, and I would do the same for them.

I blew out a deep breath and looked to Gedeyon. "No deal," I stated evenly before pushing out my fists and constricting his heart and lungs.

Gedeyon gasped, clutching his heart. Pain constricted my own heart, and my breathing cut short, but I pushed through.

Gedeyon raced toward me in a blur of movement. He shoved me to the ground and raised a clawed hand in the air. I lifted my arm to block him, his claws sinking deep into my flesh. He raked his other clawed hand across my chest, and I could have blacked out from the pain.

"If you want to die, I will make it hurt," he wheezed out as he continued to slash at me.

I tried to push him off of me. The magic to weaken his heart and lungs required too much of my strength.

Suddenly Gedeyon arched his back and fell to the ground. He slid backwards across the snow as if being pulled by the collar. Phillip stood in front of me, looking bloodied and beaten, but still intact. One of his eyes was swollen shut, and his right arm hung limply by his side, shredded. His clothes were frayed and torn. He limped towards me and dropped to the ground.

"Kill him," I whispered. My lungs were filling up with blood, and my mind grew fuzzy from my continued magic. I would not let go. Gedeyon had to die. If I couldn't kill Gedeyon on my own, Phillip would help me. He didn't have to know that it would kill me too.

I thought I saw Erik and Blake from the side of my view, along with Poppy and Gary. Hands and paws touched me.

Phillip nodded before pointing a finger out towards Gedeyon who was currently rising to his feet. "Die," Phillip commanded the soulmate, pushing power through his words.

I repeated his word, using as much power as I could muster. We both pushed our hands out towards Gedeyon, who was already moving towards us with determination. He pushed back against our magic with his own, but slowly he bent his legs before dropping to his knees. Together we were just too powerful for him. Finally.

He grabbed his head and released a resounding moan of agonizing pain. A pain that I felt thundering in my own skull. I shut my eyes tightly, pushing through.

Soon Gedeyon's cries ended, and I heard a sickening crunch.

CHAPTER 27

Gedeyon was no more, his body a mess of exploded parts. I should have felt something. Relief, shock, happiness. Instead, all I felt was a growing numbness.

Phillip collapsed beside me with a smile. The pain in my head, lungs, and heart were subsiding. So were my wounds. I stared down as they began to heal before my curious eyes. I looked over to Phillip, who looked amazed at himself.

"How?" came Blake's shocked voice above my head.

I looked up at her and then at Erik, who knelt beside me, my hand locking in his. He, too, had a gobsmacked look from viewing our rapid recovery.

"Could be our bond with you guys and our familiars. You certainly gave us a power boost there," Phillip surmised. He still lay on the ground in a weakened state, yet his face seemed so much more peaceful now.

"How'd you all get through the ward?" I asked, looking up at the cloudy sky. Light flurries fluttered down, touching my skin then melting away. I welcomed the cold covering against the heat of battle. I felt alive and well. We had won.

"I broke the ward," Phillip answered. He rose to his elbows. "I think the fighting is done."

I sat up and looked around. The fighting *had* died off. All that was left were our allies, the dead and the injured. It seemed that once the original soulmates were killed, their supporters took off into the wind.

"Did we get all the bad guys?" I asked.

Blake shook her head. "Lorenzo and demon king, Herrod, took off. Took what's left of their people with them. There was another wave of badies coming, but they left as well."

"How are the others?" I struggled to my feet, still sore, but I no longer had any open wounds. Erik steadied me, but I didn't need his help. I let him hold me up because his shocked face looked like he didn't know what else to do.

"We're fine, sis," Charles said, walking towards me with Faith by his side. Both looked battered and bruised, but nothing life threatening.

I looked past them and saw Felix and Lisa healing some of the injured. In fact, most of the active people who had the healing ability were aiding the sick.

"What about the others?" I asked, looking around.

Charles hung his head. "Mae. She didn't make it. She used up all her psychic magic in the fight. With her already being sick with the paranormal infection, I think it drained her of her life. She protected those left in town that were too young or weak to fight."

The numbness started to shrink in me, and I put a hand to my mouth, tears pricking the back of my eyes. She was like a mother to us all. I would never have gotten to this moment without her. My heart hurt, and a rush of emotions hit me. I looked over to Phillip, who was still on the ground, his jaw slack and brows wrinkled. Blake embraced him, and I saw tears fall down his cheeks, but he made no sound.

My throat felt too dry to even speak. She was our guide. She made this crazy world seem almost rational. How could she be gone? How could we not have her to provide advice or treats, direction? I couldn't cry now. If I did, I wouldn't stop.

"Who else?" I didn't want to know, but I had to hear about all our friends. They deserved my respect, no matter how hard it was to hear.

"She's gone. They can't...," I heard Ed say in a tight voice behind me. I turned and cried out upon seeing him.

He carried Mercy's lifeless body in his arms before kneeling down with her before me. Tears streaked his dirty face. "She was just a human, but she fought like she was a damn superhero," he said in a low voice, placing her down on the ground. "They can't heal her."

Phillip jumped up and moved over to her. He dropped down and gently touched her face, closing his eyes. He was trying to heal her as if he didn't believe she was gone. She remained immobile.

I wiped at the tears streaking down my face in rivulets, not even sure when I had started crying. For the time that I was banished to Ireland, she had become one of my closest friends. She was Ed's right hand. I had no idea how he would get on without her. Right now, he looked so broken. It made me cry harder.

"Where's Ahmed?" Phillip whispered, still touching Mercy's cheek. "He can grant us a wish, can't he?"

I'd never heard of a djinn bringing anyone back from the dead. I didn't think it was possible, but I was willing to try anything.

Ed lowered his head and shook it. "I saw him, and he apologized to me for the fighting he brought to my village. He'd already apologized, but he said it again like he needed to say it more than anything. He told me where he put his lamp. Said it was mine."

Joo-won walked towards us with Senna and Yuri, his sword still glowing in his hand as if he wasn't ready to give up the fight. "He died nobly. I had no understanding of how powerful a fighter he was. Ahmed was an honest man. I regret the pain we brought to his life." Joo-won looked to Ed with uncharacteristically empathetic eyes. "Even in his death, the lamp is quite valuable. You should keep it. Barter only in dire circumstances."

Ed gave a curt nod, head still hung low.

I felt almost nauseous. So many had died. Was it worth it? It had to be, but the nagging thought that the deaths were senseless still plagued at me. I understood that the soulmates had to go, but I felt at fault for allowing so many to die during that fight. I wanted so badly to contain the battle to just Gedeyon, Rima, Phillip, and me. Had I let everyone down? If it weren't for soulmates, our world would be better off. What were we supposed to be saving everyone from other than ourselves?

I left the group and began to walk through the area to see who I could help, but there were just so many harmed. There were so many hurt and not enough healers, it was almost overwhelming. I was emotionally exhausted and welcomed any return of my previous numbness. I pushed away any impending tears and blew out a depth breath. Resetting.

I stopped at Carter, who shook his head and closed the eyes of a now deceased man I didn't recognize. "We've been wrangling up all the injured we can identify as followers from the originals and put them in a containment ward. Is it really all over?" He asked with worried eyes.

I nodded.

He looked down at his hands. "Amina, I'm sorry for betraying you."

I patted his shoulder. "It wasn't your fault. Everything's okay now." I heard myself say the words, but I wasn't feeling it. I was, happily, on autopilot now.

He looked up at me, his face twisted in sorrow. "Is it? There are so many people hurt. So much damage."

I looked over at Phillip, who wasn't too far from me, already in leader mode as he began talking to some of the community leaders. "Phillip," I called. "We need to be healing. Urgent people first."

Phillip walked over to me with a raised eyebrow. "Why don't we do more than one person at a time. The original soulmates were doing mass healings. Why can't we?"

"We've never done anything like that before."

He shrugged. "Doesn't mean we can't. We both healed ourselves and at a rapid rate. We've never done that before. I'm beginning to understand that the originals being back was siphoning our true power." He offered me his hand.

I took it, giving him a skeptical look. I really had no reason to believe this would work, but at this point, it couldn't hurt, and there were too many people that needed immediate care. He closed his eyes, and I did the same. I had no idea how this worked. We weren't near a wound to hover our hand over. How would our magic know where to go?

"Stop asking why, *mi corazon*, and just do," Phillip said, reading my thoughts.

Damn him. I was going to have to put my mental wall back up when this was all over.

I let out a deep breath and raised my free hand in the air. Magic touched my exposed skin, swirling around me like a cooling breeze, lifting my curls in the air and fluttering my scarf around my neck. The both of us stood in silence for some time, ignoring any sounds around us until there was only quiet.

And then we heard exclamations.

I opened my eyes and looked around. The living were now fully healed, sitting, or standing up. Even our enemies in the containment ward were healed. Scorched and damaged earth, buildings, and plant life were refreshed and renewed. We had made everything brand new, and we didn't even break a sweat. I still felt fully energized.

The heads of everyone in the vicinity began to turn towards us, faces filled with amazement. My knees buckled, and Phillip squeezed my hand tighter. I wasn't feeling weak. There was a slight dizziness, but not in a sick way. No, it was more like a buzz from intoxication. I felt like my body was humming. Like I could do a backflip. But I didn't, because I really didn't think it would play out so well. I'd tried in elementary school and almost gave myself a concussion.

A thought entered my head, swatting away my euphoria. "Where's Brandon?" I asked Erik.

"Inside town, in the hospital," he replied, tilting his head back towards the wall.

I looked at Phillip and grabbed his hand, taking Erik's in my other before teleporting to the hospital. Once there, we were directed to Brandon's room.

I walked to the room, balling my fists. The anger and rage at what Gedeyon had done was still welling inside me. If I could have revived him and killed him again, I would have.

I didn't want to see Brandon. It hurt too much. However, I had to see if I could do anything to save him. All this power to heal; to not use it to at least try to transform Brandon back would be a waste. If we could regrow limbs and give people their sight back, it stood to reason that we could heal a loupe or mid-form were.

However, when I got into the room, I was not prepared for what I saw.

Brandon sat in his bed, looking healthy and back to his little boy form, gulping down a glass of water. Mr. Johnson sat beside his bed, shaking his head and smiling.

I ran into the room. "How?"

Johnson looked up with raised eyebrows. "He just changed back. Just now. Apparently, everyone in the hospital is healed of what brought them here," the older man said, before touching his chest. "I'm sorry for letting you down and allowing them to get to Brandon."

I shook my head before wrapping Brandon in a tight hug. "Don't place that blame on yourself. We all underestimated their reach." I ran my hand over the little boy's head. "Look at you. How are you feeling?"

Brandon smiled up at me. "Hungry." His eyes widened. "Can I have a steak? Medium rare."

I chuckled and looked around the room. "Yeah, I think he's better." I was still amazed. Did our magic really reach this far out?

Johnson stood up. "I'll see what I can make happen." He started to walk, then stopped, staring at me with curious eyes. "Any idea how this all happened?"

"I think we did this," Phillip said in a quiet voice, looking down at his hands.

Johnson paused and looked at us both, his eyes both surprised and concerned. Then he nodded as if coming to some understanding that he wasn't clueing us in on. "Well… thank you," he said before turning and leaving.

Erik sat in the chair that Johnson vacated and looked between Phillip and me with cool eyes. "How could you heal that many people at once, including through a ward to this hospital?" Erik asked.

Phillip rocked on his heels like a little kid filled with excitement. "Maybe we always could. It's just that the original soulmates detracted from our powers."

"That's a lot of power." Erik looked more concerned than impressed as he narrowed his eyes at Phillip

"You say it like it's a problem," I commented, sitting beside Brandon on the bed.

It was far from a problem. For once, I felt in control. No longer this super being who had to remain helpless. I wasn't just destroying. I was healing. The wounds Gedeyon gave me should have killed me, but I survived, fully healed on my own. Phillip and I were able to defeat the very first soulmates. Something no other soulmate pairing could do before.

Our power boosting ability had aided me beyond even what I could have imagined. Now with the original soulmates I was…invincible. It was time I fully embraced my gifts and prevented any more unnecessary loss of life.

Charles walked into the room. "I don't know what kind of boost you two got, but word on the street is, your mass healing cured even the regressed," Charles announced. He walked over to Brandon and gave him a high five. "Knew you were a survivor, kiddo."

I looked up at him in shock. "Are you serious?"

Charles nodded. "That's what they're saying. The ward where we were keeping the sick? They're saying those folks are healed. You covered the whole town." He looked over to Erik. "I'm sure if you took the test, you'd be cleared."

A thought occurred to me. Now was just as good a time as any. "How about you?"

Charles pointed to himself. "Me? I'm good."

I stood up and walked over to him. "You know what I'm talking about."

He sighed and dropped his shoulders. "I do, and like I've been saying, I don't want to be alright with my circumstances."

I shook my head. He was so stubborn. Didn't he know that this suffering only made his life worse? Didn't he know that I could help make him better? For once, I could do something good without going through so many trials and tribulations. I could right the wrongs quickly. This was what we were meant to do, and I could finally feel it as true.

I stood up and touched his cheek, pouring my magic through my fingers.

Charles stumbled back, giving me a startled look. "What did you do?"

I smiled at him. "Healed your mind. You're going to be okay now. No more stupid drug use."

Erik rose out of his chair, his eyes even colder than before. "Amina, he said he didn't want help."

I ignored him and continued to look at my brother. "But you're better now, right? Don't you feel better?"

Charles relaxed his face and flopped down at the foot of the bed. "Eh, I don't care anymore. It's all good, Sis."

"You shouldn't have done that," Erik continued, his eyes cautious. Was he worried for me or because of me?

Phillip let out a dramatic sigh and walked to the window. "Man, you're being such a buzz kill. It's not like she's going around terrorizing people. We're healing. There's nothing wrong with that. She helped her brother get peace of mind. How is that a crime?"

If the soulmates hadn't been leeching off our power, we could have defeated them easily, and none of our friends would have died. Charles wouldn't have been attacked by David and had to become a vampire.

I was done being weak. I was done with negotiations. Now, fully powered, I would stamp out any threats to us and keep innocents safe.

"There's a crowd forming in front of the hospital," Phillip stated, looking out the window.

Faith, Felix, and Lisa entered the room. Faith looked over to me with raised brows and a partial smile as if she found everything both comical and surprising. "They're all here for you. They think you both are some sort of gods for what you did."

You're a god. Gedeyon's voice rang in my head. He wasn't alive, but the memory of what he said hadn't left me. It made me instantly queasy and scared. I was no god. I was just Amina. I had a great power that I just wanted to do good with.

You can't remain good. The soulmate's voice continued. However, I would be different. I would be good. Phillip and I both would be good. We got rid of the darkness and the evil eye curse. We could stay on the right path.

I walked over to the window and stood beside Phillip, looking down at the growing crowd. They were just standing around in the cold, waiting. For us. There was a mix of those still tattered from battle and healthier looking people who had possibly come from their homes or left the hospital. It was thrilling and terrifying all at the same time. These people were mine to control. They were our followers and would do anything for us because they knew we would heal even the most impossible injuries. No one else could do what we could.

I looked over to Phillip, catching the glee in his eyes and his wide smile. He looked…crazy. I touched my face. Did I look the same?

We were happy, even giddy now, from the intoxicating power. Nothing was wrong with that. We wouldn't stray just from one fight. We'd be fine for a long time to come. But for how long? Mae thought we would be a threat. The original soulmates were good in the beginning. I was already ignoring the wishes of others and thinking I knew better.

Suddenly, things became clearer to me. I would not be another Gedeyon or Rima. I walked over to Brandon and kissed the top of his head. "Can you go to the nurse's desk for a bit? I have to talk to my friends privately."

Brandon raised a suspicious eyebrow and opened his mouth.

"Do as she says," Erik said in a stern voice, and Brandon jumped off the bed and left.

I closed the door with a swipe of my hand in the air.

Lisa frowned and scratched her head in bewilderment. "Am I missing something? What's going on?"

"We need to be put to sleep," I announced to the group. God, that sounded awful to say out loud. It certainly wasn't what I wanted, but it had to be done. I understood that now.

Phillip spun around in surprise, and I put up a hand to stop him from saying anything before I got my thoughts out in the open. "We are going to become Gedeyon and Rima and a lot sooner than we think. I believe we are more powerful than even the first. We can't be trusted. Not even this early."

Faith shook her head and waved a hand in front of her as if swatting away my words. "That's silly. You have us."

"You aren't enough. When we go bad, it'll be harder to take us down. We might hurt you. I can't risk that."

"Can't we wait until there are some signs at least?" Felix implored. His face looked almost pained.

The idea would, of course, hit a sour note with everyone. I sure didn't like the sound of it myself. I looked back at Phillip.

His face was tight, but he soon relaxed his facial muscles and dropped his shoulders as if resigned. "I think there already are signs."

Good. I wouldn't have to fight him on this idea. I honestly didn't think he would be so agreeable, but Phillip was more thoughtful than I ever gave him credit for being. He'd shown me on enough occasions that he knew how to put the needs of others before his.

"If you can find a way to mute our soulmate powers, then wake us back up. We have to do this now. It's just going to be harder the longer we prolong it," I continued, turning back to the group.

I walked over to Lisa and gave her a tight hug.

"You're taking things too far," She sniffled.

"Maybe. But better to be safe than sorry. Part of this power, part of protecting everyone, is also protecting them against us. Tell Joo-won thank you, and I hope he breaks his curse. I regret that I couldn't heal him."

Lisa nodded and looked away, her lips set in a pout.

I moved on to Faith. "This is dumb," she muttered,

refusing to hug me back as I wrapped my arms around her. "We can find another way to keep you in check."

"Please do, then wake me up. Take care of everyone here, will you?"

Faith swore and wrapped her arms around me.

I moved on to Felix, who bent over and gave me a life depleting hug, raising me off my toes. "We're going to figure this out. Quickly" he said. "Maybe the angels can help."

"Maybe, but no demon power. We've had enough dark magic on us."

Felix nodded and looked away, wiping at his eyes.

Charles grimaced and stood up. "I know you put me under some happiness spell, but I'm not going to be happy about this. Sorry, Sis." He hugged me tightly, and I rested my chin on his shoulder. "I don't know what I'm going to do without you, so I'm just going to be focusing on fixing you around the clock. I'll be a man obsessed."

"Ok, but please take care of yourself. And I don't care who you date, as long as they are good to you."

The door slammed open, and Blake walked in, closing the door behind her. "Phillip? Why did you hijack my head and tell me to come here? I have recovery to do. I am the head of the vampires. I have a job- Why all the sad faces. Lisa, why are you crying?" Blake looked around the room with wide eyes.

Phillip waved her over. "I'll catch you up."

I walked over to Erik, who shook his head and turned away. I hugged his back. "Don't be mad at me, okay?"

"You were supposed to come back to me. This is not coming back," he said, his voice stiff.

"Well, it's just a little detour. However, I don't expect you to wait. I'll understand if you get a new mate. I can't expect you to stop your life."

He shook me off of him and spun around with an incredulous look on his face. His upper lip turned up with a snarl, and his jackal flashed beneath his eyes. It was fair to say that I had pissed him off. "Don't start that. I'm waiting for you. And it won't be a long time. We have a trip to go on."

I nodded quickly, feeling even more remorseful. "But if it is, it's okay. I'll understand. I know what I'm risking by doing this."

He gently touched the side of my face and stared into my eyes with such love I thought I would stop breathing. His hazel eyes began to glisten, and his lips turned downwards. "Do you know how much I love you? How much you've changed me?"

I smiled up at him, but couldn't speak. I had no words, and I was on the verge of crying. Like soul shaking sobbing. As if sensing I was on the verge of a breakdown, he bent down and pressed his lips to mine. He kissed me as if it were the first and last time. As if he had to get in as much of me as he could to last him indefinitely.

And then I did cry. Tears streamed down my face, wetting his, and a sob full of sadness escaped my mouth. I stood back, not wanting to look at or touch him anymore. It was too painful. "I love you," I said through hiccuped breath. "Please don't ever forget that. I didn't change you. You were perfect. But you..." I wiped at my face, struggling to find the right words. My heart began to speed up, and I knew a panic attack was rearing its ugly head. I sat down on the bed and lay down, looking up at the ceiling.

From the corner of my eye, I spotted Phillip lying down on the empty bed beside mine. "Amina," he called, grinning. "It was fun while it lasted, right?"

"Sometimes," I cracked, still crying. God, would these tears never go away?

"See you in my dreams, maybe."

I snorted. "Maybe." I then turned away and looked at my friends. "Let's get this party started. You know the spell." I'd given it to them after we had our dream with the other soulmates. I never thought we would have to use it on me. I should have known better.

They formed a semicircle around us, and Charles led the chant. The pulse of their magic filled the room until my body was numb with it, floating on an imaginary cloud that rocked me into a deep sleep.

I fought against it at first. Basic human instinct. Being put under, by magic or anesthesia, always freaked me out, and I hated naps as a kid. However, after the first wave of fear and magic washed over me, I allowed my body to relax and drift away.

My last sight was Erik, breaking the chant, to mouth 'I love you.'

EPILOGUE

Once again, I found myself sitting on a bench in a city park wearing a pretty sundress.

Only this time it was daylight, and there were other people around me. Kids played in the grass, people walked their dogs. I could see cars and buses going back and forth. It was like it had been before the magic returned.

I sighed and smiled, leaning back on the bench. I sniffed the air, then squinted my eyes as I spotted a Mexican food truck farther down the street on my right. "Tacos."

"This seat taken?" came a familiar voice.

I looked up and saw a man standing there with a small box of food in his hands and two bottles of soda held between his body and arm.

Seeing his face made me want to cry, and I didn't know why. I nodded, and he grinned and sat beside me.

"I got pork tacos. Want some?" he offered.

"Hells yeah," I replied, taking a taco from his box of food.

He pushed his arm forward, and I grabbed a drink.

"This is better than the first time. Less creepy," I said before taking a bite. The taco was just as amazing as I thought it would be. This was heaven. Wait, were we in heaven?

"And this time, you remember me."

I squinted at him, feeling playful. "I mean, I remember your face but...what was your name?"

He stopped chewing. "Really?"

I laughed, feeling more joyous than I had in a long time. "No, just kidding. I remember you, Phillip."

He pretended to wipe his forehead. "Whew. You scared me for a moment. You forget enough things as it is. How's your taco?" He bit into his and then tilted his head side to side. "I think this is better than the fried chicken we had yesterday."

I lowered my taco and stared at him. "We ate together yesterday?"

He glared at me. "Tell me you're kidding."

I shook my head. I really wasn't this time. I didn't even recall seeing him yesterday. I barely remembered yesterday at all. Time was so weird now.

Phillip sighed and put his taco back into the box. "I knew you'd forget. Lately, your memory has been for shit, Mina. We hang out every damn day, and sometimes you remember, and sometimes you don't."

I frowned. My memories were really shaky right now. I couldn't tell which recollections were real and which ones were dreams. I couldn't tell if I was awake now or still asleep. "How long have we hung out?"

Phillip shrugged. "That I actually don't know. The dream world is kind of fuzzy."

I poked his arm. "So, your memory is for shit, too." I looked down at my taco. How could I taste it if I was dreaming? How did I know what was good and what was bad in the dream world? For all, I knew dirt could taste like ice cream. "Maybe because we're sleeping. Sometimes we have real dreams, and sometimes, we have controlled dreams. It's just a big jumbled up mixture."

Phillip nodded, his eyes squinting as if deep in thought. "Aren't you curious how long we've been sleeping? Doesn't it freak you out that we're even coherent sometime? I always talk to you about feeling like I'm missing out. Sometimes I wish we didn't connect like this. It just reminds me that I'm missing out on life. Although don't get me wrong, I love whenever you pop up in my dreams." He gave me a naughty grin.

I rolled my eyes. "Please tell me I didn't give in and that we haven't had anymore inappropriate dream hookups."

Phillip snorted. "Sadly, no. But patience is a virtue, and we have all the time in the world."

"Actually, my dears, your time is up," came a voice behind us.

We both turned around and saw Mae standing there with a giant smile on her face.

Phillip put his food to the side and jumped up. "Mae!" he exclaimed. "What are you doing here? I missed you." He raced over to her and embraced his godmother. I could already see his eyes filling up with tears.

I got up and walked over as well.

"You both look good in here.," she stated, hugging me.

"Did you come from heaven?" I asked her. "Why did it take you so long to come to us?"

She chuckled in my ear. "It's not easy crossing over from where I am. You both are asleep, not dead. I had to make a special request just to come visit after all this time."

"How is it there?" Phillip asked, wiping his face.

Mae gently patted his cheek, a sad smile on her lips. "Wonderful, honey." She looked at us both. "Your parents are wonderful people." She grabbed my hand. "Your father sent me a message to you. He said, 'tell my Mimi I am so proud of her and my Charlie. And your grandma Ester said she's sorry she couldn't teach you the ways of magic."

I covered my mouth with my free hand in shock. She really had talked to my father, she knew the nickname he gave me. And my grandmother really was a witch before magic returned. We'd used to joke that she had special powers, but to know it was true!

It had long been believed by many that the type of paranormal one became was due to the type of being our ancestors were during the last time of magic, before it was suppressed.

Mae let go of my hand and placed it on Phillip's shoulder. "Your parents told me to tell you to keep being strong. They have faith that you are going to continue to do great things and to help so many people. Your brother said he's glad for the time you two had together, and to let go of the anger and live well. And that he's happy."

Phillip lowered his head and dropped to the bench. "Ok," he said in a barely there voice.

"Are you happy, Mae?" I asked.

She nodded. "I hope it's been enjoyable for you here."

"Like one long forgettable vacation," I muttered.

Mae nodded, patting my shoulder. "Well, most vacations end, and so will this one. I was allowed in your dreams to tell you to wake up now."

I leaned forward to hear her better. "What? Why?"

Phillip gave her a skeptical look. "How do you know we're ready?"

Mae squeezed his hand. "Your auras are clean, they were tested. You're safe to be around. You won't hurt anyone. They did have to dampen your powers, so you don't have all the abilities you had before."

"How weak are we?"

"You're strong, but let's hope you don't run into any more evil soulmates. You won't be able to control as easily as you did before. There will be more consequences to you killing with your magic."

I raised a hand. "I'm good with that. I'm done fighting if I can help it."

Mae nodded in understanding. "Your friends searched high and low to find a spell that can suppress you, and they finally did. So, you see it's time for you to awaken so you can thank them properly." She looked around. "It's nice here. But don't stay too long. People are waiting. Well, I got to go."

"No," Phillip said, standing up. "Will we see you again?"

She tilted her head. "One day. But no time soon."

A thought popped in my head. "Should we tell Bill we saw you?"

Mae shook her head. "No need, honey. I've said all I need to." She turned and unceremoniously walked away, fading quickly into nothingness.

What did we do now? If I had bags, I would have packed them.

"Why is it dependent on us to wake up? Can't they just make us wake up?" Phillip finally said.

Fair question. "The sleeping spell puts you to sleep, but it doesn't wake you up."

Phillip swore. "Well, I must have skipped the fine print. How did I not know? So I'm guessing it must be hard for them to wake us up."

I rubbed my cheeks in thought. "So, she's telling us we've got to do it from here. How the hell do we do that?"

He shrugged and walked back to the bench. "Beats me." He grabbed a taco from his box and began to eat again like he hadn't heard anything since Mae arrived. Had he finally lost his mind? Was he just super hungry?

I stared down at him in confusion. "How can you just sit there and eat?"

"Because this taco is damn good, and we don't eat like this

anymore out in the real world. To be honest, this dream state is better than anything out there."

I crossed my arms. "This isn't the matrix. I'm not going to stay in this fake world."

"Fine, you go on."

I growled. "Just like us getting back from Ireland, I don't think I can do it without you. So, eat up, and let's go."

Phillip took a large gulp from his soda before he spoke. "No."

I swore and punched the air with my fists. "Come on, don't be a dick."

He looked up at me with sad eyes. "I'm not being a dick. I like it here. I like being with you…in here."

"Well we can hang out… in the real world. Our friendship isn't over."

He looked away, and I sat down beside him.

"What's going on, man?"

He let out a deep sigh and toss his taco back in the box, moving it onto a space on the bench. "You love him, I know it. I wasn't ever going to wear you down, even in here. But it was nice to have this time with you and no one else around."

I grabbed his hand. "I haven't said this to you because I didn't want to confuse things but…you've become a friend. A good friend. Maybe a best friend. I do love you. You are my soulmate. Sometimes your soulmate isn't the one you marry. Meeting the other soulmates showed us that." I rested a hand on his shoulder. "I think there is an amazing woman out there for you, and she's going to be your match in every way. You'll forget all about me. Although, I don't want that because I want you as my friend forever. I love you, Phillip Leal."

He chuckled, then nodded. "Okay." He looked back at me and gave me a genuine smile. "Okay."

We stared at each other for a long moment, not speaking. I was sure we were both thinking of our time together.

Our dream meetings, working together to save the prison, our magical battles against each other, the banishment to Ireland, and the fights against the first soulmates. We'd been through so much, and I would never forget it or him. He was a part of my life, and I wasn't going to fight it anymore.

"Can I call you it one last time?" He said with a soft smile.

I sighed and tapped my head against his forehead. "Sure."

He let out a deep sigh. "Well, *mi corazon,* I think it's time to go."

He closed his eyes, still holding my hand, and I did the same. We were going home again.

~

My vision was horrible when I first opened my eyes, and I had to close my eyes again before making another attempt at seeing. The third time was more successful, and when I could see, it was Erik sitting in the chair next to me reading a book.

"Reading anything good?" I asked in a hoarse voice.

He straightened up, threw the book to the floor, and embraced me, not saying a word.

"I missed you in the dream world," I whispered.

"I missed you in the real world," he chuckled before moving in to kiss me.

I leaned back. "My lips are dry, and I can't imagine the morning breath I must have."

He rolled his eyes. "Like I care, woman," he replied before kissing me.

I missed those lips, bad breath be damned.

He tapped his forehead to mine, and we didn't say anything for a long moment. Just connected in the silence, our hearts full.

Soon after, Bill came to check on me, and I was given the

clear. I wanted to tell him that we'd seen Mae, but wondered if it would hurt too much.

Thanks to the wonderful world of magic, I was able to stand without collapsing. I was tired of the bed and ready to live again.

"When can we go on that vacation you promised me?" I asked.

Erik chuckled. "As soon as you're ready."

"I'm ready now."

Erik cocked a brow. "We have time, woman."

"Okay, tomorrow then." I laughed.

"Give it at least a week," Bill stated, closing his med mage bag after he put away his tools. "By the way, there is something you should know. About Phillip.

I raised my brows in question. "He woke up, right?"

"Yes, but you should know you can't see him."

I frowned. "Why?"

"We had to move you two. You know that when the soulmates are together, they are at their most powerful. Separation makes you less strong, but in this case that's ideal. It's important that you both not be around each other unless absolutely necessary. It's safer that way. You'll still be able to connect, but just do it sparingly."

That would make sense as another layer to keep us from going all evil soulmates.

"So, he's awake? And you told him we couldn't be around each other?"

Bill nodded. "He woke up at the same time as you. Ed and Blake are with him right now. He understood. Didn't fight it." Bill gave me a sympathetic smile.

So, this was it. We were finally apart, just like I always wanted. And yet, something inside of me panged at his absence. I wasn't lying when I said he was one of my best friends now. How would it be to not see him anymore?

A sudden thought entered my mind. "If we have to be apart, we both can't be in this town."

"That's right," Bill said as they began to walk me around the room on wobbly legs.

I looked up to Erik. "We'll need to leave then. This was Phillip's town first." I really had no desire to leave Erik, but felt it selfish to ask him to come with me.

Erik frowned. "I suppose we should. I could turn the pack over to Carter."

"No," Bill cut in. "The pack is yours to continue to run. Things will remain the same. Only...only Phillip is leaving."

I widened my eyes in surprise. "What?"

"He's letting go of the town. He volunteered to. We keep the council as it is, with you as one of the leaders. Phillip stepped down. He'll come back to announce his goodbyes, and then he's leaving town."

"To go where? It was his dream to run things."

Bill shrugged. "And now it's not. He said you and Erik are better for this town than him. He's going off to see the world. He mentioned spending time with Ed."

I shook my head, still confused. "Is Blake going with him?"

"She's staying. But I'm sure he'll be back for visits."

I began to frown, but then relaxed my brows. Phillip gave up his position, his home, for me. Tears welled in my eyes, and I pressed my lips together to hold in a sob.

Thank you, I said to him telepathically.

There was a brief silence before I heard a reply.

Of course... friend. He replied back.

I snorted and blinked back my tears.

"You okay?" Erik asked with an arched brow.

I nodded. "Yep, I'm just happy."

"Sis, you're back!" Charles shouted from the doorway.

A figure darted around him, and a boy with a face I knew all too well appeared. Except he was taller.

I leaned back. "Brandon?"

The boy nodded with a wide smile.

I opened my arms, and he jogged over to me, wrapping his arms tightly around me. He was almost my height. I looked up at the others in the room. "Growth spurt?"

Charles titled, his head back and forth. "Something like that."

I narrowed my eyes at him, then moved Brandon back and looked him over. His features had changed slightly. He was less round in the face. "How old are you?"

He gave a lopsided grin. "I'm ten now."

I dropped my mouth open. "I've been asleep for over two years?"

Brandon nodded. I looked up to the rest of the people in the room, and they all confirmed my guess. I dropped my shoulders and moved back to my bed, feeling a sudden weakness overtake me, although I knew it was just me feeling overwhelmed. Two years of my life were gone. Just like that. Even though I lived a longer life than normal, two years was a lot. When I'd offered to go to sleep, I think a little part of me hoped it wouldn't be for long.

"Sleeping beauty is back!" Felix exclaimed, walking through the door. "I would have brought flowers, but your room is already practically a garden as it is, so instead, I got you a yellow chocolate icing cake." He carried a covered plate towards me. "And I made it from scratch."

My eyes widened. "My favorite."

He put the cake down on the bedside tray table. "I know."

Faith and Lisa came behind him.

"I bought you nothing," Lisa said dramatically, waving her hands in the air. "Except for all the gossip because it's been two freakin years!"

I scooted back on the bed to rest my back on my pillows. "What gossip? What did I miss? Did you help Joo-won break his curse?" I looked at Felix. "Did Francesca get her memory back?"

Faith shook a bottle of brown liquor at me. "Lady, we have so much catching up to do. It's gonna require drinks."

Bill crossed his arms with a disapproving frown. "Cake and alcohol. This is not the food she should be eating after waking up from a two-year slumber."

I pouted and clasped my hands together, blinking my eyes rapidly trying to be as pitiful as possible.

Bill sighed and then pointed at me. "A proper dinner first, then this garbage."

I threw my hands in the air. "Yea!"

"I'm so glad you're back," Lisa squealed, doing a jig.

Felix put his hands on his waist and looked around the room with a wide grin. "The Six are back together again. It feels good."

He was right, it did feel good. I'd lost so many I loved and gained more to love. Life wasn't easy, but I was still excited to live. I would confront my fears, knowing I was never alone. And having others to care for was not my weakness. I looked at my friends and new family, smiling and joking. No, they were never my weakness. They were my strength, and I was theirs. I would be ready for whatever came our way.

~

Phillip sat back on his lounge chair, reading his book. The sun spread a relaxing warmth over his skin, and he pushed up his sunglasses. He put his book down on his bare chest and looked out at the ocean past the white sand beach.

He still couldn't believe he was actually here.

He never would have thought he'd take a vacation again, let alone somewhere overseas. Yet, here he was, relaxing on the beach in perfect weather, spending his days lounging, eating and drinking, and his nights dancing to live music and flirting with pretty girls.

He was having the time of his life, and he didn't regret leaving Silver Spring. At least not yet. He had no clue what his future would hold for him. Maybe he'd join a new town. Or even a government town. He thought he had the skills to do quite well there. Maybe he could even be president one day. After all, he'd saved the world. That was something to put on a resume. Did people still have resumes anymore?

"Hey, Phil. I'm off to get more drinks," Ed announced, sitting up from his lounge seat under a wide umbrella. "Want anything?"

Phillip looked down at his empty beer and pointed a finger. "Another one of those, please."

Ed jumped up. "Right. Pray, I don't turn as red as a lobster on the way to the bar. This sun is relentless."

Phillip grinned. "I believe in you, brother," he called after Ed.

He was glad to have the presence of what he might call his best friend. It was less lonely in this paradise. He'd never thought he'd be friends with a normal human again, especially one so different from him. What did he know?

He looked back at the water and went back to his thoughts. There was a hopefulness in him that he hadn't felt in a long time. Actually, maybe ever. Sure, he lost Amina, but who was he kidding? She was never really his. He was finally okay with that. He wasn't a bad looking guy, he'd get a chance at love again.

"Excuse me," came a female voice from his left.

He looked up to see a young woman with long braids down her back. She stood nervously, wringing her hands in front of her. "Are you Phillip Leal?"

He froze. No one should know him here, at least not by his face. If someone was looking for him, it probably wasn't good. He'd thought he'd righted all his wrongs by now.

Sensing his discomfort, the woman continued. "I saw your picture on the internet. You're one half of the soulmate pair, right?"

Of course, he was some sort of celebrity now. He nodded.

She relaxed a bit. "What you guys did was amazing. I'm sorry to bother you. I'm a big fan, by the way."

He sat up, putting his book to the side. "Do you want an autograph or a picture with me?" he cracked. She was kind of cute. He wondered if she was single.

Her eyes widened. "That would be amazing, but I actually came over here for another reason." She looked nervously around the area. "I know you're probably on vacation, but I need your help. A friend of mine was killed by some corrupt ghoul cops. No one believes me that they murdered him. It happened four months ago, but they're just roaming free like nothing happened. My friend was a good guy. He didn't do what they said he did. I know because I was with him when they said the crime happened. They were some racist assholes who framed him because we don't have a lot of money and make an easy target."

Ghouls. It had to be ghouls. He freakin hated them. He didn't even have to do a truth spell to believe her. Phillip sat up. "I'm sorry to hear about your friend. How can I help?"

She looked down at her hands before looking back up at him with pain filled eyes. "I know what you can do. You right wrongs. You are super powerful. Can you help me get justice for my friend?"

Phillip frowned and looked back out at the ocean. He wasn't as powerful as he once was, but he was still plenty strong. And he had more resources now, including a familiar who was busy flying around the island at the moment.

What the hell else did he have to do? Maybe this was his purpose in life. He'd lost a brother to police corruption in the Pre-world, and he couldn't do anything about it then. Now he had power and passion.

Before he opened his mouth, he knew he would say yes. His future was starting to take shape. He would protect and fight for the innocent, and he would start with this case.

He looked up at the woman and patted the space beside him on his lounge seat. "Tell me more."

This ends the soulmate saga, but that doesn't mean there aren't other stories to tell. Did Lisa learn more about the Fae, defeat Lorenzo, and uphold her promise to Joo-won? Did Felix help Francesca get her memories back? Who is behind the new regressive drug, and will there ever be a cure for its side effects?
Stay tuned.

If you enjoyed the book, please leave a review on Amazon and Goodreads.

ABOUT THE AUTHOR

C.C. is originally from Baltimore, Maryland, and has actively written fiction since the age of eleven. She's an avid "chick lit" reader and urban fantasy fan. During her days, she works in Civil Rights for the federal government. In her free time, she sings karaoke, travels the globe, and watches too much TV…when she's not writing, of course.

To keep updated on future books and C.C.'s travel and lifestyle website, go to:

www.ccsolomon.com

Sign up for my newsletter:

CC Solomon: Nerdy Travelista Newsletter

Join me in my reader group:

Cat's Corner: New Adult Urban Fantasy and Paranormal Romance Reader Group

You can also reach C.C. at the following social media sites:

OTHER BOOKS BY CC SOLOMON

Paranormal World Series:

Mystic Bonds

Mystic Journeys

Mystic Realms: A Novella

Mystic Awakenings

Paranormal Rising Series:

Deathly Touch

Paranormal Times Series:

Mystic Memories/Dark Memories: A Novella

Dark Hauntings - *Coming Spring 2021*

Standalones

The Mission